TWISTS OF THE TALE

STEPHEN KING: "The Cat From Hell"
"I can't believe this. You hired me to hit a cat?"
"Look in the envelope, please."
It was filled with hundreds and fifties.
"Six thousand dollars. There will be another six when you bring me proof the cat is dead. . . ."

JOYCE CAROL OATES: "Nobody Knows My Name"
The sunlight shimmered on the lake. Mommy was on the cellular phone talking to a friend, and baby's sister was thinking how everything had changed. In the bright, perfectly arranged nursery two living things stirred: baby and a cat. . . .

KATHE KOJA: "Homage to Custom"
Three stories up in a battered New York tenement a young woman, a prostitute, enters the last summer of her life. While men come and go, a cat named Thunder sits on the cracking edge of her marble windowsill, dying a death of his own. . . .

DOUGLAS CLEGG: "The Five"
Coyotes howl in a Los Angeles canyon. But for a young girl, trapped with a terrible secret, the only sound is the mewing of kittens inside a wall. . . .

TANITH LEE: "Flowers for Faces, Thorns for Feet"
In a village near the roof of the world, two young women drop to all fours and run away as cats—to escape their violent fates as witches. . . .

Twists of the Tale: Cat Horror Stories

Edited by Ellen Datlow

A DELL BOOK

Published by
Dell Publishing
a division of
Bantam Doubleday Dell Publishing Group, Inc.
1540 Broadway
New York, New York 10036

Interior Design by Jeremiah B. Lighter

ISBN: 0-440-21771-7

Printed in the United States of America

Published simultaneously in Canada

November 1996

OPM   10 9 8 7 6 5 4 3 2 1

This book is dedicated to:

Gordon Van Gelder,
who said it shouldn't be done
My aunt, Evelyn Geisenheyner,
who first introduced me to the creatures

Lily and Dinah—the new batch.

ACKNOWLEDGMENTS

I would like to thank the following people for various things involved in working on this anthology: Shira Daemon, Gordon Van Gelder, Jeanne Cavelos, Lisa Tuttle, Merrilee Heifetz, Liza Landsman, Meredith Phelan, Pat Murphy, Beth Fleisher, A. R. Morlan, Anne Bobby, Eluki bes shahar, Kristin Kiser, and Jacob Hoye.

CONTENTS

Introduction

SUPPOSEDLY ONE IS either a dog person or a cat person. Dogs conjure up images of loyalty, obedience, and cheerfulness. Cats, on the other hand, conjure darker images—willfulness, self-interest, and mystery.

According to Elizabeth Marshall Thomas's *The Tribe of Tiger*, cats were domesticated by accident, as a by-product of the domestication of grass. When humans learned to harvest grain and store it inside, local mice and rats followed. In turn, the wild cat moved indoors after its natural prey and evolved into the cat as we know it today. Domestic grains, mice, rats, and cats spread through North Africa, Asia, and Europe and finally all over the world once people invented ships and learned to trade. It is also possible that they were domesticated as a baby substitute—the cry of a cat and the cry of a human baby are remarkably similar.

Since then, the domestic cat has had a curious history. Around 1000 B.C., cats were so valued by the Egyptians (for their mouse-killing abilities) that an embargo was placed on their export, and to kill one was to court the death penalty oneself. As kin to lions, which were venerated for their ferocity and identified with the sun god Ra (appearing on ancient papyrus in the form of a giant cat with a knife in its forepaws, beheading Apop, the serpent of darkness), cats were also worshiped in the form of the goddess Bast, becoming a fertility symbol for young married women. Major feline cemeteries have been discovered at Bubastis and Beni Hasan, and evidence exists that cats were buried with the same ceremony accorded humans.

Early Christianity absorbed Bast's good attributes into the Virgin Mary. An old Italian legend even claims that a cat gave birth in the stable the same time Mary did. And the *Gospel of Aradia*, collected by the nineteenth-century folklorist Charles Godfrey Leland, refers to Diana as "cat among the star mice." But Christianity also incorporated the Egyptian "bad" cat—Sekhmet, the lioness that became the Sphinx—and the Greek cat created by the goddess Diana in response to the creation of the lion by her twin Apollo.

Diana and her cat came to represent the dark phase of the Moon and the attributes of Hecate, goddess of the underworld, who presided over the evil deeds committed in the dark. Christian artists began to depict cats in their pictures of the Last Supper, sitting at the feet of Judas.

Through the tenth century, cats were valuable (again, as mousers) to the Irish, Welsh, and Saxons and were often thought of as being magical. But by the thirteenth century, the Church, threatened by the burgeoning heresies throughout Western Europe, was conducting witch hunts in order to foil what it saw as an organized conspiracy against it, and cats were found guilty by association and demonized because of their slit pupils and nocturnal habits. The overall effect was to devalue all cats. Atrocities were commonly committed: on St. John's Day, all over Europe, cats were put into sacks and baskets and burned in bonfires, the ashes taken home as good-luck charms. This practice continued in France until the end of the eighteenth century. At the coronation of Queen Elizabeth I, a dozen cats were stuffed into a wickerwork effigy of the Pope, which was paraded through the streets, then flung into a bonfire. The animals' dying shrieks were interpreted as the language of the devils within the body of the Holy Father. Cat "organs" were created—instead of pipes, twenty cats were tied by their tails to cords that were then attached to a keyboard; when the cords were pulled, the cats would meow. And the great Parisian cat massacre of the late 1730s was perpetrated by apprentices from a printing shop in retaliation for poor wages.

By the end of the eighteenth century, however, cats were faring considerably better. The French were the earliest Europeans to "rehabilitate" the cat. In the mid seventeenth century, Cardinel Richelieu kept dozens of cats at court and even left an endowment for those that survived his death. The French astronomer Joseph Jerome de Lalande named a constellation after the cat (although *Felis* didn't last the nineteenth century). Titled ladies lavished cats with attention and medals were struck in their honor. In England, the painter William Hogarth used them in his portraits, and cats were becoming "sentimentalized." In the 1800s the Royal Society for the Prevention of Cruelty to Animals was founded in Great Britain, and in 1900 the American Society for the Prevention of Cruelty to Animals was formed in New York City mainly to intervene on behalf of draft horses, but it attempted to protect all animals, including cats.

I came to know and appreciate cats later rather than earlier in my life. I grew up a dog person; my family owned a wonderful cocker spaniel and I rarely saw cats where I lived (in a large city, where no one let their animals out to roam). All I knew of these mysterious creatures was that they chased and ate mice in the weird, silent, very primitive "Farmer Gray" cartoons of my childhood and that my aunt living in West Germany would write regular letters to me reporting on her cats' antics. They (and, as a result, she) were always in trouble with the neighbors for their predilection for killing birds. It wasn't until I moved to Manhattan in the 1970s that I acquired (through a roommate) my first cat. The roommate moved in, immediately brought home two kittens, and then decided after a couple of months that she hated New York and went home to Ann Arbor, leaving me with one of the two kittens because her parents wouldn't let her take both. I was suddenly a cat owner, quickly acquiring a second, older cat (who lived to be twenty-three plus), and was soon faced with my own dead or dying birds—a roof adjoining my apartment allowed my cats limited roaming area. Since then I've always owned cats, and perhaps strangely, I expect cats to greet me whenever I visit someone's home. Judging from the stories herein, I'm not the only one with cats on her mind.

Over the years there have been several anthologies of cat stories—science fiction and fantasy cats, mystery cats, literary cats, cute cats. But because of my interest in horror, I wanted to put together a darker collection of original cat stories. The perfect cat horror story is, of course, Edgar Allan Poe's "The Black Cat"—which does not appear herein, as I feel it's been reprinted often enough. But I have included two reprints: one a classic crime tale by Stephen King, the other a never-reprinted piece by William Burroughs, originally published as a chapbook. I wanted a wide variety of stories using cats: metaphorically, as in Susan Wade's science fiction tour de force about firefighting, chaos theory, and failed relationships; poignantly, by focusing on the distressed lives of "outsiders" who live with cats such as those in the Joel Lane story and in the Koja-Malzberg collaboration; edgily humorous as in Jane Yolen's poem of flattened fauna and Michael Cadnum's tale of "The Man Who Did Cats Harm"—to put together an anthology of unusual, intriguing, and horrific cat stories, yet avoiding tortured, evil cats. Granted there is a wee bit of torture—some serious, some just weird. And there might be a couple of bad cats. (Evil? I'm not sure.) But don't forget, this *is* a horror and dark suspense anthology. So, enjoy.

Much of the material on the history of cats comes from *The Cat: A Complete Authoritative Compendium of Information About Domestic Cats* by Muriel Beadle (New York: Simon & Schuster, 1977).

A. R. Morlan

A. R. Morlan has been published in the magazines *Night Cry, The Twilight Zone, Weird Tales, The Horror Show,* and in the anthologies *Cold Shocks, Obsessions, Women of the West, The Ultimate Zombie, Love in Vein, Deadly After Dark: The Hot Blood Series, Sinestre,* and *The Year's Best Fantasy and Horror.* Her two novels, *The Amulet* and *Dark Journey,* were published in 1991.

Morlan is a cat lover. This shows in her loving portrait of a man and his cats. I was so taken with Hobart Gurney and Katz's cats that I called the author to ask if Gurney is based on a real person; the answer is yes and no. Morlan says that the character was inspired by a real barn painter (who only painted text, not pictures of cats) of advertising and all the cats depicted in the story are based on actual cats that the author has owned.

No Heaven Will Not
Ever Heaven Be . . .

A. R. MORLAN

> *There are no ordinary cats.*
> —COLETTE

NOT TOO LONG ago, it wasn't too uncommon for someone driving down Little Egypt way, where southern Illinois merges into Kentucky close to the Cumberland River, to see oh, maybe five-six Katz's Chewing Tobacco barn advertisements within a three- or four-hour drive; in his prime, Hobart Gurney was a busy man. Now, if a person wants to see Gurney's handiwork, they have to drive or fly out to New York City, or—if they're lucky—catch one of the traveling exhibitions of his work. *If* the exhibitors can get insurance—after all, Gurney was sort of the Jackson Pollock of the barn-art world; he worked with what paints he had, with an eye toward getting the job done fast and getting his pay even quicker once he was finished, so those cut-out chunks of barn wall need to be babied like they were fashioned out of spun sugar and spiderwebs—and not just flaking paint on sometimes-rotting planks. Someone once told me that the surviving Katz's barn signs had to be treated with the same sort of preservation methods as the relics unearthed from the Egyptian tombs—now *that* would've tickled old Hobart Gurney's fancy, as he might've put it.

Oh, not so much the preservation part, but the Egyptian aspect of it all, for Gurney did far more than paint Katz's Chewing Tobacco signs for a living (not to mention for a good part of his life, period); he *lived* for his "Katz's cats."

Died for them, too. But that's another story . . . one you won't read about in any of those books filled with photographs of Gurney's barn signs, or hear about on those PBS or Arts & Entertainment specials on his life and work. But the story rivals any ever told about the cat-worshiping Egyptians . . . especially since Hobart knew his cats weren't gods but loved them anyhow. And because they loved *him* back. . . .

When I first met Hobart Gurney, I thought he was just another one of those old men you see in just about every small town in the rural heartland; you've seen them—old men of less than average height, wearing pants that are too big in the waist and too long in the leg, held up by suspenders or belts snugged up so tight they can hardly breathe, with spines like shallow Cs and shoulders pinched protectively around their collarbones, the kind of old men who wear too-clean baseball caps or maybe tam-o-shanters topped with fluffy pom-poms, and no matter how often they shave, they always seem to have an eighth-inch-long near-transparent stubble dusting their parchment cheeks. The kind who shuffle and pause near curbs, then stop and stand there, lost in thought, once they step off the curb. The kind of old man who's all but invisible until he hawks up phlegm on the sidewalk not out of spite but because men *did* that sort of thing without thinking years ago.

I was adjusting the shutter speed on my camera when I heard him hawk and spit not two feet away from me— making that irritating noise that totally blows one's concentration. And it was one of those days when the clouds kept moving in front of the sun every few seconds, totally changing the amount of available natural light hitting the side of the barn whose painted side I was trying to capture . . . without thinking, I looked back over my shoulder and grumped, "You *mind*? I'm trying to adjust my camera—"

The old man just stood there, hands shoved past the wrists into his trouser pockets, a fine dark dribble of tobacco spittle still clinging to the side of his stubbled chin, staring mildly at me with hat bill–shaded pale-blue eyes. After a few false fluttering starts of his chapped-lipped mouth, he said, "No self-respectin' cat ever wants to be a model . . . you have to sorta sneak up on 'em, when they ain't payin' *you* no mind."

"Uh-huh," I said, turning my attention back to the six-foot-tall cat painted next to the neatly lettered legend: KATZ'S CHEWING TOBACCO—IT'S THE KATZ'S MEOW. This Katz's cat was one of the finest I'd seen yet—unlike other cat-logo signs, like the Chessie railroad cat, for instance, every Katz's cat was different; different color, different pose, sometimes even more than one cat per barn sign. And this one was a masterpiece: a gray tiger, the kind of animal whose fur you *know* would be soft to the touch, with each multihued hair tipped with just enough white to give the whole cat an auralike sheen, and a softly thick neck that told the world that this cat was an unneutered male, old enough to have sired a few litters of kittens but not old enough to be piss-mean or battle-scarred. A young male, maybe two, three years old. And his eyes were gentle, too; trusting eyes, of hazy green touched with a hint of yellow along the oval pupils, over a grayish-pink nose and a mouth covering barely visible fang tips. He was resting on his side, so all four of his paw pads were visible, each one colored that between gray and pink color that's a bit of each yet something not at all on the artist's color wheel. And his ombre-ringed tail was curled up and over his hind feet, resting in a relaxed curl over his hind paws. But something in his sweet face told a person that this cat would jump right up into your arms if you only patted your chest and said "Come 'ere—"

But . . . considering that this cat was mostly gray, and the barn behind him was weathering fast, I had to make sure the shutter speed was adjusted *so*, or I'd never capture this particular Katz's cat. Not the way the clouds were rolling in faster and faster—

"Don't look like Fella wants his picture took today," the tobacco-spitting old man said helpfully, as I missed yet another split-second-of-sun opportunity to capture the likeness of the reclining cat. That did it. Letting my camera flop down against my chest by the strap, I turned around and asked, "Do you own this barn? Am I supposed to pay you for taking a picture or what?"

The old man looked at me meekly, his bill-shaded eyes wide with hurt as he said around a glob of chaw, "I already got my pay for that 'un, but I 'spose you could say it's my *cat*—"

When he said that, all my irritation and impatience melted into a soggy feeling of shame mingled with heart-thumping awe—this baggy-trousered old man had to be Hobart Gurney, the sign painter responsible for all of the Katz's Tobacco signs dotting barns throughout southern Illinois and western Kentucky, the man who was still painting such signs up until a couple of years ago, stopping only when old age made it difficult for him to get up and down the ladders.

I'd seen that profile about him on CNN a few years ago, when he was painting his last or next-to-last Katz's sign, but most old men tend to look alike, especially when decked out in the ubiquitous uniform of a baseball cap and paint-splattered overalls, and at any rate, the work had impressed me more than the man who created it. . . .

Putting out my hand, I said, "Hey, sorry about what I said . . . I—I didn't mean it like that, it's just that I only have so many days of vacation left, and the weather hasn't exactly been cooperative—"

Gurney's hand was dry and firm; he shook hands until I had to withdraw my aching hand, as he replied, "No offense meant, no offense taken. I 'spect Fella will wait awhiles until the clouds see fit to cooperate with you. He's a patient one, is Fella, but shy 'round strangers." The way he said "Fella," I knew the name should be capitalized, instead of it being a generic nomenclature for the animal at hand.

Judging from the way the clouds scudded across the sun, I figured that Fella was in for a good long wait, so I motioned to the rental car parked a few yards away from the barn, inviting Gurney to share one of the cans of Pepsi in my backseat cooler. Gurney's trousers made a raspy rubbing noise when he walked, not unlike the sound a cat's tongue makes when it licks your bare arm. And when he was speaking in close quarters, his tobacco-laced breath was sort of cat fetid, too, all wild-smelling and warm. The old man positioned himself half in and half out of my car, so he could see his Fella clearly, while still keeping his body in the relative warmth of my car. Between noisy slurps of soda, he told me, "Like I said, no self-respectin' cat aims to model for you, so's the only way to get around it is to make your *own* cat. Memory's the best model they is—"

I almost choked on my Pepsi when he said that; all along, I'd assumed that Gurney had used whatever barn cats were wandering around him for his inspiration . . . but to create such accurate, personable cats from memory and imagination—

"Funny thing is, when I was hired on to work for Katz, back in the thirties, all they was interested in was gettin' their name out in front of the public, in as big letters as possible. That I added cats to the Katz's signs was my idea—didn't get paid no extra for doin' it, neither. But it seemed natural, you see? And it did get folks' attention. 'Sides, them cats, they kept me company, while I was workin'—gets mighty lonely up on that ladder, with the wind snaking down your shirt collar and no one to talk to up that high. Was sorta like when I was a boy, muckin' out my pa's barn, and the barn cats, they'd come snaking 'round my legs purrin' and sometimes jumpin' straight up onto my shoulders, so they'd hitch a free ride while I was workin'—only I didn't get 'round to givin' too many of them cats names, you see, 'cause they was always comin' or goin', or gettin' cow-crushed—oh, them cows didn't mean no harm, see, it's just they was so big and them cats too small when they'd try snuggling up wi'em on cold winter nights. But I sure did enjoy their company. Now you may laugh at this, but—" Here Gurney lowered his voice, even though there was no one else around to hear him but me and the huge painted Fella resting on the side of the abandoned barn. "—when I was a young'un, and even a *not* so young'un, I had me this dream. I wanted to be small, like a cat, for oh, maybe a night or so. Just long enough for me to snuggle down with a whole litterful of cats, four-five of 'em, all of us same-sized and warm in the hay, and we'd tangle our legs and whatnot in a warm pile, and they'd lick my face and then burrow their heads under my chin, or mine under theirs, and we'd sleep for a time. Nothing better for the insomnia than to rest with a cat purring in your ears. 'Tis true. Don't need none of them sleeping pills when you gots yourself a cat.

"That's why I took the Katz's Tobacco job when I heard of it, even though I wasn't too keen on heights. Course, it bein' the Depression was a powerful motivator, too, but the *name* Katz was just too good to pass by . . . and them not minding when I dickied with their adverts was heaven-made for me, too. Struck me funny, when them television-fellers interviewed me and all, when I was paintin' the little girls—"

Gurney's words made me remember the album of Katz's signs I kept locked in the trunk of the car (not my only set, but a spare album I used for reference, especially when coming across a barn I may have photographed before, under different lighting or seasonal circumstances); too excited to speak, I got out of the backseat and hurried for the trunk, while Gurney kept on talking about the "pup reporter" who'd interviewed him for that three-minute interview.

"—and he didn't even ask me what the cats' names was, like it didn't matter none to—"

"Were these the 'little girls'?" I asked as I flipped through the album pages until I found the dry-mounted snapshot of one of the most elaborate Katz's signs: four kittens snuggled together in a hollowed-out bed of straw, their pointed little faces curious yet subtly wary, as if they'd all burrow into the straw if you took one step closer to them. Clearly a litter of barn kittens, even if you discounted the straw bedding; these weren't Christmas-card-and-yarn-balls kittens, cavorting like live Dakin kittens for a Madison Avenue artist, but feral-type kittens, the kind you'd be lucky to coax close enough to sniff your fingers before they'd run off to hide in the farthest corners of the manure-scented barn where they were born. The kind of kitten who'd grow up slat-thin and long-tailed, slinking around corners like a fleshed-out shadow, or coming up to you from behind, as if sizing up whether or not to take a sharp-clawed swipe at your shoe before running for cover. The kind of cat you know will get kittened out before she's three years old, winding up saggy-bellied and defensive by the time she's four.

But when Gurney saw the eight-by-ten enlargement, his face lit up and his puckered lips stretched out into a broad grin, exposing what my own grandfather used to call "dime-store choppers" of an astonishing Chiclets gum uniform squareness and off-whiteness.

"You took a picture of my little girls! Usually they're tricky ones, on 'count of Prissy and Mish-Mish lookin' so much alike, but you caught 'em, by gummy, got them in just the right light—"

"Wait, wait, let me get this down," I said, reaching over the seat for the notebook and pen resting on the front passenger seat. "Now, which one is which?"

His face glowing with the kind of pride most men his age took in showing off pictures of their grandchildren (or even great-grandkids), Gurney pointed at each kitten in turn, stroking their chemically captured images with a tender, affectionate forefinger, as if chucking each under her painted chin. "This 'un's Smokey, the tiger gray, and here's Prissy—see how dainty she looks, with them fox-narrow eyes and little points on her ears?—and right next to her is Mish-Mish, even though they're both calicos, Mishy's a little more patchy-colored than usual—"

" 'Mish-Mish'?" I asked, not knowing how he'd come up with that name; Gurney's answer surprised—and touched—me.

"Got that name from the *Milwaukee Journal* Green Sheet, where they put all their funnies and little offbeat articles . . . was an article about the Middle East, and it mentioned how them A-rabs like cats so much, and how

their version of 'Kitty-kitty' was 'Mish-Mish,' which is
their lingo for peach color, on 'count of most of their
strays bein' sorta peachy-orange. See how Mish-Mish's
face is got that big splotch of peach on it? Oh, I know
we're not 'sposed to care what them A-rab folks think, on
'count of them bein' the enemy or whatnot, but you can't
fault a people who care so much for their cats too much.
Heard tell the Egyptians worshiped their cats, like gods
. . . done up their pets as mummies, the whole shebang.
So's I don't even mind when their descendants says they
hate us, long as they take care of their cats—'cause a man
who can hate a cat can't much like hisself, *I* says."

I had to laugh at that; before Gurney could go on, I
quoted Mark Twain from memory: "If man could be
crossed with the cat, it would improve the man but deteri-
orate the cat—"

Now it was Gurney's turn to laugh, until he spittle-
flecked his shirt collar before he went on, "Anyhows, next
to Mish-Mish is Tinker, only you can't tell from lookin' at
her that she's a girl, on 'count of her only bein' two colors
and all, but from personal experience, most gray cats with
white feet I've seen's been girls. Don't know why that is . . .
sorta like how you never see a white cat with black feet
and chest, like you see black cats with white socks and
bibs. Funny how nature works that way, ain't it?" Having
told me the names of the "little girls" (which I duly wrote
down in my notebook), Gurney began paging through the
rest of the album, matching heretofore anonymous painted
felines with the names that somehow made them real—
at least to the man who created them: black-bodied and
white-socked Ming, with his clear, clear green eyes and
luxurious long fur with a couple of mats along the chest;
calico Beanie with her rounded gray chin and owl-like
yellow-green eyes; dandelion-fuzzy Stan and Ollie, black-
and-white tuxedo-patterned kittens, one obviously fatter,
but both still too wobbly-limbed and tiny-eared to look
anything but pick-me-up adorable; and too many more to
remember offhand (thank goodness I had many clean pages
left in my notebook that afternoon), but once each cat was

named, I could never again look at it as just another Katz's Tobacco cat; for instance, knowing that Beanie was *Beanie* made her *into* a cat, one with a history and a personality . . . you just knew that she was full of beans when she was a kitten, getting into things, playing with her tail until she'd spun herself like a dime-store top. . . . And for a moment, Gurney's cats became more than pigment and imagination. Not unlike the work of regular canvas-easels-and-palette artists, or those natural-born billboard painters, the legendary ones who never needed to use those gridlike blueprints to create the advertisements.

It was sad, really, how that reporter had missed out on the essence of Gurney's work; all the "pup reporter" seemed to be interested in was how *long* Gurney had been at it.

As Gurney looked at the last of the barn pictures I'd taken and enlarged, he said shyly, "I feel sorta humbled by this and all . . . it's like I was one of them art-fart painter guys, in a gallery 'stead of a regular workin' Joe. . . . Oh, not that I'm not pleased . . . it's just . . . oh, I dunno. It just seems funny to have my cats all put in a book form, 'stead of them just *bein'* out where they are, in the open and all. Like they was suddenly domesticated 'stead of bein' regular barn kitties."

I didn't know how to answer that; I realized that Gurney must be astute enough to realize that his signs *were* works of art—he may have been slightly inarticulate, and most likely unschooled, but he wasn't ignorant by any means—he was obviously in a quandary; on the one hand, he was from a time when work was simply something you got paid for, period; yet on the other hand, the fact that he'd been interviewed on TV and caught me taking pictures of his efforts must have been an indication that his work *was* something special. He couldn't quite cope with having a fuss being made over something he'd considered to be paid labor.

I gently lifted the book off his lap and placed it on the seat between us before saying "I can empathize with you there . . . I work as an advertising photographer, taking pictures of products for clients, and when someone praises me for my composition, or whatever, it can be a strange feeling . . . especially since I'm just a go-between when it comes to the product and the consumer—"

Gurney's watery pale-blue eyes were darting around as I spoke, and for a moment I was afraid that I was losing his attention, but instead he surprised me by saying "I think Fella's lost his shyness . . . the sun's been shining for a good minute now."

Quickly I got out of the car and positioned myself in front of the barn; true to Gurney's word, Fella was no longer shy, but exposed in all his sunlit perfection against the sun-weathered barn. It's funny, but even though the lettering next to the cat was badly flaked, I could almost see every individual hair of the tomcat's fur.

And behind me, Hobart Gurney took a noisy slurp of his soda as he repeated, in the way of old men you find in every small town, "Yessirree, my Fella's not shy anymore. . . ."

I said good-bye to Gurney a couple of hours later, outside the adult day-care center and seniors apartment where he lived; without going in, I knew what his room must be like—single bed, with a worn ripcord bedspread, some issues of *Reader's Digest* large-print edition on the bedstand, and a doorless closet filled with not too many clothes hanging from those crochet-covered hangers, and—most depressing of all—no animals at all to keep him company. It was the sort of place where they only bring in some puppies or kittens when the local newspaper editor wants a set of human interest pictures for the inner spread during a dull news week—"Oldsters with Animals" on their afghan-covered laps.

Not the sort of place where suddenly-small men snuggle with litters of barn cats in a bed of straw. . . .

With an almost comic formality, Gurney thanked me for the Pepsi and for "letting me see the kitties" in my album. I asked him if he got out much, to see the signs in person, but instantly regretted my words when he nonchalantly spit at his feet before saying "Don't get 'round much since I turned in my driver's license . . . my hands aren't as steady as they used to be, be it with a brush or with a steering wheel. Once I almost run over a cat crossing a back road and tol' myself, 'This is it, Hobart' even though the cat, she got away okay. Wasn't worth the risk. . . ."

Not knowing what else to do, I opened the back door of the car and brought out the album; Gurney didn't want to take it at first, even though I assured him that I had another set of prints plus the negatives back in my studio in New York City. The way he brushed the outside of the album with his fingers, as if the imitation leather was soft tiger-stripe fur, was almost too much for me; knowing that I couldn't stay, couldn't see any more of this, I bid him farewell and left him standing in front of the oldsters' home, album of kitties in his hands. I know I should've done more, but what could I do? Really? I'd given him back his cats; I couldn't give him back his old life . . . and what he'd shared with me already hurt too much, especially his revelation of the smallness fantasy. I mean, how often do even people who are close to each other, like old friends, or family, reveal such intimate, deeply *need*ing things like that—especially without being asked to? Once you know things like that about a person, it gets a little hard to face them without feeling like you have a bought-from-a-comic-book-ad pair of X-ray glasses capable of peering into their soul. Nobody should be that vulnerable to another living being.

Especially one they hardly know. . . .

A few days after I met Hobart Gurney my vacation in the Midwest was over, and I returned to my studio, to turn lifeless sample products into . . . something potentially essential to people who didn't know they needed that thing until that month's issue of *Vanity Fair* or *Cosmopolitan* arrived in the mail, and they finally got around to paging through the magazine after getting home from work. Not that I felt responsible for turning the unknown *into* the essential; even when I got to keep what I photographed, it didn't mean squat to me. I could appreciate my work, respect my better efforts . . . but I never gave a pet name to a bottle of men's cologne, if you get my drift. And I envied Hobart for being able to love what he did, because he had the freedom to *do* it the way he wanted to. And because the now-defunct Katz's Chewing Tobacco people could've cared less what he painted next to their logo. (Oh, for such benign indifference when it came to *my* work!)

But I also pitied Hobart, because letting go of what you've come to love is a hard, hard thing, which makes the ending of that creative, *loving* process all the harder to take, especially when the ending is an involuntary thing. What had the old man said in the TV interview? That he was too old to climb the ladder anymore? That had to have been as bad as him realizing that he couldn't drive safely anymore. . . .

And the funny thing was, I got the feeling that if he could have climbed those ladders, he would've still been putting those man-sized cats on barns, whether Katz's paid him or not.

I honestly couldn't say the same about what *I* did for a living.

I was in the middle of shooting a series of pictures of a new women's cologne, which happened to come in a bottle that resembled a piece of industrial flotsam more than a container for a fragrance boasting "top notes of green, with cinnamon undercurrents"—whatever *that* meant, since the stuff smelled like dime-store deodorant, when my studio phone rang. I had the answering machine on Call Screening, so I could hear it while not missing out on my next shot . . . but I hurried to the phone when a tentative-sounding voice asked, "Uhm . . . are you the one who dropped Mr. Gurney off at the home a couple of months ago?"

"Yeah, you're speaking to me, not the machine—"

The woman on the other end began without preamble, "Sorry to bother you, but we found your card in Mr. Gurney's room . . . the last anyone saw of him he was carrying that album you give him under his arm, before he went for his walk, only he never went for a walk for a week before—"

The sick feeling began in my stomach and soon fanned out all over my body; as the woman in charge of the old people's home rambled on, telling me that no one in the area had seen the old man after he'd accepted a lift from someone with Canadian plates on his car, which naturally meant that he could be anywhere, but maybe headed for New York, I shook my head, even though the woman couldn't possibly see me, as I cut in "No, ma'am, don't even try looking here. He's not far away . . . I'm sure of it. If he's not still in Little Egypt, he's across the border in Kentucky . . . just look for the Katz's Tobacco signs—"

"The what?"

I pressed the receiver against my chest, muttered *You stupid old biddy* just to make myself feel better, then told her, "He painted signs, on barns . . . he's saying good-bye to the signs," and as I said the last few words, I wondered at my own choice of words . . . even as my own artist's instincts—instincts Gurney and I shared—told me that I had, indeed, chosen my words correctly.

Despite the fact that the woman from the rest home had gotten her information from me, she never bothered to call me back when Hobart Gurney's body was found, half buried in the unmown grass surrounding one of the abandoned barns bearing his loving handiwork; I found out about his death along with all the other people watching CNN that late-fall evening—the network reran the piece about his last or next-to-last sign-painting job, along with an oddly sentimental obituary that ended with a close-up of the "little girls," whose particular sign the old man's body had been found under. The camera zoomed in for a close-up of Mish-Mish, with her patchwork face of mixed tan and gray and white, with that peach-colored blotch over one eye, and she looked so poignant yet so *real* that no one watching her—be they a cat lover or not—could fail to realize what may've been more difficult to realize during that warts-and-all initial CNN interview, which plainly showed how unsophisticated and gauche Hobart Gurney may have seemed to be on the outside (so much so, perhaps, that it made underestimating his work all the easier): that Gurney was more than a great artist: He was a genius, easily on the par of Grandma Moses or anyone of her ilk.

J. C. Suarès was the first person to put out a book devoted to Katz's Cats, as Gurney's creations were to become popularly known. Many famous photographers, including Herb Ritts, Annie Leibovitz, and Avedon, took part in that collection; I wasn't one of them, but I did get in on that other collection put together for one of the AIDS charities. Then came the specials on what Gurney would've called the "art-fart" stations, and there's even been word of a postage stamp bearing his likeness, along with one of the Katz's Cats.

The irony was, I seriously doubt Gurney would've truly enjoyed all the fuss made about his work; what he'd created was too private for all *that*. Not when he'd so lovingly stroked the images of his "little girls" faces in that rental car of mine, and not when he'd so spontaneously shared that cat-size dream of his from his barn-mucking boyhood so many years—and barn cats—ago. But at least for me, there was one benefit from his life, and his work, becoming so public: It gave me an opportunity to find out what really happened to him, without my needing to visit that depressing small town where I'd met him or to actually see his all-but-empty cell-like adult day-care bedroom.

Some policemen found his body, almost covered by long, dead grass, just below the barn where he'd painted the "little girls"; he was curled on his left side, almost in a fetal position, with both hands covering his face, not unlike a cat at sleep or rest. Supposedly it was a heart attack, but that didn't account for the abrasions on his exposed face and hands; a rough, red rashlike disruption on his flesh, which was eventually dismissed as fire-ant bites. Nor did the "official" cause of death account for the blissful look on his face that the policeman in one A&E special described; you don't have to be a doctor to know that heart attacks are painful.

Nor do you need to be an expert on cats—especially *big* cats—to know what a cat's tongue can do to unprotected flesh, especially when they get it into their heads to keep licking and licking while snuggled together in a pile of warm, furry flesh.

Maybe Hobart Gurney didn't mean to say good-bye per se during that self-prescribed tour of his creations; maybe he'd just grown nostalgic after seeing the pictures I'd given to him. Funny how he took the album with him, when he'd never forgotten a single cat he'd created, but then again, no one will ever know what drove him to turn a Depression-era job taken despite an aversion to heights into something more than his life's work. Perhaps *my* decision to collect photographs of his work ultimately led to his death, which I heard about on the CNN news. But if that is so, I can't quite feel guilty about it—after all, Gurney hadn't painted cats in years; true, nothing stopped him from painting them on canvas, but I don't think that was Gurney's way at all.

Hadn't he said that what he was doing was work, something he was supposed to be doing? I doubt that the notion of painting for himself applied to his practical mind, just as I doubt that he could have foreseen a day when his cats would be severed from the very barns on which they lived, to be taken in wall-size chunks and "domesticated" in museums and art galleries all over the country.

Or . . . maybe he *did* have an inkling of what would happen, and knew that he wouldn't have his cats to himself for very much longer. . . .

And, considering what was written on his tombstone—by whom, I don't know—I don't think I'm the only person who *maybe* knows what really happened to Hobart Gurney, down in the long, dead, flattened grass below the "little girls" . . . for this is what is carved on his barn-gray tombstone:

No Heaven will not ever Heaven be, Unless my Cats are there to Welcome me.

All I can say is, I hope it was warm, and soft, and *loving*, there in the long, dead grass, with the little girls. . . .

In memory of Beanie, Ming, Fella, Ollie,
Puddin', Blackie, Cupcake, Smokie, Prissy,
Mish-Mish, Dewie, Rusty,
Precious, Lucky, Eric, Sweetheart

Nancy Kress

Nancy Kress is the author of ten books: three fantasy novels, four science fiction novels, two collections of short stories, and a book on writing fiction, *Beginnings, Middles, and Ends*. Her most recent novels are *Beggars and Choosers*, the sequel to *Beggars in Spain*, which was based on her Hugo- and Nebula-winning novella of the same title, and *Oaths and Miracles*. Her most recent story collection is *The Aliens of Earth*.

Kress's short fiction appears regularly in *Omni, Asimov's Science Fiction Magazine*, and other major magazines and anthologies. She was awarded the 1985 short-story Nebula for "Out of All Them Bright Stars." A former elementary school teacher and advertising copywriter, Kress is currently the monthly "fiction" columnist for *Writer's Digest* magazine and teaches seminars in writing science fiction. She lives in Brockport, New York.

The "Marigold Outlet" of the title is a haven for the vulnerable, the helpless. The cats who live there are not central to the story but are its fulcrum.

Marigold Outlet

NANCY KRESS

HE WAS TOO cold to sleep. Mommy put the blanket around him but the car heater was broke again and no matter how tight he pulled the blanket, he couldn't get warm. Cold air was coming from someplace down near his feet. Maybe the car was broke there, too. Maybe they would fall through to the cold road and get smooshed, like the mouse he saw yesterday at the highway rest stop. He reached for Mommy's arm.

"Timmy, not while I'm driving! We could crash!"

He took his hand away and pushed it between his knees, for warmth. His special pillowcase was there, the one that used to be blue. Mommy said he was too old to have it, but he did. She hadn't noticed the pillowcase because she was driving. They were always driving. They had been driving for two years, on and off, ever since he was five. He was so cold.

"Are we almost there?"

"No. Go to sleep."

"It's too cold to sleep."

"Well, is that my fault?" Mommy snapped. In the thin morning light her cheeks looked white and lines pulled down her face. Timmy pushed himself back across the seat, scrunching against the window. The glass was freezing.

Of course it wasn't Mommy's fault it was cold. Nothing was Mommy's fault. They had to keep ahead of Daddy, who was a bad person who would tell Timmy lies if he could find him. Tell him lies and hurt him. The cold was all Daddy's fault. Like everything else when they were between towns.

Timmy sat up straighter, to keep his cheek away from the cold window. The road started to have more houses on it, more signs. Maybe that meant they *were* nearly there. Sometimes Mommy didn't tell the whole truth. That was Daddy's fault, too.

Timmy could read some of the road signs; they'd stayed in Cedar Creek since school started and he'd had the best first-grade teacher in the school, Mr. Kennison. Everybody said he was the best. He had a lot of boys in his class. The boys in other first grades were jealous of Timmy, although of course he hadn't been Timmy in Dansville. He'd been John. He was only Timmy between towns, when they left one very fast, like they did this morning. John—Timmy—hadn't even had time to pack his rock collection. Probably he would never see Mr. Kennison again.

That made tears start, and Mommy would get mad if he cried again. She said he was too old to cry, and anyway all this was much harder on her than him and he should realize that. That's what she said. If he cried, she'd slap him again, and then *she'd* cry. Instead, Timmy hummed. Sometimes that helped. *Three blind mice. Three blind mice. They all ran after the farmer's wife . . .*

"Shut up that racket!"

He stopped humming and sounded out the road signs. Sometimes that helped, too.

SLOW CHILDREN. 20 MPH. CURVE AHEAD. And a bright yellow sign with a flower drawn on it: MARIGOLD OUTLET. Timmy sounded out that one slowly. He didn't know people were allowed to draw on road signs.

"Well! It wasn't as far as I thought after all!"

He glanced at his mother. She was smiling. He decided to risk it. "Mommy, that sign said 'Marigold Outlet.' What's an outlet?"

"A passage for something to escape, like water from a pond. We're here, Timmy."

She stopped the car. Timmy didn't see any pond. But the house was different from the other ones between towns. It was big, and very white, with lawns and woods around it. It looked rich. Not like the others. He started to hum again, but softer.

"Well, get out, can't you? I'm certainly not going to carry you!"

Slowly Timmy got out of the car. The house looked too rich. He pulled his pillowcase from between his knees and shoved it in his coat pocket. He had to be careful because it made a bulge Mommy might notice, and besides the pocket had a big hole. But he wasn't going to throw the pillowcase out, no matter how hard Mommy slapped him.

A tall, skinny woman with wire glasses hurried toward them across the lawn. She carried a cat, orange and white with thick long fur. "Betty?"

"Yes," Mommy said. "Are you Jane?"

"Yes. Welcome to Marigold Outlet. And you must be John."

"Timmy," Mommy said. She was looking hard at Jane's coat. It was pale gold fur, like the cat, and just as thick and soft. Mommy pulled her own cloth coat closer and her mouth got that thin, mean line. Timmy tried to inch away without being noticed. Jane helped by holding out the cat to him.

"Would you like to pet Boots? She's very gentle."

Boots looked at Timmy from big yellow eyes. Timmy put a hand on her head. Boots started to purr, and Timmy looked harder into her eyes. There was something in there, some deep place. He petted her again.

Mommy knocked his hand away. "If you don't *mind*, he's cold and so am I. Could we have the social amenities later?"

Jane's face changed. "Sorry. Come this way."

She led them across the lawn. On the wide clean porch, Boots jumped out of Jane's arms and strolled around the corner, out of sight. Timmy watched her go, thinking about the deep place in Boots's eyes.

The bedroom was all for himself. There was a bed with a Superman cover and two pillows and a shelf of toys and books. Timmy stopped in the doorway and looked at the floor.

"Don't touch anything," Mommy said. "It's not yours."

"Oh, no, he can play with whatever he wants," Jane said. "I just keep this for visitors."

"I don't want him getting used to what he can't have," Mommy snapped. "It's not like all of us can live like you."

Mommy was jealous, Timmy knew. Mr. Kennison had taught him that word. There were a lot of kids who weren't in Mr. Kennison's special first grade but wanted to be. They got mean to Mr. Kennison's kids, and Mr. Kennison explained that they were jealous. Mommy sounded exactly like those kids. Timmy didn't want to get slapped, so he didn't look at the toys again. He crossed the room and climbed into the Superman bed.

"Take off your shoes first, you little shit!" Mommy said. She was close to crying, Timmy saw. He pulled off his shoes. In the last house between towns, he slept in his shoes because he was afraid that Eric Cheney, who lived there always and wasn't between towns, would steal them. Eric stole everything.

"Let me show you your room," Jane said to Mommy. Mommy slammed the door. Timmy heard them move off down the hall, Mommy stomping. He wondered how long before Jane yelled at them to leave.

When he was sure Mommy wasn't coming back, Timmy climbed out of bed and onto a rocking chair. He peered out the window to look for Boots. The cat wasn't in sight. The door opened and Jane caught him.

She would hit him for being out of bed, like Mrs. Cheney at the last place. She would take away his pillow-case. She would tell Mommy . . . Timmy knelt, frozen, on the rocking chair.

"Timmy," Jane said, "what's wrong, honey? Were you looking for something?"

"No!"

She came toward him. Timmy flinched. She stopped. "Were you looking for Boots?"

How did she know? Mommy never knew what he was thinking. He looked at her warily. She smiled.

"Boots is a great cat. You can play with her in the

morning. But she has kittens, so she doesn't stay away from them long."

Timmy nodded. Kittens. They would go into that deep place in Boots's eyes. The kittens would be safe there. He wanted to see the kittens so bad, he ached.

Jane said, "If you're not sleepy, would you like to see the kittens?"

He made himself not answer. It could be a trap. She could get him to do it and then hit him for it, like Mommy sometimes did when she was too tired or too jealous. He didn't move, not so much as a bit of his face. But Jane took his hand and led him down the hallway and down a lot of stairs to the basement. Timmy started to breathe hard. Eric had taken him to the basement, too, at Mrs. Cheney's, and . . . He looked for a place to run.

But Jane just led him to a big box where Boots had four kittens sucking on her belly. Two gray, one orangey like Boots, and one all spotted black and orange and white. Timmy stroked that one's head, and when Jane didn't yell at him, he did it again.

"They're almost ready to leave Boots," Jane said. "Would you like one for your own? To keep forever?"

Immediately Timmy pulled his hand away. "Mommy wouldn't let me."

"I could talk to her . . ."

"No!" He stood. "I'm going back to bed now."

"Okay," Jane said. She was watching him, hard but not mean, the same way Mr. Kennison watched him sometimes. Used to watch him. "You can come down here to see the kittens anytime you want."

No, he couldn't. Mommy wouldn't like it. "Don't drool over things you can't have!" she would say. "Don't you make me feel bad enough already about the way we have to live? All on account of you?"

Timmy went back to bed. The Superman cover was warm and soft. It had bright colors. He was tired, but he lay awake a long time, thinking about the deep safe place in Boots's eyes.

* * *

"He's withdrawn emotionally almost to the point of non-communication," Jane said into the telephone. "And yet the rage underneath is tremendous. You can feel it."

Timmy hid in a little cupboard under the stairs and listened. This big old house had lots of places to hide. He'd had two days to find them all.

"I know what the rules are," Jane said. "Claudia, don't lecture me on the rules of this, I already know them. . . . Of course she's had a bad time. But I'm telling you, this is more than just tired resentment for a bad deal. She slaps him, she's verbally abusive, she isn't capable of any real connection with him at all. As a snap diagnosis, I'd say she's a borderline personality with narcissistic character structure. . . . No, Claudia, I don't need to be reminded not to blame the victim!"

Jane took a deep breath. She was really mad. Timmy held his pillowcase closer to his cheek. Cradled in it was a kitten, one of the grays.

"I'm sorry, Claudia. I didn't mean to lose my temper. But I'm telling you, in my professional capacity as a counselor, that this case is different. Please just check the court transcript, see how it looks to you. I mean, we both know it does happen, not every man awarded custody gets it just because he makes the money, sometimes a woman really is unfit and what she tells us could be a vengeful fabrication. . . . No, of course you won't be able to tell for sure, and it's an insult to me to think I'd contact him without the organization's permission. I resent your even suggesting it. But if you could see this kid . . . No, never. Not once. I've never heard him offer any conversation, let down his guard. I've never even seen him smile. And *she*—"

The kitten purred. Could Jane hear it? Frantically Timmy tried to muffle the purring with his pillowcase. The kitten purred louder.

"All right, Claudia. All right. Another week. But please just see what you think of the custody hearing transcript, won't you? Terry can get it for you."

Timmy squeezed the kitten in the pillowcase. It had to stop making noise. It had to, or else Jane would hear and find him where he wasn't supposed to be and then . . . His head opened up into the dark place, the place always next to him, where the bad thoughts were. Nobody must find him! He squeezed the kitten harder. It started to squawk.

"I tell you, Claudia, that Timmy is repressing dangerously, and I mean dangerously. If he doesn't find some outlet for his feelings soon—"

The bad thoughts all came rushing in. Timmy squeezed harder. The kitten stopped squawking. The cupboard was suddenly too dark, too small. He couldn't breathe.

Jane hung up the phone. He heard her footsteps walk away down the hall. The front door opened and closed. Timmy tumbled out of the cupboard. He breathed huge gasps of air. The bad thoughts slithered back into their place . . . slowly, slowly.

He reached into the cupboard and pulled out the pillowcase. The kitten came out with it, lying still. Timmy still breathed hard. He was afraid to touch it. *Don't be dead,* he thought hard at it. *Don't be dead.*

After a minute, the kitten started to move and mewl.

Timmy carried it carefully down the stairs and put it with the others in Boots's box. Boots wasn't there. He went back upstairs and sat on his bed, taking off his shoes first. He sat very quiet, not moving, not talking. If he did that he could keep the bad thoughts away, sometimes. All he had to do was go completely quiet. Not move. Not think. Just hum, and let the humming fill up the places in his mind. . . . *cut off their tails with a carving knife, you never saw such a sight in your life . . .*

After a long time Jane came into the room. "Timmy, it's almost lunch. Have you been playing here all morning?"

Timmy didn't answer.

Jane looked around the room. Timmy knew she was looking for signs of his mother. Timmy hadn't seen Mommy since dinner last night, when she yelled at Jane for having such pretty dishes. He didn't know where his mother was this morning. Jane said gently, "Would you like to have a peanut butter sandwich? And then maybe we can go see the kittens."

He looked down at his shoes, careful to move not even a little bit of his face.

He found a place outside, against the back of the garage, under a big drooping bush that made a solid cave even though there weren't any leaves on it in winter. The bush-cave was cold, but Jane had bought him a new warm coat and boots and mittens. Timmy kept them in the cave, so Mommy wouldn't make him give them back, and changed into them when he went out there. From a little hole in the bushes he could see the road sign: MARIGOLD OUTLET. But nobody could see him.

But on the third day Jane pushed aside the droopy branches and crawled into the cave. "Timmy. May I come in, please?"

He stared at her.

"I'll only stay a minute. Look, I've brought you a present. Your mother said you couldn't have a kitten to take with you when you move to your new home, so I brought you this." She put a box on the snowy ground.

"I don't want it."

"Won't you look at it first?"

Timmy didn't answer. The box was small, metal, black. There were glass-covered holes on one side, a small switch on the other, and a panel to cover the power pack. Jane pressed the switch.

A cat jumped out.

No, not out, *through*—the cat jumped right through the walls of the box. It was a big gold-colored cat, bigger and golder than Boots. Its eyes were bright green. It walked around in a circle, its tail raised high, its eyes watching everything. It started on a second circle, bigger this time, and when it walked over Timmy's knee he could see the torn knee of his jeans through its tail. The cat was made of light.

"It's a holoprojection," Jane said. "Nobody even has to know you've got it except when you want it to come out. The projector will fit in your pocket."

The cat made a third circle, then pounced on a mouse

that Timmy couldn't see. But the cat could see it. Its green eyes sparkled. It let the mouse go, chased its tail for a minute, then stopped and sat still.

Timmy reached out and pressed the switch on the box. The cat disappeared. He pressed it again and the cat reappeared, sitting on the ground. After a few minutes it started to walk in circles again.

Timmy waited until it was once more sitting still, then he crouched on the frozen ground and brought his face close to the cat's. In its eyes there was a deep place, even deeper than in Boots's eyes.

A deep safe place where nobody else could go because the cat was made of light and Timmy could press the switch.

"It's yours," Jane said. "What will you name her?"

Timmy stared at the cat, then off through the bushes at the road sign. The flower was still on it, hand-drawn, pretty.

"Timmy," Jane said again, but not making him answer, not ready to slap or yell, "what will you name her?"

"Marigold," Timmy said.

He played with Marigold every day. Not in the cave under the bushes because that wasn't secret anymore, but under the kitchen porch, where a part of the trellis was missing; in the cupboard under the stairs; behind the long sofa in the library, which smelled of musty books; at the top of the stairs to the boarded-up attic; in the woods, where it turned out there really was a creek leading out from a big pond. Never in the cellar, where Boots and the kittens were. He didn't need Boots. Marigold was better. And she never purred.

Timmy watched her for hours, all golden light and green eyes. He followed her in circles. He hummed to her: *Three blind mice. Three blind mice. They all ran after the farmer's wife . . .*

Mommy left for three days. When she came back she couldn't stand up straight and she threw up on Jane's dining room rug. Timmy, scrunched inside the sideboard next to cardboard boxes that said SOUP TUREEN and PUNCH BOWL, watched Marigold walk through the corners of the boxes in silent circles.

"Betty!" Jane said.

"So have ... your cleaning lady clean ... it up." Mommy's voice shook.

"Don't you want to know what your son's been doing for three days while you were off on a bender?"

"Sure you ... took care of him."

"Yes. I did. But don't you think that's your place?"

"Sure is, bitch. So don't ... usurp it."

Jane's voice changed. She didn't sound like the person who'd give him the cat. "Look at you. Not fit to have a son like Timmy. Do you know what you're doing to him? This running isn't to keep him from an abusive father, it's so you can justify your whiny self-pity and live off others too kind to let you rot while you've got Tim—" Jane made a funny noise and then her voice changed again, got all stiff. "I'm sorry. That was very unprofessional of me. But, Betty, you do need help. Not from me, but I know someone who could make things feel much better for you, a trusted colleague who's really very good—"

"Is he? Is he ... 'really very good,' Jane? How nice for him. Fuck you, Timmy and I are just fine. We don't need you, you tight-assed Miss Priss with your big house and dried-up tits and stupid do-goodism. You know what really bothers you, bitch? That I won't kowtow to you the way the rest of them do, the poor cunts you so graciously help ... we're out of here, Timmy and me. You won't see us again."

"You can't take Timmy away from here until Claudia sets up another identity and—"

"Oh, can't I? Timmy! Timmy, where the hell are you!"

Timmy turned off Marigold and shoved her box in his pocket. He heard his mother crashing into things in the dining room, throwing furniture, yelling. She went into the hall and he heard the cupboard under the stairs flung open. He tried to squeeze behind the PUNCH BOWL box but there was no more room in the sideboard. He jammed his pillowcase into the other pocket. The sideboard door tore open, ripping loose at one hinge, and Mommy grabbed him and pulled him out.

"Hiding and skulking!" she screamed. Her face was all twisted up and she smelled awful. "You see what I have to put up with, bitch? And you blame it on me, just like everybody always does! Hiding and skulking and eavesdropping on me so there's never any peace!" She dragged Timmy by his arm across the floor. It hurt. He tried to squirm free and that hurt more, but he didn't cry out because that would just make Mommy slap him.

"Let him go!" Jane screamed. She hit at Mommy's arm. Mommy let go. Mommy fell on the ground. Jane went on hitting her, and Jane was crying, too. Mommy put her arms around her head. Timmy crawled away, and then he felt the other person in the room, the big person, and he stopped crawling and lay still.

"What the hell is going on here?" Daddy said.

Jane got up slowly from the floor. Her glasses were broken and her skirt was torn. Her face was an ugly red. "Oh my God. Mr. Collins?"

"What the—"

"I'm sorry. Oh, I'm sorry. I'm Jane Farquhar, I phoned you to come . . ."

Daddy didn't say anything. Timmy looked all the way up at him, up the long legs and long arms, and remembered. Jane stood, smoothing her torn skirt, taking off the broken glasses.

"I'm so glad you've come, Mr. Collins. The situation here has deteriorated, your son desperately needs you. Betty simply can't . . . isn't . . ." Jane stopped.

Daddy walked over to where Mommy lay on the floor, her eyes closed. His face got red. He looked hard at Jane. "What the hell have you been doing to her? Don't you know she's sick? What the fuck's wrong with you?"

Timmy closed his eyes. But he could feel when Daddy looked at him. He could feel it.

"Timmy. You're the man here. Didn't I always tell you it's *your* job to take care of your mother?"

* * *

He sat in the woods, beside the outlet that was really just a creek. He didn't have Marigold, or his pillowcase. He didn't want anything to happen to them. He waited, humming: *you nev-er saw such a sight in your life—*

Maybe Jane would find him first, but he didn't think so. Daddy always found him, in all the towns, just like he had found him leaving Mr. Kennison's class in Dansville. That was part of how it went. Daddy found them, and then Daddy waited a little so they could get a head start between towns, and he and Mommy jumped in the car and drove away and Mommy made phone calls from booths along the road to find out from the organization where they were going between towns. But that part wasn't yet. First Daddy would find him.

"Timmy. You let me down."

"I'm sorry, Daddy," Timmy said, although it wouldn't help. It never did.

"Your mother's sick in her head. I told you that. I told you in Dansville that it was your job to keep her quiet while I closed up the house to bring you both home. That's what I said, wasn't it, Timmy?"

"Yes." He tried to think about Marigold, about the deep safe place in her eyes. But he couldn't see it, couldn't feel it. He was shivering too hard. You had to be quiet to go there.

"You let me down, Timmy. You let us both down. You know that, don't you, son?"

"Y-y-yes."

"And I can't even discipline you properly until we leave here, because of that meddling bitch Jane Farquhar. She'd interfere, all right. But you know I will discipline you when we finally do leave, don't you, Timmy? For your own sake? Don't you?"

"Y-y-yes."

"A boy who can't protect his women is going to make a mighty poor man."

Timmy didn't answer. Daddy turned and walked back along Marigold Outlet. Timmy heard his boots crunch in the snow. The shivering wouldn't stop. All the other times, he hadn't had to wait. All the other times, Daddy had gotten it over right away. He couldn't stop shivering. He was so cold.

"It's a restraining order," Jane said. A policeman stood beside her, and another man in a dark suit with a briefcase. "He's been placed in my custody pending the hearing. If either of you come within two hundred feet of him, you'll be arrested."

Mommy stood next to Daddy. She looked small next to him. She had a new dress and her hair was combed and her face was very white. Mommy didn't say anything. She never did in the times when Daddy came. She kept her eyes on the floor and smiled to herself. She and Daddy held hands.

Jane choked out, "Of all the sick psychological dependencies . . ." She stood up straighter. "Now leave, both of you."

"We won't forget this," Daddy said. "Timmy, we'll get you back, son."

"Not in this state," Jane said.

Timmy heard the cars drive away: first Mommy's, then Daddy's. That's how it always went. He would follow her close all the way home.

But this wasn't the way it always went, leaving him behind. This was different.

Jane knelt beside Timmy. "You're safe now, Timmy, do you understand? They can't come hurt you anymore. Mr. Jacobson is a lawyer, and he'll stop them, and Officer French will stop them, and so will I. You're going to be safe here with me, Timmy, do you understand?"

Timmy didn't answer. He looked at the floor.

"Would you like to go see the kittens? All three are weaned now."

All three. There had been four. Before the day in the cupboard, when the gray one purred.

Jane looked like she said something wrong. Timmy turned and walked upstairs. Marigold's box was in his pocket. He would never go see the kittens that were left again, never.

"Timmy," Jane called after him. "Won't you let me know if you need anything, honey?"

He didn't answer or turn around.

At night he woke up sweating. They weren't there. They really weren't there, not Mommy and not Daddy. They weren't sleeping in separate rooms, like they did at home, and they weren't sleeping crumpled together naked, like they did between towns. But the bad thoughts were still here, in Timmy's head, and he didn't know how to stop them. They were stronger now. Mommy wasn't there to hide from. Daddy wasn't there to hide from. All his hiding places weren't hiding places anymore, and so the bad thoughts came. . . . *cut off their tails with a carving knife, you never saw such a sight in your life* . . .

Sometimes the bad thoughts turned to bad dreams, and he woke up screaming, his pillowcase stuffed in his mouth so nobody would hear. His hands must do that when he was asleep.

Timmy got out of bed and turned on Marigold and watched her walk in circles and pounce on the invisible mouse and chase her tail. The circles were best. He could crouch down with his face near hers and see the deep safe place in her eyes.

But he couldn't ever get there. Ever, ever.

"His internal defenses are crumbling," Jane said on the phone, "but so far no real breakthrough. God, it's painful to watch. . . . He sees Dr. Lambert three times a week, but so far he hasn't said a single word to him. And he won't *eat*."

Timmy made Marigold go around and around some more. All afternoon, all evening, all the parts of the dark night he couldn't sleep. *Three blind mice* . . .

"He needs an outlet for all that rage," Jane said on the phone. "Oh, God, it's heartbreaking!"

Marigold pounced and chased and strutted in circles, her beautiful tail high.

"Timmy, honey, you've got to *eat* something."

She didn't understand. The bad thoughts fed on food, When he ate food, his mind was a strong place the bad thoughts liked to come to. When he didn't eat, his head was too funny a place for them, floating and full of light, gold-colored light like Marigold.

"Timmy, if you don't eat, we'll have to take you to the hospital. Please eat, honey, just a little."

Sometimes he could see Marigold even when the box was turned off, walking in her high-tailed circles. But turned on was better. If he ever got to that safe place in her eyes, it would be when Marigold was turned on.

"A catharsis experience," Jane said on the phone. Her voice sounded funny, hard and desperate. Timmy stayed hidden in the cupboard. She sounded like Mommy when Mommy wanted him to do something.

"Yes, I understand, Marty," Jane said. "Tonight. I'll meet you at the end of the drive."

Marigold wouldn't turn on.

Timmy sat on the floor of his room, pressing the switch. Nothing happened. He pressed it again. Nothing. He threw the box across the room, crawled after it on hands and knees, frantically pressed and pressed. Nothing.

Breathing hard, he sat very still.

The knives were kept in the kitchen. He got one, creeping silently as fog back up the stairs, and pulled off the metal cover to the projector's power pack. It was empty. Somebody had taken it out.

Timmy bent over the black metal box. Marigold was gone. The deep safe place in her eyes was gone, and only the place inside his head was left, the place where the bad thoughts came. Marigold was gone—

He screamed and threw the box across the room. He dashed after it and jumped on it, and the cat of light raced around the room, tail high. Only she wasn't there, she was dead, he had killed her in the cupboard under the stairs because she purred too loud, just like he killed Mommy and Daddy just like he wanted to kill them, plunging the knife over and over into them after they hit him running them over in the car burning them up in the fire . . . *cut off their heads with a carving knife* . . . the bad thoughts all there now because Marigold was dead and he'd killed her, stabbing her with the carving knife in his hand now until it was bent and mangled like it was now and the carpet all slashed to pieces and red with Mommy's guts—

"There, there, Timmy," Jane crooned, holding him. Dr. Lambert was there, too, big as Daddy in his winter coat. "It'll be better now, honey. It'll be better now, just cry it out. I'm here, you just needed an outlet for all that pain, there, there . . ."

An outlet. An escape. He sobbed and sobbed and fell asleep in her arms.

He didn't have to go to the hospital, Dr. Lambert said. He still had to see Dr. Lambert, but that was all right because now Timmy could talk to him. Just a little at first, and then a little more. About Mommy and Daddy and between towns. He could eat a little, too, and then a little more. Jane smiled.

But best of all, Marigold was back.

This time he didn't even need a black metal box. Marigold walked around him in big circles whenever he looked a special way out of the corner of his eye. At first she walked where Boots did, or the kittens that now were big enough to creep upstairs, struggling over the top of each step like it was a mountain. Boots or the kittens would stalk across the room and there would be Marigold right with them, a bigger cat made of gold light moving with the fur-and-bone cats. Later Marigold didn't even need Boots or the kittens. She could walk alone, anytime Timmy wanted, her tail waving and her ears twitching forward. And the best thing was, since Timmy had broken her box, Marigold had learned to talk.

"That was my outlet, Timmy," Marigold said. "I got out. I can come now whenever you want, and between times I go to the deep safe place. Breaking the box was my outlet."

"You wouldn't believe his improvement in such a short time," Jane said on the phone. "It's incredible."

Marigold twitched her ears and raised her tail at Jane.

Timmy started school, a special school where there were only six kids in his class, and he was the only one who could read. Sometimes Marigold came to school, too. A lot of days she didn't, and then Timmy had to wait till he got to Jane's to see her. School wasn't good and it wasn't bad. Mostly it didn't matter.

"He's still very withdrawn," Jane said on the phone, "and Marty Lamberton is guarded about the prognosis. But I'm optimistic." There was something wrong with her voice.

"Jane needs an outlet," Marigold told Timmy. "It would make her feel better."

"She can't have you," Timmy said. "Marigold, can't I go with you to that deep safe place you go between times?"

Marigold only smiled and disappeared. Timmy hated that. He sat completely still, the bad thoughts pushing at his mind, until Marigold came back a few hours later, twitching around the edge of a chair, walking in circles with her tail up like nothing happened.

The snow was almost melted when Jane told Timmy they had to go to court to tell Timmy's story to a nice man, a judge, who wanted to help Jane keep Timmy always. Timmy's mother and father would be there, Jane said, but they wouldn't be able to touch Timmy or even to talk to him. He musn't be afraid.

"Mommy and Daddy are already here," Marigold said, walking in circles around Jane. "Jane doesn't know. They're camped on the other side of the woods. They'll come get you whenever Daddy wants to."

Timmy started to cry.

"Oh, honey, don't," Jane said, reaching for him. Timmy pushed her away. What did she know about what Marigold said? About what Daddy could do? About anything?

He ran outside and crawled under the kitchen porch. Marigold came with him. They sat there in the dark.

Timmy whispered, "The bad thoughts are coming."

"I know," Marigold said.

"I . . ."

"You hurt," Marigold said. It was what Dr. Lambert said all the time, but Timmy never answered him because Dr. Lamberton didn't really *know*. It was just more words, like when Daddy said he needed discipline or Mommy said she was sick. Just words. But Marigold *knew*.

"You need an outlet," Marigold said. "Like when you smashed my box and let me out. Remember how good that felt?"

Timmy said, "But the bad thoughts made me do that."

"But after you did it, the bad thoughts were gone," Marigold argued. "And remember how good that felt?"

Timmy remembered. And Marigold did, too. Coming from Marigold, it wasn't just words.

"You need an outlet," Marigold said.

". . . in the best interests of the child," the judge said. He'd said a lot of other things, for two days. Timmy had stopped listening. It was just words, and he was tired, and Mommy and Daddy sat across the room on hard brown chairs and tried to smile at him. He wouldn't look at them. He wouldn't look at anybody. Marigold had refused to come to court, and Timmy was mad at her. How could she refuse to come? She was supposed to be there when he needed her.

". . . no supported evidence of paternal misconduct, and if you, Mrs. Collins, promise to receive psychiatric help, and if the conditions of full-time schooling for Timothy are met, I see no reason why the rights of the biological parents should not be the foremost consideration in—"

"No!" Jane cried. "No, you can't!"

She stood up in her chair. Timmy wished she would sit down. She looked silly, in her long skinny dress with her glasses falling off her nose.

"—failure to provide convincing testimony that the child has actually formed a bond of affection with you in any meaningful way, Ms. Farquhar—"

"He can't," Jane said. Her voice was quiet now, but

Timmy saw she was holding her hands so tight together that the skin looked white. Like Boots's paws. He looked away.

"Don't you see, Your Honor? Timmy's never learned to love. All love means to him now is pain. But he's not a cruel child and with time—"

"I've given my decision," the judge said. "You have three days to restore him to his parents, Ms. Farquhar. Case dismissed."

Jane clutched Timmy's shoulder. He didn't like it. He didn't like Mommy and Daddy looking at him, either. He wanted to get home to Marigold.

That night he took her behind the library sofa. She let him carry her now. It felt funny, carrying such a heavy cat made all of light. He could see her dimly underneath his hands. The library was cold—Jane turned the heat down at night—and smelled like nobody ever went there. Timmy liked that smell.

"They say I have to go away," he whispered to Marigold. "Back to Mommy and Daddy."

"I'll go with you," Marigold said.

"I know. But Mommy will slap me and then we'll run away and go between towns and then someplace to live and then Daddy will find me and hit me for not taking care of Mommy."

"But I'll be with you," Marigold said.

"I know," Timmy said miserably. It wasn't enough. Marigold wasn't enough. How could that be?

"The bad thoughts come hard, Marigold," Timmy said. "I want to . . ." He started to cry.

Marigold said, "Remember how good it felt when you smashed my box?"

"Take me to the deep safe place, Marigold! Take me away from the bad thoughts!"

"I can't," Marigold said.

"Take me to the deep safe place in your eyes!"

"I can't." Marigold twitched her tail. "But you can, Timmy."

"I'm afraid," Timmy sobbed.

"Remember how good you felt afterward?"

Marigold looked at him. In the darkness behind the sofa her eyes were very green. Timmy could see the deep safe place in them.

"The bad thoughts are here, Marigold!"

"You need an outlet," Marigold said, in Jane's voice. She started to purr, which she'd never done before. The purring sounded just like humming. It had words in it, Marigold's words so they must be true: . . . *never saw such a sight in your life* . . .

Timmy crept to the kitchen. The knives were there, with the sharp edges for cutting off the blind mice's tails. He took two, one for each hand, because he didn't need to carry Marigold anymore, she scampered happily next to him. Timmy and Marigold went down the cellar. Timmy hadn't been there since his first weeks at Jane's. The bad thoughts pushed him hard, hurting him inside the way Daddy hurt him—

The box beside the furnace was empty.

Marigold said, "Jane gave the kittens to good homes when they got too big." Timmy looked at her. Her face didn't show him anything: He couldn't stand that.

"Marigold, the bad thoughts are coming. I can't stop them, they *hurt*—"

This time Marigold didn't answer, which was worse. Oh, much worse. Timmy went upstairs, then upstairs again, to the bedrooms.

Jane slept on her back, with her mouth open. She snored. Without her glasses, her face looked empty. The bad thoughts hurt Timmy so much, he thought he would scream.

Timmy raised the knife. He looked at Jane snoring with her mouth open. Only she wasn't snoring, she was smiling, walking across the lawn with Boots in her arms. *Would you like to pet Boots? She's very gentle. Would you like a kitten for your own? To keep forever? Would you like another peanut-butter-and-jelly sandwich, honey?*

"I can't," Timmy whispered.

"Go on, Timmy," Marigold said, only now she had

Mommy's voice, mad and hurrying. *Come on, Timmy, for cripe's sake, can't you do anything right, you little shit—*

The bad thoughts burned him. Stabbing and kicking and burning and blood and their brains spilling out and their arms gone and their guts on the floor . . . *cut off their heads with a carving knife . . .*

"Remember how good it felt last time?" Marigold said. "Afterward?"

This is for you, Jane said. *Your mother said you couldn't have a kitten when you move to your new house, so I brought you this. You press the button here—*

. . . never saw such a sight in your life . . .

And then Timmy saw it.

It was right there, right in Marigold's eyes. Killing her box *had* felt good last time, had been the outlet, the escape, the way in. The way to Marigold, who was always there, who would never leave him or kick him or hurt him the way the bad thoughts hurt him. The outlet was the way to the safe place deep in Marigold's eyes, and the bad thoughts tried to confuse him because they were bad thoughts. He had smashed Marigold's box, but that had only set Marigold free. Free to show Timmy the safe place, where the bad thoughts could never go—the such a sight he never saw in his life—

"Thank you," Timmy said. He said it out loud and then raised the sharp knife to his own throat. Marigold smiled. Timmy pushed hard and then someone was screaming, two people were screaming, but it didn't matter because he wouldn't ever have to hear them again and the bad thoughts were gone and he had reached the deep place inside Marigold's eyes, the place the three blind mice had run, the place where Boots and the kittens would be there always and of course so would his cat, *his* cat, the place Timmy made because no one else could make it for him. The safe place. Marigold Outlet.

Susan Wade

Susan Wade's short fiction has appeared in *Amazing Stories; The Magazine of Fantasy and Science Fiction; First for Women; Snow White; Blood Red; Black Thorn; White Rose; Ruby Slippers; Golden Tears;* and *Off Limits.*

Her first novel, *Walking Rain,* a sort of magical realist/thriller hybrid, was recently published. Her second novel is tentatively called *Northern Lights* and is, Wade says, "contemporary with a hint of magical realism (animal enchanters and a fairy tale figure prominently) about a complicated issue of child custody." She lives in Austin, Texas.

"White Rook, Black Pawn" is a tour de force about firefighting, physics, chess, and divorcing parents.

White Rook, Black Pawn

SUSAN WADE

ELLIOT FRANKLIN FIRST noticed the odd behavior of the cats a week after his wife took their daughter and went to her parents' house in Dallas.

"Just for the rest of the summer," Rita had said. "So Anna can take dance lessons from Madame Duprée. This studio is doing her no real good, even you can see that."

Elliot didn't see anything wrong with the Dance Theatre School, other than the fact that they spelled theater with an "re" instead of an "er." Especially at Annie's age.

Annie's dance school wasn't the real issue, but he had learned that pointing such things out to Rita would not improve matters. So he settled for Annie's assurance that *of course* she could dial long distance by herself and *of course* she remembered his work number.

"And besides, it's Station 12 of the Austin Fire Department," she added, "so I can look it up in case I forget. Which I won't."

"And you know which shift I'm—"

"B-shift," she had said, her gray eyes condemning him for doubting her seven-year-old abilities. "Besides, I *always* remember your work schedule, Daddy."

"It's just that I'm going to miss you," Elliot said apologetically. "A whole lot."

Annie hugged him. "Me, too, Daddy. But it's only six weeks."

He knew where she had picked up that phrase. It was Rita's answer to every objection he had raised. And he couldn't bring himself to warn Annie that it might be a lie.

Rita never had adapted to Austin; she was a North

Dallas girl to her bones. Elliot suspected that only a spasm of youthful rebellion had led her to marry him. Once it passed, she became relentless in her discontent over living here.

He had turned thirty-six in June. The birthday that made him too old to join any other major fire department. During the four days after Rita announced her plans, he had moments when he suspected her of waiting until he was stuck in Austin before moving back to Dallas for good.

If she hadn't come home by the time school started, he'd know she was leaving him. If he accused her of it before then, she would insist that nothing was wrong and that he was paranoid.

Elliot believed that living with Rita for eight years could breed paranoia in the sanest of men. But that was another argument entirely, the one he generally thought of as their "Who's crazier?" fight.

So, in the end, he had let them go: his discontented wife and his only child. He had even conspired in his own defeat, obediently loading the bags in the trunk of the Buick and gloomily watching as they drove down the suburban street and out of his sight.

He spent the next week in unrelieved dejection, punctuated by a single bright spot when he called his father-in-law's house in Dallas and was actually permitted to speak to Annie. His other calls met with abrupt termination at the hands of Roger Waller, Rita's father. "She's taking a nap," he would say, or, "They're at the studio for Anna's lessons." He always hung up before Elliot could leave a message.

Elliot pulled his shifts that week like always—twenty-four on and forty-eight off—and paid bills and shopped for groceries. But he had the growing conviction that he had lost his daughter for good.

It wasn't until Saturday evening, after another foiled attempt to call Annie, that he realized she might have written to him. He hunted for the mail key for twenty minutes before unearthing it from a basket on the hall table.

A long summer twilight had succeeded the torturously

searing day, and the first cool wind of the evening rose as he walked down the hill to the P.O. box. The creek that ran under the road at that point was surprisingly full considering how hot it had been lately.

Elliot extracted a week's worth of mail from the jammed box. As he stood there sorting the junk from the bills, something flickered at the edge of his field of vision, a swift, shadowy movement along the pavement. It made the hair on his neck prickle.

He turned his head to look closer, but the tall sycamores and oaks that grew along the creek had shaded the dusk into darkness. At first, he couldn't make anything out.

He stood there without moving, and, as his eyes adjusted, a strange tableau came into focus.

A pair of large storm drains bracketed the bottom of the road where it curved to bridge the stream. Evenly arrayed in front of the storm drain across from him were close to a dozen black cats. Solid black. Each cat was holding a distinct posture in a specific spot, so the group looked like a platoon of soldiers frozen at their posts.

The small, gaunt adolescents were ranged in front of the older cats, sitting with tails curled neatly around their black bodies, ears alert, eyes forward. The larger cats had more varied stances, but there was still a strange regularity to their positions. An enormous, sleek tom with oversized ears that gave him a foxy look sat on the curb above the drain as if surveying the ranks. On either side, two cats sat settled back on their haunches, each with one paw up, claws bared.

Definitely odd. Elliot had noticed the stray cats in the neighborhood before, of course. With the creek and undeveloped wooded area behind the houses here, they saw lots of wild animals—'possums and raccoons and hundreds of squirrels. But he'd never seen the feral cats assemble like this.

Something else flickered at the periphery of his vision. Very slowly, Elliot turned, making sure to keep the tableau of black cats in his line of sight.

In front of the drain on this side, another group had convened. The cats in the second group were all solid white. In contrast to the orderly ranks of the blacks, the white cats' positions looked scattered and chaotic.

The two companies faced each other across the street, motionless and unblinking. Elliot noticed that one of the white cats looked off-sides—a medium-size female with half an ear missing. She was sitting, tail up, a good six feet away from the rest of her phalanx.

Not one of the cats moved.

It was the weirdest damn thing Elliot had ever seen.

Without any warning, the ragged-eared white cat swooped diagonally across the street. She snatched an adolescent from the ranks of the blacks, seizing its head in her mouth and skittering past the enemy flank into the creek bed beyond.

It happened at lightning speed, soundlessly, without even a cry from the victim. But Elliot thought he heard the kitten's neck bones crack as the white cat disappeared into the shadows.

He peered after her, trying to track her progress, but the fading light defeated him. By the time he looked back at the street, the tableaux of cats had melted away as if they had never been there.

"Maybe I'm seeing things," he said. His voice sounded rusty. He cleared his throat and turned back toward the house.

The white marauder sat atop the wall of the bridge behind him, calmly licking blood from her snowy fur.

Elliot dropped his mail. The cat looked up at him for a moment, then resumed her unhurried grooming.

"I get it," Elliot whispered. "White rook to Queen's pawn three. Is that it?"

Finished removing the dark blood from her chest, the white cat merely flicked her tail and vanished into the twilight.

Elliot's shift started the following day, technically at noon, but it was a tradition to relieve the guys on the preceding shift early, so he went in at eleven.

Station 12 had a big territory, covering northeast

Austin from Lamar Boulevard to IH 35, and ran a lot of calls. Most were medical—usually heart attacks; sometimes stabbings or shootings. But they ran a lot of fires, too.

That shift was the busiest Elliot could remember, and it wasn't even a full moon. The biggie was a box alarm that came in at 4:04 in the morning. The tone sounded—a loud "wuuuh-aanh"—and caught him deep in REM sleep. Elliot usually came alert fast, but this call caught him at the wrong time, and later he couldn't remember a thing that happened before they got to the fire.

It was in one of the row-style apartment complexes that speckle Austin's north side, twenty units in an L-shape two-story building. It looked to be a real burn. Reflections from the engine's warning lights skated across the face of the building, flashing orange and red on the darkened windows, like sparks. Mesmerizing.

Then somebody yelled, and it registered on Elliot that twenty or so residents were milling around by the curb with flashlights. Touie had pulled the engine up in front of the row of units that were engaged and was looking at him.

Touie said sharply, "Franklin! You okay?"

Elliot snapped to and got on the radio. "Engine 12 is out. Assuming I.C. We've got an apartment complex with heavy smoke showing upstairs. Second-in engine needs to lay five-inch line. We'll be pulling rack lines."

Vasquez was already scrambling to pull the engine's hoses, and Elliot jumped to help her, while Touie got ready to pump water. Voigt grabbed one of the lines and headed for the stairs.

"Is everybody out?" Elliot called to one of the civilians, a big guy in jeans who looked as if he was wide awake. "Where'd it start?"

The guy said, "In the apartment next to mine, we think," and pointed to the door upstairs on the end. "Three eighty-five. The smoke alarms went off—I think everyone heard 'em."

"Count heads," Elliot told him. "Check apartment numbers. We'll search, but try to make sure everybody's accounted for." Some unsourced anxiety was chewing on him. He got on the radio again. "Voigt! They think it started in apartment three eighty-five—"

Voigt was halfway up the stairs, his turn-out jacket flapping open as he dragged a flat tail of uncharged 1½-inch line behind him.

"Get your gear on right and give me an interior size-up, Voigt," Elliot said.

Voigt stopped in front of the open door that was spilling smoke. His voice came back loud and excited. "It's not bad—we can nail it here."

Then Voigt stumbled back against the upstairs railing, swearing. Seconds later, a white cat came hurtling down the stairs. It had half an ear missing, Elliot noticed as it darted diagonally across the parking lot and disappeared into the landscaping. At the sight of the ragged ear, his anxiety flared.

Something clicked into place for him—a safety inspection they'd made here months ago. He yelled, "Negative, Voigt! I want cut-off lines in the unit next door. Block it!"

The civilian in blue jeans came up. "Janet says the people in three eighty-five are on vacation—we're pretty sure everybody's out here."

Elliot gave the man a thumbs-up and ran for the stairs, pulling line. "Vasquez—get in place, but don't put any water on it. Voigt and I'll pull ceilings in the side unit. We've got to stop the spread in the attic."

Touie was opening the valve on the engine. Voigt was still standing in the doorway of the apartment, but at least he was fastening his jacket. Vasquez brought the pike poles upstairs, then went back to pull another rack line without being told. She was a good hand.

Elliot moved inside the affected apartment; it was completely masked in billowing black smoke. He couldn't see how far up into the attics the fire had spread.

"I'm telling you, we can nail it," Voigt said from farther in.

"Voigt," Elliot called to him, "save the John Wayne crap. Get next door with me and help me pull ceiling."

"But only part of the kitchen—" Voigt said.

"Do it like I told you, Voigt." Elliot grabbed a pike pole and ran to the apartment on the other side. "Or you'll be signing a twenty."

Elliot could hear the sirens that meant the next company was out; he might be relieved as In-Charge anytime. Smoke was already trickling from the vents. He stabbed the pull-down hook into the drywall overhead and yanked, his shoulder joints complaining. *Getting old, Elliot.* Then Voigt was next to him, stabbing with his hook, too. With the first hole overhead, heat blasted out. But no flames here yet—they were in time.

"We're dicking around over here while it burns!" Voigt yelled at him. "We coulda nailed it right there!"

Elliot didn't waste time answering. It took them several minutes to pull a trench across the ceiling. Touie reported that the second-in engine was catching a plug on their way in, to lay a supply line.

Elliot sent extra hands from their company in for a building search while Touie helped one of the tailboard men from 15 hook up the supply line. Within seconds, the hydrant was open, pumping extra water to the engine for the rack lines they were using.

Elliot got Voigt into position on the cut-off line in the second unit.

"This is shit," Voigt said, shooting a little water up into the attic. "Nothing's happening."

"Just wait," Elliot called. He grabbed the other line and ran to three eighty-five, which was burning like a dog. The place was black with smoke and hot as hell.

Vasquez was in position on her line, waiting like he'd told her.

"Let's knock it down!" he said.

They dived in, spraying water in a wide-fog pattern ahead of them. As they hit the dining room, the orange flames gave a flickering hellish light. The water they were pumping was boiling into steam, making it hotter than ever.

He was worried about a flashover. A fire that got really hot could go from a contained blaze in one area to a spontaneous ignition of the entire room in seconds.

Turn-out gear couldn't protect you from a flashover; it just melted onto your body and fried you. More steam built up. The heat was fierce.

"Getting too hot?" he said.

"It'll be okay," Vasquez called. Her voice sounded fuzzy behind the faceplate.

Then it vented through the roof. He could tell because the smoke started clearing and the flames flared higher. But the place cooled down some—the heat was pouring out of the hole. Then the flames started fading.

"We're getting it!" Vasquez shouted.

Touie's voice came over the radio. "Can you get out here, I.C.? We got some sparking on the roof."

One of the guys from 15 came in. Elliot left him and Vasquez and ran down to the first landing.

Fire was gouting through the roof of three eighty-five. Sparks shot up into the darkness and drifted lazily across the roof.

Shit. As dry as it'd been, they were ripe for grass fires. And part of the roof farther along was starting to smolder.

The civilians were screaming and rushing around downstairs. Inside the helmet, the sound of his own breathing was louder than their screams, louder even than the radio chatter. "Try to calm 'em down," he told Touie as he ran down and grabbed the nozzle of the booster line mounted on the roof of the engine. The rubber line unreeled behind him as he climbed, soaking down the roof on either side of the breakout as he went. His own sweat was scalding him inside the gear, and he felt slow and stupid. Completely incapable of calculating the variables of this burn.

Chaos, he thought. Fires are fucking *chaos.*

Clouds of steam were billowing through the gap in three eighty-five's roof. "You all right inside?" Elliot called, still soaking the roof.

"We're getting it," Voigt yelled.

"No shit," Vasquez called back. She sounded like she was smiling. "Don't sweat it, Franklin. Looks like a clean stop."

Something made Elliot turn his head. Draped along one of the stairwell banisters was a sleek black cat. It stared at Elliot and gave a satisfied yawn, pink tongue curling delicately around its sharp white fangs.

Elliot got a spidery feeling along his back. This cat looked familiar.

He turned back. This fire was out. "Shut it down," Elliot called to Voigt and Vasquez.

Dvarik, the chief from Battalion 4, showed up then, pausing to give the cat a chuck under the chin. Elliot had a lot of respect for Dvarik, an old smoke-eater who'd been fighting fires since the '40s. He expected the chief to relieve him, but Dvarik only asked, "What's the size-up, Franklin? We need a second alarm on this?"

"Think we've got it knocked down, Chief," Elliot said.

"Civilians all out?"

"We're running a manpower team through now," Elliot said, just as one of the guys from 15 reported back that the building was clear.

"What's the loss?" Dvarik asked.

"Two units," Voigt said. It sounded like an accusation. "And that goddamn cat scratched the shit out of me."

Dvarik's mouth twitched.

"Mostly smoke and water damage on two of 'em." That was Vasquez.

"Good call, going in on either side," Dvarik said, before Elliot could respond. "I've inspected out here— there're holes in the attic firewells. If you'd gone in frontal, you could have lost the whole row."

"Thanks, Chief," Elliot said. For once, Voigt kept his mouth shut.

"Pull your people out for rehab," Dvarik told him. "We'll start salvage in a few minutes."

The black cat jumped down from the banister and started rubbing itself against Elliot's boots, purring loudly.

Run reports and a last-minute call made Elliot late home from his shift. He got home around two in the afternoon,

exhausted. They hadn't gotten more than an hour of unin-
terrupted sleep all night.

When he paused on the front steps to pick up the
paper, something dived past his ear, droning like a tiny
propeller airplane. A hummingbird. It buzzed around
Rita's hummingbird feeder for a few minutes, then darted
off. Elliot unhooked the feeder, feeling guilty that he'd let
it go dry. He glanced around the yard.

The grass was parched and brown around the edges.
He went inside and refilled the feeder. Then he hung it
from the porch roof and dragged out the sprinkler and
hose. Water pressure was low. As he fiddled with the set-
tings to try to reach the thirsty fringes of the lawn, he noticed one of the gangly black kittens curled up behind the
row of canna lilies near the faucet, watching him listlessly.

"You look half starved, fella," Elliot said to him.

The kitten rose to a crouch, and its body tensed, as if
it were getting ready to bolt.

"What's with you guys, anyway?" Elliot said. "What
are you up to?"

The kitten made no sound, but he could see its ribs
heave with its rapid breathing.

He went inside and opened a can of tuna, which he
carried back out and tucked behind the honeysuckle bush
at the end of the row of cannas. The black kitten watched
warily from the shadow of the broad bananalike leaves.

"It's okay," Elliot said. "It's safe to come eat."

The kitten watched him, motionless.

Exhaustion crept around Elliot like a fog. He gave up
and went inside, unable even to manage a shower before
he crashed.

But his sleep was fretful; he dreamed of fighting a
white flame that leapt catlike from roofs and windows
onto the people around him, leaving blackened, twisted
corpses in its wake.

On Tuesday morning, he called his father-in-law's house
again. This time Annie answered the phone.

"Annie!" he said. "How are you, sweetheart?"

"Hi, Daddy," she said. "It's great up here. Grandpa's taking me ice-skating in a little while and then to the toy store. He says I can have any Barbie set I want."

"You want a Barbie doll?" Elliot asked. She had always preferred train sets and baseball cards to dolls.

"Of course," she said, with an inflection he recognized. A note-perfect mimicry of Rita, even to the drawn-out "o" that made "course" a two-syllable word. "Elizabeth says if I have the Action Barbie Beach Condo, I can come to her house and play."

"Who's Elizabeth?" Elliot asked.

"Oh, Daaad-dy," she said.

Another of Rita's speech mannerisms, one that had always embarrassed Elliot. Hearing it from Annie made his teeth clench.

"Elizabeth Lesterfield." Her awed tone was the one formerly reserved for Nolan Ryan. "She lives down the street, next to the park. She has eight Skippers, five Kens, and *sixteen* Barbies."

He was at a loss for an answer at first. "That's nice. Listen, Annie-bug, I was thinking I could drive up and take you to the zoo—"

"Grandpa took me yesterday," she said.

He hesitated. "Well, to Six Flags, then—"

"We're going there tomorrow," Annie said. Someone spoke in the room on the other end of the line. "Grandpa says we have to go now," Annie said. "Bye, Daddy."

"Good-bye, sweetheart—I love you," Elliot said, but the line was already dead.

After talking to Annie, he went out to water the lawn. The grass looked more alive, but it was getting shaggy. He'd have to mow it soon.

The black kitten was in its lair under the cannas again. Elliot glanced behind the honeysuckle bush. The tuna can had been polished clean.

"Guess you were pretty hungry, huh, Butch?" he said as he hooked up the hose. "Just let me get the sprinkler going and I'll get you another can, okay?"

The young cat watched him unblinkingly, ears alert, but this time it wasn't poised for flight.

"I always was a sucker for the underdog," Elliot said as he set the sprinkler out. "Oh, pardon me. Maybe you prefer under*cat*? But the point is—maybe we're on the same side, you and me. Trying to impose order on chaos. What are your thoughts, Butch?"

The cat settled down in a lionlike sprawl. Elliot heard the faint rumble of a purr.

After he gave Butch another can of tuna, he went inside and made a stab at cleaning out the desk in the spare room upstairs that served as his office. Twenty minutes in, he found an old origami kit of Annie's in one of the drawers.

He ended up spending the afternoon folding origami cats out of small squares of black and silver paper.

He walked down to check the mail around dusk. The street was quiet. It was past time for afternoon traffic, and most people were busy indoors. What would they be doing? Fixing supper, reading the paper, watching TV? Elliot glanced at the windows of the houses, bright oblongs in the summer twilight, but couldn't project himself inside. The parts of his life that were normal had migrated to Dallas.

Sprinklers were working overtime to resuscitate the parched lawns, and crickets creaked loudly. No personal mail, but there was a brightly colored postcard from Terra Toys announcing a Summer Discovery display. If Annie had been home, he would have taken her there tomorrow, on the way back from their morning swim at Barton Springs.

The concrete wall of the bridge had fresh gang marks painted on it, strange chicken-scratch hex signs. Elliot hitched himself up onto the wall near the mailboxes and waited to see what would happen.

White assembled first this time.

He almost missed them at first, because the mailboxes partly blocked his view of the storm drain on this side. But the cats were there. Their positions had changed since last time.

After a minute, the blacks took their places. Their front line looked raggedy now that they were missing a pawn. Butch was the scrawniest of the adolescents, the runt. He didn't acknowledge Elliot at all, just stared straight ahead.

Elliot's neck tensed. The blacks were definitely outmatched; the white pawns were bigger and there were more of them, although the major pieces on both sides appeared to be pretty even.

The pawn next to Butch made the first move. It was a larger cat, though still adolescent, and its original position looked to be B-three. It took two deliberate steps forward, moving well ahead of the uneven front line.

A defensive move? Or the beginning of some long setup?

Then, lured by the prospect of an easy capture, the ragged-eared female leapt from white's ranks.

He was so focused on the cats that he didn't notice the Bronco until it was on top of them. It caught the white marauder in a glancing blow, spinning her body into the gutter.

Elliot called out, startled. The blue Bronco didn't even slow down. By the time it turned the corner, the rest of the cats had vanished. Elliot thought the black pawn had been caught by the truck's rear wheel and knocked into the storm drain.

The white cat lay motionless against the curb, the breeze barely ruffling her snowy fur.

"A sacrifice play," he said. "Some hot move your buddies made there, Butch." The sound of his voice fell into the silence and died.

He walked slowly back up the street through the twilight. Once at the house, he went upstairs and carefully arranged his origami cats into two phalanxes, facing each other across the burnished teak surface of his desk.

Voigt called in sick for B's next shift, which ended up being as calm as their previous shift had been chaotic. An honest-to-God peaceful day at Station 12.

Elliot mulled that over. Before the last shift, white had taken a black pawn, and afterward they'd had that big fire in the apartment with the white cat inside it. Yesterday, the blacks had scored a victory, and now Station 12 hadn't run a single call all day.

Was there some connection there? Or was he just imagining things?

He hadn't imagined seeing the cats at the fire—Voigt had stayed home because the scratches on his throat had gotten infected. But cats were everywhere. Those two had probably just been scared pets. As for the wild cats by the storm drains—maybe his eyes had been fooled by twilight shadows.

It was so slow at the station that evening that Touie talked Elliot into playing chess with him. Elliot used to enjoy their games, but since the business with the cats had started, the shifting patterns of the black and white pieces on the board made him uneasy.

"You're going to have to do something about Voigt," Touie said as he moved his King's knight out.

"Why?" Elliot responded automatically, moving a pawn. "He's hopeless. A cowboy. Nothing'll change that."

"Yeah, but if you don't kick his butt up between his ears next time he starts to shuck one of your orders, you're both gonna end up in deep kim-chee."

Touie was right; Elliot knew it. But he didn't have the energy to deal with Voigt's posturing right now. No matter what he tried to concentrate on, his mind kept circling back to Annie and Rita.

Okay, so he and Rita didn't see eye-to-eye on everything. Lots of couples muddled along in spite of that. He was a faithful, hardworking husband; he had always been a good provider. And he spent a lot of his off-hours with Annie, taking her swimming and to the Children's Museum, on hikes and to the Nature Center. He was a good father; he pitched in around the house; what else did Rita want?

He tried to think what he should have done differently, what his wife needed that he hadn't given her. Ten moves into the chess game, he still hadn't figured it out.

"Your mind's wandering," Touie said disgustedly, and took Elliot's knight. "What's with you lately, anyway?"

Elliot hunched his shoulders, then let them drop, trying to work the tension out. "Rita took Annie and went to Dallas."

Touie looked up from the board. "She coming back?"

Elliot shrugged.

"Sorry to hear it," Touie said, and moved his rook.

Elliot studied the board, trying to concentrate. But no matter how he played it, Touie was going to take his Queen in three moves.

When he called Dallas that evening, Rita answered. Her voice had a forced cheerfulness to it. He recognized the tone from parties that made her uncomfortable, like the time they'd gone to Touie's for a barbecue. He probably sounded the same way when they went to ballet openings.

"Hi," he said. "It's me."

A pause. "Oh."

"How're things?" A stupid question. But it was all he could come up with.

"Fine," she said.

"Good. That's good. Listen, I wanted to ask you—"

"You mean you actually want to talk to *me* for once?" she said. "Well, miracles never cease."

"You got a point, Rita? Then make it."

He heard the way she sucked her breath in and could picture her fingers trembling on the phone. He never spoke harshly to her, because she couldn't hack it. But he wasn't long on patience right now.

She drew in another audible breath. "The *point*," she said clearly, "is that you've called—what?—maybe ten times to talk to Anna? And haven't asked to talk to me *once*."

"What was there to say?" he asked. "You wouldn't listen to me while you were in the same room with me. I didn't figure you'd changed your mind since you got to Dallas."

"What do you mean I wouldn't listen—"

"Just that," he said shortly. "I asked you over and over not to go, and you blew me off."

"I—"

"And don't bother saying you only went up there for Annie's dance lessons, because it won't wash. You just didn't have the guts to tell me you wanted out."

The pause lasted longer this time.

"Maybe I don't want out," Rita said. Her voice was faint and frightened.

Elliot clenched his eyes shut. "What *do* you want, Rita? I've been trying to figure it out for eight years, and I still can't make sense of any damn thing you do. So *tell* me, for Christ's sake."

"I just did," she said. "We've been gone two weeks, and this is the first time you called to talk to me. Doesn't that tell you something, Elliot?"

"What—"

"I want to be *visible*, goddamn you, Elliot! Is that too much to ask? Is it?"

"I—"

The receiver made a sharp accusatory click in his ear as she hung up.

That night he couldn't sleep. He kept hearing stealthy padded footfalls on the roof above his bed, full of furtive advances, skittering slides, and occasional leaps. Cat maneuvers.

After a while, he could almost picture them overhead, the graceful, deadly ballet as they moved through their ritualized battle training. They were tireless; the sound of their advance-and-retreat never stopped. He became convinced he could distinguish the sound of Butch's paws from the others.

Lying in the dark, listening, his vision of their dance became so clear he could no longer tell whether he was awake and hallucinating or asleep and dreaming.

In the end, he had to take his pillow and go downstairs to sleep on the couch.

* * *

Elliot hung around the station after his next shift, trying to get someone on C-shift to swap with him, so he could have the whole weekend off.

At first, he didn't get any takers; everybody already had plans. Then the captain checked the schedule and realized that Elliot was due to be off on Labor Day.

"Got a family reunion coming up. My parents really want us to be there," the captain said. "I'll get your shift covered if you'll cover me for Labor Day."

It was a crappy deal, but Elliot took it anyway. By Thursday's shift, word had gotten around the whole station that he had big plans for the weekend.

He shaved with special care Friday morning. As he stood lathered up in front of the mirror in the barracks-style bathroom of the station, he was thinking about what Rita had said on the phone.

She'd made it sound like she wanted more of his attention. And it was true that he and Annie did things together more often than he and Rita did. Or even all three of them together.

So why didn't she go places with him and Annie? He nicked himself with the razor and winced. Because they liked outdoorsy stuff, the kind of pastimes that made her whine and nag to go home early. He realized that he and Annie had gradually become conspirators. They still invited Rita to go swimming with them or out to play volleyball at Pease Park. The trick was that they made the invitations sound unappealing.

He washed the leftover shaving cream off his face, then stared at himself in the mirror.

He liked to *do* things. To him, climbing Enchanted Rock was fun. Rita's idea of fun was to go to an art film where she could sit in air-conditioned darkness and drink fancy mineral water.

Was he supposed to trade his kind of fun for hers? Forget that. And he wasn't sure he wanted to be responsible for her fun anyway—why couldn't she just grow a life of her own? Annie had, and she was only seven years old.

Peterson walked by the open door and noticed him

standing in front of the mirror. "Hey, Franklin, you beautiful yet? You know you got to pretty up if you wanna get laid. Whoooh-ee, don't he look nice?"

"What would you know about pretty, Peterson?" Touie hollered. "Your mama told me you got bit by a ugly snake as a child and you ain't never recovered."

All of them piled on then, even Vasquez, who was usually pretty quiet. They were taking odds on Elliot getting lucky and razzing him about whether he was really going to spend the weekend with his wife.

Elliot managed to laugh it off. If he let their needling get to him, he'd never hear the end of it.

But the ribbing made him resent the whole situation even more. Why was Rita so unreasonable?

That afternoon, he reserved tickets for the Rangers game, then stopped at a convenience store for dry cat food and a dozen cans of tuna.

He opened a can of tuna, then took it, the box of cat food, and an oversized bowl from the cabinet—one of Annie's old cereal bowls, he noted with a pang—and went out front. Butch wasn't in his usual spot behind the cannas.

"Butch?" Elliot said.

He heard the scratchy sound of purring behind him and looked around. Butch was draped along the edge of the porch roof, close to the hummingbird feeder.

"Keeping an eye out for birds, huh, fella? Come on down and eat this instead." He set the tuna behind the honeysuckle bush and opened the cat food. Butch dropped down to land lightly on the grass, watching Elliot closely.

"I'm going to Dallas for a couple of days, buddy," he said. "Sorry about the dry cat food." He shook a generous amount into the cereal bowl, set it next to the tuna, and stepped away. "There'll be more tuna when I get back."

Butch edged toward the bush, still watching him carefully.

"I've got to go see my little girl," Elliot explained. "I've got tickets to a Rangers game. Annie'll love that. At least, she used to love baseball."

Butch started eating, his ears swiveled back toward Elliot as if listening to every word.

"Too bad Ryan isn't pitching anymore," Elliot said. "If he were, I know Annie couldn't resist. He's her hero. But she's different lately. Since they went to Dallas, you know."

Butch was inhaling the tuna with neat, efficient little jerks of his head.

"So, Butch—you guys going to kick some tail tonight?" Elliot said. "The good guys going to win?"

The cat's ears twitched.

"Will Rita let Annie go to the game with me?" Elliot asked softly. "Can we work things out?"

Roger Waller and his wife owned one of the most ostentatious homes in Highland Park. Elliot felt self-conscious parking his battered Subaru in front of the enormous colonial later that evening. The traffic coming through Dallas had been heavy, and it was nearly eight o'clock.

Unsure of his reception, he left his overnight bag in the car and went to the door. When he pressed the bell, discreet chimes played two bars of "The Bells of St. Mary's."

Annie answered the door. "Daddy!" she squealed, and launched herself at him.

Elliot swung her up and around, delighted. "How's my girl?" he said, and before she could answer, "I sure have missed you."

She rested her chin on his shoulder and sighed contentedly. "Me, too, Daddy." Then she wriggled down. "Come and see my Barbies," she commanded, and dragged him inside by the hand.

"Okay," he said. "In a sec. First I have to talk to your mother."

She stopped and looked at him in confusion. "But—"

"Just for a minute, Annie-girl," he said firmly.

Roger Waller appeared in the door of the foyer. "Elliot," he said calmly, and offered his hand.

"Evening, sir," Elliot said and shook. "I was just explaining to Annie that I need to talk to Rita about something before I come see her Barbies."

"I'm afraid Rita's not here just now," Roger said.

"She had a date," Annie blurted.

Roger frowned at her. "Anna, that's inaccurate. Run upstairs and play now. Your father will come up in a little while."

Annie went without protest, which surprised Elliot. She did pause at the top of the stairs for a prison-yard whisper. "*Soon*, Daddy."

"Okay, sweetheart," he said and looked at his father-in-law.

Roger gestured toward the den. "Come have a cup of coffee, Elliot. We need to talk."

Elliot stayed in a hotel that night, paying $120 for a room at a Marriott that was reasonably close to the Wallers' house. Roger had agreed without hesitation when Elliot suggested taking Annie to the baseball game. Roger went so far as to say he was sure she would prefer being with her father on Saturday to making another trip to Six Flags.

When Elliot mentioned that he had gotten three tickets to the game instead of two, Roger had said, "Good. I can't speak for Rita, of course, but I do think you've been a little slow to assert yourself with her. She went to a play with an old friend from S.M.U. tonight. I believe she's trying to convince herself she isn't miserable without you."

At a loss, Elliot had muttered, "Thank you, sir."

"Not at all," his father-in-law said. "I'll let Rita know about Anna's visit with you. Come to lunch tomorrow—you can invite Rita to the game yourself then."

So that's what Elliot had done. Now, seated at his mother-in-law's linen-swathed table, Elliot wished he'd been quick enough to suggest that he take Rita and Annie out to eat instead.

Marianne had just served their plates with delicate scoops of shrimp salad mounded in halved avocados, watercress salad, and hot cheese biscuits the size of quarters.

Elliot tried to pin the avocado with his fork so he

could slice it, but it slid sideways until it was dangerously close to the edge of his plate. He could already picture the slimy smear it would leave on Marianne's snowy table-cloth. He settled for a bite of watercress instead and snuck a look at his wife.

Her hair was a dark, gorgeous red, and her skin was pale and perfect. Today there were shadows under her eyes and her mouth had a tendency to droop at the corners. When they had first met, that air of tragic vulnerability had driven him to absurd heights of gallantry. Why did it only irritate the hell out of him now?

He suffered through lunch at Marianne's table for nothing. Rita turned him down on the baseball game.

The game wasn't a complete wash; Annie hadn't changed so much that she didn't enjoy it. And as far as Elliot was concerned, there were few things more wonderful than live baseball. And this day was damn near perfect: The home-town crowd was enthusiastic, and the Rangers were having a good day.

But there were subtle signs of the changes in his daughter. She had worn a dress, for one thing. It was a simple red jumper, true, but her little flat shoes matched it. And she was carrying a purse.

Why on earth would Annie want a purse? Pockets had always satisfied her before now. One of their household rules required Elliot to evacuate the pockets of Annie's clothes before they were washed, a rule in force ever since Rita had run across a live garter snake in Annie's corduroys. That had been after one of their fossil-hunting trips along Shoal Creek. Annie had confided to him later, when he went upstairs to console her in her banishment, that finding the trilobite had distracted her, and she just stuck the snake in her pocket and *forgot*.

She had turned those cloud-gray eyes on him and said, "Why's she so mad at me, Daddy? It's just a garter snake."

And he had been in the center, seeing the event from both sides at once: how frightened Rita had been to find a live snake in her laundry basket, and how unreasonable her mother's fear seemed to Annie.

Now he was the outlander, the one who couldn't understand how the other two felt about anything. He didn't like it.

Annie had been paying more attention to the game than he had. She jumped to her feet and caught the wave as it passed around them, leaving him alone in a sea of leaping bodies.

He persuaded Rita to go to dinner with him after Annie was in bed. At Roger's suggestion, they tried a high-end Italian restaurant that was too heavy on romantic atmosphere for comfort.

Elliot ordered shrimp scampi and Rita some pasta dish with eggplant and mushrooms. He watched her familiar mannerisms: the way she folded her napkin in half before placing it in her lap, the studious dip of her upper lip as she tasted the wine before approving it. He watched her, aware of every detail of her appearance, and thought, I'm having dinner with my ex-wife.

The thought left him disoriented and dizzy, like the time he'd been concussed by falling debris in a skyscraper fire, unable to get his bearings or sense which direction gravity should flow.

"I want you and Annie to come home," he blurted, aware as soon as he said it that it was a mistake.

"At least you said 'you and Annie,' " she replied. "I suppose I should be grateful you included me."

He sighed, and was relieved that the waiter brought their salads then.

After the waiter left, he said carefully, "I'm trying to understand why you decided to leave. But I want our family together again. I'm sorry if I didn't say it right."

"I can't come home until I'm sure it's the right thing for me."

"Why not?" he asked. "Why can't we work on things together? That would make more sense, wouldn't it?"

She shook her head. The candlelight gilded her hair to

glowing embers, and he had a momentary vision of her as a stunning stranger.

"I can't, Elliot," she said. "Don't you see—I won't have the guts to leave again. So I can't come back until I'm sure it's the best thing for me."

"What about what's best for Annie?" he said.

She looked at him levelly.

"That's a perfect example of why it's hard for me to tell you anything, Elliot," she said. "You're so self-contained—nothing ever gets to you. Nothing ever really matters to you—except maybe Annie. Certainly not *me*. That's one of the reasons I left—it was getting so I couldn't fool myself there was anything between us anymore."

"Whoa—words of one syllable?" he said. It was an old joke, one that dated back to the time they first knew each other, when he had been tutoring her in physics.

It won him a faint smile. "Do you remember," she said, "how we used to go to breakfast together after our eight o'clock physics class? We'd sit in that booth at Kerbey for hours—we couldn't stop talking to each other."

He nodded.

"Whatever happened to that? Where did that burning desire to share yourself with me go? I'd really like to know, Elliot."

He thought about it, struggling to come up with a genuine answer that would also please her. "It's—I guess it's because you're so entwined in my life now that it seems silly for me to explain it to you."

She nodded gravely. "That would make sense . . . if I had the least idea of what your life is really like."

"What?" He could feel the old outrage beginning to burn in his chest. She was speaking the secret language of women, that incomprehensible tongue that always made him feel as if she saw the world with an entire dimension added, one he couldn't perceive. It was like the difference between color vision and black and white. And if you were color-blind, you could never understand what a color-sighted person was talking about, what they saw. No matter how hard you tried.

Their food came, and he took a bite of his shrimp. It tasted like congealed library paste.

"You go to work," Rita said, "and when you come home, it's like that twenty-four hours has been excised from your life. Oh, you might tell me something about station politics, like that time Loettner tried to back-stab you to the captain, but you never tell me anything real about what you do. If I hadn't recognized the dent in your helmet on the news last month, I wouldn't even have known you were treated for smoke inhalation."

The unjustness of it choked him, and he coughed. "What I do isn't all neat and polite, Rita. I don't invest pension funds all morning and take power lunches at Turtle Creek. What do you want? For me to come home and live the chaos and filth of fighting fires all over again?"

"What chaos? I don't know anything about what fighting fires is like," she said. "And that's just one symptom of what's really wrong, Elliot. You hold too much distance between us."

He looked her in the eye. "Are you sure it's me who's distant, Rita? If our marriage is distant, I think it's partly because you *like* it that way."

"There's no point to—"

"And it damn sure won't help our marriage for me to haul my job home with me. Believe me, you don't want to hear it. 'Gee, Rita, I dragged three dead teenagers out of a torched crack house first thing this morning, I got to see them with all their skin burned off so they looked like hunks of raw meat that were charred around the edges. How was *your* day, hon?' "

Rita's fingers were trembling on her dinner fork, and she had tipped her head down so he couldn't see her eyes anymore.

"Makes for lovely dinner-table conversation, don't you think?"

Rita dropped her fork. "I want to go now," she said.

She didn't speak to him at all during the drive back to her father's house. Her silence gathered around him like heat building before a flashover, a harbinger of destruction.

* * *

After he got back from Dallas, he started recording the cats' skirmishes in a spiral notebook he bought at the drugstore. He picked it up from an enormous display of school supplies. Seeing them depressed him. Rita probably already had Annie enrolled at some fancy private school in Dallas.

He was now able to readily distinguish individuals among the two groups of cats. The black Queen was a large, pregnant female with green eyes and longish hair; the black Bishop was the tom who looked like a miniature panther, with sleek dark fur and neat rounded ears set almost flat against his head. Knowing them made it easier to discern the tactical effect of their maneuvers.

He brought home one of the big fire-station maps, with its detailed grids of Station 12's territory, and used his company of origami cats to mark the various fire sites. When the burn got away from them, he used a silver cat marker; when they made great stops, he used a black. Within a few days, the maps looked like one of the cats' battle arrays.

They weren't really playing chess, he understood that now—except in the sense that chess was also ritualized battle. But he could use chess as a model to understand what their conflict signified. With his maps, he could almost grasp the strategies at work, the forces at play that—once understood—would let him predict white's next move.

At first, he only tracked his own station's fire activity against the cat battles, but within a week, he realized that fires throughout the whole city were affected.

There was only one thing to do: He brought home maps of other stations' territories and stocked up on origami paper.

Elliot was eating dinner on the front porch, because the dining table was covered with maps. He offered his half-eaten hamburger to Butch, who was sprawled across three of Rita's prized daylilies. Butch sniffed politely but didn't take the food. His black fur had a deep blue cast in the afternoon sunlight. He had grown considerably in recent weeks and no longer looked like a kitten.

"I don't blame you," Elliot said. "I've got to start planning better, instead of eating this crap."

But lately he couldn't seem to get a grocery list written, and the last time he'd gone to the store, he'd found himself standing in the produce department, staring blankly at the mounds of lettuce.

A dark-eyed young woman with a baby strapped across her chest was watching him anxiously. "Are you all right, sir?" she had asked, her voice filled with concern. He had thanked her and retreated, leaving his partly filled cart behind.

Since Butch didn't want it, Elliot dumped the burger in the kitchen garbage bag, which was starting to stink. He carried it out to the curb and dumped it; he'd left the trash cans out so long last week that somebody had stolen them.

A knock on the door woke him up at six the next morning.

Elliot tumbled off the couch, where he had been sleeping lately, and scrubbed a hand across his face. The knocking came again, more insistent this time. He answered the door still in his boxers.

It was their across-the-street neighbor—what was his name?—the university professor who drove the Saab. The Brit with the accent Rita always found so charming. He'd probably come to complain about the lawn. Elliot abandoned the effort to dredge up the man's name and said, "Yeah?"

"Oops," the neighbor said cheerfully. "Sorry to wake you, but those damned cats have been at the refuse again." He waved toward the street. "They've got yours all over the road this morning. We really ought to round up the lot of them and put them down, if you ask me."

Elliot stepped out on the porch and looked at the street. The trash bag was shredded on one side, and garbage was strewn all over the driveway and along the gutters. Probably white's retribution against him for feeding one of their rivals.

Or maybe they were making a power play on black's safe haven. "Did you see the cats? What color were they?"

"No, but I'm certain it was cats. The dogs only get at it when they can easily dump the contents out. When the bags are clawed that way, it's the cats. There are simply dozens of them running wild hereabouts, you know."

"Yeah, I know," Elliot said. "Two different packs of them. And they're all either solid black or solid white. It's the strangest thing."

The man laughed. What a phony. "Not strange at all, really. In fact, they're likely all from the same breeding group. Based on the pattern of dominant versus recessive genes for coloration, if a white cat isn't white, it's black."

"Excuse me?" Elliot said.

"It's rather like a double negative," the man said. "If the genome pattern tells the body once that its fur should be white, then it is. But if the code tells it *twice*, then it's as if the switch for white is flipped on and then off again. And, voilà! A black cat. Perfectly suited for flinging in the paths of one's enemies or riding on the tail of one's broom, according to one's taste."

"Like two wrongs making a right," Elliot said. "Is that what you're telling me?"

The neighbor—this phony charmer of other men's wives—looked taken aback. "Well, not precisely—" he began.

"Never mind," Elliot said. "I'll figure it out." He went back into the house.

"But—aren't you going to collect that mess?" the neighbor asked.

Elliot shut the door without answering.

That evening, the black Queen returned, bringing a new litter of pawns with her, and Butch advanced to the position of Queen's rook.

His fire map was covered with origami cats now, their paper bodies making complex patterns across the gridwork of city blocks. He was certain that when the white cats won, fires broke out all over the city, a rash of arson and accidents. And black victories created an artificial calm. But it was only after the abrupt cessation of the awful flash floods in San Antonio in mid-August that he realized the cats' battles were connected to larger, more significant events, as well.

Elliot started carrying the notebook with him everywhere, jotting down the news as he heard it or read it and matching the action of the cats' conflict with external events. True, the patterns were subtle, but they were perfectly clear to anyone who was plotting them carefully.

Touie noticed the notebook and started bugging him about it, asking why he was always hunched over that journal and never played chess or volleyball anymore.

Elliot knew better than to talk about his discovery. He trusted Touie, but there were too many chaotic forces present in the world for him to reveal prematurely what he had learned. Look at all the evidence of the eternal struggle: the black-and-white chess pieces, the black-and-white hexagons on the volleyball, the black-and-white floor tiles at the station.

And added to it the evidence that he was accumulating in his notebook. After the sacrifice play black made that cost white its second rook, three men in Mexico City were finally indicted for the Yogurt Shop Murders. When white revenged itself by entrapping and taking the black Queen's bishop, Mexican authorities refused to honor U.S. law enforcement's extradition papers on the indicted men.

When white followed up on its advantage and menaced black's Queen in a brief skirmish, the President's health-care proposal was killed in committee. Then black battled back to take white's remaining Knight in a beautifully executed bait-and-capture move. A compromise program was presented, voted out of committee, and passed by the House within the week.

There was more: six climbers who died in an avalanche on the Italian side of the Alps, eruptions of gang violence in East Austin, raging forest fires in California. After black victories, A.P.D. announced that its Neighborhood Partners Unit had engineered a peace pact between the warring Austin gangs, and sixteen teenage hikers who'd been presumed dead were rescued from the California fire.

The ripples spread out from his neighborhood and his life in ever-widening circles.

Elliot bought a fifty-pound bag of cat food and began feeding the whole crew of black cats. His house seemed to be their safe turf; he never saw the white cats anywhere near it. So he set up a shelter for the blacks behind his garage, on the premise that if they were better fed than their rivals, they would win more frequently. And somehow their winning was connected to his own: winning Rita back, having his family again.

So far the advantage was slight—most of the feral cats were good scavengers and hunters—but come winter . . .

It wasn't until the third week of August that he started to wonder what would happen if he intervened in their struggle directly.

Next shift, they were second-in on a box alarm in Engine 20's territory—a four-plex in Dove Springs. Smoke and flames were showing by the time they got there, but black had won the night before, so Elliot wasn't too worried.

Antonio Garza was In-Charge. "Missing residents," he shouted at them before their engine even stopped moving. "Search and rescue—move it."

Elliot and Voigt ran toward the building. Garza sent the rest of their engine company to pull another main line up to the second floor. They were going straight in on the fire.

"See—Garza's no wimp," Voigt said. "He's gonna nail this sucker head-on."

"This place was built to code," Elliot said. "Makes a difference."

"Yeah, right. To wimps."

Elliot longed to boot Voigt into next week and then ask him who the wimp was. No time for it now. But later—

They split up on the second floor, taking a unit apiece.

It was smoke city in the apartment. Even with the air

pack on, Elliot was breathing the burnt-hair-and-charcoal smell of the fire, and he couldn't see a damn thing.

He broke out in a sweat instantly from the heat. The place must be burning like a dog. But it was oddly quiet inside. The only thing he heard was his own breathing and the gentle whoosh of air through the regulator.

Elliot had spent three years on a manpower team before his first promotion. He always did search-and-rescue by the book, crawling along with his right hand on the wall while he felt around with his free hand, never bypassing any door or opening. Fifteen minutes of air before he'd have to backtrack, going out the same laborious way he'd come in. Trying to free-hand it would get you lost, and getting lost would get you killed.

It was getting hotter in the apartment, the air starting to sear him through his turn-out gear. Under his jacket, the Nomex uniform shirt felt as if it was being ironed with him inside it.

The trouble was he couldn't be sure how hot was too hot. The chaos of burn had too many variables.

He probably ought to get out now, but he had a few minutes of air left. And Garza'd said there were missing residents. He was in no mood for digging charcoaled people out of the rubble today—or even for removing corpses without a mark on them.

In all the smoke he couldn't be certain, but he thought he was in one of the back bedrooms when he found the closet. A blanket had been stuffed under the crack of its doors, and the edges of the cloth were smoldering.

Elliot stomped on the blanket, then jerked the door open. He could see for a second before the smoke rushed in. A kid maybe eight years old was huddled inside, crying.

Elliot grabbed the kid and tucked her face against his chest, then headed back out in a racing crab-scuttle, keeping low, his left hand tracing the walls. He got on his radio and said, "Engine 12—I've found a victim—coming out. Request EMS."

The kid was coughing bad now, and struggling, making Elliot's adrenaline level pump. The Vibralert on his regulator went off, humming against his faceplate. Four minutes of air left. He'd thought he was moving at top speed, but the adrenaline gave him an extra burst.

Then he could see the door.

He tightened his grip on the kid and ran, still crouching as low as he could to keep her away from the worst smoke. He ran down the stairs, dashed past the fire line, and laid her gently on the grass.

The kid was still squirming and coughing, so Elliot figured she was in pretty good shape. A guy from 20 ran up with the bag and slapped oxygen on her before the kid got her eyes open.

"Can you breathe?" the guy from 20 asked. "What hurts?"

Her face was covered with black smudge and she was gasping.

"What's your name? Do you live here?"

Elliot's Vibralert stopped wiggling. Out of air. He hunched down next to the kid and stripped his helmet off. She grabbed his arm and shoved her oxygen mask aside.

"I thought—" she gasped out "—was going to get burned up—" She coughed so hard that tears squeezed from her eyes and mixed into a muddy mess on her face. The other firefighter pushed the mask back on her, and this time she let it stay. "Could hear the fire—getting closer," she told Elliot, her voice faint behind the mask. "I called and called, but nobody came—"

He dragged his gloves off and held her hand. Her fingers were icy with shock, but her grip was fiercely strong. "I came," he told her. "We got you out. You're safe now."

That's when he saw Butch perched on top of the oxygen bag, watching them both with a smug look.

In his twelve years with the department, Elliot had never rescued a human being before. Pets, sure, corpses, yeah, but never a live person. Since smoke alarms had become so prevalent, most people woke up and got out before fires became dangerous. Either that, or the firefighters ended up "rescuing" a dead body.

This kid had been smart and lucky. Smart enough to hide in the closet when she couldn't get out of the house . . . and lucky that they'd gotten to her in time. But the guys made a big deal over Elliot, saying he was bound to get a citation for it.

Once their shift was over at noon, everyone in the company insisted on taking Elliot out to celebrate. They ended up at the Filling Station on Barton Springs Road, sitting around the horseshoe-shaped bar in a rowdy, gleeful mob, taking turns buying Elliot shots of imported tequila.

Even Chief Edwards stopped by and bought everybody a round. "A toast," he said, lifting his beer bottle in Elliot's direction. "Franklin, not everybody gets the chance to show what they're made of. Today you showed you've got the right stuff. So, here's to Franklin—a cool hand."

The company hooted and hollered and slapped Elliot on the back. After the fifth shot, he lost all sensation in his throat and drinking them got easier.

Around four o'clock, the bar manager came out and asked them to settle down a little, because they were disturbing the other customers. At four-thirty, she cut them off. Grumbling a little, just about everyone headed home.

He and Touie stayed and had something to eat after the others left. Elliot needed time to sober up enough to drive.

"Say, Touie. You noticed a lot of cats lately?"

"What're you talking about?" Touie was making a log cabin by stacking wooden matches on the table. He laid the matches with such precision that the walls of the structure looked machined.

"At incidents," Elliot said. His voice sounded muffled and far away to him. "Cats at every fire. Black ones and white ones. They were at the fire today."

"Yeah, I seen some cats. Cats're everywhere. What d'you expect?"

"But there's always these particular cats—it's weird, Touie. These black cats that are like the forces of order or something, always around when we make a good stop. Or like today, when I got the kid out. And then there're these white cats that are the forces of chaos—always at torch jobs and burns that are getting away from us—"

"You're telling me they're the cats of chaos?" Touie laughed so hard, sweat popped out on his forehead. When Elliot didn't join in, Touie gradually got himself under control, then looked at him assessingly. "You are shit-faced, man. Seriously shit-faced."

"But, Touie—you said you saw 'em today. And remember the white cat that scratched Voigt so bad? It came from inside the burning apartment—"

"So? Cats're everywhere," Touie said again. "And besides, I got nothing against any cat that messes Voigt up."

Just then, the waitress brought their burgers.

"Get some food in you," Touie told him. "Before you start talking that shit again. You're about to give me a cat *pho*bia, Mr. Hero."

By nightfall, Elliot had a terrible hangover, but he had promised to call Annie to hear about her dance recital. He couldn't think of a way to bring up the rescue without sounding boastful, so he said nothing, just listened to Annie's chatter about Elizabeth Lesterfield and her new tutu and all the Barbie crap Roger had bought for her—and how Mommy said she and Elizabeth could go to school together at St. Michael's.

"You don't want to come home to Austin for school?" Elliot asked before he could stop himself. Then he added, "No, never mind, Annie-girl—I'll talk to your mom about that."

"Okay. But, Daddy—"

"Yes?" The flash of hope nearly choked him—maybe she *did* want to come home.

"Would you please call me 'Anna' instead of 'Annie'?"

"Sure, sweetie," Elliot managed to say. He had to clear his throat before he could go on. "Whatever you like."

"Then Anna, please," she said. It felt as if each clear note of her voice were being nailed into his gut. "It sounds more dignified, don't you think?"

* * *

She would grow up to be just like Rita—gorged on things while she starved for attention. He considered that as he drove to work on Thursday. He had screwed up his chance at reconciling with Rita, and in doing so, he'd wrecked Annie's chances, too. She was going to grow up warped by Barbie crap. That and all the Waller precepts that assured her it was more important to be fragile and pretty than it was to be self-sufficient and strong.

Elliot got to work around eleven-thirty, which made him late relieving Durham, but nobody bitched.

Touie was cooking that week. He'd made his famous red beans and rice, so everybody ate lunch together. There was a lot of talk about Elliot's rescue and when he might get his citation. Vasquez had cut out the article and picture—the one of him squatting by the little girl, with her hand on his arm—from the newspaper. She'd even glued it to a piece of posterboard and gotten it laminated.

She offered it to Elliot, saying "For your scrapbook, Franklin."

He was touched and embarrassed. "Thanks." He couldn't think of anything else to say. Vasquez didn't seem to mind.

"So you're riding pretty high, huh, Lieutenant?" Peterson said, a faint edge of sarcasm in his voice. "How's it feel to be a hero?"

Elliot shrugged and took a bite of red beans. Not even Touie's cooking appealed to him. Nothing tasted good anymore.

"Talk to us, man," Peterson said. "Tell us how it felt to be a hero—to rescue the kid and know she was gonna make it."

Elliot looked around the table, hoping for some help. They were all watching him, waiting for him to say something. Even Touie.

Elliot cleared his throat. "It felt weird."

"Being a hero felt weird?" Peterson said. "C'mon, Lieutenant!"

Everyone else waited.

"She said she could hear the fire coming. She kept

calling for someone to come get her, and nobody came. I keep thinking—" He broke off and looked around, but they were all quiet. "I can't stop thinking how easily it could have gone the other way. I was running out of air— what if I'd turned around sooner? What if the fire had come and burned her up before I got a new air pack and went back in?"

The faces around the table were serious now, and none of them would meet his eyes. "I keep thinking," he said, "we're fighting a losing battle here. There's more force to chaos than there is to order—that's just how the universe works. The deck's stacked against us."

Nobody moved or spoke.

Then Touie said, "Hey, eat up, folks. Food's getting cold. Don't you appreciate my cooking?"

Once the normal lunchtime chatter revived, Elliot slipped out. He went into the bunkroom, sat on his bed, and stared at the locker. Everything was sliding away from him. Annie would start school in Dallas, and then Rita would say that they couldn't move her during the school year. He'd go up or she'd come down on weekends, if he wasn't working.

But she'd forget fast, kids always did. She'd forget about hunting for fossils along the creekbed, forget about going swimming every summer morning in the icy water of Barton Springs. The pleasures of baseball would evaporate from her memory like sprinkler water on a hot sidewalk.

And Rita? He hardly recognized her anymore.

Somebody opened the door behind him. Elliot didn't look around.

"Hey, Franklin?" It was Voigt. He came around and sat down on the next bunk, facing Elliot. "Hey, you're a good hand, Franklin. I shouldn't've called you a wimp the other day."

"It's not important."

"Just wanted to say it." But Voigt didn't leave. After a minute he added, "Touie says your old lady left you, took the kid."

Elliot couldn't help it; he flinched.

"Hey, man," Voigt said, "I know it's hard. Same thing happened to me last year, see? I wouldn't've given you shit like that if I knew you were going through something. See, I know how hard it is—our families, man, that's the main thing. When my old lady left, I nearly lost it. I really thought about taking my shotgun and blowing myself away."

Elliot would have given anything to stop Voigt from telling him this, but he couldn't seem to form any words of his own.

Voigt was tracing the mortar lines on the room's brick wall with one finger. "But, man, just hang in there. Right now, you think there's no hope, but you wait and see. Things start getting a little shaky up there in Dallas— her car breaks down or her new boyfriend dumps her— any little change in the status quo, and bam! She's back. That's how it happened for me. And me and my old lady, we never been better."

Elliot stared at him. "What did you say?"

"Me and my wife never been—"

"No, before that—about the status quo."

Voigt shrugged. "It's that chaos stuff you were talking about before. See, things start to get shaky for her, something changes—'cause something's always changing—and she'll come home."

Elliot was stunned. Here he'd been fighting so hard to preserve order—the *present* order—and he'd failed to realize that the whole status quo of his life had already changed. Now the status quo consisted of Rita and Annie living in Dallas.

Voigt slapped Elliot on the shoulder. "So hang in, man. Something's sure to shift and then everything'll turn around."

The tone sounded, and the dispatcher said, "Box alarm at 2385 Morningside. Apartment fire."

They were second-in. The whole top row of the apartments was obscured by smoke. Elliot couldn't make sense of what he was seeing. Lines ran up the stairs, but he couldn't see anybody, didn't hear anything over the radio about what people were doing.

"Who's I.C.?" Touie shouted as they pulled up. "What orders?"

Nobody answered. "Lay a supply line," Elliot told him, and jumped out of the engine. Voigt and Vasquez jumped off the back, and the three of them ran toward the stairs.

The driver from Engine 16—his jacket said "Reynolds"—was supporting a woman in shorts and a bathing-suit top who had big white patches of blister on her bare shoulders. Her hair was singed off on one side and she looked wild, her eyes dark and round. A young girl, maybe twelve or thirteen, was standing next to them.

Reynolds shook the woman. "Ma'am, you have to tell us which apartment. We're searching, but where do you think he would be?"

"You In-Charge?" Elliot asked him. "What's the status?"

Reynolds didn't look around. "He wasn't in there with you—where should we look?"

The young girl said, "We don't know. He's always hiding, isn't he, Mom?"

The woman was crying silently now, her mouth wide open in a scream, with no sound coming out. Strings of spit hung between her teeth.

Elliot looked at the girl. "Hide where?"

"He likes to crawl in the pantry. Sometimes he sneaks out to Tommy's house to play video."

"Which unit is Tommys?" Reynolds's voice was shaking.

The girl was shaking her head. "Don't know. We only just moved here—he wouldn't tell me. And last week I found him clear across the complex in the laundry room—"

"We'll find him," Elliot said. "Engine 12 assuming I.C. Vasquez, start a search on all units in this row—a small child who likes to hide is missing. You got that? Take the other radio. And check all the cupboards. Voigt, come on."

He should have backed off and taken over the command station, but it didn't look like 16 had even set one up. When he and Voigt got to the top of the stairs, he saw why. The company's lieutenant was down, unconscious, with no helmet on. All the hair on his face was burned off, and his breathing sounded labored.

Vasquez was right behind them. Elliot signaled her and Voigt to take the man down for treatment, then he followed the tangled lines inside.

One of 16's firefighters was shooting water into the apartment from about ten feet in. "What happened to your lieutenant?" Elliot yelled.

The guy didn't look around. "He kicked the door in without his gear all the way on—think he breathed fire. But Reynolds got him—and I need help in here. Could you get 'em to step up the pressure in the hose?"

"Sonuvabitch," Elliot said. He got on the radio and asked Dispatch for EMS and more units while he peered through the black smoke and steam, trying to get a size-up. The fire looked to have originated in the kitchen, where it had burned up through the ceiling into the attic. These units were more of that '80s building boom—probably subcode, with defective firewalls. The water this guy was laying out was probably pushing the fire into the attics of other apartments.

"Be right back," he said.

He ran next door to assess the spread, telling Reynolds to get more hand lines up and functioning. Reynolds just kept talking to the woman. The guy was fucking useless.

The neighboring apartment was already black with smoke; Elliot went on to the next one, kicking the door open.

Butch was waiting just inside, his body in a tense crouch. He yowled when he saw Elliot.

"This the place to stop it?" Elliot said, looking up. Faint puffs of smoke were pulsing from the A/C vents.

This room's status quo was about to change.

What had he told the others at lunch? That they were

fighting a losing battle? Well, there was at least one way to remedy that.

For an instant, he could see the kid, a boy with dark, round eyes, very young, hiding somewhere and listening to the fire eat toward him—No.

Elliot shook his head, rejecting the image. No, that boy was off somewhere else, climbing trees or playing video games. The picture blurred and metamorphosed into Annie, her mouth pinched up like Rita's, saying "Please call me Anna."

"Engine 12 to I.C.—supply line is laid," Touie said.

"Three units searched—no luck on the kid so far." That was Vasquez, on the radio, too, sounding grim.

"That kid's run off somewhere," Elliot told her.

Voigt rushed in behind Elliot, nearly tripping over Butch.

"Where do you want us?"

Elliot looked down at the cat, who was watching him expectantly. "So much for conservative tactics," he said softly. "Sorry, buddy. White pawn takes black rook."

"What?" Voigt yelled. Sweat was pouring off his face behind the faceplate. "What's the order?"

Elliot took his arm and shoved him out onto the landing.

Beyond Voigt, Elliot could see the woman and her daughter huddled at the base of the stairs. The woman's face was contorted, and he could see her shoulders shaking, but the white noise of rushing water masked any sound.

"Let's nail it," he said, louder this time.

Voigt looked at him disbelievingly and shook his head. "What?"

"Step to and run that hose in head-on," Elliot yelled, pointing into the first apartment. "We're gonna nail this sucker!"

Voigt's face cleared. He grabbed a line and dived into the smoke.

Elliot looked around for Butch, but the cat was gone. He guessed one of the whites would turn up soon. And he ought to establish a command station; knocking this one down was going to take a while.

He turned and backed slowly down the stairs, watching the chaos unfold.

For my brother, Daryl, firefighter and philosopher.

Gahan Wilson

Gahan Wilson lives in the New York area. His work has appeared in periodicals as diverse as *Playboy, The New Yorker, Weird Tales, Gourmet, Punch, Paris Match,* and the cover of *Newsweek.* Selections from this accumulation have appeared in over fifteen cartoon collections, most recently in *Still Weird.* Wilson has also written children's books and has had adult fiction published in *Playboy, Omni, The Magazine of Fantasy and Science Fiction,* and numerous anthologies. He has authored two mystery novels, done graphic novels on Edgar Allan Poe and Ambrose Bierce, and has completed his first animated movie, a gruesome short called *Gahan Wilson's Diner.* His CD-Rom game, *Gahan Wilson's Ultimate Haunted House,* has been wildly successful and he is currently working on another game.

"Best Friends" takes a peek into an unusual symbiosis between two species.

Best Friends

GAHAN WILSON

GOD, LOVE YOU to death, darling! Always forget *completely* how much, how deeply.

What an absolutely adorable hat.

Isn't this *hideous* rain totally ghastly? Poor Muffin has positively given up because of it, you know. Just sits there brooding by the window, glaring out at all those silly drops thumping down on the terrace and *won't* listen to a single word I say about cheering up.

Here we are.

Stop here, driver. *Here!* By that little green awning with the fat doorman, damn it! Only now it's way back there. You may keep the change, not that you deserve it.

Christ, it's absolutely beyond belief the sort of people one finds driving cabs these days! Did you see that shitty, third world glare he had the nerve to give me? He's probably got the makings of some idiotic bomb stuffed into his trunk with the explosives cooked up out of cow crap or whatever it is the papers say they use. I suppose we should all be grateful the bastards can't afford proper explosives.

Let's for God's sake get inside before we're both soaked.

Oh, dear, now I get a look at it I really do wish I hadn't suggested this restaurant. I'm afraid it's caught on altogether far too well. Will you just look at all these ghastly *people*, for God's sake. Do you know *any* of them?

My *God*, honestly, do you *see* the hair on that woman?

It slipped my mind one's actually starting to read about this place in the *papers*. Who was with whom and where they sat and what they ate and was it well prepared and did they look adoringly at one another and did they fuck at the end of the day?

Well, high time, here somebody comes to look after us at last.

Yes, Andre, so good to see you. Yes, it has been too long. Yes, that table will do quite nicely; you've remembered it's one of my favorites. I'll sit on the banquette and Miss Tournier will sit on the chair. Thank you, Andre.

As if he'd dare give me anything but a satisfactory table, darling. Just let him try and he'd see the fur fly and doesn't he know it!

God, it's been *years*, hasn't it? Positively *ages*, for heaven's sake! Now you *must* tell me all that's happened and leave absolutely nothing out. For instance: You *did* leave him, didn't you? Charles, I mean?

Good! I knew you'd come to your senses, given enough time. Just *knew* it. You're a sensible girl, Melanie, darling. Always have been. I don't care what they say.

Yes, Jacques. Good afternoon. Yes, I'll have my usual but I don't know what Mademoiselle Tournier will have. What would you care for, darling? Kir Royal. There you are, Jacques. No, I think we'll have the menu a little bit later, thank you just the same.

I simply can't believe it. Did you see that, darling? Did you see how he positively *pushed* that damned menu at us? Honestly, it's gotten so this is almost a fucking Greek restaurant. I feel as if I'm sitting at some greasy *counter* with *workmen* and things like that all over the place, for God's sake. The staff will be walking around in their shirtsleeves wearing aprons the next thing you know. Really!

Anyhow, enough of that. It's not worth our time, let's go on to something that *matters*.

What happened with Charles, darling? Did you get rid of him on your own, or was it Cissy's doing?

Oh, good for you! Did it all by yourself, did you? Cissy must have been that proud. He wasn't worthy of you, darling, but of course you know that. How absolutely marvelous of you to kick him out on his ass, the bastard, the shit.

I only wish I could say the same about the way I handled things between Howard and myself. I suppose you've heard something of it, most everyone seems to. Unfortunately.

Of course, the whole business has been profoundly embarrassing. I'm usually pretty good about finishing off entanglements, as you know, but not this time. I'm afraid poor Howard really had my number.

God, did you hear that?

Did you hear me *say* that?

Poor Howard, indeed! He still *has* my number, or would have if he were still alive. I might as well face it, it'll be months before I manage to work that son of a bitch completely out of my system. Positively months. I just know it.

It was those sad eyes of his that always did me in, darling. I couldn't help it, no matter what unforgivably stinking, crappy thing he did, those goddamn sad eyes of his always managed to get right through to me. *Always*, damn it! Honestly, he was *such* a waif.

Anyway, when Muffin saw I was floundering she came to my rescue and made a quick end to it. She was marvelous, of course, simply marvelous.

Honestly, you really should have seen the look on Howard's face, I tell you it was a perfect scream! I don't think I've ever *seen* anyone so completely and absolutely astonished.

No sad looks from him *then*, darling—no time for that act with Muffin coming at him from every direction like a little white blur—only bulging eyes and a gaping mouth and his hands flailing every which way trying to bat her off!

The astounding, the absolutely remarkable thing is that she never actually touched the bastard! Didn't leave so much as one tiny scratch to get people thinking.

And it was such fun, you see, because I knew just what she was up to. It was like watching a movie on the late show that I'd seen before in a theater.

She maneuvered him so neatly, darling! She positively *herded* him just as if she were a dear little sheepdog. All the way from the bar across the carpet to the terrace and over the railing and down he went to land, kerplunk, on a taxi parked in front of our building.

I just hope its driver was like that clod that bungled us over here, I really do. The impact mashed the cab's top in completely and set that quaint sign on its roof to blinking over and over and over like a yellow Christmas tree ornament. And there was Howard gaping up at me from the middle of the ruin.

Of course now his sad look was playing on *my* side, darling. That was sweet, I can tell you. They asked around and learned how gloomy poor Howard had always been, how blue, and of course they saw how sympathetic and understanding I'd been to him, and death by suicide it was!

If only all life's problems could be solved so simply.

So it's over, and so is he. Over with a vengeance. Over in spades. Thank *God* for Muffin is all I can say.

We are so lucky, aren't we?

Oh, shit, here comes Jacques with his bloody menu again. Are you sure you're up to it, dear? Very well, then. Actually I don't even need the damned thing because I know exactly what I want.

I'll have the grilled turbot, Jacques, with that nice mustard sauce. You know the one I mean.

Well, if it doesn't happen to be on your precious menu today I'm sure you can have the chef make it up, can't you? Would you like that, darling? Good. You'll enjoy it. And a nice bottle of Meursault, Jacques. And would you like a nice little salad, darling? And a nice little salad, Jacques. Yes, for both of us. Of course for both of us. Something light, naturally. Thank you, Jacques.

Muffin still hasn't quite *entirely* forgiven me for my lapse. Her brooding isn't altogether because of the rain, I'm afraid, but I don't blame her. After all, it hasn't been a full three weeks since it happened and, besides, she *is* starting to soften. She even gave me really rather a sweet look this morning just before I left the apartment to meet you. We'll patch things up. Muffin and I always patch things up.

Of course, there are some that can't.

You've heard about Maddy and Clara.

You really haven't? My God, where have you *been*, darling? I thought absolutely *everyone* knew about it. Oh, of course, you were in the South of France. And it's obvious you haven't read this morning's *Post*.

Well, I hadn't expected I'd have to do it, but I'd better bring you up to speed before I can tell you about what happened last night. Then I'll tell you about what I'd like us to do.

Actually it's really something we absolutely *must* do, as I'm sure you'll agree once you've heard the story.

We really must do it.

It seems poor Maddy went head over heels for this man she met vacationing in Rio last winter. She fell absolutely and *hopelessly* in love with him, poor dear, and couldn't get over it no matter how hard she tried. Just went totally silly over him, gaga as a schoolgirl.

God, you should have seen her with him, it was horrible, absolutely ghastly, to see a grown-up female like Maddy gaping at this perfectly ordinary man with an unbelievably adoring simper spread over her face. I mean it positively made you want to puke, to throw up right then and there, all over the two of them.

Clara put up with it for quite some time. Everybody's agreed completely that she really was extremely tolerant and very, *very* understanding, but the damned thing just kept going on and on and getting worse and worse and Maddy kept falling deeper and deeper in love, and it was becoming increasingly obvious that Clara was running out of patience, and naturally we were all becoming quite worried about what she might do.

We all know you can only push them just so far.

Maddy called me up and asked if we couldn't have tea at the Pierre, you know, in that funny room with the *trompe l'œil* walls and ceiling? Because she wanted to talk about what was happening and of course I jumped at the chance because, like everybody else, I was dying to know all the gory details.

God, she was so *pale*, poor dear, so *frightened*. I hate to see a pretty woman so distraught, don't you? I mean she was actually chewing her lips and plucking at her fingers, for God's sake! And her eyes never stopped darting, looking up along the balcony and the staircase, shooting quick, searching looks at the floor and the doorways.

She was wearing a long-sleeved dress and it wasn't *like* Maddy to wear a long-sleeved dress. Not with her beautiful arms, certainly not during a heat wave. She must have noticed I'd noticed, because after she'd done all this peering around the room she rested one arm on the table and then pulled its long sleeve back and showed me a crisscrossing of white bandages and nasty red scratch marks stretching out from under them.

She glared down at her arm with this perfectly *fierce* frown on her face—something right out of *Medea*, I can assure you—and said in a perfect hiss: "*Clara* did this to me! There will *always* be scars!"

Then she positively jerked her sleeve back down over those bandages and things and went on and on about how unfair Clara had been and how she wasn't going to take it anymore and about how she was a grown-up woman and could do what she pleased if she wanted to and all the rest of that tiresome garbage.

I did what usually works in situations like this: I let her go on until she'd run down a little and then I tried talking sensibly to her. I told her how much she owed Clara, how much we *all* owed our darlings, and I was even unkind enough to ask her flat out in plain English how she thought she would manage if she *did* leave Clara for the man she'd met in Rio.

"I mean, is he rich, darling?" I asked her. "Is he *that* rich?"

She turned and pouted at me.

"No," she said. "He thinks *I'm* rich."

"Of course he does, darling," I told her. "*All* the men

do. That's how come we get our choice of them, don't you see?"

But she didn't see, and all my advice did was to set her off again on a new tirade, which ended with her leaning close to me and whispering the most appalling thing! The most perfectly awful thing!

But here are our salads. Thank you, Jacques. Yes, the wine is excellent, Jacques.

Wait a second, darling, until he's out of earshot.

The silly bitch told me she planned to kill Clara!

Oh, I'm sorry, dear, I can see now I should have led up to it a bit more. Padded the approach. Please do excuse my thoughtlessness, but it's just that this has been the most *awful* business for me and it's got me thoroughly upset. Of course, that's really no excuse.

I shouldn't have been so abrupt.

Have some more wine.

Better?

Well, I tried again to talk sense to her, even after that, though it seemed perfectly hopeless. She had that crazy, glazed look people get when they're absolutely determined to do the stupidest, silliest thing possible, so in the end all I asked of her was not to do anything drastic for at least a little while and—after what seemed hours—I wore her down and she agreed she'd think things over once or twice again and call me in a few days and then we'd have another little talk about it all.

So I felt rather smug when we parted.

This wine isn't really all that good after the first few sips, is it? I do believe Jacques's losing his touch. I think I really might permanently cross this place off my list, don't you think?

Anyway, it was over a full week when a call came, but it wasn't the one I was hoping for, to say the least.

I was profoundly asleep as it's just possible I'd had a touch too much to drink, and the ringing of that pretty bedside phone Andre gave me—you do remember Andre, don't you? He was a count and I've never had anything to do with counts since—hauled me out of the depths of some god-awful dream so that I was really only half awake when I'd managed to put the receiver to my ear so at first I couldn't make any sense of what I was hearing and I suppose I kept saying "What is it?" in this slurry, muzzy voice a half-dozen times until it dawned on me at last that it wasn't a human voice at all on the other end of the line!

It was a mewing, darling, the saddest, sweetest little mewing you ever heard. Going on and on in the most pathetic way possible. It wasn't a few more seconds before I recognized it, and then the most ghastly chill ran through me from my toes to the crown of my head because, of course, it was Clara. Maddy's little Clara.

But after that I thought: My God, she's calling me for help! and I knew I'd *never* been so touched. It was—I'm afraid I'm getting quite teary-eyed just talking about it— positively the most wonderful thing that ever happened to me in all my life.

The trust.

The idea that she thought of me first.

Excuse me but I've positively *got* to dab my eyes.

That's better.

"Don't worry, sweetness!" I said into the phone, gently as I could. "Don't worry, little dearest! I'll be right over!"

I was as good as my word, darling. I got up and dressed though it was the middle of the night and taxied right over to Maddy and Clara's building where I proceeded to bully the doorman and then the building manager in turn when the doorman woke him up—great sleepy hulks, both of them—and we finally all took the elevator to Maddy and Clara's apartment, after ringing it God knows how many times, and opened the door.

Well, you simply wouldn't believe the smell, dear. Totally extraordinary. The whole place reeked, simply reeked. It moved out at you like a wall.

The doorman took one choking gulp of it, then turned and puked his guts out on the floor of the hall. The manager just kept saying "Jesus, Jesus, Jesus," over and over again until I ached to slap his silly fat face until he shut up.

But then I heard that little mew and Clara stepped timidly into the light coming from the hallway and trotted right over to my feet looking up at me in the most pathetic way, and I leaned down and picked her up and kissed her poor, sad little face right on its nose in spite of the terrible, *terrible* stench of her which she hadn't been able to lick away in spite, I'm sure, of the most heroic attempts to do so.

I barged right into the living room while the babbling manager staggered along behind me as there wasn't any doubt where the smell was coming from and there was Maddy sprawled out on the carpet like a swastika right in the middle of an impossibly huge splash of dried blood that they'll never, *ever* manage to scrub away.

What was left of Maddy was lying there, that is, because it was obvious that poor Clara had been forced to eat quite a bit of her over the last week or so.

I simply can't imagine why someone hasn't had the brains to come up with cat food packed in a container the poor dears could open themselves in case of an emergency, can you? Then so many of these distasteful things you hear about simply wouldn't have to happen.

Anyhow, Maddy had absolutely no face left and her lovely slip had been reduced to red ribbons all gone stiff. I suppose poor Clara had been forced to tear it apart so that she could get at the rest of her after she'd finished off all of the exposed soft parts.

Absolutely ghastly.

Of course, I knew perfectly well it wasn't just hunger that made Clara take away *all* those bits and pieces. Hunger wouldn't explain why the whole throat was completely missing, darling, even those tough, rubbery chunks that must be *hideous* to chew and swallow if you've only got tiny teeth and a little pink mouth to work with.

I'm sure it will never dawn on those stupid policemen that if there'd *been* a throat then there would have been its original wound for all to see and it might have given them a problem with their theory that Maddy had sliced her neck open with the chef's knife clutched in her hand because she'd been so sad about her friend from Rio.

It's not likely, but one of them might have even been smart enough to take a good look at that wound and wonder if a certain little pussycat had been very angry at her mistress for trying to chop her up with that same knife.

But there was no original wound to look at because Clara had eaten it all up, clever little thing.

Ah, good—here's the fish at last. Yes, of course we want it boned.

Thank you, Jacques. We'll do our very best to enjoy it, never fear.

My God, the lazy bastards will be asking us to *cook our lunches* the next thing you know!

Now, then—as to why I asked if you were free today, darling.

There's a girl I've spotted working in that small perfume counter at Bergdorf's. You know, the little discreet one they've tucked in a corner far away from that cabash they've got spread over all those other rooms?

I've chatted with her quite a bit and noticed her looking sidewise at my jewels and my furs. She loves the way I buy the most expensive stuff without a thought and I know she'd give *anything* to be able to do it herself.

Absolutely anything.

Of course you remember how *that* felt, don't you, dear? God knows I certainly do!

Why don't we go over there after lunch and you can look at her and we can sort of feel her out together?

She's very pretty.

She's like us.

I think she'd be absolutely perfect for Clara!

Nicholas Royle

Nicholas Royle was born in 1963 in South Manchester, England, and now lives in London. Since 1984 he has published stories in *Interzone, Dark Voices, Obsessions, Narrow Houses, Little Deaths, The Year's Best Horror Stories, Best New Horror,* and *The Year's Best Fantasy and Horror.* His first novel, *Counterparts,* has recently been published in the United States His second, *Saxophone Dreams,* has recently been published in England.

Royle's short fiction successfully roams the boundaries between horror, fantasy, and science fiction. "Skin Deep" is a dark suspense story of male gamesmanship in which there can only be losers.

Skin Deep

NICHOLAS ROYLE

HENDERSON ONLY AGREED to go on the expedition because he thought Elizabeth was going along, so when he turned up at the Washington service area on the A1(M) and found only Bloor waiting to meet him, he felt like a child with an empty Christmas box. It was important, however, not to show too much disappointment, given that Elizabeth was Graham Bloor's wife. Bloor waited for Henderson to ask, then explained.

"Elizabeth wasn't feeling up to it at the last minute," he said, flicking ash from his cigarette into the little foil tray that sat on the plastic tabletop between the two men. "Women's things, you know." He placed the cigarette between his lips with his forefinger and thumb. Henderson wasn't sure if he mistrusted *all* men who held their cigarettes in this particular way, or if it was just Bloor. Certainly the man wouldn't win any charm contests, and Henderson *was* screwing his wife.

"So it's just the two of us, then," Henderson said, eyes sliding across Bloor's heavy, jowly features to the other tables in the cafeteria. Apart from a couple of thickset lorry drivers sipping scalding tea from greasy mugs and a sales rep in a gray double-breasted suit taking dainty bites round the edge of a white bread sandwich, they were the only customers. It was still early, not long after eight. The only two kitchen staff—women in their forties with tight curly perms and pink housecoats—were leaning against opposite sides of a doorway chattering in low voices.

"Looks like it, doesn't it?" Bloor said, picking his

cigarette out from between his lips for the last time before grinding it out in the ashtray.

The plan was for Henderson to leave his car in the carpark and go with Bloor. The idea had appealed to him when it had included Elizabeth sitting in the passenger seat. He had imagined sitting in the back and watching the soft spring of hairs on the back of her neck. She would have put her hair up especially, because she was no slouch when it came to understanding her own appeal. But with Elizabeth left at home—she and Bloor shared a sizable detached house in Gosforth—it was sadly inevitable that Henderson should take the seat alongside Bloor. He drove the Mercedes the way Elizabeth said he made love—fast, undeviating, and without a backward glance. The way he dangled his arm out of the window was telling.

As Bloor put more miles between them and the service area, Henderson became increasingly miserable. Not even the bleak splendor of the Borders cheered him up, unable as he was to think of anything other than Elizabeth arching her back catlike in bed.

She complained unceasingly about Bloor, his habits and the way he treated her; the oily manner he adopted with female shop assistants and waitresses, the unshakable confidence that she was his and would never leave him. And in that, at least, he appeared to be right, not that Henderson felt able to criticize her for staying: Bloor's success in various businesses had provided comforts aplenty; they wanted for nothing on the material side, and Elizabeth was a material girl. Henderson knew this—she would pick at the cloth of his lapel disdainfully and frown at his chain-store shoes—but it in no way colored his feelings for her. She was a deeply attractive woman, and Henderson knew he had to be doing a lot better than he was as a business studies lecturer to lure her away from her Gosforth lair for more than a night at a time. He didn't blame her, because he would have done the same in her position.

"So where are we heading?" Henderson asked to break the silence.

"The Highlands, of course." Bloor pressed the cigar lighter home.

"I know, but whereabouts?"

"Oh, I forget the name. Someplace. We'll leave the car and go on foot. Find somewhere to pitch the tent when it gets dark. And hopefully get lucky either tonight or tomorrow."

"But there's no guarantee, is there? That we'll find one." Henderson's heart was sinking still further at the prospect of more than a single night spent with Bloor.

"No guarantee, that's right, but plenty of incentive. Curtin's offering two grand. His client must be offering double that."

"Christ," said Henderson. "Why would anybody pay four grand for a stuffed cat?" He looked out of the window at the passing outposts of Scots pine, wondering again about the ethics of the job.

"It's not just any old cat. The wild cat's as rare as rocking horse droppings. Two grand though, eh? Not bad for a couple of days' work. And it's like I said: fifty-fifty."

"What about Elizabeth's share?" Henderson asked.

"What share? Would you expect to get paid if you'd stayed at home?"

Henderson bristled with righteous anger. Elizabeth was entitled to her share, and he'd no doubt she'd still be expecting it. She'd helped with the research after all, picked the most likely spot to yield a wild cat. He'd offer her part of his share when they got back, assuming of course they found one of the damn things and managed to catch it and kill it without damaging the pelt. Curtin had made it quite clear to Bloor that if the cat was disfigured he wouldn't pay them a penny. Quite why he was being so fussy was a mystery to Henderson, who never would have expected taxidermists to adhere so strictly to whatever moral code prevented the man substituting a swatch of tabby fur. Maybe his client was enough of an expert to be able to tell the difference: Why else would he offer such silly money? The wild cat's basic color was yellowish gray and while five out of ten domestic strays could match that, they wouldn't have the wild cat's strong black vertical bars and dorsal stripe, nor its broad, bushy tail, which the text-books—and Elizabeth—had taught them was the surest means of identification. The last thing they wanted to do was turn up at Curtin's with a feral moggy.

Henderson, though, had had grave doubts about the expedition's viability. Indeed, he had needed to be convinced the wild cat actually existed, having grown up with the idea that the British Isles were devoid of any genuine wildlife. And then the books Elizabeth had trucked back from Newcastle Library all said how elusive the wild cat was and how the closest encounter you could reasonably hope for was a set of pawprints in fresh snow, or twin mirrors startled in car headlamps. Systematic tracking, the naturalists wrote, would very rarely produce a result.

So when Bloor swung the wheel of the Merc in a wide arc and scrunched to a halt in pinecones and dirt at the edge of the unmetaled road in the Middle of Nowhere, Highland region, Henderson felt their chances were minimal.

"Got everything?" Bloor asked before locking the car.

Henderson nodded, hefting his rucksack and peering up the track. Bloor bent down and tucked the keys under a rear wheel arch.

"No point carrying anything we don't have to," he said, "and who's going to nick it out here? Let's go. We have to go as quietly as we can. They're very shy."

"Do you really think we'll find one?" Henderson asked.

"I'm not going home without one." And with that he immediately got into his stride. Henderson followed him into the semigloom of the forest. Once he'd gotten used to the sound of their passage, Henderson listened for other noises but the forest remained silent: no clouds of flies buzzing in stray patches of sunlight, no tiny creatures scratching through the undergrowth, and, most surprising of all, no birds clattering through the tops of the trees. He didn't get too close to Bloor but was careful not to lose sight of his broad shoulders rising and falling twenty yards in front.

"It's getting dark," he shouted forward when he realized the trees had started to close in around them.

"Ssh." Bloor flapped a hand in the air. "Wild cats are nocturnal," he said, catching his breath when Henderson had drawn level. "The darker it gets the better our chances, but we've got to be quiet."

They set off again, Henderson bringing up the rear, thinking about Elizabeth. They'd met two years previously holidaying on Paxos. Henderson had been struck by the unmistakable look of a bored wife when he'd happened to take breakfast on a couple of occasions at the same time as she and Bloor. He followed them one evening to a taverna that was well off the tourist trail and sat in a dim corner with a bowl of olives and a bottle of white wine. Bloor tucked into course after course while Elizabeth looked over his shoulder and once or twice crossed sightlines with Henderson. Walking back to the hotel, she looked back a couple of times and he was there at the edge of the surf, trousers rolled up, jacket slung over his shoulder with calculated nonchalance. So when she came downstairs half an hour after going up with Bloor to find Henderson drinking alone in the bar, neither of them was really surprised.

Henderson ordered another bottle of wine and they shared it with a round of conversational hide-and-seek.

"You do the shopping together every Thursday evening," Henderson guessed. "You push the trolley and load in all the basic stuff while he marches in front picking up vacuum packs of continental sausages and firelighters for the barbecues you never get round to having."

"You circle programs in the *Radio Times*," she said, raising her glass to her painted lips, "then forget to watch them, sitting there listening to music instead and nursing a bottle of beer. Old jazz stuff probably or movie soundtracks. Comfort music."

"And then when I do remember to set the video for something," he continued, "I never watch it but record the next thing over the top of it instead. I have tapes filled with the ends of shows I wanted to watch."

"You don't go to singles bars—" She crossed her legs,

dress riding up. "—but you do watch women in pubs, always married women. You try to catch their eye when their husband goes to the toilet."

"You take long, long showers after he's gone to work, loving the feel of the water on your body. Then you might stretch out on that extravagant sheepskin rug in the living room."

"Like a cat," she added, draining her glass. And so they wandered down to the sea, talked some nonsense about the stars, and returned to the hotel, to Henderson's single room. She showered and slipped back to her own room before dawn with Bloor none the wiser.

In the week that remained it was inevitable that Henderson should get drawn into the group; it was the only way to escape suspicion. Henderson cultivated the other man's friendship at the same time as screwing his wife, who suddenly developed a taste for long solitary walks, usually to deserted stretches of coastline but occasionally just up to Henderson's room on the top floor. Bloor, though already a successful businessman, was attracted to the older, unflashy lecturer, and would sit for hours fascinated by his theories, the names he dropped so casually: dinner with the head of the CBI, invitations to the wedding of the ICI chief executive's daughter.

"How much of it is true?" Elizabeth asked on one of their walks.

"Enough," he said. "The rest is just confidence."

Henderson played him like a fish, paying out line when he praised Bloor's acumen, comparing his strategies to those of top-flight Germans and Japanese, tactfully offering advice like a speechwriter deferring to a senior minister. Bloor glowed and bubbled for the remainder of the Greek holiday, persistently cracking terrible jokes about the name of the island. "Do you know this is where they make the stuffing?" He would grin and splutter from the dregs of yet another bottle of ouzo. "Paxos," he'd repeat time after time. "Paxos, Paxos." And trail off in incomprehensible mutterings, Elizabeth's hand on his arm (her other under the table on Henderson's linen trousers) and a smile on Henderson's lips.

They were booked back on the same charter and Bloor actually suggested to Elizabeth that she sit with Henderson rather than suffer the smoking section. At Gatwick they made plans for Henderson to come up to Newcastle as soon as his teaching schedule would allow. In fact, he was to make many more trips up the A1 than the ones Bloor would know about. After a weekend as their guest in Gosforth he'd come up again on the Wednesday night, every other week his Thursday being completely free, and get a room at the St. Mary's in Whitley Bay, where Elizabeth would join him once Bloor was out of the way at work. They'd walk along the windswept beach as far as Cullercoats and make jokes about how it compared to Paxos. Neither of them spoke of love—except Elizabeth when talking about Bloor ("He does love me, you know")— and yet there was clearly a need of some kind on both sides. She would get on the phone to Henderson when Bloor was called away at short notice, as he was with increasing frequency, to Copenhagen and Brussels, and Henderson's car would find itself pressed into more and more demanding service.

They snatched a weekend together in Alnwick when Bloor was in London. He left long, whining messages on the answerphone, which they heard when Henderson accompanied Elizabeth back to the house before driving back down to Leicester. Where was she? Why hadn't she called him back? Then he'd wheedle: "Don't worry, darling. I just hope you're having a nice time. I'll see you when I get back." It gave Henderson no little grim pleasure as he motored south to think that at some point Bloor would pass him going north on the opposite carriageway. He had begun to feel jealous of the man and started inventing excuses to avoid coming up for weekends at their house; no longer could he easily bear seeing them together. He didn't know if Bloor had put on weight or if he just *saw* him as fatter, slower, and more complacent. After all, for all her abandon in bed at Whitley Bay, Elizabeth was still married to the man.

The expedition had been on the cards for a few weeks, ever since Bloor had bumped into his old friend Curtin at a Rotarians dinner and the taxidermist had raised the subject of wild cats. Elizabeth did her research and suddenly the trip was on, but minus one person.

Bloor had come to a halt and Henderson caught up with him.

"Isn't it getting too dark to see one now even if there are any?" Henderson asked, wiping sweat from his forehead.

"Not if you're looking." Bloor hitched his rucksack up his back. Heavier than Henderson's, it contained the tent, a primus stove, and some provisions. "We're more likely to see evidence of a cat before we see the cat itself. The carcass of a hare or a buzzard. Try and keep an eye out."

There was a note of sarcasm in his voice that Henderson had not heard before and didn't much care for. It occurred to him that apart from moments when she'd slipped to the loo, it was the first time he'd been in the company of Bloor without Elizabeth.

Around 11:30 P.M., still having seen no trace of their quarry, they found a tiny clearing and set up camp, Bloor pitching the tent while Henderson got the primus going. The sky above the pines was an indigo velvet pincushion.

"I envy you sometimes," Bloor said as they sat back after a fairly basic meal of beans with minifrankfurters, followed by an apple each. "Being single."

"Oh?" Henderson said neutrally.

"Well, you know, the freedom. You can do what you like." Bloor leered, waggling his eyebrows.

Henderson thought about his response. "I suppose so, although I don't really have much time for any of that."

Bloor said, "Is that right?" and for the first time Henderson wondered whether he might possibly suspect. "I thought with your job there would be a lot of free time and what with all those nubile young students hanging around you could be, you know, making the most of it while you still can." He tapped a cigarette out of his Camel softpack and continued: "Only I'm beginning to wonder if I'm past it. You know. I'm forty-six, not as fit as I was. I don't know if I still satisfy Elizabeth." He stared at Henderson, then placed the cigarette between his lips, and spun the wheel on his Bic lighter. "She's still a young woman."

"I don't think age comes into it," Henderson said.

"No, I don't suppose it does." Bloor flicked ash over the primus. "I mean, look at you. You're older than both of us."

"Put together." Henderson laughed, but it was a nervous laugh and he couldn't imagine that Bloor wouldn't spot it and start working things out, if he hadn't already.

For a few minutes the only sound in the night, apart from the occasional hoot of an owl, was the hiss of Bloor dragging on his cigarette. Then he spoke again. "I've got something I want to ask you," he said, and Henderson's stomach muscles clenched. "Would you . . . and tell me if you think I shouldn't even have asked . . . but would you sleep with Elizabeth, if she wanted you to?"

Henderson was speechless.

Bloor stubbed out his cigarette. "Okay, look, I shouldn't have asked. Forget I said anything, okay?"

Henderson still couldn't find the right words.

"It's been a long day," Bloor was saying. "I think we both need some sleep. We've got to find that damn cat tomorrow, and the earlier we get up the more chance we'll have." So saying, he crawled into the tiny two-man tent.

"I'm going to sit up for a while," Henderson said because he couldn't face climbing into the tent while Bloor was still awake. "I won't be long."

Henderson woke at dawn, shivering and hungry, to discover that Bloor was already up. His sleeping bag had been rolled and folded into a tiny pouch and his rucksack stood ready to go. Henderson dragged himself out of his own sleeping bag and took a swig from a bottle of mineral water he kept tucked away. He pulled on some clothes and halfheartedly performed a couple of push-ups. Bloor appeared while he was taking a leak at the edge of the clearing, and they set off soon after without either of them having ventured more than a "good morning."

Midmorning they came across a rabbit or, more precisely, its skin. Something had eaten all the meat—odd bones lay scattered around—and tossed the skin aside, expertly turned inside out. Bloor took it in his hand and held it up so that the skin fell back over itself like a glove puppet.

"Wild cat," he said.

"Really?"

"They can be vicious," he added, turning the rabbit skin so that the head, which was still intact, flopped this way and that. "Mind you, a domestic cat can do this just as easily."

They pressed on deeper into the forest. Bloor stayed in front and Henderson stared as hard as he could into the soft light between the boles of tall pines, because the sooner they found the cat, the sooner they could get back home. Surprisingly it bothered him that he couldn't get to a phone to ask her how she was feeling. Her periods were generally over fairly quick, two or three days at most, and although she suffered a little, she, and Henderson, always celebrated their arrival as proof that they'd got away with it for another month. They took precautions, but, because of the circumstances, they worried a little when it got to three weeks.

It was just before they were going to stop for food, around 6 P.M., that they came across the weasel. It had been skinned as cleanly as the rabbit. Bloor held it up triumphantly, appearing to scent success and money.

"Curtin couldn't have done a better job himself," he said as he turned the skin over in his hands.

"What do you mean?"

"This is what he does. He skins the animal—dead, obviously—and then uses the carcass to make a mold, usually in fiberglass, unless it's something this small."

During their reconstituted meal Bloor continued.

"He invited me to spend a day at his workshop when

he was mounting a puma he got from the zoo. The puma died of old age and he was commissioned to mount it for a museum somewhere in Wales. It takes weeks to do a big cat apparently, but I was there on the day he skinned it."

Bloor pushed his paper plate away and lit a cigarette. The shadows around the clearing were thickening as the sky was gradually leached of daylight.

"He hung the carcass upside-down from a chain fixed to a beam, and it's amazing how easily the skin comes away. He'd pull a bit and it would unravel a further inch or so, then he'd take the scalpel and delicately free it from the fat and gristle. It's bizarre when you see the skinned carcass with its bug eyes and exposed muscle and tendons. It's beautiful in a way."

Henderson rigged up the little kettle on the primus to have an excuse to look away from Bloor, whose face had taken on a look of mixed revulsion and fascination.

"What does he do with the carcass?" Henderson asked.

"He calls up the knackers' yard, who come along and take it away. Unless it's something small like a bird, or that weasel, in which case he slings it into the field. Apparently there's a lot of fat foxes round where he has his workshop."

"So the stuffed animal you see in a museum isn't an animal at all. It's just the skin with some kind of cast inside?"

"Exactly. He generally uses expanding foam. You could pick up a tiger with one hand, they're so light."

"It's a bit disappointing, isn't it?"

"Not really. It depends where you think the essence of the animal really is: in the carcass or in the skin. Because once you've skinned an animal, all you've got on the one hand is a lump of meat, and on the other you've got the skin, which was all you saw while it was alive, after all."

"But it's only skin deep."

"Aren't we all, though?" Bloor said with a grimace, plucking his cigarette from between his lips. "What would you rather see in a museum, or in your front room for that matter, a bloody carcass or a stuffed skin? I know which I find more attractive."

Henderson wasn't entirely convinced by Bloor's logic. Obviously, the carefully prepared, titivated thing in the glass case was more attractive, but if you'd slung the beast's beating heart in the bin and scraped all trace of its brains from its skull, how could you still call it an animal, albeit a stuffed one?

"What about my wife?" Bloor asked suddenly from out of the shadows. "Don't you find her attractive?"

Henderson cast around for a way to answer but ended up spluttering: "I don't know. I haven't, you know, I don't see her in that light. She's your wife."

"But she's a beautiful woman. Surely you find her attractive?"

"Well, yes, she's attractive, of course. But I don't see how it's relevant."

"Just making a point," Bloor said, sucking on his cigarette and causing the end to glow as it crept farther toward his lips. "We only see the surface of things, you see."

The blue flame on the primus sputtered and died.

"Shit," said Henderson. The water hadn't yet boiled. "Have you got another gas canister?"

"Over there." Bloor pointed toward his rucksack. "Side pocket."

Henderson got the wrong side, fiddled around in one of the pockets, and found nothing. "Chuck me a torch, will you?"

Bloor lobbed him the thin pencil torch he kept in his jacket and Henderson peered into the rucksack.

The redness was shocking.

Stuffed into a zip-up compartment that had not been fastened were several screwed-up tissues, all spotted and streaked with dried blood. Some instinct told him to conceal his discovery from Bloor, but the sight of blood had set his heart thumping and he had to remain bent over the rucksack even after he'd located the new canister.

Bloor's disembodied voice brought him back to his senses. "Can't you find it?"

"Got it," he said, twisting round to the little stove and fixing the new canister in place as Bloor dampened his

cigarette butt and flicked it into the darkness. "Call of nature," Henderson said, getting up and disappearing into
the trees.

He needed to get away from Bloor for a moment to
take in what he'd just seen. Clearly, the most likely expla-
nation was that Bloor had had a nosebleed and had kept
the tissues in his rucksack rather than litter the countryside
(despite his tendency to drop cigarette ends). But something was nagging at Henderson, plucking at his brain:
hadn't Bloor seemed just a little bit too knowledgeable in
the business of skinning animals, and where for that matter had he been to so early in the morning?

"Something wrong?"

Henderson jumped. Bloor was a few feet behind him
and would have seen that Henderson was just standing
there, no trickle of water between his legs.

"Can't seem to go," he said, miming zipping up his
fly. Bloor grunted, lit a cigarette, and turned to look into
the forest. It was very dark by now, like an old house, the
tree trunks like table legs. The whole place was deathly
silent apart from the occasional floorboard creak as an
owl alighted on a high branch.

"It's out there somewhere," Bloor said.

Something is, certainly, thought Henderson. Even if
it was only the hidden animal in Bloor, the dark side of
his character that enjoyed tearing small creatures apart.
Though, presumably, if he was responsible, he was doing
it either to frighten Henderson or to convince him that the
wild cat was within their grasp and thereby persuade him
to go deeper with him into the forest, and into the night.

Henderson was suddenly convinced that Bloor knew
exactly what was going on with Elizabeth.

The two men stood there staring into the gloom.
Bloor spat on his spent cigarette and flicked it into the forest where it was accepted silently by the carpet of needles.

When they'd packed up and were heading off again
Henderson followed close behind Bloor, extremely tense,
wondering what he would say next. He felt like a small
boy with an angry, unpredictable father, and, like a child,

he didn't seem to possess the courage either to run away or talk straight. As they walked, Henderson even started thinking that the whole premise for the jaunt could have been made up: there was no deal with Curtin and they were as likely to find a tiger as a wild cat in this godforsaken corner of the highlands. He felt a strong urge to call off the search and return home: Bloor was no more the country boy than he was, but the other man at least had the advantage of knowing where they were going. Henderson started watching his surroundings with greater interest—the way the hills on his left seemed to rise to three distinct peaks; the change from pure pine forest to a mixture of larch and Scots pine—so that he felt a little less dependent on Bloor.

"What's next, then, Graham?" he heard himself asking, to make it seem as if he still believed they were actually hunting wild cat and everything was normal.

"Black panthers," Bloor replied without a moment's hesitation. "They've been seen just outside Worcester."

"That's ridiculous. There are no big cats in England."

"What do you know about it?" Bloor spun round and glared at Henderson. "Hmm?" His dimpled chin jutted forward. "What do you know?"

Henderson watched Bloor's eyes, but it was too dark to distinguish pupil from iris, so they were just black holes.

"Curtin knows a woman called Meech, a photographer, who lives down there and she saw one. Okay?"

Bloor's sarcastic tone tipped the scales a fraction and Henderson felt some power flow his way; just a drop but he lapped it up. "A black panther?" he said.

"Well, it was black, it was a cat, and it was the size of an Alsatian, so what do you suggest?" Bloor took out a cigarette and bathed his face in a cup of orange fire to light it.

"She could have been mistaken."

"She's a wildlife photographer."

"Did she get a picture of it?"

Bloor dragged on his cigarette and blew a column of smoke directly into Henderson's face. "She wasn't quick enough."

"Shame," said Henderson, stepping around Bloor and taking the lead for the first time. There was no path, but he marched off in what had been a straight line for the last twenty minutes. After a moment he heard Bloor mutter something and start following. Henderson hid his growing unease with a confident stride, but he knew he didn't possess the bluff to carry it off for very long. If Bloor was lying about the black panther he'd done so convincingly.

They marched for another half hour. There could have been dozens of wild cats watching them from the trees for all Henderson was aware. His mind was focused exclusively on Bloor and he didn't slow his pace until the shout came: "We'll stop here." In the renewed quiet Bloor's breath chugged like an idling locomotive. "We need some rest," he added as if he now needed to justify his orders. "It's mental as well as physical. If we're not alert we don't stand a chance."

He had echoed Henderson's own conviction, but the older man was unable to prevent himself falling asleep next to Bloor in the two-man tent, and when he awoke Bloor was gone. The power shift, if it had happened at all, had been reversed. Bloor was out there somewhere either tracking rabbits and mice and gutting them with his bare hands, or he was watching Henderson from behind a tree. Maybe he was genuinely searching for the wild cat, but there were too many maybes: Henderson had had enough. If he was right and Bloor knew about them, then Elizabeth needed to know; otherwise she'd be at a disadvantage when Bloor got back to Gosforth.

There wouldn't be a phone for miles. The only thing for it was for Henderson to retrace their steps to the car and get the hell out. It wouldn't take more than a couple of hours to bomb it down to Newcastle. He could be with her—quick glance at his watch—by 7 A.M. He was sure enough of Bloor's knowledge not to take the not inconsiderable risk of stealing his car.

Henderson started packing his rucksack, suddenly terrified that Bloor would return and catch him in the act, but he had a thought and scribbled a quick note telling Bloor he'd woken up early and gone looking for him. He took from his own bag only the essentials and slipped out of the tent. The note could buy him an extra hour or two, enough time for Elizabeth to pack a bag and leave with him if she wanted to. It wouldn't be ideal, but at least she'd have a choice.

He crept through the trees for the first hundred yards in case Bloor was close by, then broke into a steady run, ducking and darting between the trunks. It was still dark but he was surprised by the clear tracks they'd left the day before: the path was easy to follow. Cresting a rise he stopped dead, blood hammering in his chest, sweat trickling down from his scalp. Twenty yards away, crouched down between the lines of trees, ears flattened against its skull and broad tail beating on the soft forest floor, was a cat. A wild cat. It bared its bone-white teeth in Henderson's direction, then, with a twitch, was gone, swallowed up by the darkness. Henderson started breathing again, exhilarated and privileged to have been allowed those two seconds' intimacy. He suddenly felt overwhelmingly grateful they had not found a wild cat: *He* couldn't have killed it and he would have been unable to prevent himself staying Bloor's arm.

The wild cat had gone and Henderson was free to do the same. He slipped between the thin trunks like a wraith, glancing up at the three hills on his right, the sky beginning to glow with the soft breath of dawn. He ran, just ran, and whether he possessed a keener sense of direction than he realized, or did it simply because he had to, he covered the distance and tumbled out of the forest, which seemed to snap shut behind him. The Mercedes gleamed in the early light. Henderson bent down and reached under the wheel arch for the keys, found them, almost dropped them, flung the door open, started the engine, and spat gravel at the dark line of trees already receding in the rearview mirror. Somewhere in that lot was Bloor, sitting by the tent waiting for Henderson to come back, he hoped.

The house was quiet. Set back from the road and protected by high hedges, you couldn't even hear the traffic unless you made an effort. Getting no response ringing the bell, Henderson went round to the back—vaulting a high white wooden gate—and found the kitchen door open. He called Elizabeth's name but could only hear the blood rushing in his ears. The kitchen was clean, devoid of signs of breakfast, and the wall clock read 9:25. The return trip had taken only a little longer than expected. She would normally be up and have had breakfast, although Bloor's absence would obviously allow for a change in routine should she wish it.

Henderson made his way into the hallway, fingering the banister rail as if it were made of china.

"Elizabeth," he called once more, and was disturbed to hear his voice break. He felt his face burning red and a little knot in his stomach tightening.

He stood silently on the landing for a couple of beats. The house was still. An impossible draft brushed the back of his neck and a ripple ran over his scalp, pulling the smallest hairs erect. He took another step toward Elizabeth's bedroom, pushed open the door, and stood on the threshold.

Amid a jumble of mad thoughts and a nauseous sinking sensation, he wondered how long he'd known at the back of his mind that this was what he would find. He approached the bed, determined to retain enough strength in his legs to stay standing.

He took her in his arms and was careful not to hold her too tight in case the stitching broke. As he sat on the bed rocking gently forward and back, forward and back, he thought with infinite sadness that here was a woman he could have loved, if he didn't already. Flooding through came the realization that subconsciously he had strongly desired her separation from Bloor. Each time he looked at her—the puckered skin round the eyes, the lopsided mouth—he pictured Bloor at work. He relaxed his hold.

Later, outside by the white gate he'd vaulted to gain entrance to the grounds, he found a large bundle of sacking material. It was damp and sticky to the touch but gently he peeled the layers away to get at what lay inside, which he then lifted out and cradled in his arms, unmoved by the powerful smell and seeping fluids.

The sun crossed the sky slowly, passing the overhead, burning only dully through the gathering scraps of cloud. The house remained silent apart from the creak of Henderson, upstairs once more, rocking to and fro on the bed, sheets sliding, slats groaning.

"Curtin told me that's how he started," said Bloor.

Henderson tensed but didn't let go. He turned his head enough to see Bloor in the doorway hugging the slippery carcass to his chest, tears tumbling from his ravaged, poisoned eyes.

"Mounting the things he loved—his dog and his cats—because he couldn't bear it when they went away. It must be different with pets," he added blankly. "Which one of us has her now, do you think?"

Henderson traced his finger over her skin, stretched tight across the mere shape of her shoulder.

He made no other reply.

Kathe Koja and Barry N. Malzberg

Kathe Koja is the author of the novels *The Cipher, Bad Brains, Skin, Strange Angels,* and *Kink,* and also short stories that have appeared, since 1988, in *Omni, The Magazine of Fantasy and Science Fiction, Asimov's Science Fiction Magazine, The Year's Best Science Fiction, The Year's Best Fantasy and Horror,* and in many original anthologies. *The Cipher* won the Bram Stoker Award, given by the Horror Writers Association, for first novel. Koja lives in a suburb of Detroit with her husband, the artist and photographer Rick Lieder, and her son, Aaron.

Barry N. Malzberg, the author of the novels *Beyond Apollo, Herovit's World, The Remaking of Sigmund Freud, Galaxies,* and many others, has published short stories, since 1967, through the entire range of science fiction and mystery markets and was the first winner, for *Beyond Apollo* in 1973, of the John W. Campbell Memorial Award. His fiction continues to be nominated for various awards; a recent story, "Understanding Entropy," was nominated for the 1994 Nebula Award.

Kathe Koja and Barry N. Malzberg began collaborating in 1992 and their stories have appeared in *Omni, F&SF,* and several original anthologies. They have completed a novel, *God of the Mountains.*

"Homage to Custom" is an extraordinarily effective amalgam of both Kojas' and Malzberg's writing styles. It illustrates scenes from the interconnected lives of a whore and the stray cat that follows her home.

Homage to Custom

KATHE KOJA AND BARRY N. MALZBERG

THE WHORE'S CAT had been diagnosed as having feline diabetes, but maybe, the whore thought, it was just a bad diet. Or the heat. Or the cold, or the dirty litter box, or the smell of the apartment, third-floor walkup in Hell's Kitchen: put one foot in front of the other and in a minute, two minutes, ten minutes you were yelping like a puppy dog, squeaking like a kitten, grinding like a stone. You were rolling like a wheel, Jack: pop the squirt and then the wallet although it was better to make them pay first because if they didn't pay first they never paid at all and who needs that?—who needs it, they did, that was who: on the bed and on the floor, on the table like lunch, gleam and glimmer, stutter and dump, chill spilled opium of the heart and the whore's cat on the edge of the real marble windowsills, real cracked and broken marble pink as the cat's disdainful little tongue whisking busy at private parts, pink as an itchy vulva, pink as the inside of her own dry eyelids when, as this morning, she had had no sleep all night.

Not that she was that busy, no. Not that there was a line to enter the third-floor walkup, a line to enter her: no and no and what difference did it make anyway? Off days, slow days but they always found her, these dumb pathetic guys, even guys *this* dumb could figure it out; maybe they got the scent, maybe they tracked her the way her cat could find a cockroach in the kitchen in the dark and once they tracked her, once they found her, what? Icky-sticky, teeny-weeny and all they wanted was a blowjob, all they wanted was to see a cunt they hadn't seen before. All cats are gray in the dark, except when they're not. She had given up fucking in cars when it got too dangerous, just like she almost always made them wear rubbers; she didn't like things that were dangerous. Like feline diabetes.

"What the fuck is feline diabetes?" she asked the vet.

"I told you," he said. White room, silver instruments, his white doctor's coat stippled with shed fur, dog hair, cat hair. "Last time. Remember?"

"Humor me," she said. You son of a bitch, she thought, I am to you what they are to me, just another couple bucks in a line of money, you son of a bitch you won't even look at me when you talk.

"It's a blood disorder," he said. "A malfunction, bad chemistry. It's complicated to explain but essentially that's the diagnosis."

All right, she was too stupid to understand a diagnosis; sure, right. Her bare knees crossed against the slick plastic chair, her cat on the table, her hand on the warm still curve, bone under fur. "Will she die?"

"They all die," the vet said. "You know that."

"Don't get smart with me," she said, cold furious fingers still gentle on the cat's lusterless fur. "*We* all die too, but I bet you still want me to pay the bill, right? The diabetes," quieter but no less cold. "Will it kill her."

"Him," said the vet. "I keep telling you. He's a male, a neutered male."

A neutered male. Well, who else would follow her home on the street, trail up the three sets of stairs, cry at her padlocked door all night until she took pity and hauled him in? "It figures," she said and could have said more, a lot more but what would be the point in that? The vet wouldn't understand and if he did it would only be worse. He didn't look like the kind of guy who went with hookers but when did they?—any of them, some of them might be, must be vets, doctors, lawyers, whatever, and there was no one look among them, no sure way to tell. Some of them looked like creeps and were, some of them looked nicer and weren't, and most of them looked like nothing at all, they were just guys with a hard-on and a problem and the hard-on *was* the problem just like the media was the message or whatever they used to say and anyway none of them ever said any of it to her. They never said much at all past *How much* or *You got a place?* Yeah, I got a place, asshole, right here under this bunny-fur jacket, right here where it's warm and dark and wet and shiny, shiny like the eyes of the cat on the table, shiny like the needle going into the cat and oh! hear his screech, one horrid little cry and she flinched as the needle entered the cat, flinched as the vet pulled it free and "Does it hurt?" she said, eyes damp, hands trembling on the cat trembling under her touch. "Does it?"

"Sure it hurts," the vet said. "It's an injection." Wiping his hands, discarding the needle, they were careful here, cats could get AIDS too. A lot of things could make cats sick, people thought they were hardy animals, rough-and-tumble garbage-can eaters but that just wasn't true, they were fragile, fragile little things who got hurt and got terrible illnesses and anything else was a lie, a misconception believed into truth. Have you heard the one about the cat who ate nothing but rat poison? And lived? Have you heard about the cat who ate rat poison and died and died? How about the one with the whore and the heart of gold? How did that one go over in Hell's Kitchen in the damp of the moon, dark of the night, whimper of the cat on the sill like the last lonely edge of the end of the world: tell me another, oh tell me please another one of those.

At night, when the cat was out prowling the city, the whore could think herself into his skin, could by imagination contain the sensibility of the animal as he moved through the bricks and stones, the unseen networks of the ruined city by the river. From the doorways one could see loiterers, lurkers, abandoned people with guns and knives looking for meat, any meat, cat meat . . . as above in the bowl of the sky the sallow and deadly lights of the poisoned atmosphere clung to the breath of strangers: but oblivious to all of this the cat worked his way through the corridors, slim and small and disinterested in any trauma not resulting directly in a meal, seeking as itself was sought by that one true fate. Thunder—the cat's name, given by the whore on that first night of his coming, when he had crawled and sniffed his way through her apartment, marking with swift determined swipes the edges of the tables, the legs of the chairs—*this is mine, this belongs to me* and he marked the whore as well, rubbed himself against her skin, less caress than order: *mine*—and the city his as well, knowing as he knew his mission, neutered or not and sometimes it was a stupefied female whom he would pin against the bricks or the dirt or the pavement and bite to a kind of frenzied attention; sometimes it was fish heads and ravaged scraps from which he would tear small and smaller pieces, aching little lumps against the stringent logic of his teeth; sometimes it was rats or dying mice seized and scattered, carried to drop and pounce and seize again; but whatever the cat consumed gave him no peace, chewing his way through the halls and passages of the city, staring at strangers, half-trance doze to wake: to crawl in, then out again through her window into the palm of darkness and begin the hunt anew and none of it, the whore knew, annealed the cloven and austere heart of the cat, gave Thunder what he sought through those flat and anonymous nights: climbing back through the window, fur matted, whiskers wrenched, nose and muzzle scabbed and bloody to lie in silence, lie beside her in the bed, lie like some returned extension of her own unhappy, exhausted heart in bands of harsh sunlight that warmed neither, that gave nothing but the news of another hungry day.

This was the last summer of the whore's life, she could feel baking like the sun into her bones some notion of her own mortality growing within her, first a pinpoint, then a cast wedge, finally a spear of light: lying on, in, beneath that bed with its blue sheets faded and marked by semen, that slab of mattress stage and theater, operating theater, theater of pain and, thirty-seven and desperate, thirty-seven going on ninety-nine, the whore could hear the men catch their breath at the apex of orgasm, welded to that stunned departing vision of themselves as they tumbled into the venomous boneyard of dead sex and possibility and in the arc of their bodies—hairy, flabby, ugly, moist—in that one whooping spasm of breath before climax she could hear her own death like a voice calling down a corridor, the clear and final bell of her own last passage caught with their come and rolling then, thighs spasmed like a cat's claws turned to grasp, sucking and clamoring at them to extension, culmination, extinction she could feel the men, then herself die and die and die against her, breath and death of their orgasms melding with that perfect vision of her own passing which she could see as a beating bird in the sky, bird in the shape of a heart, heart in the grasp of a consummation more perfect because unknown.

Twisting her head from side to side, all the faces empty, all the eyes the same, their sounds one sound made against her and as piteous as that of the cat meowing its claim and clamor on the stairs outside her door the night it had followed her home: head on the pillow, pillow on the bed, bed the shore of lost hope and all the mariners, all the little sailors come to sail her warm red inner sea: fleet's in! and out, and gone. But never for long. Overseeing the city, pinned under their climactic throbs and grunts, the whore felt in this painful darkening summer all the weight of her collisions and expulsions, every cock, every spurt, every pair of hairy, pebbled balls as if in perfect and sequential order, taking it all in again as prerequisite to letting it all go. Small and fragile life, life like the cat's in the street, granted then yanked from her and tossed down all of the steps and turnings of her own implausible possibility: in the mingled come, sweat, stink of money, the small dry wail of her stricken cat and in her own vague and drier sobs, sobs of her thirty-seventh year, thirty-eighth year, sobs of all knowledge taken and lost the whore felt that she was coming to a new kind of knowledge, some fresh vision available only to eyes that were yet to be.

But at other times—times when Thunder was about the city and she his imagined passenger, times when she lay parched in the sheets unable to wake or sleep, come or go, hunched like all the johns in the shape, the question mark of her own condition—at those other times the whore grasped, however imperfectly, the fact that she knew or would know nothing at all, that she and her cat were only two aspects of the same numbed witness, agents and repositories to consequences which they could not understand but to which they could only respond as a mouth responds to a breast, to the taste of meat, to the pull of respiration, respond in the kind of thrall which like the Cheyne-Stokes arias of the johns took them only farther into darkness, farther from the place they knew as light.

Sometimes, early times, she and Thunder had gone tricking together, cat fur and bunny fur, four legs and two: moving quickly on the streets, sometimes ducking into a bar, sometimes finding their trade while still outdoors, in the rain and the clumps of endless trash, in the heat and the arid shade. Most of the time the johns did not even notice the cat until the arrangements were made, the preliminaries concluded, all the cute shit cut and dried and then somewhere on the way to the walkup or sometimes on the stairs would come the questions: that your cat, lady? Is a cat part of the deal? Sometimes the johns did not care at all, a few of them even liked the idea of the cat coming along, made their empty little jokes about paying extra or twice the pussy, a few more turned sullen and even refused to continue the deal but: regardless of the preliminaries almost all would turn shy during the fucking, when it was clear that paid or not the cat was absolutely part of the deal and would leave the room only when the whore did. Some pretended to be unaffected but none, she saw, knew, felt and was glad, none were indifferent and when she did her humping with Thunder in the room it was to his stare that she would respond, not the mouths and fingers and meaty thrusts but the cool, pale, neutral gaze of the cat regarding all of this as if from some high and holy place.

Once, only once had the cat actively interfered, pouncing as if on prey upon the shoulders of a john as he worked and barked his way toward climax: the silent leap

and the cry of pain and then heaving upward, bucking the
cat from his back but even in his shock and deflation the
john had left his mark: that cloudy leaking stain of jism,
smeared across her thigh and as he bolted cursing for his
clothes *Keep the money*, he had said even though she had
not offered him a refund, *keep the fucking money lady,
just leave me out of this, just leave me alone. You're crazy,
you know that, stone fucking crazy* and this had been the
night she had become the passenger, had dreamed of the
cat's shadow flicking from wall to wall, rising as it had
risen above the helpless, astonished john, settle as if settling on prey, food, meat on the street and who was really
the passenger here, who was carrying whom?—oh tricking
with your cat, maybe that was crazy, maybe the john was
right but what difference did that make, what weight
could such a judgment ever hold? It was the cat's judgment that mattered, the cat's and her own, her life beaten
and forced against great shores of inconsequence and loss,
her knowledge of that loss through the days and nights, the
dreams of dogs and men, knives and Thunder, riding along
with him as he tricked along with her, watching as she
reached again and again that same dreary self-awareness
in that same damp-streaked and changeless bed: *stone
fucking crazy* and so what, so what? Light and shadow,
woman and cat, pussy and pussy and pussy forever and
ever, world without end, end of all time, so what, so what?
Streaks of light, gobbets of come: that your cat, lady? and
so what if it is?

In these difficult, endless, exhausting weeks, aching legs
and lower back, yeast infections and swollen glands the
whore felt the prophecy of her own death settling with
ever-greater conviction into her heart, then brain, then
moist unhappy cunt from which she made for these peri-
lous years such an equivocal living. Like a secret message,
a hidden sign, once the code was broken you saw it everywhere: in the crap and detritus of the street, in the cup of
cold coffee you drank on the move, in the eyes of your cat
as it watched you fuck another one, take another customer

home; that rush of breath, of orgasm and death riding pillion, her eyes behind the cat's eyes staring at her from the cracking edge of the marble sill, fault line, DMZ, noman's-land of bare buttocks and sweaty fingers, of dirt and stink and the waiting silence as the john dressed again, became again what he had been before he entered the room: his presence left forever behind, less than memory, noted only by the cat as with that brief economical motion he marked his feline scent over and over to drown the human spoor and every time the last one, every time the legs of the table, the palms of the whore wiped clean, reanointed, reprieved until the next time, and the next time, and the last time for today.

It was on one of those final evenings that Thunder, gone from the apartment where the whore lay, curled comma in the bed, made his way far up the river, strayed under the Washington Bridge and while sniffing in his incurious but dedicated fashion the trash and the scraps, the sticks and the bones, was set upon by a pack of dogs. Born strays or abandoned, gone foraging: and the whore in her bed pulling knees closer to chin, eyes open in that linkage, ears to hear the roving tread of the dogs, then their growls and snaffles, their stumbling emergence from the trees: and then their sighting of Thunder and in this moment, hooked to a kind of attention so profound that it might have been the shape of her own murderer come through the door, the whore watched Thunder fall to the barking of the dogs, the clamoring of their claws and teeth and there was nothing the whore could do; her thrall as absolute as that of the entrapped and discharging johns, her helplessness to equal theirs as their breath announced the moment of dissolution, Thunder's dissolution, her own grievous and exhausted spillage when at last she would give it all back, gush and spatter, splatter and leak: and neutered or not, diabetes or not Thunder died with difficulty and in great defiance, clawing at the dogs, clawing as the whore clawed at her own legs, writhing in the bed as if overwhelmed by passion, overwhelmed by death as the pack at last drove Thunder to the ground, the swelter of the dogs and try as

she could the whore could not emerge, could not escape:
her life like Thunder's lived only between ellipses of doom,
from this to that wounding, hanging in suspension, claw
and scratch and make them wear a rubber but the pack is
many, oh so many and their spoor is ineradicable, you can
never get rid of the smell, the smell, the smell, lying in the
bed, rolling sideways to vomit as she saw what the dogs
had left there beneath the bridge, vomit till she was empty,
empty enough to rise.

It is not clear if this was the evening she went out into
the streets in the wake of that death to seek and succumb
to her murderer, or if this was some evenings later; the
records remain unclear; who records the passing of a whore?
Only at the end, when he mounted her and brought his
weapon to the task did she find in the pain and the terror
that seed of closure, the understanding of not time but des-
tiny: the knifed heart, the heaving cry, their mingled cries
as penetration broke to deeper blood and in the froth and
suspension of her death she did not see the enormous head
of judgment bent before her, eyes soft and green as a cat's,
full as a cat's, measuring as a cat's as she let it all go, blood
and semen, fishhook dawn, Thunder's body the template
for the emptiness which she must now become.

"Will he die?" the vet said. "Well, we all die so of course I
guess he'll die too. But not soon," the vet said. "Not all
that soon."

Not soon enough, the whore thought, nothing is ever
soon enough and out then to the indifferent streets, Thunder resentful in her arms, her heart and cunt so empty now
that they could have seized the world, encompassed the cat
like some changeling child, consumed the Queen of the
Cats herself: catch, clutch and stammer, full then empty,
empty then gone to the music of the barking dogs by the
river, by the geometries of closure marked like scent on the
flesh itself.

Douglas Clegg

Douglas Clegg was born in Virginia, but has lived in the Los Angeles area for over ten years. He has published several novels, including *Dark of the Eye, You Come When I Call You, The Children's Hour,* and *Colony.* He has had stories in the anthologies *Little Deaths, Love in Vein, Forbidden Acts, Phobias II, Southern-Fried Horror,* and *The Year's Best Fantasy and Horror: Eighth Annual Collection,* and in the magazines *Cemetery Dance, Deathrealm,* and *Palace Corbie.*

In "The Five," a troubled young girl is drawn to a litter of kittens. I asked Clegg what he thought of the seeming connection between children and cats. About his own experience with felines, he says, "In a way, cats express the kind of conditional love that permeates many moderately unhealthy families. When I was a kid, I never entirely trusted the cat, even though I loved her. If she got under my covers, she terrorized me, via my feet. If she stared at me too long, I was afraid she was reading my inner thoughts. I felt as a kid that cats communicated telepathically to people. It's very weird, and makes me think I could use a good therapist, except as an adult, my relationship with my cat is a good deal healthier—coincidentally, it also is healthier with my family."

The Five

DOUGLAS CLEGG

1

THE WALL WAS up against the carport, and Naomi, who was just beginning the gangly phase, stretched out across it like she was trying to climb up the side of the house to the roof. She heard the sound first. She knew about the cat, the wild one that lived out in the Wash. Somehow, it had survived the pack of coyotes that roamed there, and she had thought she saw it come near the house a few times before. But there was no mistaking the sounds of kitten mewling, and so she presented the problem to her father. "They'll die in there."

"No," he said. "The mother cat knows what she's doing. She's got the kittens there so the coyotes won't get them. When they're old enough, she'll bring them out. They're animals, Nomy, they go by instinct and nature. The mother cat knows best. The wall's sturdy enough, too. Walls are good, safe places from predators."

"What's a predator?"

"Anything that's a threat. Anything that might eat a cat."

"Like a coyote?"

"Exactly."

"Where's the father cat?"

"At work."

He showed Naomi where the weak part of the wall was, and how to press her ear up against it with a glass. Her eyes went wide and squinty, alternately, and she accidentally dropped the glass, which broke.

He said, "You'll have to clean that up."

She was barefoot and had to step carefully around it, and the oil spots from the car, over to get the broom. She took a few swipes at the broken glass and then leaned against the wall again. Her father was, by this time, just starting up the lawn mower in the side yard. She wanted to ask him more about the cat, but he was preoccupied, and since (she'd been warned) this was one of his few days off for the summer, she decided not to bother him. She went indoors and told her mother about the cat and the kittens and her mother was more concerned. Her mother had helped her rescue a family of opossums at the roadside out near Hemet—the mother opossum had been hit by a car, and although Naomi knew that the babies were probably doomed, she and her mother gathered them up in a grocery bag and took them to a nearby vet who promised to do his best and that had been that. Her mother was much more sentimental about animals than her father, and went outside with her immediately to examine the wall.

"There's the hole near the drainpipe. I don't know how she did it, but she squeezed in there. Good for her. She protected her children." Naomi's mother pointed up to beneath the eaves, where the pipe only partially covered a hole that her father had put into the wall accidentally when he was repairing the roof.

"I've seen her before," Naomi said, "the mother cat. She watches gophers over in the field. She's very tough looking. Father says she's doing it because of instinct."

Her mother looked from Naomi over to her husband, mowing. "It's his day off and he mows. We see him at breakfast and before bed, and on his day off he mows."

"It's his instinct," Naomi said. The air was smoky with lawn mower exhaust and fresh-drawn grass; motes of dust and dandelion fluff sprayed across the yellow day.

She thought about the kittens all afternoon, and wondered how many there were.

"I think several," her mother told her. "Maybe five."

"Why don't people have babies all at once like that?"

Her mother laughed. "Some do. They're crazy. Trust me, when you're ready to have children, you won't want several at once."

"I can't wait to have babies," Naomi said. "When I have babies, I'll protect them just like the mom cat."

"You're much too young to think that."

"You had me when you were eighteen."

"So, you have nine more years to go and you need to pick up a husband along the way."

Her father, who had been listening to all this even while he read the paper, said, "I don't think it's right to encourage her, Jean."

Her mother glanced at her father and then back at Naomi.

The living room was all done in blues, and Naomi sometimes felt it was a vast sea, and she was floating on a cushion, and her parents were miles away, underwater.

Her father, his voice bubbling and indistinct, said something about something or other that they'd told her before about something to do with something, but Naomi had known when to block him out, when to put him beneath the waves.

She climbed the drainpipe just after dinner, with a flashlight held in her mouth, making her feel as if she would throw up any second. She grasped one edge of roof, and cut her fingers on the sharp metal of the pipe, and lodged her left foot in the space between the pipe and the wall. She directed the flashlight down the hole, and saw a pair of fierce red eyes, and movement. Nothing more than that. The eyes scared her a bit, and she tried to pull her foot free so she could shimmy down, but her foot was caught. The mother cat moved up into the hole until its face was right near hers. Naomi heard a low growl that didn't sound like a cat at all. She dropped the flashlight and felt a claw swipe across her face. She managed to get her foot free and dropped five feet to the ground, landing on her rear. She felt a sharp pain in her legs.

Her mother came outside at the noise and ran to get

her. "Damn it," her mother gasped, "what in God's name are you going?" She rushed to Naomi, lifting her up.

"My leg." It hurt so much she didn't want to move at all, but her mother carried her into the light of the carport. She was trailing blood. It didn't spurt out like she thought it might, but just came in dribs and drabs like the rain when it was spitting.

"It's glass," her mother said. She removed it; Naomi didn't have time to cry out. Tears were seeping from her eyes. The pain in her leg, just along the calf, was burning.

Her father had heard the shouting, and he came out, too. He was in white boxer shorts and a faded gray T-shirt. He said, "What's going on here?"

"She cut herself," her mother said.

"I told her to sweep up the glass," he said, and then turned to her, and more softly said, "Didn't I tell you to clean up the broken glass, Nomy?"

Naomi could barely see him for her tears. She looked from one to the other, and then back, but it was all a blur.

"We've got to take her to the emergency room."

Her father said, "Yeah, and who's coming up with the three hundred bucks?"

Her mother said nothing.

"We can sew it up here, can't we?"

Her mother seemed about to say something. Almost a sound came out of her mouth. Then, after a moment, she said, "I guess I could. Jesus, Dan. What if this were worse?"

"It's just a cut. It's only glass. You know how to put in stitches."

Her mother asked her, "Sweetie, is that all right with you?"

"If it's what my father wants," she said.

Her father said, "She always calls me that. Isn't that strange? 'My father.' Why is she like this?"

Her mother ignored him. She felt the warmth of her mother's hand on her damp cheek. "It's okay to cry when things hurt."

"She never looks me in the eye, either. You ever notice that? You're Mommy, but I get 'my father.' Christ."

Her father said something else, but even the sounds were starting to blur because Naomi thought she heard the kittens mewling in the wall, just the other side, and they were getting louder and louder.

Even later, when her mother took out her sewing kit and told her it wouldn't hurt as much as it looked like, even then, she thought she heard them.

2

The stitches came out a week later, and although there was a broad white scar, it wasn't so bad. She could still jump rope, although she felt a gentle tugging. She hadn't been outside much—she'd got a fever, which, according to her mother, was from an infection in her leg. But all she'd had to do was lie around and watch *I Love Lucy* reruns, and eat Saltines and guzzle cola. Not the worst thing, she figured. As soon as she was able, she went out to check on the kittens.

She had a can of tuna with her—she knew cats loved it, and her mother would never miss it. She set up the stepladder and climbed up.

But the hole was no longer there.

It had been sealed up. White plaster was spread across it.

She asked her mother about it.

"They got old enough to leave," her mother said, "and so the mom cat took them back out to the field to hunt mice."

"What about the coyotes?"

"Wild cats are usually smarter than coyotes. Really, honey. They're fine."

3

Although she wasn't ever supposed to go into the field that adjoined her father's property, Naomi untangled her way through the blackberry and boysenberry vines, and went anyway. The grass in the field was high and yellow; foxtails shot out at her and embedded themselves in her socks. She picked them out carefully. There was an old rusted-out tractor in the middle of the field, and she found several small stiff balloons near it. She kept searching through the grass. Something moved along the mound where the grass grew thickest. A great tree, dead from lightning, stood guardian of this spot. A peregrine falcon sat at its highest point. Naomi looked around for the cats. The grass quivered. The falcon flew off across the field, down toward the orange groves.

She saw two ears rise slowly above the grass.

A coyote was not four feet away from her. Its yellow-brown head came into view. It was beautiful.

She stood still for several seconds.

She had never seen a coyote this close.

And then the animal turned and ran off down the field, toward the Wash.

Naomi had been holding her breath the whole time, not realizing it. The sun was up and boiling, and she looked back across to her house. It seemed too far away. She sat down in the grass for a minute, feeling the leftover heat of fever break across her forehead. She cupped her hands together as if she was praying and laid her head against them. She whispered into the dry earth, "Don't let anything hurt the kittens."

When she awoke, the sun was all the way across the sky. Ants crawled across her hands; some were in her hair. She had to brush them out. She felt like she'd been sleeping for years, it had been that peaceful. Her mother was calling to her from the backyard. She stood, brushed dirt and insects from her, and ran in the direction of the familiar voice. She jumped around the thorny vines, but her leg started to hurt again, so she ended up limping her way up the driveway. She went along the side of the carport to get to the back gate, when something leapt out in front of her.

It was the mother cat. Snarling.

Naomi froze.

The mother cat watched her.
Naomi looked around for the kittens but saw none.
And then she heard them.
She followed the sound.
Pressed her ear against the carport wall.
She heard them.
Inside the wall.
The five.

4

When her father got home from work, he went in and sat in front of the television to watch the ten o'clock news. Naomi was supposed to be getting ready for bed, but she had been pressing herself up against the wall in the living room, because she thought she heard something moving behind it. She wandered into the den, following the sounds. Her father glanced at her, then at the television. The noise in the wall seemed to stop at the entrance to the den.

Naomi stood there, leaning against the doorjamb. "You didn't take the kittens out, did you?"

He looked at her. His eyes seemed to be sunken into the shriveled skin around them; his eyeglasses magnified them until she felt he was staring right through her.

"Nomy?" he asked.

"You left them in the wall."

He grinned. "Don't be silly. I took them out. All five. Set them down. The mother carried them into the vines. Don't be silly."

"I heard them. I saw the big cat. She was angry."

"Don't be silly," he said, more firmly. He took his glasses off.

She realized that she was alone in the room with him, and she didn't like it. She never liked being alone with him. Not inside the house.

She ran down the hall to her mother's room. Her mother was lying on the bed in her slip, reading a book. She set it down.

Naomi climbed up on the bed. "Mommy, I have a question."

Her mother patted a space beside her. Naomi scooted closer. She lay down, resting her head on her mother's arm.

"It's about the kittens in the wall."

Naomi looked up at the ceiling, which was all white, and thought she saw clouds moving across it, almost forming a face.

"What I want to know," she said, "is did the cat take the kittens out before he covered the hole?"

Her mother said, "Why?"

"I heard the kittens earlier."

"Before dinner?"

Naomi nodded. The cloud face in the ceiling melted away.

"You didn't tell me you heard them."

"I was really angry. I thought you lied to me."

"I wouldn't lie to you."

"I asked my father, and he said I was being silly."

"Well, it's not silly if you thought you heard them. But you must've imagined it. I saw them leave. With the mom cat."

"I saw her, too. She looked angry. She looked like she was mad at me for letting her babies get put in the wall like that."

"Oh," her mother said, stroking her fine, dark hair, "cats don't think things like that. She was probably just asking for milk. Maybe she's getting tamer. Maybe one day she and all the kittens, grown up, will come back because you were so nice to them."

"I was sure I heard them."

"Maybe you wanted to hear them."

Naomi was fairly confused, but had never known her mother to lie.

Her mother said, "You got sunburned today."

"I saw a coyote in the field."

"You went in the field?"

"I was looking for the kittens."

"Oh, you. Don't tell your father."

* * *

In the morning, she returned to the carport wall. She pressed a drinking glass to it, and then applied her ear.

Nothing.

No sound.

She tapped on the wall with her fingers.

No sound.

And then . . . something.

Almost nothing.

Almost a whine.

And then, as if a dam had burst, the screaming, shrieking of small kittens and the sound of frantic clawing.

She almost dropped the glass, but remembering her leg she caught it in time. *I wouldn't lie to you,* she heard her mother say, a memory.

I wouldn't lie to you.

She put the glass up to the wall.

Nothing.

Silence.

Sound of her own heart, beating rapidly.

5

That night, she lay in bed, unable to sleep. In the daylight, she would be all right, but at night she had to stay up because of things in the dark. She thought she had forgotten how to breathe; then realized she was still inhaling and exhaling.

About one in the morning, her door opened.

Someone stood there, so she had to close her eyes.

She counted her breaths and hoped it wouldn't be him.

She felt the kiss on her forehead.

That, and the touching her on the outside of the blanket, was all he ever did, the nighttime father, but it was enough to make her wish she were dead and wonder where her mother was to protect her.

But as she lay there, she heard them again.

The kittens.

Mewling sweetly, for tuna or milk.

They had traveled to find her, through the small spaces within the walls, to find her and tell her they were all right.

She fell asleep before the door opened again, listening to them, wondering if they were happy, if they were catching the mice that she knew occasionally crawled into other holes and vents and cracks. The five were still there, her kittens, her kittens, and she knew it would turn out fine now.

6

"What's wrong with her?"

"Well, Dan, if we'd taken her to the hospital instead of letting the infection go like that . . ."

"And somebody would've accused us of child abuse. That's all that ever happens anymore. And it's not some infection, Jean. Look at her. Why is she doing that?"

"I think she's sick. Her fever's back."

"What's gotten into her?"

Naomi heard them, but paid no attention, because the kittens were getting louder. They were three months old now, and they sounded more like cats. They played there, behind the diamond-shaped wallpaper in the kitchen, just behind the toaster. One had caught a mouse or something, and they were playing with it—she could hear the frightened squeaks. She pressed the palms of her hands against the wallpaper, trying to open up the wall, but no matter how much she pressed, nothing gave.

Her father said, "She shouldn't be crawling around like that. She looks like an animal."

"Sweetie," her mother said, stroking her hair, "don't you think you need to get back in bed?"

She glanced up at her mother. "I love them," she said, unable to control an enormous smile, "I love them so much, Mommy."

Her mother wasn't looking at her. She said, "I'm taking her to a doctor right now."

"Hello, Naomi." The doctor was bald and sweet looking, like a grandfather.

"Hello," she replied.

"That leg's healing okay. Looks like whoever stitched it did it right."

"Mommy did it. She used to be a nurse."

"I know. She used to work with me. Did you know that?"

No reply.

"What seems to be the problem?" he asked. He put the stethoscope against her chest. She breathed in and out. Then a funny-looking thermometer, which he called a "gun," went in her ear. Lights in her eyes. A tongue depressor slipped to the back of her throat, almost gagging her.

"I don't know," she said finally.

"Your mommy's really worried."

"I don't know why."

"She says you listen to the walls."

Naomi shook her head. "Not the walls. The five."

"Five what?"

"Kittens. Each of them know me. I love them so much."

"How did the kittens get there?"

She looked at him, unsure if she should trust him. "I can't tell you."

"All right, then."

He gave her a shot in the arm, which she didn't feel at all. She thought that was strange, so she told him.

"Not at all?"

"I didn't even feel it."

He put his hand under his chin. Then he reached to her arm and pinched.

"Did you feel that?"

She shook her head.

Then he went over to a counter on the other side of

the room. He returned with a plastic bottle. He took the lid off and held it under her nose. "Smell this."

She sniffed.

"Sniff again," he said.

She sniffed hard.

"What does it smell like?"

"I dunno. Water, maybe?"

He was trying to smile at her response, she could tell, but couldn't quite do it. "Is there anything you want to tell me?" he asked.

"About what?"

"Anything. Your mommy or daddy. How you feel about things."

She thought a minute. "Nope."

And that was it. He took her out to the waiting area where her mother was sitting. Then she was asked to sit and wait while her mother had a checkup, too.

On the way home, in the car, her mother was in a mood. "Are you playing games?"

"Uh-uh."

"I think you are. Are you trying to destroy this family? Because if you are, young lady, if you are . . ." Her mother's hands were shaking so hard, she had to pull the car over to the side of the road and park.

Naomi began to say something, but she saw that her mother wasn't listening, so she shut her mouth.

And as her mother started lecturing her, Naomi realized that she could barely hear a word her mother said.

7

The nights were peaceful. She could press her ear against the wall and hear them, playing and hunting and crawling around one another. She kept trying to think up good names for them, but each time she came up with something, she forgot which was which.

Then, when the bedroom door opened—which didn't

happen very often anymore—she listened to the cats (for they had grown in size), and sometimes, if she closed her eyes really tight, she could almost imagine what they looked like. All gray tabbies like their mother, of course, but one with a little bit of white in a star pattern on its chest, and two of them had green eyes, while the rest had blue. One had gotten very fat from all the mice and roaches it had devoured over the past weeks, and another seemed all skin and bones and, yet, not deprived at all.

8

One day, a woman in a suit came by. She had some manila files in her hand. Naomi's mother and father were very tense.

The woman asked several questions, mainly to her parents, but Naomi was listening for the sound of the five.

"Naomi?" her father said. "Answer the lady, please."

Naomi looked up; her father's voice had gotten really small, like it was caught in a jar somewhere and couldn't get out. She looked at the lady and then to her mother. Her mother's forehead held beads of sweat.

"Yes, ma'am." She looked back to the lady.

"How are you feeling, dear?"

Naomi said, "Fine."

"You were sick for a while."

Naomi nodded. "I'm better now. It was the flu."

"Have you had a good summer vacation?"

Naomi cocked her head to the side; she squinted her eyes. "Can you hear them?"

The lady said, "Who?"

"All of them. They just caught something. Maybe a mouse. Maybe a sparrow got in. I thought I heard one. Didn't you?"

9

After the lady left, her father exploded with rage. "I am so sick and tired of you running our lives like this!"

Who was he talking to? Naomi heard the runt of the litter tearing at the bird's wings, feathers flying. The five could be brutal sometimes. They stalked their prey like lions and brought a bird or mouse down quickly, but then played with it until the small creature died of fear more than anything. Something beautiful about that—about taking something so small and playing with it.

"There are no fucking cats in the fucking walls," her father's voice intruded. He came over to her, lifted her up from under her arms. "I am going to tell you what happened to those kittens, right now," he said.

Her mother said, "Jesus, Dan, you're going to hurt her like that," but the voices rushed beneath some invisible glass, caught, silent.

Her father began screaming something—she knew by the movements of his mouth—but all she heard was the one she was calling Scamp tussle over the sparrow's head. Yowler tore at the beak with her claws, but lost most of the skull, which Scamp took down in one gulp. Hugo ignored them—he was not one to join in when food was being torn apart—he preferred to lick the bones clean later, after the carcass was stripped.

"I'm going to show you once and for all," her father's voice came back, and she was being dragged out the back door, around to the carport wall. He dropped her to the ground and went around the wall, into the carport; she heard Fiona whisper something to Zelda about some centipedes that she had trapped in a spiderweb behind the wall at the back of the refrigerator.

Her father came back around the corner with a large hammer.

"You just watch what you see," he said, and slammed the hammer into the wall, down where the kittens had once been born. Back and forth, he worked the hammer, chips of wall flew up, and beneath them, chicken wire, and there, in a small mound, surrounded with bits of cloth and newspaper, were small dried things.

"See?" her father said, poking at them with his hammer. From one, a dozen wriggling gray-white maggots emerged. "Do you fucking see them?" he shouted, his voice receding again.

She looked at them, all stiff and bony and withered like apricots. Her heart was beating fast; she thought something wet came up her throat; light was flickering. Were they the bodies of the mice that the five had caught, in storage for a future meal?

And then she thought she was going to faint. She saw pinpricks of darkness play along the edge of her vision and then an eclipse came over the sun. The world faded; her father faded; and she reached her hand into the new hole in the wall and pressed her head through too. Her whole body seemed to move forward, and she saw pipes and wires and dust as she went.

10

"I can hear her," her mother said, "I think she made a noise."

Her father said nothing. After a minute, "For three days, she does her weird, unintelligible sounds, and now she snarls her upper lip and you think she's on the road to recovery."

"She said something. Honey? Are you trying to say something?"

But Naomi didn't care to speak with them at the moment. She held Hugo in her lap, stroking him carefully, carefully, because he didn't like his fur ruffled. Scamp was playing with the ball of thread; the others slept, piled together.

"Look at her," her father said.

"Sweetie?" her mother said, beyond the wall. "Are you trying to talk? Is there something you want to say?"

"You think holding her is going to help?" her father said. "You think she's ever going to get better if you coddle her like that? All that rocking back and forth—she knows what she's doing. She's not stupid."

Zelda rolled on her back and stretched out, a great yawn escaping her jaws. Her whiskers brushed against Naomi's ankle. It tickled.

"Sweetie?" her mother asked.

"She's just doing this," her father said, "it's all for attention. And look at you, giving it to her. She's just doing this to hurt us."

"No, look at her lips. She's trying to say something, look, Dan. My God, she's trying to talk. Oh, sweetie, Nomy, baby, tell Mommy what's wrong. Are you okay? Baby?"

On the other side of the wall, Naomi pressed her face into the dust-covered fur and listened to the purring, the gentle and steady hum beneath the skin that was like a lullaby. It was warm there, with the five, with the walls around them.

Her father said, "My God, she's starting in again."

"Shut up, Dan. Let her."

"I can't stand this. How can you sit there and cradle her and not scream out loud when she does this?"

"Maybe I care about her," her mother said.

Naomi mewled and rocked and mewled and rocked, safe from predators, safe in the wall.

She watched as one of the cats sat up, her hackles rising, hunting some creature that had the misfortune of entering this most secret and wonderful domain.

Michael Cadnum

Michael Cadnum lives in northern California and is an award-winning poet. His most recent collection of poetry is *The Cities We Will Never See*. He has also published nine novels, including *Saint Peter's Wolf, Ghostwright, Skyscape, The Judas Glass, Calling Home, Taking It,* and *Zero at the Bone* (the latter three aimed at young adults).

Cadnum's short stories have appeared in *Antioch Review* and *Beloit Fiction Journal,* and in the anthologies *Black Thorn, White Rose* and *Ruby Slippers, Golden Tears*. His short stories are invariably clever, quick, and nasty. Herewith, Karl, a man with a problem.

The Man Who Did Cats Harm

MICHAEL CADNUM

WITH KARL IT wasn't a question of a cat having nine lives. With Karl it was a question of the cat being basically dead as soon as it was Karl's cat. And it wasn't Karl getting mad and nailing the animal, in spite of what you have probably heard.

Karl was a kindhearted person, in his way, but if you confused him he got upset and it didn't matter that he had no business throwing things and hollering. The moon doesn't ask and the sun doesn't and Karl doesn't.

Sometimes Karl would get up at night when he couldn't sleep, which was pretty frequently because of the problems you have all heard about, and he'd pour out a little Carnation milk onto a coffee saucer, the kind with a little recess in it for the cup to fit into. And one of Karl's cats would be there lapping up that extra-thick nutrition, the sort you are supposed to thin out with water or at least some instant coffee; Karl doesn't thin things out.

Because of the firearms Karl swears he hates but keeps around anyway you might say it's the sort of existence we would find reckless, with the big empty swimming pool in the backyard out with the billboards leaning up against the timber saw and all the other items of property Karl bids for at the auctions.

But I have seen cats looking happy at Karl's place. He had a half dozen or so, and they slept in the sun on the porch next to the gumball machine, and on the roof where it was repaired from the earthquake, a long tarred-in crack that soaked up heat and let a cat feel safe from the scrub jays. The birds think a cat is there as a figure of future amusement, if they can ever get around to stooping so low.

Karl liked his cats, but he lost a lot of money in the competition for the new TV station, the one he bid on with the forged license and then actually tried to lay the foundation for before the TV company went Chapter 11.

When the stove gas leaked and killed everything but Karl, it wasn't his fault some of the lost animals were cats.

And then when he threw a tire iron across the dried-up Japanese pond because he thought a drug enforcement investigator might be out there in the poison oak, it was a plain accident that a neighbor's Russian blue was out there stalking gophers. That was the one that got him in the newspapers again, because by this time Karl was notorious in the old sense of the word, meaning someone who would pay to not be so famous if he could. Then there was the case of Nine Lives liver-flavored that had to be recalled with Karl as yet another consumer victim, and it was plain that Karl was going to go down in history as a man who did cats harm.

For a while Karl would tell his ex-wife that it wasn't fair, and she agreed that it wasn't, but she was caught up in her radio show, the one about you and your home appliances, so she couldn't be seen with him anymore. Karl would tell everybody how much he liked cats, and even break into ordinary conversations about the smog with something like "There's nothing like a cat," or, "What's a day without a cat?" But this sort of thing got him in worse trouble, after the drug people quit their investigation and the humane society started working on tips that Karl was cutting up cats for stew.

Then Karl decided he would not stand in the way of public opinion and actually tried to be mean to a cat or two now and then, joking a little, hollering at a tomcat who used to go around howling and beating up dogs. One day Karl shouted at what he thought was a cat on the sidewalk, but it was only a hat blown off a visiting professor by the wind.

But it was only when I myself decided that Karl was a decent and misunderstood man, and determined despite all thought of calamity that a woman's touch was what he deserved, that Karl began the descent into what I have come to refer to as his own darkest hour.

My cat and I moved in, and I made bell pepper omelettes and I made raisin bread with dates in the bread machine, but my cat, which I had left unnamed because I don't believe that humans should project their own thoughts and hopes onto feline elegance, would always be right under Karl. If Karl went to sit down the cat was there. When Karl took a step in the dark the cat was there. When Karl put down the case of stewed tomatoes the cat was there, and getting in a worse and worse mood.

I told Karl that a cat is a graceful creature but not necessarily intelligent. I told him that cats do not get together and discuss a man like Karl. I did at one time wonder, as a child, what cat mothers told kittens about the trials of congress with human beings, but now I know they are both devoid of discourse and wouldn't say much about us anyway if they could.

Karl said, "Lee Anna, I know all this, but the animal is looking at me even now," and indeed it was, if you can say that a cat ever really looks at anything. Which a cat does, of course, especially if it's a thing a cat could eat.

So Karl began leaving early to do his pickups and came home looking over his shoulder because once or twice the cat dropped out of the date palm onto his back, just playfully, bounding away in a second. But I knew what Karl meant when he said that the cat hated him.

It was when the cat was trapped under the hood of the Studebaker pickup that I realized the scope of the problem. It was one of Karl's vintage vehicles, the sort that got him in the Sunday magazine, although this wasn't one of the nicer ones, being a little sun-bleached and worn from being waxed so much so that it was going pink on white. Karl started the engine. And there was a howl.

This was an unmistakable feline tumult. Karl turned off the ignition. His eyes were wild. He got out of the truck.

He got back in. He started the engine and backed out of the driveway, hearing the cat howling all the way, and sure that he could ignore it because it was all in his mind.

It was the morning that the toxic spill closed Interstate 80 and the street outside our house was full of traffic, not even letting Karl back out into it, everyone in a hurry and stuck.

This meant that when Karl finally opened the hood to check on what was making the noise, the cat jumped out. It clung to Karl's face, and the Channel 2 news got some good footage, which they use to this day when they need a tape of bloopers and mishaps. The ambulance came and took Karl away.

I made a determination. I think the animal is our glimpse of a world without guilt and human contrivance, but given the choice between the life and dignity of a man like Karl and a cat, I decided to throw in my future with Karl.

It's true that the world is not what it was. I have heard people complain that people don't have, say, handwriting the way they used to, how everyone writes in a sort of creeping scribble. And I have complained myself how even criminals are getting worse, actually shouting obscenities, for example, on the way to the getaway car.

I would add the fact that cats are wise to something these days, either because they are genetically developing or for some other reason. All I know is that when I gave the cat, which I had left unsoiled by a name, just the smallest amount of painkiller my own personal troubles began. It wasn't just that the fluid was poison; mayonnaise is poison if you eat too much or leave it sitting out on the counter. It was a practical choice that I regretted, but I also felt that Karl might do something worse to the cat when he got back from Kaiser Hospital, the new one they opened next to the estuary.

Things did not go as I had planned.

When Karl found me I was weak from the blood loss, and I was sure that I could end all my days right there with a clear conscience. When Karl sat by my side in intensive care those long days while my sutures healed, I knew what a pearl he was, and I determined not to return until the cat had found a new home, far from where we reside.

Karl would buy a nice new cat carrier to carry the cat, and he would take the cat in the truck to Modesto or Tracy or Stockton, far to the east. He would let the cat go in farm country around cows and sheep.

The news of Karl's accident off the bridge moved me from the postoperative unit to the cardiac wing, and when I heard they were dragging the American River for Karl, a nice man from psychiatry held my hand.

When Karl was helped into my room you can imagine the tears of joy and the promises of devotion we made. The cat never returned, presumably lost in the current, but the damage was done in the eyes of those of us who remembered Karl as he used to be, earthily debonair if overly impulsive.

I do want to thank the thousands who have sent greetings and encouragement to us. The donations, however small, have made me hope that soon we will have reached our high-water mark of sorrow. Karl is well. And when he comes out of his special carrier for his condensed milk I can see a trace of the old Karl there in his eyes, the Karl the psychiatrists swear will return, if Karl has not critically injured himself before then by the way he washes.

Michael Marshall Smith

Michael Marshall Smith was born in England in 1965, lived in the United States, South Africa, and Australia for his first ten years, then returned to the UK. He now lives in North London, working sporadically as a corporate scriptwriter and graphic designer. His favorite things include cats, pomme frites, malls, winter, and cats.

Smith burst onto the horror scene in 1990 by winning the British Fantasy Award for short story and for Best Newcomer, as a result of his first published story, "The Man Who Drew Cats." He again won for Best Short Story in 1991 and was nominated in 1992. His short fiction has been published in the *Dark Voices* anthology series, *Darklands 1 & 2*, *The Mammoth Book of Zombies*, *The Mammoth Book of Werewolves,* and *The Mammoth Book of Frankenstein*, *Touch Wood: Narrow Houses 2,* in *The Best New Horror* series, and in *The Year's Best Fantasy and Horror* series. His work has also been published in the magazines *Omni, Exuberance, Chills,* and *Peeping Tom.* He has published two novels, *Only Forward* and *Spares*.

"Not Waving" is about love, guilt, and the choices that sometimes trap us. Smith comments on the story's most unusual—and one of its most painful—aspects, "I wrote about bulimia because a friend of mine was a sufferer—though I should stress she bore no relationship whatsoever to the character in the story. I guess I wanted to try to capture the strange combination of strength and weakness that the condition seems to confer on people, without making it the sole focus of the story; not least because that combination of strength and weakness is there in all of us. Also, that it is the condition of which one appears to be trapped—much like the relationship of the narrator."

Not Waving

MICHAEL MARSHALL SMITH

SOMETIMES WHEN WE'RE in a car, driving country roads in autumn, I see sparse poppies splashed in among the grasses and it makes me want to cut my throat and let the blood spill out of the window to make more poppies, many more, until the roadside is a blaze of red.

Instead I light a cigarette and watch the road, and in a while the poppies will be behind us, as they always are.

On the morning of 10th October I was in a state of reasonably high excitement. I was at home, and I was supposed to be working. What I was mainly doing, however, was sitting thrumming at my desk, leaping to my feet whenever I heard the sound of traffic outside the window. When I wasn't doing that I was peeking at the two large cardboard boxes that were sitting in the middle of the floor.

The two large boxes contained, respectively, a new computer and a new monitor. After a year or so of containing my natural wirehead need to own the brightest and best in high-specification consumer goods, I'd finally succumbed and upgraded my machine. Credit card in hand, I'd picked up the phone and ordered myself a piece of science fiction, in the shape of a computer that not only went like a train but also had built-in telecommunications and *speech recognition*. The future was finally here, and sitting on my living room floor.

However.

While I had £3000 worth of Mac and monitor, what I didn't have was the £15 cable that connected the two together. The manufacturer, it transpired, felt it constituted an optional extra despite the fact that without it the two system components were little more than bulky white ornaments of a particularly tantalizing and frustrating kind. The cable had to be ordered separately, and there weren't any in the country at the moment. They were all in Belgium.

I was only told this a week after I ordered the system, and I strove to make my feelings on the matter clear to my supplier, during the further week in which they playfully promised to deliver the system first on one day, then another, all such promises evaporating like the morning dew. The two boxes had finally made it to my door the day before and, by a bizarre coincidence, the cables had today crawled tired and overwrought into the supplier's warehouse. My contact at Callhaven Direct knew just how firmly one of those cables had my name on it and had phoned to grudgingly admit they were available. I'd immediately called my courier firm, which I occasionally used to send design roughs to clients. Callhaven had offered, but I somehow sensed that they wouldn't quite get round to it *today,* and I'd waited long enough. The bike firm I used specializes in riders who look as if they've been chucked out of the Hell's Angels for being too tough. A large man in leathers turning up in Callhaven's offices, with instructions not to leave without my cable, was just the sort of incentive I felt they needed. And so I was waiting, drinking endless cups of coffee, for such a person to arrive at the flat, brandishing said component above his head in triumph.

When the buzzer finally went I nearly fell off my chair. The entry phone in our building was fashioned with waking the dead in mind, and I swear the walls vibrate. Without bothering to check who it was I left the flat and pounded down the stairs to the front door, swinging it open with, I suspect, a look of joy upon my face. I get a lot of pleasure out of technology. It's a bit sad, I know—God knows Nancy has told me so often enough—but hell, it's my life.

Standing on the step was a leather convention, topped with a shining black helmet. The biker was a lot slighter than their usual type, but quite tall. Tall enough to have done the job, evidently.

"Bloody marvelous," I said. "Is that a cable?"

"Sure is," the biker said indistinctly. A hand raised the visor on the helmet, and I saw with some surprise that it was a woman. "They didn't seem too keen to let it go."

I laughed and took the package from her. Sure enough, it said AV adapter cable on the outside.

"You've made my day," I said a little wildly, "and I'm more than tempted to kiss you."

"That seems rather forward," the girl said, reaching up to her helmet. "But a cup of coffee would be nice. I've been driving since five this morning and my tongue feels like it's made of brick."

Slightly taken aback, I hesitated for a moment. I'd never had a motorcycle courier in for tea before. Also, it meant a delay before I could ravage through the boxes and start connecting things up. But it was still only eleven in the morning, and another fifteen minutes wouldn't harm. I was also, I guess, a little pleased at the thought of such an unusual encounter.

"You would be," I said with Arthurian courtliness, "most welcome."

"Thank you, kind sir," the courier said, and pulled her helmet off. A great deal of dark brown hair spilled out around her face, and she swung her head to clear it. Her face was strong, with a wide mouth and vivid green eyes that had a smile already in them. The morning sun caught chestnut gleams in her hair as she stood with extraordinary grace on the doorstep. Bloody hell, I thought for a moment, the cable unregarded in my hand. Then I stood to one side to let her into the house.

It turned out her name was Alice, and she stood looking at the books on the shelves as I made a couple of cups of coffee.

"Your girlfriend's in Personnel," she said.

"How did you guess?" I said, handing her a cup. She indicated the raft of books on Human Resource Develop-

ment and Stating the Bleeding Obvious in 5 Minutes a
Day, which take up half our shelves.

"You don't look the type. Is this it?" She pointed her
mug at the two boxes on the floor. I nodded sheepishly.
"Well," she said, "aren't you going to open them?"

I glanced up at her, surprised. Her face was turned
toward me, a small smile at the corners of her mouth. Her
skin was the pale tawny color that goes with rich hair, I
noticed, and flawless. I shrugged, slightly embarrassed.

"I guess so," I said noncommittally. "I've got some
work I ought to do first."

"Rubbish," she said firmly. "Let's have a look."

And so I bent down and pulled open the boxes, while
she settled down on the sofa to watch. What was odd was
that I didn't mind doing it. Normally, when I'm doing
something that's very much to do with me and the things I
enjoy, I have to do it alone. Other people seldom understand the things that give you the most pleasure, and I for
one would rather not have them around to undermine the
occasion.

But Alice seemed genuinely interested, and ten minutes
later I had the system sitting on the desk. I pressed the button and the familiar tone rang out as the machine set about
booting up. Alice was standing to one side of me, sipping
the remains of her coffee, and we both took a startled step
back at the vibrancy of the tone ringing from the monitor's
stereo speakers. In the meantime I'd babbled about voice
recognition and video output, the half-gigabyte hard disk
and CD-ROM. She'd listened, and even asked questions,
questions that followed from what I was saying rather than
to simply set me up to drivel on some more. It wasn't that
she knew a vast amount about computers. She just understood what was exciting about them.

When the screen threw up the standard message saying all was well we looked at each other.

"You're not going to get much work done today, are
you?" she said.

"Probably not," I agreed, and she laughed.

Just then a protracted squawking noise erupted from

the sofa, and I jumped. The courier rolled her eyes and reached over to pick up her unit. A voice of stunning brutality informed her that she had to pick something up from the other side of town, urgently, like five minutes ago, and why wasn't she there already, darlin'?

"Grr," she said, like a little tiger, and reached for her helmet. "Duty calls."

"But I haven't told you about the telecommunications yet," I said, joking.

"Some other time," she said.

I saw her out, and we stood for a moment on the doorstep. I was wondering what to say. I didn't know her, and would never see her again, but wanted to thank her for sharing something with me. Then I noticed one of the local cats ambling past the bottom of the steps. I love cats, but Nancy doesn't, so we don't have one. Just one of the little compromises you make, I guess. I recognized this particular cat and had long since given up hope of appealing to it. I pointlessly made the sound universally employed for gaining cats' attention, with no result. It glanced up at me wearily and then continued to cruise on by.

After a look at me Alice sat down on her heels and made the same noise. The cat immediately stopped in its tracks and looked at her. She made the noise again and the cat turned, glanced down the street for no apparent reason, and then confidently made its way up the steps to weave in and out of her legs.

"That is truly amazing," I said. "He is not a friendly cat."

She took the cat in her arms and stood up.

"Oh, I don't know," she said. The cat sat up against her chest, looking around benignly. I reached out to rub its nose and felt the warm vibration of a purr. The two of us made a fuss of him for a few moments, and then she put him down. She replaced her helmet, climbed on her bike, and then, with a wave, set off.

Back in the flat I tidied away the boxes, anal-retentive that I am, before settling down to immerse myself in the new machine. On impulse I called Nancy, to let her know the system had finally arrived.

I got one of her assistants instead. She didn't put me on hold, and I heard Nancy say "Tell him I'll call him back" in the background. I said good-bye to Trish with fairly good grace, trying not to mind.

Voice recognition software hadn't been included, it turned out, nor anything to put in the CD-ROM drive. The telecommunications functions wouldn't work without an expensive add-on, which Callhaven didn't expect for four to six weeks. Apart from that, it was great.

Nancy cooked that evening. We tended to take it in turns, though she was much better at it than me. Nancy is good at most things. She's accomplished.

There's a lot of infighting in the world of Personnel, it would appear, and Nancy was in feisty form that evening, having outmaneuvered some coworker. I drank a glass of red wine and leaned against the counter while she whirled ingredients around. She told me about her day, and I listened and laughed. I didn't tell her much about mine, only that it had gone okay. Her threshold for hearing about the world of freelance graphic design was pretty low. She'd listen with relatively good grace if I really had to get something out of my system, but she didn't understand it and didn't seem to want to. No reason why she should, of course. I didn't mention the new computer sitting on my desk, and neither did she.

Dinner was very good. It was chicken, but she'd done something intriguing to it with spices. I ate as much as I could, but there was a little left. I tried to get her to finish it, but she wouldn't. I reassured her that she hadn't eaten too much, in the way that sometimes seemed to help, but her mood dipped and she didn't have any dessert. I steered her toward the sofa and took the stuff out to wash up and make some coffee.

While I was standing at the sink, scrubbing the plates and thinking vaguely about the mountain of things I had to do the next day, I noticed a cat sitting on a wall across the street. It was a sort of very dark brown color, almost black, and I hadn't seen it before. It was crouched down, watching a twittering bird with that catty concentration that combines complete attention with the sense that they might at any moment break off and wash their foot instead. The bird eventually fluttered chaotically off and the cat watched it for a moment before sitting upright, as if drawing a line under that particular diversion.

Then the cat's head turned, and it looked straight at me. It was a good twenty yards away, but I could see its eyes very clearly. It kept looking, and after a while I laughed, slightly taken aback. I even looked away for a moment, but when I looked back it was still there, still looking.

The kettle boiled and I turned to tip water into a couple of mugs of Nescafé. When I glanced out of the window on the way out of the kitchen the cat was gone.

Nancy wasn't in the lounge when I got there, so I settled on the sofa and lit a cigarette. After about five minutes the toilet flushed upstairs, and I sighed.

My reassurances hadn't done any good at all.

A couple of days came and went, with the usual flurry of deadlines and redrafts. I went to a social evening at Nancy's office and spent a few hours being ignored and patronized by her power-dressed colleagues, while she stood and sparkled in the center. I messed up a print job and had to cover the cost of doing it again. Good things happened, too, I guess, but it's the others that stick in your mind.

One afternoon the buzzer went and I wandered absentmindedly downstairs to get the door. As I opened it I saw a flick of brown hair and saw that it was Alice.

"Hello there," I said, strangely pleased.

"Hello yourself." She smiled. "Got a parcel for you." I took it and looked at the label. Color proofs from the repro house. Yawn. She must have been looking at my face, because she laughed. "Nothing very exciting, then."

"Hardly." After I'd signed the delivery note, I looked up at her. She was still smiling, I think, though it was difficult to tell. Her face looked as if it always was.

"Well," she said, "I can either go straight to Peckham to pick up something else that's dull, or you can tell me about the telecommunications features."

Very surprised, I stared at her for a moment, then stepped back to let her in.

"Bastards," she said indignantly when I told her about the things that hadn't been shipped with the machine, and she looked genuinely annoyed. I told her about the telecoms stuff anyway, as we sat on the sofa and drank coffee. Mainly we just chatted, but not for very long, and when she got to the end of the road on her bike she turned and waved before turning the corner.

That night Nancy went to Sainsbury's on the way home from work. I caught her eye as she unpacked the biscuits and brownies, potato chips and pastries, but she just stared back at me, and I looked away. She was having a hard time at work. Deflecting my gaze to the window, I noticed the dark cat was sitting on the wall opposite. It wasn't doing much, simply peering vaguely this way and that, watching things I couldn't see. It seemed to look up at the window for a moment, but then leapt down off the wall and wandered away down the street.

I cooked dinner and Nancy didn't eat much, but she stayed in the kitchen when I went into the living room to finish off a job. When I made our cups of tea to drink in bed I noticed that the bin had been emptied, and the gray bag stood, neatly tied, to one side. When I nudged it with my foot it rustled, full of empty packets. Upstairs the bathroom door was pulled shut, and the key turned in the lock.

I saw Alice a few more times in the next few weeks. A couple of major jobs were reaching crisis point at the same time, and there seemed to be a semiconstant flurry of bikes coming up to the house. On three or four of those occasions it was Alice whom I saw when I opened the door.

Apart from one, when she had to turn straight around on pain of death, she came in for a coffee each time. We'd chat about this and that, and when the voice recognition software finally arrived I showed her how it worked. I had a rip-off copy, from a friend who'd sourced it from the States. You had to do an impersonation of an American accent to get the machine to understand anything you said, and my attempts to do so made Alice laugh a lot. Which is curious, because it made Nancy merely sniff and ask me whether I'd put the new computer on the insurance.

Nancy was having a bit of a hard time, those couple of weeks. Her so-called boss was dumping more and more responsibility onto her while stalwartly refusing to give her more credit. Nancy's world was very real to her, and she relentlessly kept me up to date on it: the doings of her boss were more familiar to me by then than the activities of most of my friends. She got her company car upgraded, which was a nice thing. She screeched up to the house one evening in something small and red and sporty, and hollered up to the window. I scampered down and she took us hurtling around North London, driving with her customary verve and confidence. On impulse we stopped at an Italian restaurant we sometimes went to, and they miraculously had a table. Over coffee we took each other's hands and said we loved one another, which we hadn't done for a while.

When we parked outside the house I saw the dark cat sitting under a tree on the other side of the street. I pointed it out to Nancy but, as I've said, she doesn't really like cats, and merely shrugged. She went in first and as I turned to close the door I saw the cat was still sitting there, a black shape in the half-light. I wondered who it belonged to, and wished that it was ours.

A couple of days later I was walking down the street late afternoon when I noticed a motorbike parked outside Sad Café. I seemed to have become sensitized to bikes over the previous few weeks: probably because I'd used so many couriers. "Sad" wasn't the café's real name, but what Nancy and I used to call it, when we used to traipse hung-over down the road on Sunday mornings on a quest for a cooked breakfast. The first time we'd slumped over a Formica table in there we had been slowly surrounded by middle-aged men in zip-up jackets and beige bobble hats, a party of mentally subnormal teenagers with broken glasses, and old women on the verge of death. The pathos attack we'd suffered had nearly finished us off, and it had been Sad Café ever since. We hadn't been there in a while: Nancy usually had work in the evenings in those days, even at weekends, and fried breakfasts appeared to be off the map again.

The bike resting outside made me glance inside the window, and with a shock of recognition I saw Alice in there, sitting at a table nursing a mug of something or other. I nearly walked on, but then thought what the hell, and stepped inside. Alice looked startled to see me, but then relaxed, and I sat down and ordered a cup of tea.

She'd finished for the day, it turned out, and was killing time before heading off for home. I was at a loose end myself: Nancy was out for the evening, entertaining clients. It was very odd seeing Alice for the first time outside the flat, and strange seeing her not in working hours. Possibly it was that which made the next thing coalesce in front of us.

Before we knew how the idea had arisen, we were wheeling her bike down the road to prop it up outside the Bengal Lancer, Kentish Town's bravest stab in the direction of a decent restaurant. I loitered awkwardly to one side while she stood in the street, took off her leathers, and packed them into the bike's carrier. She was wearing jeans and a green sweatshirt underneath, a green that matched her eyes. Then she ran her hands through her hair, said "Close enough for rock and roll," and strode toward the door. Momentarily reminded of Nancy's standard hour and a half preparation before going out, I followed her into the restaurant.

We took our time and had about four courses, and by the end were absolutely stuffed. We talked of things beyond computers and design, but I can't remember what. We had a bottle of wine, a gallon of coffee, and smoked most of a packet of cigarettes. When we were done I stood outside again, more relaxed this time, as she climbed back

into her work clothes. She waved as she rode off, and I
watched her go, and then turned and walked for home.

It was a nice meal. It was also the big mistake. The
next time I rang for a bike, I asked for Alice by name.
After that, it seemed the natural thing to do. Alice also
seemed to end up doing more of the deliveries to me, more
than you could put down to chance.

If we hadn't gone for that meal, perhaps it wouldn't
have happened. Nothing was said, and no glances exchanged: I didn't note the date in my diary.

But we were falling in love.

The following night Nancy and I had a row, the first full-
blown one in a while. We rarely argued. She was a good
manager.

This one was short, and also very odd. It was quite
late and I was sitting in the lounge, trying to work up the
energy to turn on the television. I didn't have much hope
for what I would find on it but was too tired to read. I'd
been listening to music before and was staring at the
stereo, half mesmerized by the green and red points of
LEDs. Nancy was working at the table in the kitchen,
which was dark apart from the lamp that shed yellow light
over her papers.

Suddenly she marched into the living room, already at
maximum temper, and shouted incoherently at me. Shocked,
I half stood, brow furrowed as I tried to work out what she
was saying. In retrospect I was probably slightly asleep,
and her anger frightened me with its harsh intensity, seeming to fill the room.

She was shouting at me for getting a cat. There was
no point me denying it, because she'd seen it. She'd seen
the cat under the table in the kitchen, it was in there still,
and I was to go and throw it out. I knew how much she
disliked cats, and anyway, how could I do it without asking her, and the whole thing was a classic example of what
a selfish and hateful man I was.

It took me a while to get to the bottom of this and
start denying it. I was too baffled to get angry. In the end I

went with her into the kitchen and looked under the table. By then I was getting a little spooked, to be honest. We also looked in the hallway, the bedroom, and the bathroom. Then we looked in the kitchen again and in the living room.

There was, of course, no cat.

I sat Nancy on the sofa and brought in a couple of hot drinks. She was still shaking, though her anger was gone. I tried to talk to her, to work out what exactly was wrong. Her reaction was disproportionate, misdirected: I'm not sure even she knew what it was about. The cat, of course, could have been nothing more than a discarded shoe seen in near darkness, maybe even her own foot moving in the darkness. After leaving my parents' house, where there had always been a cat, I'd often startled myself by thinking I saw them in similar ways.

She didn't seem especially convinced but did calm a little. She was so timid and quiet, and as always I found it difficult to reconcile her as she was then with her as Corporate Woman, as she was for so much of the time. I turned the fire on and we sat in front of it and talked, and even discussed her eating. Nobody else knew about that, apart from me. I didn't understand it, not really. I sensed that it was something to do with feelings of lack of control, of trying to shape herself and her world, but couldn't get much closer than that. There appeared to be nothing I could do except listen, but I suppose that was better than nothing.

We went to bed a little later and made careful, gentle love. As she relaxed toward sleep, huddled in my arms, I caught myself for the first time feeling for her something that was a little like pity.

Alice and I had dinner again about a week later. This time it was less of an accident and took place farther from home. I had an early-evening meeting in town, and by coincidence Alice would be in the area at around about the same time. I told Nancy I might up having dinner with my client, but she didn't seem to hear. She was preoccupied, some new power struggle at work edging toward resolution.

Though it was several weeks since the previous occasion, it didn't feel at all strange seeing Alice in the evening, not least because we'd talked to each other often in the meantime. She'd started having two cups of coffee, rather than one, each time she dropped something off, and had once phoned me for advice on computers. She was thinking of getting one herself, I wasn't really sure what for.

While it didn't feel odd, I was aware of what I was doing. Meeting another woman for dinner, basically, and looking forward to it. When I talked to her my feelings and what I did seemed more important, as if they were a part of someone worth talking to. Some part of me felt that was more important than a little economy with the truth. To be honest, I tried not to think too hard about it.

When I got home Nancy was sitting in the living room, reading.

"How was your meeting?" she asked.

"Fine," I replied. "Fine."

"Good," she said, and went back to scanning her magazine. I could have tried to make conversation, but knew it would have come out tinny and forced. In the end I went to bed and lay tightly curled on my side, wide awake.

I was just drifting off to sleep when I heard a low voice in the silence, speaking next to my ear.

"Go away," it said. "Go away."

I opened my eyes, expecting I don't know what. Nancy's face, I suppose, hanging over mine. There was no one there. I was relaxing slightly, prepared to believe it had been a fragment of a dream, when I heard her voice again, saying the same words in the same low tone.

Carefully I climbed out of bed and crept toward the kitchen. Through it I could see into the living room, where Nancy was standing in front of the main window in the darkness. She was looking out at something in the street.

"Go away," she said again, softly.

I turned round and went back to bed.

* * *

A couple of weeks passed. Time seemed to do that, that autumn. I was very immersed, what with one thing and another. Each day held something that fixed my attention and pulled me through it. I'd look up, and a week would have gone by, with me having barely noticed.

One of the things that held my attention, and became a regular part of most days, was talking to Alice. We talked about things that Nancy and I never touched upon, things Nancy simply didn't understand or care about. Alice read, for example. Nancy read, too, in that she studied memos, and reports, and boned up on the current corporate claptrap being imported from the States. She didn't read books, though, or paragraphs even. She read sentences, to strip from them what she needed to do her job, find out what was on television, or hold her own on current affairs. Every sentence was a bullet point, and she read to acquire information.

Alice read for its own sake. She wrote, too, hence her growing interest in computers. I mentioned once that I'd written a few articles, years back, before I settled on being a barely competent graphic designer instead. She said she'd written some stories and, after regular nagging from me, diffidently gave me copies. I don't know anything about fiction from a professional point of view, so I don't know how innovative or clever they were. But they gripped my attention, and I read them more than once, and that's good enough for me. I told her so, and she seemed pleased.

We spoke most days and saw each other a couple of times a week. She delivered things to me, or picked them up, and sometimes I chanced by Sad Café when she was sipping a cup of tea. It was all very low key, very friendly.

Nancy and I got on with each other, in an occasional, space-sharing sort of way. She had her friends, and I had mine. Sometimes we saw them together, and performed, as a social pair. We looked good together, like a series of stills from a lifestyle magazine. Life, if that's what it was, went on. Her eating vacillated between not good and bad, and I carried on being bleakly accepting of the fact that there didn't seem much I could do to help. So much of our lives seemed geared up to perpetuating her idea of how two young people should live that I somehow didn't feel that I could call our bluff, point out what was living beneath the stones in our house. I also didn't mention the night I'd seen her in the lounge. There didn't seem any way of bringing it up.

Apart from having Alice to chat to, the other good news was the new cat in the neighborhood. When I glanced out of the living room window sometimes it would be there, ambling smoothly past or plonked down on the pavement, watching movement in the air. It had a habit of sitting in the middle of the road, daring traffic to give it any trouble, as if the cat knew what the road was for but was having no truck with it. This was a field once, the twitch of her tail seemed to say, and as far as I'm concerned it still is.

One morning I was walking back from the corner shop, clutching some cigarettes and milk, and came upon the cat, perched on a wall. If you like cats there's something rather depressing about having them run away from you, so I approached cautiously. I wanted to get to at least within a yard of this one before it went shooting off into hyperspace.

To my delight, it didn't move away at all. When I got up next to her she stood up, and I thought that was it, but it turned out to be just a recognition that I was there. She was quite happy to be stroked and to have the fur on her head runkled, and responded to having her chest rubbed with a purr so deep it was almost below the threshold of hearing. Now that I was closer I could see the chestnut gleams in the dark brown of her fur. She was a very beautiful cat.

After a couple of minutes of this I moved away, thinking I ought to get on, but the cat immediately jumped off the wall and wove in figure eights about my feet, pressing up against my calves. I find it difficult enough to walk away from a cat at the best of times. When they're being ultra-friendly it's impossible. So I bent down and tickled, and talked fond nonsense. I finally got to my door and looked

back to see her, still sitting on the pavement. She was looking around as if wondering what to do next, after all that
excitement. I had to fight down the impulse to wave.

I closed the door behind me, feeling for a moment
very lonely, and then went back upstairs to work.

Then one Friday night Alice and I met again, and things
changed.

Nancy was out at yet another work get-together. Her
organization seemed to like running the social lives of its
staff, like some rabid church, intent on infiltrating every
activity of its disciples. Nancy mentioned the event in a
way that made it clear that my attendance was far from
mandatory, and I was quite happy to oblige. I do my best
at these things but doubt I look as if I'm having the time of
my life.

I didn't have anything else on, so I just flopped about
the house for a while, reading and watching television. It
was easier to relax when Nancy wasn't there, when we
weren't busy being a Couple. I couldn't settle, though. I
kept thinking how pleasant it would be not to feel that way,
that it would be nice to want your girlfriend to be home so
you could laze about together. It didn't work that way with
Nancy, not anymore. Getting her to consider a lie-in on one
particular Saturday was a major project in itself. I probably
hadn't tried very hard in a while, either. She got up, I got
up. I'd been developed as a human resource.

My reading grew fitful and in the end I grabbed my
coat and went for a walk down streets that were dark and
cold. A few couples and lone figures floated down the
roads, in midevening transit between pubs and Chinese
restaurants. The very formlessness of the activity around
me, its random wandering, made me feel quietly content.
The room in which Nancy and her colleagues stood, ro-
botically passing business catchphrases up and down the
hierarchy, leapt into my mind, though I'd no idea where it
was. I thought quietly to myself that I would much rather
be here than there.

Then for a moment I felt the whole of London spread

out around me, and my contentment faded away. Nancy had somewhere to go. All I had was miles of finite roads in winter light, black houses leaning in toward each other. I could walk, and I could run, and in the end I would come to the boundaries, the edge of the city. When I reached them there would be nothing I could do except turn around and come back into the city. I couldn't feel anything beyond the gates, couldn't believe anything was there. It wasn't some yearning for the countryside or far climes: I like London, and the great outdoors irritates me. It was more a sense that a place that should hold endless possibilities had been tamed by something, bleached out by my lack of imagination, by the limits of my life.

I headed down the Kentish Town Road toward Camden, so wrapped up in heroic melancholy that I nearly got myself run over at the junction with Prince of Wales Road. Rather shaken, I stumbled back onto the curb, dazed by a passing flash of yellow light and a blurred obscenity. Fuck that, I thought, and crossed at a different place, sending me down a different road, toward a different evening.

Camden was, as ever, trying to prove that there was still a place for hippie throwback losers in the 1990s, and I skirted the purposeful crowds and ended up in a back road instead.

And it was there that I saw Alice. When I saw her I felt my heart lurch, and I stopped in my tracks. She was walking along the road, dressed in a long skirt and dark blouse, hands in pockets. She appeared to be alone and was wandering down the street much as I was, looking around but in a world of her own. It was too welcome a coincidence not to take advantage of and, careful not to surprise her, I crossed the road and met her on the other side.

We spent the next three hours in a noisy, smoky pub. The only seats were very close together, crowded round one corner of a table in the center of the room. We drank a lot, but the alcohol didn't seem to function in the way it usually did. I didn't get drunk but simply felt warmer and more relaxed. The reeling crowds of locals gave us ample ammunition to talk about, until we were going fast enough not to need any help at all. We just drank, and talked, and talked and drank, and the bell for last orders came as a complete surprise.

When we walked out of the pub some of the alcohol kicked suddenly in, and we stumbled in unison on an unexpected step, to fall together laughing and shh-ing. Without even discussing it we knew that neither of us felt like going home yet, and we ended up down by the canal instead. We walked slowly past the backs of houses and speculated what might be going on beyond the curtains, we looked up at the sky and pointed out stars, we listened to the quiet splashes of occasional ducks coming into land. After about fifteen minutes we found a bench and sat down for a cigarette.

When she'd put her lighter back in her pocket Alice's hand fell near mine. I was very conscious of it being there, of the smallness of the distance mine would have to travel, and I smoked left-handed so as not to move it. I wasn't forgetting myself. I still knew Nancy existed, knew how my life was set up. But I didn't move my hand.

Then, like a chess game of perfect simplicity and naturalness, the conversation took us there.

I said that work seemed to be slackening off, after the busy period of the last couple of months. Alice said that she hoped it didn't drop off too much. So that I can continue to afford expensive computers that don't do quite what I expect? I asked.

"No," she replied, "so that I can keep coming to see you." I turned and looked at her. She looked nervous but defiant, and her hand moved the inch that put it on top of mine.

"You might as well know," she said. "If you don't already. There are three important things in my life at the moment. My bike, my stories, and you."

People don't change their lives: evenings do. There are nights that have their own momentum, their own purpose and agenda. They come from nowhere and take people with them. That's why you can never understand, the next day, quite how you came to do what you did. Because it wasn't you who did it. It was the evening.

My life stopped that evening, and started up again, and everything was a different color.

We sat on the bench for another two hours, wrapped up close to each other. We admitted when we'd first thought about each other, and laughed quietly about the distance we'd kept. After weeks of denying what I felt, of simply not realizing, I couldn't let go of her hand now that I had it. It felt so extraordinary to be that close to her, to feel the texture of her skin on mine and her nails against my palm. People change when you get that near to them, become much more real. If you're already in love with them then they expand to fill the world.

In the end we got on to Nancy. We were bound to, sooner or later. Alice asked how I felt about her, and I tried to explain, tried to understand myself. In the end we let the topic lapse.

"It's not going to be easy," I said, squeezing her hand. I was thinking glumly to myself that it might not happen at all. Knowing the way Nancy would react, it looked like a very high mountain to climb. Alice glanced at me and then turned back toward the canal.

A big cat was sitting there, peering out over the water. First moving myself even closer to Alice, so that strands of her hair tickled against my face, I made a noise at the cat. It turned to look at us and then ambled over toward the bench.

"I do like a friendly cat," I said, reaching out to stroke its head.

Alice smiled and then made a noise of her own. I was a bit puzzled that she wasn't looking at the cat when she made it, until I saw that another was making its way out of the shadows. This one was smaller and more lithe, and walked right up to the bench. I was, I suppose, still a little befuddled with drink, and when Alice turned to look in a different direction it took me a moment to catch up. A third cat was coming down the canal walk in our direction, followed by another.

When a fifth emerged from the bushes behind our bench, I turned and stared at Alice. She was already looking at me, a smile on her lips like the first one of hers I'd seen. She laughed at the expression on my face and then made her noise again. The cats around us sat to attention, and two more appeared from the other direction, almost trotting in their haste to join the collection. We were now so outnumbered that I felt rather beset.

When the next one appeared I had to ask.

"Alice, what's going on?"

She smiled very softly, like a painting, and leaned her head against my shoulder.

"A long time ago," she said, as if making up a story for a child, "none of this was here. There was no canal, no streets and houses, and all around was trees, and grass." One of the cats round the bench briefly licked one of its paws, and I saw another couple padding out of the darkness toward us. "The big people have changed all of that. They've cut down the trees, and buried the grass, and they've even leveled the ground. There used to be a hill here, a hill that was steep on one side but gentle on the other. They've taken all that away, and made it look like this. It's not that it's so bad. It's just different. The cats still remember the way it was."

It was a nice story, and yet another indication of how we thought in the same way. But it couldn't be true, and it didn't explain all the cats around us. There were now about twenty, and somehow that was too many. Not for me, but for common sense. Where the hell were they all coming from?

"But they didn't have cats in those days," I said nervously. "Not like this. This kind of cat is modern, surely. An import, or crossbreed."

She shook her head. "That's what they say," she said, "and that's what people think. They've always been here. It's just that people haven't always known."

"Alice, what are you talking about?" I was beginning to get really spooked by the number of cats milling softly around. They were still coming, in ones and twos, and now surrounded us for yards around. The stretch of canal was dark apart from soft glints of moonlight off the water, and the lines of the banks and walkway seemed somehow stark, sketched out, as if modeled on a computer screen. They'd been rendered well and looked convincing, but something wasn't quite right about the way they sat together, as if some angle was one degree out.

"A thousand years ago cats used to come to this hill, because it was their meeting place. They would come and discuss their business, and then they would go away. This was their place, and it still is. But they don't mind us."

"Why?"

"Because I love you," she said, and kissed me for the first time.

It was ten minutes before I looked up again. Only two cats were left. I pulled my arm tighter around Alice and thought how simply and unutterably happy I was.

"Was that all true?" I asked, pretending to be a child.

"No," she said, and smiled. "It was just a story." She pushed her nose up against mine and nuzzled, and our heads melted into one.

At two o'clock I realized I was going to have to go home, and we got up and walked slowly back to the road. I waited shivering with her for a minicab, and endured the driver's histrionic sighing as we said good-bye. I stood on the corner and waved until the cab was out of sight, and then turned and walked home.

It wasn't until I turned into our road and saw that the lights were still on in our house that I realized just how real the evening had been. As I walked up the steps the door opened. Nancy stood there in a dressing gown, looking angry and frightened.

"Where the hell have you *been*?" she said. I straightened my shoulders and girded myself up to lie.

I apologized. I told her I'd been out drinking with Howard, lying calmly and with a convincing determination. I didn't even feel bad about it, except in a self-serving, academic sort of way.

Some switch had been finally thrown in my mind, and as we lay in bed afterward I realized that I wasn't in bed with my girlfriend anymore. There was just someone in my bed. When Nancy rolled toward me, her body open in a way that suggested that she might not be thinking of going to sleep, I felt my chest tighten with something that felt like dread. I found a way of suggesting that I might be a bit drunk for anything other than unconsciousness, and she curled up beside me and went to sleep instead. I lay awake for an hour, feeling as if I were lying on a slab of marble in a room open to the sky.

Breakfast the next morning was a festival of leaden politeness. The kitchen seemed very bright, and noise rebounded harshly off the walls. Nancy was in a good mood, but there was nothing I could do except smile tight smiles and talk much louder than usual, waiting for her to go to work.

The next ten days were both dismal and the best days of my life. Alice and I managed to see each other every couple of days, occasionally for an evening but more often just for a cup of coffee. We didn't do any more than talk, and hold hands, and sometimes kiss. Our kisses were brief, a kind of sketching out of the way things could be. Bad starts will always undermine a relationship, for fear it could happen again. So we were restrained and honest with each other, and it was wonderful, but it was also difficult.

Being home was no fun at all. Nancy hadn't changed, but I had, and so I didn't know her anymore. It was like having a complete stranger living in your house, a stranger who was all the worse for reminding you of someone you once loved. The things that were the closest to the way they used to be were the things that made me most irritable, and I found myself avoiding anything that might promote them.

Something had to be done, and it had to be done by me. The problem was gearing myself up to it. Nancy and I had been living together for four years. Most of our friends assumed we'd be engaged before long: I'd already heard a few jokes. We knew each other very well, and that does count for something. As I moved warily around Nancy during those weeks, trying not to seem too close, I was also conscious of how much we had shared together, of how affectionate a part of me still felt toward her. She was a friend, and I cared about her. I didn't want her to be hurt.

My relationship with Nancy wasn't completely straightforward. I wasn't just her boyfriend, I was her brother and father, too. I knew some of the reasons her eating was as bad as it was, things no one else would ever know. I'd talked it through with her, and knew how to live with it, knew how to not make her feel any worse. She needed support, and I was the only person there to give it. Ripping that away when she was already having such a bad time would be very difficult to forgive.

And so things went on, for a little while. I saw Alice when I could, but always in the end I would have to go, and we would part, and each time it felt more and more arbitrary and I found it harder to remember why I should have to leave. I grew terrified of saying her name in my sleep, or of letting something slip, and felt as if I were living my life on stage in front of a predatory audience waiting for a mistake. I'd go out for walks in the evening and walk as slowly up the road as possible, stopping to talk to the cat, stroking her for as long as she liked and walking up and down the pavement with her, doing anything to avoid going back into the house.

I spent most of the second week looking forward to the Saturday. At the beginning of each week Nancy announced she would be going on a team-building day at the weekend. She explained to me what was involved, the chasm of evangelical corporate vacuity into which she and her colleagues were cheerfully leaping. She was talking to me a lot more at the time, wanting to share her life. I tried, but I couldn't really listen. All I could think about was that I was due to be driving up to Cambridge that day, to drop work off at a client's. I'd assumed that I'd be going alone. With Nancy firmly occupied somewhere else, another possibility sprang to mind.

When I saw Alice for coffee that afternoon I asked if she'd like to come. The warmth of her reply helped me through the evenings of the week, and we talked about it every day. The plan was that I'd ring home early evening, when Nancy was back from her day, and say that I'd run into someone up there and wouldn't be back until late. It was a bending of our unspoken doing-things-by-the-book rule, but it had to be done. Alice and I needed a longer period with each other, and I needed to build myself up to what had to be done.

By midevening on Friday I was at fever pitch. I was pacing round the house not settling at anything, so much in my own little world that it took me a while to notice that something was up with Nancy, too.

She was sitting in the living room, going over some papers, but kept glancing angrily out of the window as if expecting to see someone. When I asked her about it, slightly irritably, she denied she was doing it, and then ten minutes later I saw her do it again. I retreated to the kitchen and did something dull to a shelf that I'd been putting off for months. When Nancy stalked in to make some more coffee she saw what I was doing and seemed genuinely touched that I'd finally got around to it. My smile of self-deprecating good-naturedness felt as if it were stretched across the lips of a corpse.

Then she was back out in the lounge again, glaring nervously out of the window, as if fearing imminent invasion from a Martian army. It reminded me of the night I'd seen her standing by the window, which I had found rather spooky. She was looking very flaky that evening, and I'd run out of pity. I simply found it irritating, and hated myself for that.

Eventually, finally, at long last, it was time for bed. Nancy went ahead and I volunteered to close windows and tidy ashtrays. It's funny how you seem most solicitous and endearing when you don't want to be there at all.

What I actually wanted was a few moments to wrap a present I was going to give to Alice. When I heard the bathroom door shut I leapt for the filing cabinet and took

out the book. I grabbed tape and paper from a drawer and
started wrapping. As I folded I glanced out of the window
and saw the cat sitting outside in the road, and smiled to
myself. With Alice I'd be able to have a cat of my own,
could work with furry company and doze with a warm
bundle on my lap. The bathroom door opened again and I
paused, ready for instant action. When Nancy's feet had
padded safely into the bedroom, I continued wrapping.
When it was done I slipped the present in a drawer and
took out the card I was going to give with it, already com-
posing in my head the message for the inside.

"Mark?"

I nearly died when I heard Nancy's voice. She was
striding through the kitchen toward me, and the card was
still lying on my desk. I quickly drew a sheaf of papers
toward me and covered it, but only just in time. Heart
beating horribly, feeling almost dizzy, I turned to look at
her, trying to haul an expression of bland normality across
my face.

"What's this?" she demanded, holding her hand up in
front of me. It was dark in the room, and I couldn't see at
first. Then I saw. It was a hair. A dark brown hair.

"It looks like a hair," I said carefully, shuffling papers
on the desk.

"I know what it fucking is," she snapped. "It was in
the bed. I wonder how it got there."

Jesus Christ, I thought. She knows.

I stared at her with my mouth clamped shut and wa-
vered on the edge of telling the truth, of getting it over
with. I thought it would happen some other, calmer, way,
but you never know. Perhaps this was the pause into
which I had to drop the information that I was in love
with someone else.

Then, belatedly, I realized that Alice had never been
in the bedroom. Even since the night of the canal she'd
only ever been in the living room and the downstairs hall.
Maybe the kitchen, but certainly not the bedroom. I
blinked at Nancy, confused.

"It's that bloody cat," she shouted, instantly livid in

the way that always disarmed and frightened me. "It's been on our fucking bed."

"What cat?"

"The cat who's always fucking outside. Your little *friend*." She sneered violently, face almost unrecognizable. "You've had it in here."

"I haven't. What are you talking about?"

"Don't you deny, don't you—"

Unable to finish, Nancy simply threw herself at me and smashed me across the face. Shocked, I stumbled backward and she whacked me across the chin, and then pummeled her fists against my chest as I struggled to grab hold of her hands. She was trying to say something but it keep breaking up into furious sobs. In the end, before I could catch her hands, she took a step backward and stood very still. She stared at me for a moment, and then turned and walked quickly out of the room.

I spent the night on the sofa and was awake long after the last long, moaning sound had floated out to me from the bedroom. It may sound like selfish evasion, but I really felt I couldn't go to comfort her. The only way I could make her feel better was by lying, so in the end I stayed away.

I had plenty of time to finish writing the card to Alice, but found it difficult to remember exactly what I'd been going to say. In the end I struggled into a shallow, cramped sleep, and when I woke Nancy was already gone for the day.

I felt tired and hollow as I drove to meet Alice in the center of town. I still didn't actually know where she lived, or even her phone number. She hadn't volunteered the information, and I could always contact her via the courier firm. I was content with that until I could enter her life without any skulking around.

I remember very clearly the way she looked, standing on the pavement and watching out for my car. She was wearing a long black woolen skirt and a thick sweater of various chestnut colors. Her hair was backlit by morning light, and when she smiled as I pulled over toward her I had a moment of plunging doubt. I don't have any right to be with her, I thought. I already have someone, and Alice is far and away too wonderful. But she put her arms around me, and kissed my nose, and the feeling went away.

I have never driven so slowly on a motorway as that morning with Alice. I'd put some tapes in the car, music I knew we both liked, but they never made it out of the glove compartment. They simply weren't necessary. I sat in the slow lane and pootled along at sixty miles an hour, and we talked or sat in silence, sometimes glancing across at each other and grinning.

The road cuts through several hills, and when we reached the first cutting we both gasped at once. The embankment was a blaze of poppies, nodding in a gathering wind, and when we'd left them behind I turned to Alice and for the first time said I loved her. She stared at me for a long time, and in the end I had to glance away at the road. When I looked back she was looking straight ahead and smiling, her eyes shining with held-back tears.

My meeting took just under fifteen minutes. I think my client was rather taken aback, but who cares. We spent the rest of the day walking around the shops, picking up books and looking at them, stopping for two cups of tea. As we came laughing out of a record store she slung her arm around my back, and very conscious of what I was doing, I put mine around her shoulders. Though she was tall it felt comfortable, and there it stayed.

By about five I was getting tense, and we pulled into another café to have more tea, and so I could make my phone call. I left Alice sitting at the table waiting to order and went to the other side of the restaurant to use the booth. As I listened to the phone ringing I willed myself to be calm, and turned my back on the room to concentrate on what I was saying.

"Hello?"

When Nancy answered I barely recognized her. Her voice was like that of a querulously frightened old woman who'd not been expecting a call. I nearly put the phone down, but she realized who it was and immediately started crying.

It took me about twenty minutes to calm her even a

little. She'd left the team-building at lunchtime, claiming illness. Then she'd gone to Sainsbury's. She had eaten two Sara Lee chocolate cakes, a fudge roll, a packet of cereal, and three packets of biscuits. She'd gone to the bathroom, vomited, and then started again. I think she'd been sick again at least once, but I couldn't really make sense of part of what she said. It was so mixed up with abject apologies to me that the sentences became confused, and I couldn't tell whether she was talking about the night before or about the half-eaten packet of Jell-O she still had in her hand.

Feeling a little frightened and completely unaware of anything outside the cubicle I was standing in, I did what I could to focus her until what she was saying made a little more sense. I gave up trying to say that no apology was needed for last night and in the end just told her everything was all right. She promised to stop eating for a while and to watch television instead. I said I'd be back as soon as I could.

I had to. I loved her. There was nothing else I could do.

When the last of my change was gone I told her to take care and slowly replaced the handset. I stared at the wood paneling in front of me and gradually became aware of the noise from the restaurant on the other side of the glass door behind me. Eventually I turned and looked out.

Alice was sitting at the table, watching the passing throng. She looked beautiful, and strong, and about two thousand miles away.

We drove back to London in silence. Most of the talking was done in the restaurant. It didn't take very long. I said I couldn't leave Nancy in the state that she was in, and Alice nodded once, tightly, and put her cigarettes in her bag.

She said that she'd sort of known, perhaps even before we'd got to Cambridge. I got angry then, and said she couldn't have done, because I hadn't known myself. She got angry back when I said we'd still be friends, and she was in the right, I suppose. It was a stupid thing for me to say.

Awkwardly I asked if she'd be all right, and she said, yes, in the sense that she'd survive. I tried to explain that was the difference, that Nancy might not be able to. She shrugged and said that was the other difference: Nancy would never have to find out if she could. The more we talked the more my head felt it was going to explode, the more my eyes felt as if they could burst with the pain and run in bloody lines down my cold cheeks. In the end she grew businesslike and paid the bill, and we walked slowly back to the car.

Neither of us could bring ourselves to small talk in the car, and for the most part the only sound was that of the wheels upon the road. It was dark by then, and rain began to fall before we'd been on the motorway for very long. When we passed through the first cut in the hillside, I felt the poppies all around us, heads battered down by the falling water. Alice turned to me.

"I did know."

"How," I said, trying not to cry, trying to watch what the cars behind me were doing.

"When you said you loved me, you sounded so unhappy."

I dropped her in town, on the corner where I'd picked her up. She said a few things to help me, to make me feel less bad about what I'd done. Then she walked off around the corner, and I never saw her again.

When I'd parked outside the house I sat for a moment, trying to pull myself together. Nancy would need to see me looking whole and at her disposal. I got out and locked the door, looking around halfheartedly for the cat. It wasn't there.

Nancy opened the door with a shy smile, and I followed her into the kitchen. As I hugged her and told her everything was all right, I gazed blankly over her shoulder around the room. The kitchen was immaculate, no sign left of the afternoon's festivities. The rubbish had been taken out, and something was bubbling on the stove. She'd cooked me dinner.

She didn't eat but sat at the table with me. The chicken was okay, but not up to her usual standard. There was a lot of meat but it was tough, and for once there was a little too much spice. It tasted odd, to be honest. She noticed a look on my face and said she'd gone to a different butcher. We talked a little about her afternoon, but she was feeling much better. She seemed more interested in discussing the way her office reorganization was shaping up.

Afterward she went through into the lounge and turned the television on, and I set about making coffee and washing up, moving woodenly around the kitchen as if on abandoned rails. As Nancy's favorite inanity boomed out from the living room I looked around for a bin bag to shovel the remains of my dinner into, but she'd obviously used them all. Sighing with a complete lack of feeling, I opened the back door and went downstairs to put it directly into the bin.

There were two sacks by the bin, both tied with Nancy's distinctive knot. I undid the nearest and opened it a little. Then, just before I pushed the bones off my plate, something in the bag caught my eye. A patch of darkness amid the garish wrappers of high-calorie comfort foods. An oddly shaped piece of thick fabric, perhaps. I pulled the edge of the bag back a little farther to look, and the light from the kitchen window above fell across the contents of the bag.

The darkness changed to a rich chestnut brown flecked with red, and I saw it wasn't fabric at all.

We moved six months later, after we got engaged. I was glad to move. The flat never felt like home again. Sometimes I go back and stand in that street, remembering the weeks in which I stared out of the window, pointlessly watching the road. I called the courier firm after a couple of days. I was expecting a stonewall and knew it was unlikely they'd give an address. But they denied she'd ever worked there at all.

After a couple of years Nancy and I had our first child, and she'll be eight this November. She has a sister now. Some evenings I'll leave them with their mother and go out for a walk. I'll walk with heavy calm through black streets beneath featureless houses and sometimes go down to the canal. I sit on the bench and close my eyes, and sometimes I think I can see it. Sometimes I think I can feel the way it was when a hill was there and meetings were held in secret.

In the end I always stand up slowly and walk the streets back to the house. The hill has gone and things have changed, and it's not like that anymore. No matter how long I sit and wait, the cats will never come.

William S. Burroughs

William S. Burroughs, the author of *Naked Lunch*, *Junky*, *Queer*, *Cities of the Red Night*, *The Place of Dead Roads*, *The Western Lands*, *Interzone*, *The Cat Inside*, *My Education: A Book of Dreams*, a nonfiction work, and most recently *Ghost of Chance*, is a member of the American Academy and Institute of Arts and Letters and a Commandeur de l'Ordre des Arts et Lettres of France. In 1993 Volume 1 of *The Letters of William S. Burroughs* was edited by Oliver Harris and *El Hombre Invisible: A Portrait of William Burroughs*, edited by Barry Miles, was published.

William Burroughs is a writer of varied enthusiasms, one of which is cats. The "Ruski" of the title was in reality an orphan cat who adopted Burroughs in the early 1980s, transforming the author (who had never had a pet) into a friend of all cats. Here Ruski plays a different role.

Ruski

WILLIAM S. BURROUGHS

THEY CALLED HIM the Great Gatsby. Came from nowhere, rented a big house, and started giving big parties, plenty of good booze and chow. It wasn't long before
they found out his bounty was not exactly free. He levied a
toll on his guests and that toll was known as Ruski. Ruski
was a purple-gray cat. The color is known as Russian blue,
so he called his cat Ruski.

"You see, he's a KGB colonel and bucking for
general."

They thought this was funny at first; someone would
say something and he would ask, "What do you think
about that, Ruski?" and translate Ruski's answer back,
which was always tactless and insulting.

And Ruski had questions for the guests . . . personal
questions.

"Ruski wants to know if you two have made up yet."
Addressed to a discreet gay couple who thought nobody
knew about them.

And medical questions.

"He wants to know if it is possible for a qualified surgeon to mistake a vein for a tendon."

Doctor Stein flushed with rage. He had escaped a mal-
practice suit through the protective silence of his fellow
doctors.

And Ruski *hissed* at the doctor. There was some uncanny bond between him and that animal.

And financial questions. "Ruski wants to know if
you're unloading Park Utah Mines on your friends while
you slide out from under before it caves in."

And legal questions. Needless to say by now every-body is dead fed up with Ruski.

But some kept coming for the free food and liquor. And no doubt they wanted to be in on the finale.

"Will no one rid us of this cursed Ruski?"

"Ruski is sulking because he hasn't been promoted. I keep telling him he must pull some brilliant coup."

"You see the 5-26 chaps with their—" He inclined his head to Ruski. "—cousins?" "Oh yes, of course . . . the *American* cousins—" Doesn't Ruski express himself well "—are onto a very interesting gold leak via . . . Laos is it? To Hong Kong."

So if Ruski can intercept Operation Gas Leak . . . "He calls it OGLe, now isn't that cute??"

A room full of agents with their bare poker faces hanging out. Then Ruski goes behind the sofa and comes out with a piece of poisoned meat and drops it at the CIA man's feet. The man's face goes black with rage . . . an inarticulate snarl breaks from him and I expect to see a mushroom cloud burst out the top of his head and he lashes out at Ruski with a loaded cane. Ruski's skull cracks like an egg, spattering the guests with blood and brains. A woman snatches up her mink stole.

"You beast!" she screams at the CIA man, and there is a general walkout. They all wanted Ruski dead but they didn't want to be associated with the act like Henry II didn't want to be implicated in the offing of lousy Becket (they say that under his hair shirt he was crawling with lice, a walking affront to sanitation).

A year later I ran into the CIA man at the Parade Bar in Tangiers. He had lost weight and his hands shook. I noticed he would reach down to the floor from time to time with a stroking movement.

So I think what the hell, I don't have to pussyfoot around with this spook on the skids.

"Say, do you remember Ruski?"

He smiled. "Of course. It's time we went home to din-ner, isn't it, Ruski?"

He walks out. The bartender shrugs.

"The ghost cat. No one can figure out if he really believes it . . . could be just an act."

"He believes it," I said. "You see, I know Ruski very well. Ruski is my cat . . . always was, old sport."

Jane Yolen

Jane Yolen has well over 150 books out, most of them for children and young adults. Her most recent publications include the illustrated fairy tales *Good Griselle* and *The Girl in the Golden Bower*, as well as the young-adult fantasy novels *The Wild Hunt* and *Passager*. Yolen is also the editor of her own imprint with the book publisher Harcourt, Brace and has edited anthologies, including, most recently, *Xanadu 3*. She has had stories chosen for *The Year's Best Horror* twice and has been in *The Year's Best Fantasy and Horror* for her stories and poems several times. She says, "There is a talking cat in *The Wild Hunt* who is something of a manipulative horror, but very beautiful. And many cat poems in my poetry collection *Raining Cats and Dogs*. Over the years I have run through (but not over) a number of cats. My last cat, Amber, died at Christmas 1991, and I haven't had the heart or the energy to get another." She and her husband have homes in Massachusetts and Scotland and travel often in between.

There is an actual book called *Flattened Fauna* that is both serious classification guide to roadkill and humorous in its grisly way. Its companion volume is *What Bird Did That?*, also for automobile drivers. I kid you not.

Flattened Fauna
Poem # 37: Cats

JANE YOLEN

1.
Imprint:
a coroner's mark,
macadam outlined
with pussy's failure,
a blemish of a life,
a simple stain.

2.
Crows:
black as priests,
their absolution
is final,
their forgiveness
in the beak.

3.
Bones:
each a small coffin
cradling marrow,
each a small boat
across a river,
a finger pointing blame.

4.
Skin:
broken bag,
spillage,
the final way
to skin a.

5.
Blood:
drunk by the thirsty road,
sucked in by cement,
drained, drawn,
decanted,
the sub-
traction.

6.
Cry:
It was too quick for a cry,
except the wind cries
above the road,
the crows cry
above their meal,
the child cries
in her bed.

Storm Constantine

Storm Constantine has written nine fantasy and science fiction novels, including the Wraeththu trilogy, *Enchantments of Flesh and Spirit, Bewitchments of Love and Hate,* and *Fulfillments of Fate and Desires.* Her tenth novel, *Stalking Tender Prey,* is a contemporary dark fantasy, inspired by the mythology of fallen angels.

Constantine's short fiction has appeared in *Interzone* and in the anthologies *Black Thorn, White Rose* and *New Worlds 1.* She writes full time, manages a rock band, and works for various other bands as a writer for their information services and fanzines. She lives in the historic county of Staffordshire in the United Kingdom, where the stately home and its baroque monuments are to be found, which provided the inspiration for this story.

Much of Constantine's fiction moves gracefully between science fiction and fantasy and often contains "techno-goth" sensibilities. "Of a Cat, But Her Skin" is most definitely fantasy and invokes the power of the cat and its relationship to the female and to the occult.

Of a Cat, But Her Skin

STORM CONSTANTINE

SHE RAN INTO the shadows of the trees, downhill, down the worn paths. He called after her "Nina! Nina!" She ignored it. Her sandaled feet hit the bare earth. Another afternoon ruined, another scene. Am I mad? Only anger, exasperation, gave her the strength and the freedom to run away. And that too would be brief. Still, the experience while it lasted was exhilarating. He did not run after her, knowing she would return eventually, contrite.

Soon her chest began to ache and she slowed her pace to a walk, panting heavily. She felt shaky at the exertion, but tingling, too. For minutes, maybe an hour, she was free. Free of him, her weakness. This was a deserted part of the garden, far from the restored Victorian tearooms, the landscaped formal pleasances, the slowly moving river. Nina preferred this kind of scenery, with its great old trees, hugged by lush grass, too green to be real, perhaps nurtured by unhealthy secrets buried deep. Woody nightshade tumbled across the path, bearing dark purple velvety flowers, with spears of shocking yellow at their hearts. Amaradulcis; the bittersweet poison. It seemed no one had walked here for years. Sunlight came down through the high canopy of oak and beech, stroking raw perfume from the herbs and grasses. Nina paused and took a deep breath. In such an idyll as this, could the real world with all its terrors, cruelties, and abuses ever intrude? She felt protected, tranquil, as if the path had closed behind her. Scott would call this yet another symptom of her "dreaminess," as he referred to it. "You're too dreamy; that's your trouble."

Perhaps it was true, but if so, why should that be seen as a flaw?

The trees receded and revealed a small glade, ceilinged by ancient branches. A green room. The path seemed to end here. At the center of the clearing was a weathered black monument; there were many of them scattered around the grounds of the old house. Some had been defaced over the years, others restored. This one appeared unmarked by human vandalism, but neither had it recently been cleaned. A stone dais of two steps supported a wide, four-sided obelisk. Crouched on the apex was the statue of a lean cat. It was frozen in a pose of alertness, a hunter's stoop, forever gazing back along the path, as if waiting to pounce. Nina sat down on the steps and put her hot face into her hands. What am I going to do? She had asked herself this question many times. The constant arguments with Scott, the groundless accusations, the pestilent silences that gnawed away at her resolve would never go away; she knew that. And yet she felt so powerless, in a financial and emotional sense. She had some money of her own, but not much. She was an illustrator of children's books but was neither well known nor well paid. Scott, a successful designer, held the reins of her life; she was trapped in the traces. But there were good days, weren't there? And she did love him, despite his jealousies, which were fretful and anxious, and therefore cruel. She knew the problem was his and that it ran very deep. Sometimes, in dark moments of bare honesty, he would weep like a child in fear and frustration. Because of this, she could never leave him. He was a casualty of his own life.

The argument that afternoon had been senseless, as usual. They were taking a couple of well-earned weeks off work, renting a cottage in the country only a short distance from the city where they lived. So far, they had spent every day exploring local historical sights. Both of them were interested in the past. Admittedly, things had been fine until today, no arguments at all. But something had ignited his temper. The paintings in the hall of Elwood Grange. Nina had admired them: fading reminders of a past age; lords and ladies of haughty mien, long dead, staring down at the milling masses for eternity, disdainful of those who came to pick over their remains. Without thinking, she had remarked that one of the couples portrayed were very striking for their time. "They have an almost twentieth-century look," she'd said. "They look like a couple of rock stars, or perhaps people who run a dodgy religion!" Her light comments were a grave mistake.

Scott said nothing at first and then, outside on the wide, sweeping steps, with the heat of summer baking the arms and bare heads of the tourists, he'd presented his sulk to her. Nina had been confused at first. What had she done? She could think of nothing. Nina was used to living her life by walking on eggshells and had become very adept at doing so. If the fragile shells broke nowadays, it was rarely because of anything she'd actually said or done, but something generated in the hot, aching nest of Scott's fecund paranoia.

"What is it?" she'd asked, wondering if someone else inside the Grange had upset him.

He'd walked off, between a stand of yews, toward the river. She'd followed. "What is it?"

Eventually, the time came for him to wheel round on her. "You always like men who are nothing like me! I don't know why you're with me! You're just sponging off me!"

Nina was aghast. Weariness was invoked immediately as her body reacted in its accustomed manner to verbal attack. "I don't know what you mean," she said.

Scott made an explosive sound. "That pretty fucker in the painting!" He strode off.

Nina followed. "Scott! Don't be absurd!"

They had argued all the way to the river, along the gravel path, past the gazebo and the folly Grecian temple. Eventually, like a chemical flooding her system, something clicked on in Nina's mind. Enough! She almost felt the physical change.

Uttering a wordless cry, she'd fled, prompting curious stares from other tourists.

What now? Nina leaned back against the cool stone. It

was so peaceful here. She wondered at the significance of
the place. Why the narrow path through the trees to this
glade, why the monument dominated by a cat? Scott had
the guidebook in his jacket pocket. She wished she'd kept it
in her shoulder bag. There was a definite presence to this
place, something brooding, and yet she did not feel discomfitted by it. If anything, it echoed her mood. She felt strongly
that she would not be pursued here and even doubted
whether any other tourists would appear along the path.
This was her time and, for these scant moments, her place.
It happened to her sometimes. Just when she needed them,
she found sanctuaries. It could be an empty car park, a deserted alley, a wooden bench in a park. But whenever she
found them, she experienced an encompassing feeling of security, and apartness. Had this only happened to her since
she'd lived with Scott? She couldn't remember.

Nina stood up and jumped off the steps, walked
around the clearing, looking up at the monument. She'd
always wanted a cat, but Scott didn't like them. She felt
unable to persevere, sure that if she acquired a kitten, it
would suffer at Scott's hands. He wouldn't be overtly
cruel, but she envisioned it would not be allowed in at
night and most of the house would be off-limits to it.
There would be complaints about mess and smells and
hair. Might as well not have one. She realized, with bitter
regret, that was her answer to everything. Easier to give in,
to let him have his way. The tense atmosphere in the house
when she defied him seemed to burn her skin. She could
not bear it.

Behind the monument, the stone was lichened and
damp, and it seemed to be less weathered. Details of carvings could easily be discerned. Nina mounted the steps
again, slippery here with moss, and put her fingers against
the stone. A legend written here. Message from the past. She
traced the word "mau." There was a carving of the sun and
moon, and the words "who shall play with a wooded
prey." Perhaps the person who built the monument had not
liked cats. Nina examined the other sides of the obelisk, but
all the engravings were in Greek or Latin. On the most dete-

riorated side, that facing the path, she thought she discerned Egyptian hieroglyphics. An eclectic arcanum. Nina smiled. She had already read in the guidebook about how one of the nineteenth-century earls of the estate had dabbled in the dark arts. Who, in the aristocracy, hadn't done at that time? she wondered. It seemed to have been fairly prevalent then. Gleeful tourist pamphlets sermonized about the mysterious trips abroad, the exposure to exotic belief systems, the desire to transcend the mundane in lives shorn by wealth of petty worries. Nina and Scott had visited many estates in order to search for the folly clues left by past incumbents who'd not been able to resist leaving proof of their obsessions behind, for those who chose to look for them. Nina had rarely felt anything unusual in these places, and she was sensitive to atmospheres.

Now she stroked the damp, cool stone of the monument and wondered. Her imagination supplied a history for it. The obelisk would have been commissioned by the woman in painting, she of the petrol-blue gown, the heavy brows, the modern features. She had been a witch, of course, a cocelebrant with her partner of arcane delights. The guidebook spoke of earls and scholarly mysticism; the true sorcery remained secret. Nina smiled. Here, the cat, symbol of woman in her most terrifying aspect. Not she of claw and fang and raised cry, nor of motherhood and nurturing, but she of the night, of treachery sheathed with eloquence, of the ability to torture without compassion, of stealth, hidden beauty and disdain, the allure that could wither men's hearts, destroy them. Nina was sure that these were the things men feared existed unseen in women. Although they could never witness the true witcheries of female kind, which Nina thought were intensely personal and impossible to articulate, men found the potential of their existence all the more fascinating and terrifying. She felt that men were always trying to guess what went on in the secret selves of women. Groping to understand a virtually alien species, they imagined they knew the hearts of women, but they could never actually be sure whether the secrets existed or not. And yet, even as they feared, and

struck out in every way at the object of their terror, they
yearned for their dark suppositions to be realized. The
goddess beneath the skin. The potent, unspoken strange-
ness that separated women from men was, Nina believed,
the very thing that bound men to them. The cat, the familiar of darkness, was perhaps the most enduring symbol
of this secret power. Nina wondered if that was why she
was so drawn to the animal. She herself felt very much in
tune with all that the cat represented. The dark, vengeful
sibling of the bright, yielding girl. She Who Must Not Be
Unleashed. Nina wondered whether she was alone in feeling the presence of this coiled inner self, an aspect of her
being she had to control with a firm hand, or whether all
women felt her crouching there inside. Nina had never unleashed the cruel one, and never wanted to, fearful she'd
be unable to hide it inside herself again afterward. But in
moments of emotional crisis, she was always conscious of
the coiled one's presence, her voice.

She smiled and patted the stone, said, "Mau!" The feline: a symbol of liberty, because no animal is as opposed
to restraint as a cat. Let any unwelcome intruder tread the
path to her grove with caution.

He was still waiting for her, sitting on the bank of the lazy
river, throwing stones into the central current. Nina walked
up behind him. She felt excoriated yet vigorous. Her weariness was not rekindled by the sight of his back, rigid with
misery. She experienced, in a moment of blinding clarity, a
supreme yet serene pity for the man. He would not, and
could not, ever grow up emotionally, and yet the strengths
of childhood had died in him. She sat down beside him.
He turned to look at her, censure in his face. She could not
care about it. "Are you hungry?" she asked. "Let's go eat."

He did not mention the argument, which was unusual. She thought he looked at her with wary puzzlement
throughout the rest of the day.

The following morning, they drove back to the city. Nina
felt removed from reality; she could not stop daydreaming.

Scott, as if sensing her mood, was temperate. They addressed one another across a tidy boundary. They were supposed to have stayed in the cottage for another day, but rain had come—a downpour—too heavy to walk out in. And the rooms of the cottage were gloomy; too small for people with sensitive skins to occupy together.

Nina was relieved to get home—she always was—but regretted not being able to investigate the cat monument further. That evening, she browsed through the guidebook to Elwood Grange. The house itself was not that remarkable, she thought, and the grounds predictable, but for the hidden place where the monument stood. The obelisk was not listed in the index of follies to be found at Elwood, but a map of the gardens showed that the book was out of date and that the glade with the monument had not been open to the public when it had been published. Flicking through the pages, Nina noticed a photograph of the painting that had caused her argument with Scott. Lady Sydelle and Rufus, Earl of Thurlow. They had been young when the portrait had been painted. Dark garments, dashing, almost foreign-looking features, glossy black hair. They had to be brother and sister, of course, not husband and wife as she'd first thought. The background, like their clothes, was dark; a dusky landscape. Only their white faces and hands glowed from the picture. Lady Sydelle's fingers were curled over something on her lap. Nina lifted the book to hold the photograph close to her table lamp. Her heart contracted. There was a cat on the lady's lap. Nina lowered the book. She had to see the picture again, and the monument. She felt as if she had discovered something marvelous. She glanced across at Scott, who was reading yesterday's paper, a can of beer open by his chair. He was back at work next week. So was Nina, although she didn't have to leave the house for it. She had a children's book to illustrate, and the deadline had almost crept up on her. Still, she could justify a trip out to make sketches. The book was about a witch and her cat.

She mentioned it to Scott in bed. "I'm thinking of going back to Elwood Grange. I'm so behind with my work.

Lack of inspiration, I think, and I saw some great places at Elwood to use in my illos."

"It's a long way for you to drive alone," he said, which was a mild complaint for him.

"I'll take a friend with me," Nina lied.

After Scott had left for work, Nina telephoned Elwood Grange and spoke to the tourist office. Would they be open that day? No. On Mondays, the Grange was closed to the public. Nina expressed disappointment, mentioned her work. The woman on the other end of the phone hesitated for only a moment. "Ah, well, perhaps we can make an exception in that case," she said.

Nina told her she could be at the Grange in two hours, perhaps sooner if the traffic wasn't bad. The only companion she took with her was the guidebook to the Grange, which lay on the passenger seat beside her. She wanted to be home before Scott got back from work, as she hadn't mentioned her trip to him again this morning. Seemed best not to.

The woman Nina had spoken to on the phone was called Lydia Hunt, and had apparently appointed herself as Nina's personal guide for the visit. Nina was disappointed. She'd wanted to roam around alone, but perhaps that had been too much to hope for. Before looking round the house, they had a cup of coffee in Lydia's office, and Nina talked about her work. Lydia thought one of her children might own a book that Nina had illustrated. "People have come here before to research material for books," Lydia said.

Nina nodded. "These old places have their histories, don't they. It's fascinating. A wealth of material to be plundered!"

Lydia smiled. "Mmm. A lot of the old stories are exaggerated for publicity purposes, I think."

"So tell me about Lady Sydelle," Nina prompted, smiling in complicity over her coffee cup.

Lydia laughed. "Ah yes! Of course you would be interested in her!" She gestured with one hand; a confident,

attractive woman, Nina thought. "Lady Sydelle is my favorite character as well. She never married, even though
she was a very beautiful woman, and I imagine local gal-
lants must have thronged her threshold. The money, too,
would have been attractive to them."

"And what were her secrets? I suppose she had some,
or they were invented for her?"

"Her brother, the earl, was rumored to be rather
a rakehell. Well, to put it bluntly, he was an occultist." Lydia pulled a sour face. "Misguided boy! It was he who
commissioned the zodiac ceiling in the music room and the
two Eleusinian folly shrines in the grounds. Lady Sydelle is
not associated with her brother's rather insalubrious pur-
suits, but she did erect the tantalizing obscure obelisk in
the gardens after his death."

"The cat monument," Nina hurriedly interrupted.
She felt breathless, almost faint.

Lydia nodded. "It's actually called the Cat Stane. We
only opened up that part of the gardens last season, and
there's still work to be done there. Scholars presume the
Stane's a bitter joke about Rufus's exploits—the melding
of mystical symbols from several ancient cultures, none of
them making much sense. It's supposed Sydelle was skepti-
cal about the whole thing. She was very fond of Rufus, naturally, and took his death badly. Still, it's an odd memorial."

"How did he die?" The atmosphere in the room
seemed to have become tense. Nina found herself thinking
that, at one time, the servants of Lady Sydelle had occupied
this area of the house; whispers would have been exchanged
here in times of crisis. Perhaps they still bled from the walls.

Lydia shrugged. "Accounts vary, I'm afraid. His neck
was broken. Some say it was caused by a hunting accident,
others that he tumbled headlong down the main stairs in
a drunken stupor. Whatever happened, he lived for nearly a week after the incident. Sydelle nursed him herself
apparently."

"No other legends?"

Lydia narrowed her eyes. "You're looking for mysteries!"

Nina forced a laugh. "Of course I am!"

"Lady Sydelle never divulged her secrets, I'm afraid. After Rufus died, she lived alone here to an advanced age and died peacefully in her sleep. There are no diaries, no local legends. Nothing. She was a respectable woman."

"But the Stane . . ."

Lydia stood up. "Would you like to see it again?"

"Yes." Nina put down her coffee cup and followed Lydia to the door. "Could I see Sydelle's rooms?"

"If you wish, although she left little mark on them. The furniture is late Jacobean, and other people lived there after she died. Her bedroom is part of the guided tour— you've undoubtedly already seen it—but I can show you her parlor, if you like. It's only available for view by appointment."

"Why?"

"The wife of the present earl uses it as an office. But the family are never in residence when the Grange is open to the public."

Nina felt downhearted by the time she and Lydia went out into the gardens. It was a dull day but the lush verdure of high summer was unsuppressed by the louring sky. The green was startling, acidic. The gardens held far more presence than the house itself. Nina had felt nothing in the rooms Lydia had shown her. No shade of Sydelle persisted there.

The two women took a slow stroll down to the obelisk. Nina had collected her sketching pad from the car, intent on making a few quick drawings, even though it seemed her impressions of the monument might have been misguided. Lydia talked about how there was debate whether this untamed area of the gardens should be cleared or not.

"No, it shouldn't be touched!" Nina said.

"I agree," Lydia replied. "It's a pleasant walk."

A cool breeze fretted the leaves of the trees overhead; there was a sense of agitation in the air. Then the monument became visible around a corner.

It is here! Nina thought. The spirit of the place! I wasn't wrong.

"The monument will be cleaned in the autumn, restored," Lydia said.

Nina mounted the steps, wondering whether her guide would approve of that, and touched the stone. "I like it the way it is."

Lydia peered at the hieroglyphics. "It's a shame some of the inscriptions are damaged. This one was perhaps the most intriguing."

"What did it say? Do you know?"

"It is still readable, just, if you can translate the symbols. I understand it says something like 'what can you own of a cat but her skin.' "

"How true," Nina murmured, holding the words in her mind.

Lydia gave her an odd glance. Perhaps she was beginning to think her visitor was a little too intense. "Well, shall I leave you to your drawing? Call back into the office before you leave and have another drink." She glanced at the sky. "Don't stay out here if it rains!"

"Thank you," Nina said.

Lydia hesitated, as if she were about to say something, and then retreated up the path without speaking. Nina did not move for a few moments, so that the atmosphere could close behind Lydia's departing figure. Then she moved back from the monument, so that she could look up at the cat. Perhaps she should have brought a camera with her. The animal looked as if it was waiting for something. Nina's hand moved quickly over the pages of her sketch pad. She meant to draw faithful representations of the obelisk but was continually drawn to depict the somber figure of a woman standing just behind the stone. Her skin prickled. She felt that soon the figure would manifest before her. Lady Sydelle; her hand against the cold stone of her private statement. What is your secret? Nina whispered. Tell me. She felt the answer was relevant to her own life. It was no coincidence she'd found this place.

Nina basked in the atmosphere of the glade; it was like rolling over and over in fur. When the rain came, she covered her sketch pad with her jacket and threw out her arms to the sky, let the fast, heavy drops fall onto her. Rain pattered against the foliage around her. She heard distant thunder. Nina shivered, glanced at her watch. What was she doing? If she didn't leave quickly, Scott would be home before her. Where had the afternoon gone?

There was no time to share another coffee with Lydia Hunt, but Nina briefly put her head round the door of the woman's office and thanked her for her help. "My pleasure," said Lydia. There was no offer of a repeat visit. She seemed affronted by the sight of Nina's soaked clothes and hair.

Nina raced down the country lanes, away from Elwood Grange. She felt excited, as if she were going to meet a new lover, which of course she was not. Sad to be so excited about nothing. She pushed a cassette into the tape player, but the music was intrusive. She turned it off. Lady Sydelle, what happened in your life? Nina felt that she knew. The lady had never married, and the brother had been a rogue. Women of that time had little freedom, bound by convention, by financial dependence. Even the privileged were subject to such restraints. The closeness of the two figures in the portrait was surely unnatural for brother and sister? Was that it, then? Incest? But how could she murder a man she loved? The thought came into Nina's head so forcefully, she had to slow down.

Oh my God . . .

Nina pulled into the next passing place and stopped the car. She leaned her forehead against the steering wheel. It seemed so obvious to her. Sydelle had both loved and hated her brother Rufus. Her emotions had been complex, beyond simple understanding. Magic. Darkness. A cat upon the stairs. A fall. Nina heard the cry, echoing. The footsteps of servants and a tall, slim figure in the shadows at the top of the stairs; a white face, watchful. The figure turned away from the chaotic scene of yelling servants, of blood upon the marble floor below. Something small ran ahead of her up the dimly lit corridor. A black shape, a cat. Of course she nursed him. Of course. "Who shall play with a wounded prey." She would have kissed his paralyzed body. Her cat would have sat upon his chest, tasted his breath. Her soul was her own; dark and potent, full of repressed power, a power that had been repressed in women for centuries. He could direct her physical body, but her soul, her mind, no! What could he own of her, but her skin?

The sky was so dark, it was like twilight. Nina started the car, switched on the windshield wipers, resumed her journey. On the motorway, she turned on the cassette tape. Faster cars hissed by her. She felt relaxed, at ease.

Scott was already home by the time Nina let herself into the house. "Hi!" she called brightly. Scott appeared in the hall, wiping his hands on a towel.

"My God, what happened?" Nina cried. His face was bleeding, scratched.

"Where the hell have you been?" Scott demanded, ignoring her question.

"I told you: Elwood." Nina went to look at his cuts. "You look like you've been attacked!"

Scott pulled away from her. "I have! How many times do I have to tell you to check all doors and windows are locked before you go out? You left the kitchen window wide open. It's lucky we have anything left in the house! Anyone could have got in. As it was, we did have a visitor. I found it making itself at home in my chair. Bloody animal!"

"A cat!" Nina said. She wanted to laugh, but managed to repress the urge.

"I don't know what you're grinning at. Damn thing nearly took my eye out when I tried to get rid of it."

"I'm sorry; you're right. I should have checked the windows. I always forget!" Nina breezed past him into the kitchen, noticing his expression of surprise. Normally, she would have curled in on herself, refused to apologize, cringed away from his angry words, which would, of course, have invoked more of them. "Have you started dinner?"

Scott trailed into the kitchen behind her. "No . . ." He knew Nina sometimes bitterly resented doing all the cooking, but she would never say so. He went out to work; she worked at home. It only seemed fair she should cook the meals. She didn't have an hour's drive home through heavy traffic. "What's wrong?" he asked.

Nina shrugged. "Nothing. I feel fine."

"You seem . . . hyped up about something."

"No. I'm not. Shall we order a pizza?"

"If you like." Scott felt uneasy. Buried anxieties patted at their grilles in the depths of his mind.

Nina went to the phone. "What did you do with the cat?"

"It went out the way it came in. Knocked two plants off. I cleared up the mess."

Nina ordered dinner. She felt as if she were about to burst. As she put down the phone, she said, "Scott, I want a cat."

He looked confused. "What?"

"You heard. I was going to mention it tonight. I've always wanted one."

Scott shook his head. "Nina, don't be ridiculous. Who would look after it when we go away? It's such a responsibility. And what about the smell, the . . ."

"Scott, I want a cat."

"I don't think . . ."

"And I'm going to have one." She wondered why she had ever given in so easily to Scott's wishes. What had she been frightened of? It seemed ridiculous now. Scott's strategies involved attack; he was powerless when she attacked first. She marched into the lounge and threw herself down on the sofa.

"You're in a weird mood," Scott said, following her into the room. "Where have you really been? Who were you with!"

Nina threw up her hands and uttered an inarticulate sound of outrage. "I've been to Elwood Grange, alone!"

"I don't believe you! Someone's been saying something to you! You're not yourself."

"Oh, shut up!" Nina's voice was low with contempt. "Do you know, I'm sick of the way things are! I'm sick of your jealousy and your pompous behavior. Do you really think if I had a lover, I'd put up with you! Do me a favor! Things have got to change."

Meekly Scott sat down, staring at her with round, shocked eyes. Nina was staggered by his submissive posture; he was like a dog fearing a slap. She had expected a thunderous row and had braced herself for it. Scott's reaction was the last thing she'd anticipated.

"You're not going to leave me, are you?" he said. It was a child's fear of abandonment.

Nina didn't answer immediately. Was she? She realized she'd always had the choice of walking out. She didn't have to put up with things she didn't like. Lady Sydelle had perhaps not had that choice. Nina had an income, albeit small, but she was not totally dependent. She had become used to a certain standard of living, that was all. "I hope we can sort things out," she said eventually.

The rain came down all night, but the air was hot. Nina opened the bedroom windows wide, and water came in to puddle on the windowsills. Scott made a complaint. Nina told him she'd wipe the water up in the morning. He said nothing more. She decided to make love to him, and let him cling to her afterward. "I love you," he said. "I love you so much." She stroked his hair. Began to doze.

Something jolted her awake. In the darkness, with the sound of rain persistent against the night, the scent of it coming into the room, Nina saw a dark shape on the bed. She was frightened for only a moment. The dark shape stretched out, advanced toward her slowly. So long and lean. Then she heard it purring. Nina pulled the cat toward her, hugged its wet fur against her naked breasts, inhaled its musky perfume. The animal continued to purr rapturously, limp in her arms.

Scott woke up, turned on the lamp, looked at her.

Her face was buried in the black pelt. It was an enormous cat. I don't know her, he thought, I don't know anything about her. He felt that she, like the cat, could leap away from him, out through the window into the wet darkness, knocking things over, breaking things as she went. She turned her head and smiled at him.

"Here's my cat!"

"It's the same one," Scott said in distaste. "The one that scratched me."

"I know. You threw her out, but she's come back." Nina kissed the cat's brow.

Scott risked a strained grin. "It must belong to someone. It's in such good condition. You can't just . . . keep it."

Nina laughed. "No, I can't. No one can own a cat. But she'll stay with me. I know she will."

Scott looked at the muddy paw marks on the pale duvet. He said nothing. Something seemed to have come into the house, something more than a cat.

"She'll stay with me because she wants to," Nina said in a low voice. "And that is the only reason why any two creatures should stay together."

Scott experienced a stab of panic. "Are *we* all right?" he asked.

Nina stared at him for a few moments, stroking the cat's head. Then she nodded. "I think so. Go back to sleep." The cat curled up beside her, and presently she leaned over Scott and turned off the lamp. Rich purrs filled the darkness. Nina thought of the glade at Elwood Grange, the monument, the shadow of a long-dead woman against the stone. Was the obelisk bare of its guardian now? She wondered whether she should go back and see, but perhaps that would be disrespectful toward the power blossoming within her. It was a stupid thought anyway. The stone cat would still be crouched upon the stone, staring back along the lonely path. The statue was still there, but the spirit wasn't. The spirit had moved on to seek another hearth. Had found it.

Lucy Taylor

Lucy Taylor is a full-time writer, a former resident of Florida, now living in the hills outside Boulder, Colorado, with her five cats. Her horror fiction has appeared in *Hotter Blood, Deadly After Dark: Hot Blood 4, Northern Frights, Bizarre Dreams, Splatterpunks 2, High Fantastic, Little Deaths, Book of the Dead 4, The Mammoth Book of Erotic Horror, The Year's Best Fantasy and Horror,* and other anthologies. Her work has also been published in the magazines *Pulphouse, Palace Corbie, Cemetery Dance, Bizarre Bazaar 1992* and *1993,* and *Bizarre Sex and Other Crimes of Passion.* Her short work has been collected in *Unnatural Acts, Close to the Bone,* and *Unnatural Acts and Other Stories.* Her first novel, *The Safety of Unknown Cities* (expanded from the short story of the same title), was a nominee for the Bram Stoker Award.

This traditional ghost story is a departure for Taylor, who has become known for writing visceral erotic horror. It takes place in an insane asylum in Scotland and demonstrates Taylor's versatility as she writes about a woman named Plush.

Walled

LUCY TAYLOR

IT WAS JUST after the twenty-second anniversary of her confinement in Dunlop House Hospital on Glasgow's Carrick Glenn Road that Plush awoke one night and heard the sound of something mewling, trapped inside the wall.

She thought at first it was a young child crying, and, for an instant, it felt as if her heart stuttered to a stop.

She lay there, mesmerized by the sound, which wrenched at her guilt-filled heart with notes as keen and piercing as a shard of bone.

"Forgive me," she whispered, praying it might be Colleen who cried out to her in the darkness.

But no, not a child at all. A cat . . .

. . . *inside the wall.*

A dream, she thought, or some kind of auditory hallucination, although, during all her years here, Plush had never been one of those patients who heard otherworldly voices, alien music crooning odes to suicide and mutilation and cantos to atrocity. Her madness, what little had not been leeched out of her by nearly two decades of stultifying confinement, was of a different nature.

When the sound continued, Plush got out of bed and tiptoed to the single window that overlooked the street. Moving about quietly at night was a habit she'd acquired from the years she'd shared a room with light-sleeping Geraldine, whose stroke the month before had resulted in Plush's relocation to a single room in the north wing of the building. She raised the shade and peered out between wrought-iron grillwork of a sufficiently rococo design— vines ornamented with spirals and cunning coils—to suggest more artistic whimsy than a method of ensuring that the occupants of Dunlop House stayed caged.

At this hour, the steep and winding Carrick Glenn Road was hushed and nearly empty. Wind-whipped litter rustled along the pavement. A pair of punk-haired women, lipsticked and leather-clad, rocked inebriatedly in each other's arms outside the lesbian jazz club across the street.

Plush took in every crannied door and ledge, each bare branch of the scrawny elm outside the Take-Away shop a few doors down.

There was no cat.

The sounds of feline distress had not diminished, though, nor was Plush any less clear as to their source.

Muffled by the bricks, but still unmistakable, the cries emanated from the wall behind her bed.

Quietly Plush pushed the twin bed away from the wall. She got down on her hands and knees and crept along the floorboards, searching for some niche or crevice where a cat might hide.

There was no such nook, no acceptably spacious cranny. No place a mouse, much less a cat, could crawl.

And yet the cries persisted.

Plush found herself weeping with despair and helplessness. The sound reminded her of what she wanted to forget: that she, too, was a prisoner. Whatever the circumstances of the animal inside the wall, she was in no more position to help the wretched creature than she was to free herself.

Nonetheless, she put her lips against the cold brick and whispered, "It's all right. Be brave. I'll help you."

Although she had been admitted to Dunlop House twenty-two years earlier, Plush was certain that she had, in fact, gone mad not prior to but in the course of her incarceration there.

Madness of monotony and boredom had caught up to her within the very walls of the asylum that purported to be capable of healing her, its claim on her mind increasing exponentially the more closely it was bracketed by the visits of tutting and bespectacled doctors claiming to possess a cure.

But what Plush considered sanity, her doctors regarded as clear proof of its absence, and by the time, according to their standards, she was sufficiently dulled and grounded by captivity to pass for sane on their bleak terms, they found her case no longer of sufficient interest to contemplate release.

Neither affluent nor educated and female besides (three conditions that added up to near hopelessness of anyone's taking her plight seriously), Plush was the eldest daughter of a cattle farmer and his wife from Stromness on the island of Orkney off Scotland's northern coast. A peculiar and reclusive child, she was close only with her grandfather Mooney, a fisherman who claimed to have seen a vision of the Virgin Mary while being held in a Japanese prison camp in World War II.

No one gave much credence to Mooney's tale, except for Plush, who'd experienced enough visions of her own to perceive such things as ordinary. She had her own name, in fact, for the dull and limited range of perception most people seemed confined to: the Narrows.

She had few words, however, to describe the miracles that sometimes visited her, but would wander the shore alone for hours beside the glittering North Sea, eyes slitted down to the thinness of incisions, bedazzled by the swirl and glamour of her private universe, the haunted murmuring of the wind, the baleful lamentations of the tides.

And, as an artist paints his or her most secret mindscapes, so Plush's thoughts unfurled like so much blank canvas and let the Universe scrawl across her senses its mysteries and magic, lush secrets that bewitched and titillated, and appalling, wondrous doodles of the perverse and blasphemous.

When her sight was at its keenest, she could slip between the sea and sky at the horizon fold where they converged like silken labia and penetrate a realm of arcane geometry, where time unfurled in bends and coils and seasons were spawned, not in straight lines but spirals, the future turning in upon itself to birth the past and present, all

three as singularly knit as a single wave that breaks into
several smaller ones upon colliding with the shore.

"A simpleton," the neighbors said behind her back,
and "touched in the head," muttered her own mother, but
Plush knew it was they who lacked for vision, they whose
sight was so limited as to be just short of blind.

They saw the Narrows only. She gazed into the whole
of time and God's design.

Thus she had thrived, a charmed captive to her private dance, until, when she was fifteen, a squall churned
with fatal suddenness across the North Sea, drowning
Mooney and half a dozen other fishermen. Grief and lone-
liness made Plush unwary, heedless. Over the next few
months, she sought comfort in the arms of any boy who
offered her a moment's consolation, conceived a child by
one of them, and was summarily evicted from the house
by her mother, who said, "No daughter of mine is going to
bear a bastard and raise it in my house."

Plush took a job waiting tables at the Braes Hotel and
moved into a small stone cottage near the sea, where she
gave birth, a few months later, to a daughter whom she
named Colleen. The baby was a comfort and a joy and
Plush enjoyed two years of relative tranquillity—until the
day a woman appeared from Children's Aid, acting upon a
complaint from Plush's mother, who had charged her
daughter with being mentally unfit to raise a child and had
decided to seek custody.

Plush was distraught, hysterical. She left her job and
took to wandering the shore alone, bereft of visions now,
beseeching God with panicked prayers to let her keep her
daughter.

In the Orkneys, the winter days are eye-blink brief,
and darkness never fully concedes its hold upon the land.
It was in February, while Plush was meandering along the
chilly shore, that Mooney first emerged from the sea to
greet her. He wore work pants and an old patched sweater,
as if he'd just gotten up from in front of the fire at home,
but his form was gossamer and radiant, shot through with
smoky light.

"Tell no one that you've seen me, but come back alone and walk with me tomorrow," Mooney said. "Be brave. I'll help you."

And he merged back into the glimmer of the sea.

Plush's ecstasy knew no containment. So much so, that she felt compelled to share it. The next day when she came to the shore, she brought Colleen along. The toddler shrieked and clutched at her mother's hand when she saw the old man's spectral outline separate itself from the sparkle of the water and approach them.

The old man's ghost came forward a few paces and then stopped. His edges seemed to bleed away, sucked into the sea like layers of cotton candy licked by an eager child.

He stared at her and appeared to sigh and back away.

"Wait! Don't leave!" Plush cried out.

She charged into the sea, dragging the child behind her. The toddler struggled and screamed as the sea spilled over her, knocking her down.

Plush lifted Colleen up and floated the child in front of her. Oblivious to the danger, she waded deeper. She could see the wraith not more than a few yards ahead now, skimming the pewter water like a low-flying gannet, but more and more of it was fast dissolving, draining into the nearly colorless crease of the horizon.

Tall walls of slate-colored sea crashed over her, cold brine rushing into her throat, numbing her lungs and stopping her breath, and that was when two fishermen who'd been out checking oyster pots grabbed Plush and lifted up Colleen's small corpse and took them both to shore.

They had not, of course, seen Mooney. They had only seen a woman battling her way into deep surf, dragging her child facedown through the waves, and they were keen to testify as to the horror of it.

Plush was accused of murder and of attempted suicide. Police were summoned, then a battalion of doctors. A trial was held in Inverness on Scotland's mainland. Plush was deemed criminally insane and sent to Glasgow.

Thus she languished for the next two decades in the two-hundred-year-old house on Carrick Glenn Road that had served, in the previous century, as a monastery. In such an atmosphere, beset with guilt and boredom, Plush's visions, once her refuge, had seeped away like rare perfume decimated by the stench of offal. The bleak and sterile Narrows had opened up and sucked Plush down as surely as the cold North Sea had claimed her daughter.

There were no more visions now, no more universe of runes and thralldom, of rotting life and lushly flowering death. Only the stultifying half-life of what others deemed reality and her own burden of self-blame . . .

. . . until the night the cat cried out behind the wall and opened up a tiny rent in the fabric of the Narrows.

In the mornings, inmates of Dunlop House were encouraged to spend time in the dayroom, a dingy and bespotted parlor where visitations took place. There were splotches on the walls—the most unsavory of ochers and the gray of clotted sperm—and a heart-shaped stain where a lovestruck schizophrenic had once painted her and her lover's names inside a heart described by her own menstrual blood.

Nearly a fortnight had passed since Plush first heard the cat. The cries were no feebler now than at the outset, though more sporadic, coming at all hours of the night to torment her waking time and permeate her dreaming.

"Is someone keeping a cat?" she asked Sister Lorna, gazing at the nun's gaunt, pinched face, pale and shiny as a well-licked lollipop. "I thought I heard one yowling yesterday."

She tried to sound as offhand about this as possible, but one does not spend two decades removed from normal society and still retain the skills of artifice and guile.

Sister Lorna made a you-poor-benighted-dear face and said, "You know perfectly well there are no animals in here."

Plush tried to look forlorn as she said, "Perhaps I'm only lonely and my ears are playing tricks. I do miss Geraldine so much. I was wondering if I might visit her."

Sister Lorna made a small froggy harrumph, her cue that she felt the request to be an imposition on her already frayed good nature, and said, "Geraldine's still very ill. She might not be ready for visitors. And her face . . . the stroke has left her changed, you understand."

Plush nodded, but her persistence wore Sister Lorna down. Thus, a few days later, a nurse escorted her to Geraldine's bedside in the hospital wing of the asylum, where her former roommate lay with one half of her face apparently in peaceful slumber, the other half contorted in a silent, simian howl.

Plush knew the stroke had destroyed the nerves in one side of Geraldine's face, but she'd been unprepared for the extent of the damage. She'd never dreamed that anything so terrible could befall dear Geraldine who, after all, was a witch, the former Queen of the Lothian Wiccan Order. She had romped skyclad through pagan rituals in her fashionable Edinburgh home and claimed, before she poisoned her drunkard husband into a coma, to converse with the spirits of Aleister Crowley and Saint Magnus. Now she was merely pitiful and old and, until her stroke, had spent most of her time reading the mysteries and history books her children dutifully sent over. Geraldine also functioned as Dunlop House's unofficial librarian. For those who wouldn't read or didn't dare expend the effort for fear of draining minds already sadly overtaxed she was a source of information, rumor, history.

Now, as Plush stared down at her old friend with frank distress, the woman's good eye popped open and a silver trail of saliva threaded its way out of the corner of the dead half of her mouth.

"Here you go, m'dear."

A nurse brought Geraldine her lunch: a bowl of lentil soup and buttered roll, a small, hard brick of cheese. Geraldine complained that it was difficult for her to eat, what with half her face unworkable, so Plush broke up the bread into tiny bits and spooned green broth into the good side of Geraldine's mouth, wiping her face clean after each spoonful.

"Enough," Geraldine said finally, pushing the food away. She fixed hawkish, deep-set eyes on Plush and mumbled in her slurred, stroke-victim's voice, "Something's wrong with you. You got that lost-dog look."

Plush, already close to tears, blurted out, "The new room that they put me in after you got sick ... there's something in there with me ... something *alive*."

She was afraid that Geraldine would laugh. Instead, she asked, "Which room is it you're in?"

"First floor," said Plush, "on the corner."

"North wing?"

"Yes."

Geraldine touched a palsied finger to a chin porcine with bristles.

"And would it be ... by any chance ... a cat that you'd be hearin'?"

At that, Plush's hand trembled so that lentil soup leaked down onto the bed. "How is it that you know?"

Geraldine gave a ragged smile. "Ah, so it's true. There *was* a cat."

"What do you mean was? Have you heard it for yourself?"

"Not I, for which I thank sweet Gaia. Just something that I read had happened back when Dunlop House was being built. I had no reason to think it true, but now, with this, the story in the history book would seem to be confirmed."

Plush hated it when her old friend spoke in riddles. "I don't understand."

"Ah," said Geraldine, while the good half of her face smiled and the other half toffee-pulled into something approximating morbid glee, "you weren't aware that Dunlop House was founded on the blood of an innocent creature?"

"What do you ..."

Geraldine shook her gray Medusa locks and grinned a gap-toothed double-double-toil-and-trouble grin. "Don't look so frightened. You've not gone mad. It *is* a cat you're hearin', sure as day."

"But ... we ought to tell someone, oughtn't we? We ought to get it out."

"It's dead, you goose. Been dead two hundred seven years, since this hellhole was first built."

"But how . . ."

"Bricking a live cat up inside a wall . . . it was a fiendish custom that got started in the Middle Ages. The besotted Christian savages thought a cat had supernatural powers, so they'd sacrifice one to ensure good fortune for the building and all who lived or worked there."

"Are you sure?"

"I've read a lot of history books these thirty years since I put strychnine in the old man's haggis," said Geraldine. "A lot I do forget, but not so terrible a thing as this. A cat was bricked up in the corner of the north wall, to bring good fortune to the Dunlop family and their building."

"All those years," said Plush, appalled. "But I tell you, it's alive. I hear it crying."

"It died two hundred seven years ago," said Geraldine. "What you hear, if you hear anything at all, then it's a ghost."

"I've got to help it."

"It's *dead*," said Geraldine. "Even if its ghost cries out, you leave it be."

That night when the mewling started, Plush pushed her bed to one side and put her ear against the wall. A cat, a baby, whatever . . . the creature was in terrible distress. She listened to the cries and whispered back consolements. Pain called to pain. Plush's skin began to roil. Gooseflesh ebbed and flowed along her arms.

She closed her eyes.

For a moment, she had a glimpse beyond the Narrows, of Colleen's small form being battered by the sea. Colleen's arms were up above her head. Bright water spattered between her fingers like golden needles, but the child's back was turned, and Plush couldn't tell if she was merely romping in the sea or gripped by mortal fear.

Plush pressed her mouth against the wall. "I'll get you out," she whispered.

From her shoe, she took the spoon she'd used for feeding Geraldine and wedged the handle between two bricks, nicking the most minuscule of indentations in the mortar. A few grains of plaster dusted down. She scraped again. The mortar was ancient, crumbly.

Plush pushed the bed back into place, lay down.

Be brave. I'll help you.

It was a start.

By the end of the week, Plush's night-long labors had been rewarded with four loosened bricks, all of which she had been able to dislodge and then replace by morning. She'd also swiped a butter knife from the kitchen while the cook was in the loo and kept it hidden, along with Geraldine's spoon, inside one of the sturdy black shoes her sister Belle had sent her for Christmas. The work was tedious and painstaking and many times Plush thought of giving up. But then the cat would cry again, and tears would course along Plush's plump cheeks, and she'd think of Mooney and of the baby daughter she had given to the sea, and how that child must call for her across the Void, and she'd resume her work.

There were no more escapes, however briefly, from the Narrows now, except one day when Plush, returning to her room after the evening meal, saw someone had tossed a scarf upon her bed. She reached up for the light switch, then stopped.

The scarf on the bed stirred, uncoiled itself into something vaguely feline, catlike and yet like no cat, spectral or otherwise, that Plush had ever seen. Its fur, the color of dark marmalade, was intact only in part. Portions of its fragmented anatomy were visible through parchment skin, tissue-paper thin, and when it leapt from bed to floor, Plush saw its head was still unformed, less cat than lumpen papier-mâché mask with mouth and cheekbones missing.

"Oh, God," she said, and reached out to offer comfort to the creature.

At once the ill-formed thing froze with alarm and hackled up what hair it had to raise. It bounded round the room in panicked flight, then leapt up and was gone.

Into the wall . . .

* * *

"Wake up," said Sister Lorna. "You sleep too much these days." The nun pulled back Plush's windowshades, let midmorning light spring across the room like yellow tigers. "Be packin' up your things today. You'll be gettin' a new room tomorrow and a roommate."

Plush rolled over, still half wedded to a dream in which a flock of skeletal gulls, their tiny bones luminous in the moonlight, plucked Colleen's body from the sea and carried it aloft, wheeling and dipping so that the child's head hung down, revealing empty eye sockets nibbled clean by fishes.

The ghost gulls swooped into the bedroom and tore at Sister Lorna's head, and Plush blinked hard and came awake in terror.

"What?"

"I said you'll be gettin' a new roommate."

"But why?"

As if embarrassed to concede that one of Dunlop House's inmates had made an escape of sorts, Sister Lorna lowered her eyes to her spare bosom and said, "Geraldine won't be coming back anymore. She . . . went home last night."

An image came to Plush: of Geraldine's soul spiraling smaller and smaller like the whorls of a Nautilus shell and of that world outside the Narrows where her visions had once led. Gone now, the gateway closed to her.

"She died."

The translation from euphemism to hard fact irritated Sister Lorna, who began to brush away imaginary lint from her starched shoulders with rapid swatting motions.

"In any case," she said, "we've decided to use the single rooms for short-term stays, those who'll be gettin' out eventually. So we'll be movin' you to a double room tomorrow."

Bleak despair dogged Plush throughout the day. That night, the moment that the lights went out, she pushed her bed aside, removed the bricks she'd already loosened, and went to work.

Two hundred seven years away, the cat began to

yowl. The sound trembled through Plush's nailbeds, shivered through the tiny hairs inside her ears.

She labored at the bricks and prayed and dug with butter knife and spoon and fingernails.

The removal of the four key bricks made easier the weakening of the surrounding ones. By ocher dawn, Plush had opened up a foot-wide section of the wall. The floor was covered with a thick layer of plaster, Plush's hands and face dusted with grit.

The cat's wailing sounded so loud now she could not believe no one else heard, that all of Dunlop House was not awakened by the cries.

Plush thrust her hands into the hole she'd dug and reached in as far as she could stretch.

"Where *are* you?"

Her hand brushed something stiff and dry that made her think of desiccated flowers pressed between the pages of a book. She gasped and pulled back, tried again. It yielded slightly to her touch, not brick at all, but . . .

Carefully she reached both arms inside the wall and loosened and withdrew the object she had labored so hard to unearth—the body of a cat, preserved and mummified by its centuries inside the wall.

Plush turned it gently in her hands and marveled at it, this thing of almost unreal loveliness and horror. Gossamer ears, translucent, flattened to the head, paws perfectly preserved, right down to the nubs of claws where it had tried to dig its way to freedom. The eyes were gone, of course, sucked dry by dehydration. Plush gazed into the black and vacant holes and thought she glimpsed the swirl of stars in unknown cosmos, heard strike the first melodious chords of lost and alien sound . . .

. . . and tried without success to follow.

She pulled the wondrous remnant to her chest and rocked it as she used to do Colleen, singing softly. It shivered, almost as if on the verge of awakening beneath her hands. Then its reexposure to the air proved too much and it crumbled into powder.

A dead thing—less than that, a pile of dust—lifeless as its empty eyes.

"No!" Plush let the dusty fragments sift through her fingers. She put her face into her hands and cried until her sobbing was interrupted by the softest of meows.

She feared she might have fantasized the sound, but looked up anyway.

A cat, translucent calico, its thick fur an undulating tapestry of auburns, was grooming itself on her bed. Preening, corkscrewing its lithe tail in round G-clefs of pleasure. The creature was complete this time, as perfect as it must have been the day the builders of Dunlop House snatched it for its awful fate.

Plush beheld the sight in awe. How long since she had seen a living animal except on the street outside her window!

And yet, not alive at all, of course.

The ghost completed washing one patterned paw, then stretched up in an S-shape, opening its mouth in a stupendous yawn. It leapt down off the bed, caressing Plush's legs, her buttocks, breadmaking in the soft flesh of her belly without leaving indentations.

"Go home," Plush whispered. "You don't belong here any longer. Go."

The cat swished out smoky figure-eights around her wrists. Its calico design unfurled into a plume of patterned fog, which leapt past Plush . . .

. . . into the wall.

"No. Go *home*."

Plush reached out to try to touch the vision one last time—her fingers came back damp. She put her fingers to her mouth and tasted salt and moisture.

The section of the wall that Plush had opened pulsed brightly, appeared to widen. Plush pushed her hand into the rent.

For some other bend in time, she heard the tide and smelled it, the beating of the sea on rocky shores, the tang of brine . . .

inside the wall

. . . and felt it roll across her then, the extending ripples of an endless shore, where Mooney and Colleen and Geraldine and a multitude of souls washed up like interwoven strands of some vast and undulating carpet before dispersing back again into the whole.

Plush pushed her head and arms inside the opening in the wall and found herself swept into a flow much fiercer than anything the sea had ever shown her. The current of the dead seized her and pulled her in, swept her up in their chilly torrent, and the dead flowed past and through her, tugging at her soul, and she gave in to their entreaties and let her mind sink into the cool dark of their oceanic realm.

"I'll help you, Mummy," Colleen said, approaching her. *"Be brave."*

When Sister Lorna came to take Plush to her new room a few hours later, she found her leaning up against the opened wall, breathing still and strong of heart, but limp and mute, with eyes so blind a light shone directly into them produced no observable reaction. And when they took her to the hospital wing and put her in the bed where Geraldine had died, it was the wraith cat who slipped from behind the wall one final time and padded along the corridors to follow after, not to where they took her body but into sacred realms of mirth and awe where Plush's empty eyes saw holiness.

Stephen King

Stephen King needs little introduction. Since publication of his first novel, *Carrie,* King has been entertaining readers and defying detractors by writing exactly what he wants to write, when he wants to write it. And that includes the occasional short story that has appeared in such varied venues as *Playboy* and *Omni, The Magazine of Fantasy and Science Fiction, Cemetery Dance,* and *The New Yorker.* He won the O. Henry Award and the World Fantasy Award in 1995 for his story "The Man in the Black Suit."

"The Cat from Hell," originally published in *Cavalier,* is a dark little crime drama with a cat playing a prominent and obstructionist role.

The Cat from Hell

STEPHEN KING

HALSTON THOUGHT THE old man in the wheelchair looked sick, terrified, and ready to die. He had experience in seeing such things. Death was Halston's business; he had brought it to eighteen men and six women in his career as an independent hitter. He knew the death look.

The house—mansion, actually—was cold and quiet. The only sounds were the low snap of the fire on the big stone hearth and the low whine of the November wind outside.

"I want you to make a kill," the old man said. His voice was quavery and high, peevish. "I understand that is what you do."

"Who did you talk to?" Halston asked.

"With a man named Saul Loggia. He says you know him."

Halston nodded. If Loggia was the go-between, it was all right. And if there was a bug in the room, anything the old man—Drogan—said was entrapment.

"Who do you want hit?"

Drogan pressed a button on the console built into the arm of his wheelchair and it buzzed forward. Closeup, Halston could smell the yellow odors of fear, age, and urine all mixed. They disgusted him, but he made no sign. His face was still and smooth.

"Your victim is right behind you," Drogan said softly.

Halston moved quickly. His reflexes were his life and they were always set on a filed pin. He was off the couch, falling to one knee, turning, hand inside his specially tailored sport coat, gripping the handle of the short-barreled

.45 hybrid that hung below his armpit in a spring-loaded holster that laid it in his palm at a touch. A moment later it was out and pointed at . . . a cat.

For a moment Halston and the cat stared at each other. It was a strange moment for Halston, who was an unimaginative man with no superstitions. For that one moment as he knelt on the floor with the gun pointed, he felt that he knew this cat, although if he had ever seen one with such unusual markings he surely would have remembered.

Its face was an even split: half black, half white. The dividing line ran from the top of its flat skull and down its nose to its mouth, straight-arrow. Its eyes were huge in the gloom, and caught in each nearly circular black pupil was a prism of firelight, like a sullen coal of hate.

And the thought echoed back to Halston: *We know each other, you and I.*

Then it passed. He put the gun away and stood up. "I ought to kill you for that, old man. I don't take a joke."

"And I don't make them," Drogan said. "Sit down. Look in here." He had taken a fat envelope out from beneath the blanket that covered his legs.

Halston sat. The cat, which had been crouched on the back of the sofa, jumped lightly down into his lap. It looked up at Halston for a moment with those huge dark eyes, the pupils surrounded by thin green-gold rings, and then it settled down and began to purr.

Halston looked at Drogan questioningly.

"He's very friendly," Drogan said. "At first. Nice friendly pussy has killed three people in this household. That leaves only me. I am old, I am sick . . . but I prefer to die in my own time."

"I can't believe this," Halston said. "You hired me to hit a cat?"

"Look in the envelope, please."

Halston did. It was filled with hundreds and fifties, all of them old. "How much is it?"

"Six thousand dollars. There will be another six when you bring me proof that the cat is dead. Mr. Loggia said twelve thousand was your usual fee?"

Halston nodded, his hand automatically stroking the cat in his lap. It was asleep, still purring. Halston liked cats. They were the only animals he did like, as a matter of fact. They got along on their own. God—if there was one—had made them into perfect, aloof killing machines. Cats were the hitters of the animal world, and Halston gave them his respect.

"I need not explain anything, but I will," Drogan said. "Forewarned is forearmed, they say, and I would not want you to go into this lightly. And I seem to need to justify myself. So you'll not think I'm insane."

Halston nodded again. He had already decided to make this peculiar hit, and no further talk was needed. But if Drogan wanted to talk, he would listen.

"First of all, you know who I am? Where the money comes from?"

"Drogan Pharmaceuticals."

"Yes. One of the biggest drug companies in the world. And the cornerstone of our financial success has been this." From the pocket of his robe he handed Halston a small, unmarked vial of pills. "Tri-Dormal-phenobarbin, compound G. Prescribed almost exclusively for the terminally ill. It's extremely habit-forming, you see. It's a combination painkiller, tranquilizer, and mild hallucinogen. It is remarkably helpful in helping the terminally ill face their conditions and adjust to them."

"Do you take it?" Halston asked.

Drogan ignored the question. "It is widely prescribed throughout the world. It's a synthetic, was developed in the fifties at our New Jersey labs. Our testing was confined almost solely to cats, because of the unique quality of the feline nervous system."

"How many did you wipe out?"

Drogan stiffened. "That is an unfair and prejudicial way to put it."

Halston shrugged.

"In the four-year testing period which led to FDA approval of Tri-Dormal-G, about fifteen thousand cats . . . uh, expired."

Halston whistled. About four thousand cats a year. "And now you think this one's back to get you, huh?"

"I don't feel guilty in the slightest," Drogan said, but that quavering, petulant note was back in his voice. "Fifteen thousand test animals died so that hundreds of thousands of human beings—"

"Never mind that," Halston said. Justifications bored him.

"That cat came here seven months ago. I've never liked cats. Nasty, disease-bearing animals . . . always out in the fields . . . crawling around in barns . . . picking up God knows what germs in their fur . . . always trying to bring something with its insides falling out into the house for you to look at . . . it was my sister who wanted to take it in. She found out. She paid." He looked at the cat sleeping on Halston's lap with dead hate.

"You said the cat killed three people."

Drogan began to speak. The cat dozed and purred on Halston's lap under the soft, scratching strokes of Halston's strong and expert killer's fingers. Occasionally a pine knot would explode on the hearth, making it tense like a series of steel springs covered with hide and muscle. Outside the wind whined around the big stone house far out in the Connecticut countryside. There was winter in that wind's throat. The old man's voice droned on and on.

Seven months ago there had been four of them here—Drogan, his sister Amanda, who at seventy-four was two years Drogan's elder, her lifelong friend Carolyn Broadmoor ("of the Westchester Broadmoors," Drogan said), who was badly afflicted with emphysema, and Dick Gage, a hired man who had been with the Drogan family for twenty years. Gage, who was past sixty himself, drove the big Lincoln Mark IV, cooked, served the evening sherry. A day maid came in. The four of them had lived this way for nearly two years, a dull collection of old people and their family retainer. Their only pleasures were *The Hollywood Squares* and waiting to see who would outlive whom.

Then the cat had come.

"It was Gage who saw it first, whining and skulking

around the house. He tried to drive it away. He threw sticks and small rocks at it, and hit it several times. But it wouldn't go. It smelled the food, of course. It was little more than a bag of bones. People put them out beside the road to die at the end of the summer season, you know. A terrible, inhumane thing."

"Better to fry their nerves?" Halston asked.

Drogan ignored that and went on. He hated cats. He always had. When the cat refused to be driven away, he had instructed Gage to put out poisoned food. Large, tempting dishes of Calo cat food spiked with Tri-Dormal-G, as a matter of fact. The cat ignored the food. At that point Amanda Drogan had noticed the cat and had insisted they take it in. Drogan had protested vehemently, but Amanda had gotten her way. She always did, apparently.

"But she found out," Drogan said. "She brought it inside herself, in her arms. It was purring, just as it is now. But it wouldn't come near me. It never has . . . yet. She poured it a saucer of milk. 'Oh, look at the poor thing, it's starving,' she cooed. She and Carolyn both cooed over it. Disgusting. It was their way of getting back at me, of course. They knew the way I've felt about felines ever since the Tri-Dormal-G testing program twenty years ago. They enjoyed teasing me, baiting me with it." He looked at Halston grimly. "But they paid."

In mid-May, Gage had gotten up to set breakfast and had found Amanda Drogan lying at the foot of the main stairs in a litter of broken crockery and Little Friskies. Her eyes bulged sightlessly up at the ceiling. She had bled a great deal from the mouth and nose. Her back was broken, both legs were broken, and her neck had been literally shattered like glass.

"It slept in her room," Drogan said. "She treated it like a baby . . . 'Is oo hungwy, darwing? Does oo need to go out and do poopoos?' Obscene, coming from an old battle-ax like my sister. I think it woke her up, meowing. She got his dish. She used to say that Sam didn't really like his Friskies unless they were wetted down with a little milk. So she was planning to go downstairs. The cat was rubbing against her legs. She was old, not too steady on her feet. Half asleep. They got to the head of the stairs and the cat got in front of her . . . tripped her . . ."

Yes, it could have happened that way, Halston thought. In his mind's eye he saw the old woman falling forward and outward, too shocked to scream. The Friskies spraying out as she tumbled head over heels to the bottom, the bowl smashing. At last she comes to rest at the bottom, the old bones shattered, the eyes glaring, the nose and ears trickling blood. And the purring cat begins to work its way down the stairs, contentedly munching Little Friskies . . .

"What did the coroner say?" he asked Drogan.

"Death by accident, of course. But I knew."

"Why didn't you get rid of the cat then? With Amanda gone?"

Because Carolyn Broadmoor had threatened to leave if he did, apparently. She was hysterical, obsessed with the subject. She was a sick woman, and she was nutty on the subject of spiritualism. A Hartford medium had told her (for a mere twenty dollars) that Amanda's soul had entered Sam's feline body. Sam had been Amanda's, she told Drogan, and if Sam went, *she* went.

Halston, who had become something of an expert at reading between the lines of human lives, suspected that Drogan and the old Broadmoor bird had been lovers long ago, and the old dude was reluctant to let her go over a cat.

"It would have been the same as suicide," Drogan said. "In her mind she was still a wealthy woman, perfectly capable of packing up that cat and going to New York or London or even Monte Carlo with it. In fact she was the last of a great family, living on a pittance as a result of a number of bad investments in the sixties. She lived on the second floor here in a specially controlled, super-humidified room. The woman was seventy, Mr. Halston. She was a heavy smoker until the last two years of her life, and the emphysema was very bad. I wanted her here, and if the cat had to stay . . ."

Halston nodded and then glanced meaningfully at his watch.

"Near the end of June, she died in the night. The doctor seemed to take it as a matter of course . . . just came and wrote out the death certificate and that was the end of it. But the cat was in the room. Gage told me."

"We all have to go sometime, man," Halston said.

"Of course. That's what the doctor said. But I knew. I remembered. Cats like to get babies and old people when they're asleep. And steal their breath."

"An old wives' tale."

"Based on fact, like most so-called old wives' tales," Drogan replied. "Cats like to knead soft things with their paws, you see. A pillow, a thick shag rug . . . or a blanket. A crib blanket or an old person's blanket. The extra weight on a person who's weak to start with . . ."

Drogan trailed off, and Halston thought about it. Carolyn Broadmoor asleep in her bedroom, the breath rasping in and out of her damaged lungs, the sound nearly lost in the whisper of special humidifiers and air conditioners. The cat with the queer black-and-white markings leaps silently onto her spinster's bed and stares at her old and wrinkle-grooved face with those lambent, black-and-green eyes. It creeps onto her thin chest and settles its weight there, purring . . . and the breathing slows . . . slows . . . and the cat purrs as the old woman slowly smothers beneath its weight on her chest.

He was not an imaginative man, but Halston shivered a little.

"Drogan," he said, continuing to stroke the purring cat. "Why don't you just have it put away? A vet would give it the gas for twenty dollars."

Drogan said, "The funeral was on the first day of July, I had Carolyn buried in our cemetery plot next to my sister. The way she would have wanted it. On July third I called Gage to this room and handed him a wicker basket . . . a picnic hamper sort of thing. Do you know what I mean?"

Halston nodded.

"I told him to put the cat in it and take it to a vet in Milford and have it put to sleep. He said, 'Yes, sir,' took the basket, and went out. Very like him. I never saw him alive again. There was an accident on the turnpike. The Lincoln was driven into a bridge abutment at better than sixty miles an hour. Dick Gage was killed instantly. When they found him there were scratches on his face."

Halston was silent as the picture of how it might have been formed in his brain again. No sound in the room but the peaceful crackle of the fire and the peaceful purr of the cat in his lap. He and the cat together before the fire would make a good illustration for that Edgar Guest poem, the one that goes: "The cat on my lap, the hearth's good fire/ . . . A happy man, should you enquire."

Dick Gage moving the Lincoln down the turnpike toward Milford, beating the speed limit by maybe five miles an hour. The wicker basket beside him—a picnic hamper sort of thing. The chauffeur is watching traffic, maybe he's passing a big cab-over Jimmy and he doesn't notice the peculiar black-on-one-side, white-on-the-other face that pokes out of one side of the basket. Out of the driver's side. He doesn't notice because he's passing the big trailer truck and that's when the cat jumps onto his face, spitting and clawing, its talons raking into one eye, puncturing it, deflating it, blinding it. Sixty and the hum of the Lincoln's big motor and the other paw is hooked over the bridge of the nose, digging in with exquisite, damning pain—maybe the Lincoln starts to veer right, into the path of the Jimmy, and its airhorn blares ear-shatteringly, but Gage can't hear it because the cat is yowling, the cat is spread-eagled over his face like some huge furry black spider, ears laid back, green eyes glaring like spotlights from hell, back legs jittering and digging into the soft flesh of the old man's neck. The car veers wildly back the other way. The bridge abutment looms. The cat jumps down and the Lincoln, a shiny black torpedo, hits the cement and goes up like a bomb.

Halston swallowed hard and heard a dry click in his throat. "And the cat came back?"

Drogan nodded. "A week later. On the day Dick Gage was buried, as a matter of fact. Just like the old song says. The cat came back."

"It survived a car crash at sixty? Hard to believe."

"They say each one has nine lives. When it comes back . . . that's when I started to wonder if it might not be a . . . a . . ."

"Hellcat?" Halston suggested softly.

"For want of a better word, yes. A sort of demon sent . . ."

"To punish you."

"I don't know. But I'm afraid of it. I feed it, or rather, the woman who comes in to do for me feeds it. She doesn't like it either. She says that face is a curse of God. Of course, she's local." The old man tried to smile and failed. "I want you to kill it. I've lived with it for the last four months. It skulks around in the shadows. It looks at me. It seems to be . . . waiting. I lock myself in my room every night and still I wonder if I'm going to wake up one early morning and find it . . . curled up on my chest . . . and purring."

The wind whined lonesomely outside and made a strange hooting noise in the stone chimney.

"At last I got in touch with Saul Loggia. He recommended you. He called you a stick, I believe."

"A one-stick. That means I work on my own."

"Yes. He said you'd never been busted, or even suspected. He said you always seem to land on your feet . . . like a cat."

Halston looked at the old man in the wheelchair. And suddenly his long-fingered, muscular hands were lingering just above the cat's neck.

"I'll do it now, if you want me to," he said softly. "I'll snap its neck. It won't even know—"

"No!" Drogan cried. He drew in a long, shuddering breath. Color had come up in his sallow cheeks. "Not . . . not here. Take it away."

Halston smiled humorlessly. He began to stroke the sleeping cat's head and shoulders and back very gently again. "All right," he said. "I accept the contract. Do you want the body?"

"No. Kill it. Bury it." He paused. He hunched forward in the wheelchair like some ancient buzzard. "Bring me the tail," he said. "So I can throw it in the fire and watch it burn."

Halston drove a 1973 Plymouth with a custom Cyclone Spoiler engine. The car was jacked and blocked, and rode with the hood pointing down at the road at a twenty-degree angle. He had rebuilt the differential and the rear end himself. The shift was a Pensy, the linkage was Hearst. It sat on huge Bobby Unser Wide Ovals and had a top end of a little past one-sixty.

He left the Drogan house at a little past 9:30. A cold rind of crescent moon rode overhead through the tattering November clouds. He rode with all the windows open, because that yellow stench of age and terror seemed to have settled into his clothes and he didn't like it. The cold was hard and sharp, eventually numbing, but it was good. It was blowing that yellow stench away.

He got off the turnpike at Placer's Glen and drove through the silent town, which was guarded by a single yellow blinker at the intersection, at a thoroughly respectable thirty-five. Out of town, moving up S.R. 35, he opened the Plymouth up a little, letting her walk. The tuned Spoiler engine purred like the cat had purred on his lap earlier this evening. Halston grinned at the simile. They moved between frost-white November fields full of skeleton cornstalks at a little over seventy.

The cat was in a double-thickness shopping bag, tied at the top with heavy twine. The bag was in the passenger bucket seat. The cat had been sleepy and purring when Halston put it in, and it had purred through the entire ride. It sensed, perhaps, that Halston liked it and felt at home with it. Like himself, the cat was a one-stick.

Strange hit, Halston thought, and was surprised to find that he was taking it seriously *as* a hit. Maybe the strangest thing about it was that he actually liked the cat, felt a kinship with it. If it had managed to get rid of those three old crocks, more power to it . . . especially Gage, who had been taking it to Milford for a terminal date with a crew-cut veterinarian who would have been more than happy to bundle it into a ceramic-lined gas chamber the size of a microwave oven. He felt a kinship but no urge to renege on the hit. He would do it the courtesy of killing it quickly and well. He would park off the road beside one of those November-barren fields and take it out of the bag and stroke it and then snap its neck and sever its tail with his pocketknife. And, he thought, the body I'll bury honorably, saving it from the scavengers. I can't save it from the worms, but I can save it from the maggots.

He was thinking these things as the car moved through the night like a dark blue ghost and that was when the cat walked in front of his eyes, up on the dashboard, tail raised arrogantly, its black-and-white face turned toward him, its mouth seeming to grin at him.

"Sssssshhhh—" Halston hissed. He glanced to his right and caught a glimpse of the double-thickness shopping bag, a hole chewed—or clawed—in its side. Looked ahead again . . . and the cat lifted a paw and batted playfully at him. The paw skidded across Halston's forehead. He jerked away from it and the Plymouth's big tires wailed on the road as it swung erratically from one side of the narrow blacktop to the other.

Halston batted at the cat on the dashboard with his fist. It was blocking his field of vision. It spat at him, arching its back, but it didn't move. Halston swung again, and instead of shrinking away, it leaped at him.

Gage, he thought. *Just like Gage*—

He stamped the brake. The cat was on his head, blocking his vision with its furry belly, clawing at him, gouging at him. Halston held the wheel grimly. He struck the cat once, twice, a third time. And suddenly the road was gone, the Plymouth was running down into the ditch, thudding up and down on its shocks. Then, impact, throwing him forward against his seat belt, and the last sound he heard was the cat yowling inhumanly, the voice of a woman in pain or in the throes of sexual climax.

He struck it with his closed fists and felt only the springy, yielding flex of its muscles.

Then, second impact. And darkness.

* * *

The moon was down. It was an hour before dawn.

The Plymouth lay in a ravine curdled with ground-mist. Tangled in its grille was a snarled length of barbed wire. The hood had come unlatched, and tendrils of steam from the breached radiator drifted out of the opening to mingle with the mist.

No feeling in his legs.

He looked down and saw that the Plymouth's firewall had caved in with the impact. The back of that big Cyclone Spoiler engine block had smashed into his legs, pinning them.

Outside, in the distance, the predatory squawk of an owl dropping onto some small, scurrying animal.

Inside, close, the steady purr of the cat.

It seemed to be grinning, like Alice's Cheshire had in Wonderland.

As Halston watched it stood up, arched its back, and stretched. In a sudden limber movement like rippled silk, it leaped to his shoulder. Halston tried to lift his hands to push it off.

His arms wouldn't move.

Spinal shock, he thought. *Paralyzed. Maybe temporary. More likely permanent.*

The cat purred in his ear like thunder.

"Get off me," Halston said. His voice was hoarse and dry. The cat tensed for a moment and then settled back. Suddenly its paw batted Halston's cheek, and the claws were out this time. Hot lines of pain down to his throat. And the warm trickle of blood.

Pain.

Feeling.

He ordered his head to move to the right, and it complied. For a moment his face was buried in smooth, dry fur. Halston snapped at the cat. It made a startled, disgruntled sound in its throat—*yowk!*—and leaped onto the seat. It stared up at him angrily, ears laid back.

"Wasn't supposed to do that, was I?" Halston croaked. The cat opened its mouth and hissed at him. Looking at that strange, schizophrenic face, Halston could understand how Drogan might have thought it was a hellcat. It—

His thoughts broke off as he became aware of a dull, tingling feeling in both hands and forearms.

Feeling. Coming back. Pins and needles.

The cat leaped at his face, claws out, spitting.

Halston shut his eyes and opened his mouth. He bit at the cat's belly and got nothing but fur. The cat's front claws were clasped on his ears, digging in. The pain was enormous, brightly excruciating. Halston tried to raise his hands. They twitched but would not quite come out of his lap.

He bent his head forward and began to shake it back and forth, like a man shaking soap out of his eyes. Hissing and squalling, the cat held on. Halston could feel blood trickling down his cheeks. It was hard to get his breath. The cat's chest was pressed over his nose. It was possible to get some air in by mouth, but not much. What he did get came through fur. His ears felt as if they had been doused with lighter fluid and then set on fire.

He snapped his head back and cried out in agony—he must have sustained a whiplash when the Plymouth hit. But the cat hadn't been expecting the reverse and it flew off. Halston heard it thud down in the back seat.

A trickle of blood ran in his eye. He tried again to move his hands, to raise one of them and wipe the blood away.

They trembled in his lap, but he was still unable to actually move them. He thought of the .45 special in its holster under his left arm.

If I can get to my piece, kitty, the rest of your nine lives are going in a lump sum.

More tingles now. Dull throbs of pain from his feet, buried and surely shattered under the engine block, zips and tingles from his legs—it felt exactly the way a limb that you've slept on does when it's starting to wake up. At that moment Halston didn't care about his feet. It was enough to know that his spine wasn't severed, that he wasn't going to finish out his life as a dead lump of body attached to a talking head.

Maybe I had a few lives left myself.

Take care of the cat. That was the first thing. *Then get out of the wreck*—maybe someone would come along, that would solve both problems at once. Not likely at 4:30 in the morning on a back road like this one, but barely possible. And—

And what was the cat doing back there?

He didn't like having it on his face, but he didn't like having it behind him and out of sight, either. He tried the rearview mirror, but that was useless. The crash had knocked it awry and all it reflected was the grassy ravine he had finished up in.

A sound from behind him, like low, ripping cloth.

Purring.

Hellcat my ass. It's gone to sleep back there.

And even if it hadn't, even if it was somehow planning murder, what could it do? It was a skinny little thing, probably weighed all of four pounds soaking wet. And soon . . . soon he would be able to move his hands enough to get his gun. He was sure of it.

Halston sat and waited. Feeling continued to flood back into his body in a series of pins-and-needles incursions. Absurdly (or maybe in instinctive reaction to his close brush with death) he got an erection for a minute or so. *Be kind of hard to beat off under present circumstances,* he thought.

A dawn-line was appearing in the eastern sky. Somewhere a bird sang.

Halston tried his hands again and got them to move an eighth of an inch before they fell back.

Not yet. But soon.

A soft thud on the seatback beside him. Halston turned his head and looked into the black-white face, the glowing eyes with their huge dark pupils.

Halston spoke to it.

"I have never blown a hit once I took it on, kitty. This could be a first. I'm getting my hands back. Five minutes, ten at most. You want my advice? Go out the window. They're all open. Go out and take your tail with you."

The cat stared at him.

Halston tried his hands again. They came up, trembling wildly. Half an inch. An inch. He let them fall back limply. They slipped off his lap and thudded to the Plymouth's seat. They glimmered there palely, like large tropical spiders.

The cat was grinning at him.

Did I make a mistake? he wondered confusedly. He was a creature of hunch, and the feeling that he had made one was suddenly overwhelming. Then the cat's body tensed, and even as it leaped, Halston knew what it was going to do and he opened his mouth to scream.

The cat landed on Halston's crotch, claws out, digging.

At that moment, Halston wished he *had* been paralyzed. The pain was gigantic, terrible. He had never suspected that there could be such pain in the world. The cat was a spitting coiled spring of fury, clawing at his balls.

Halston *did* scream, his mouth yawning open, and that was when the cat changed direction and leaped at his face, leaped at his mouth. And at that moment Halston knew that it was something more than a cat. It was something possessed of a malign, murderous intent.

He caught one last glimpse of that black-and-white face below the flattened ears, its eyes enormous and filled with lunatic hate. It had gotten rid of the three old people and now it was going to get rid of John Halston.

It rammed into his mouth, a furry projectile. He gagged on it. Its front claws pinwheeled, tattering his tongue like a piece of liver. His stomach recoiled and he vomited. The vomit ran down into his windpipe, clogging it, and he began to choke.

In this extremity, his will to survive overcame the last of the impact paralysis. He brought his hands up slowly to grasp the cat. *Oh my God*, he thought.

The cat was forcing its way into his mouth, flattening its body, squirming, working itself farther and farther in. He could feel his jaws creaking wider and wider to admit it.

He reached to grab it, yank it out, destroy it . . . and his hands clasped only the cat's tail.

Somehow it had gotten its entire body into his mouth. Its strange, black-and-white face must be crammed into his very throat.

A terrible thick gagging sound came from Halston's throat, which was swelling like a flexible length of garden hose.

His body twitched. His hands fell back into his lap and the fingers drummed senselessly on his thighs. His eyes sheened over, then glazed. They stared out through the Plymouth's windshield blankly at the coming dawn.

Protruding from his open mouth was two inches of bushy tail ... half black, half white. It switched lazily back and forth.

It disappeared.

A bird cried somewhere again. Dawn came in breathless silence then, over the frost-rimmed fields of rural Connecticut.

The farmer's name was Will Reuss.

He was on his way to Placer's Glen to get the inspection sticker renewed on his farm truck when he saw the late-morning sun twinkle on something in the ravine beside the road. He pulled over and saw the Plymouth lying at a drunken, canted angle in the ditch, barbed wire tangled in its grille like a snarl of steel knitting.

He worked his way down and then sucked in his breath sharply. "Holy moley," he muttered to the bright November day. There was a guy sitting bolt upright behind the wheel, eyes open and glaring emptily into eternity. The Roper organization was never going to include him in its presidential poll again. His face was smeared with blood. He was still wearing his seat belt.

The driver's door had been crimped shut, but Reuss managed to get it open by yanking with both hands. He leaned in and unstrapped the seat belt, planning to check for ID. He was reaching for the coat when he noticed that the dead guy's shirt was rippling, just above the belt buckle. Rippling ... and bulging. Splotches of blood began to bloom there like sinister roses.

"What the Christ?" He reached out, grasped the dead man's shirt, and pulled it up.

Will Reuss looked—and screamed.

Above Halston's navel, a ragged hole had been clawed in his flesh. Looking out was the gore-streaked black-and-white face of a cat, its eyes huge and glaring.

Reuss staggered back, shrieking, hands clapped to his face. A score of crows took cawing wing from a nearby field.

The cat forced its body out and stretched in obscene languor.

Then it leaped out the open window. Reuss caught sight of it moving through the high dead grass and then it was gone.

It seemed to be in a hurry, he later told a reporter from the local paper.

As if it had unfinished business.

Ray Vukcevich

Ray Vukcevich has sold fiction to *Aboriginal SF*, *Asimov's Science Fiction Magazine*, *The Magazine of Fantasy and Science Fiction*, *Pulphouse*, and others. He is a research assistant for the Institute of Cognitive and Decision Sciences at the University of Oregon and is currently working on a novel.

"Catch" is an odd little story that takes place in a world like and unlike our own.

Catch

RAY VUKCEVICH

YOUR FACE, I say, is a wild animal this morning, Lucy, and I'm glad it's caged. Her scowl is so deep I can't imagine she's ever been without it. Her yellow hair is a frumpy halo around her wire mask. My remark doesn't amuse her.

I know what I did. I just don't know why it pissed her off, and if I don't know, insensitive bastard that I am, she certainly isn't going to tell me.

She lifts the cat over her head and hurls it at me. Hurls it hard. I catch it and underhand it back to her. The cat is gray on top and snowy white below and mostly limp, its eyes rolled back in its head and its coated tongue hanging loose out of one side of its mouth. I know from experience that it will die soon, and its alarm collar will go off, and one of us will toss it into the ditch that runs between us. A fresh angry bundle of teeth and claws will drop from the hatch in the ceiling, and we'll toss the new cat back and forth between us until our staggered breaks and someone takes our places. The idea is to keep the animals in motion twenty-four hours a day.

In this profession, we wear canvas shirts and gloves and wire cages over our faces. I sometimes dream we've lost our jobs, Lucy and me. What a nightmare. What else do we know?

My replacement comes in behind me. He takes up the straw broom and dips it into the water in the ditch that runs through the toss-box and sweeps at the smeared feces and urine staining the floor and walls. A moment later, the buzzer sounds, and he puts the broom back in the corner. I step aside, and Lucy tosses the cat to him. I slip out of the box and into the catacomb for my fifteen-minute break before moving on to the next box.

Lucy and I work an hour on and fifteen minutes off all day long. As we move from toss-box to toss-box, our paths cross and recross. I'll be out of phase with her for half an hour, probably just long enough for her to work up a real rage.

The catacomb is a labyrinth of wide tunnels dotted with concrete boxes. There is a metal chute running from the roof to the top of each box. The boxes are evenly spaced, and there is a lightbulb for every box, but not all the bulbs are alive so there are gaps in the harsh light. The boxes are small rooms, and there is a wooden door on each side so catchers can be replaced without interrupting the tossing. The concrete walls of the tunnels, like the concrete walls of the boxes, are streaked black and white and beaded with moisture. The floors are roughened concrete. Everything smells like wet rocks and dead things.

So what did I do?

While Lucy dressed for work this morning, I played with our infant daughter, Megan, tossing her into the air and catching her again, blowing bubbles into her stomach while she pulled my hair and giggled until she got the hiccups.

When Lucy came in, I tossed the baby in a high arc across the room to her. Megan tumbled in a perfect backward somersault in the air. Lucy went dead white. She snatched Megan out of the air and hugged the child to her chest.

"Nice catch," I said.

"Don't you ever," Lucy said, her voice all husky and dangerous, "ever do that again, Desmond! Not ever."

Then she stomped out, taking Megan with her.

What the hell? I'd known there was no chance whatever that Lucy would miss. She's a professional. My trusting her to catch the love of my life, the apple of my eye, Daddy's little girl, was, I thought, a pretty big compliment. Lucy didn't buy it. In fact, she didn't even let me explain at all, said instead, oh shut up, Desmond, just shut up, and off we went to work silent, stewing, our hurt feelings like a sack of broken toys between us.

Now she's not speaking to me. It's going to be a long day.

The buzzer sounds, and I move into the next box. I do my duty with the broom, and when the buzzer sounds again I replace the catcher. The cat here is a howling orange monster, and I have my hands full. When the animal is this fresh, the tossing technique looks a lot like volleyball. You don't want to be too close to the thing for very long.

By the time Lucy takes her place across from me, I've established a rhythm and am even able to put a little spin on the cat now and then. I have to hand it to Lucy. She catches up quickly, and soon we have the animal sailing smoothly between us.

The animals go through stages as we toss and catch them. First defiance, then resistance, followed by resignation, then despair, and finally death. This one is probably somewhere in the resistance stage, not fighting wildly, but watching for an opening to do some damage. I put one hand on the cat's chest and the other under its bottom and send it across to Lucy in a sitting position. Not to be outdone, she sends it back still sitting but upside-down now. Maybe the silly positions have done the trick. Whatever. I can feel the animal slip into the resignation stage.

I toss the cat tumbling head over heels, a weak howl and a loose string of saliva trailing behind it. Is Lucy ever going to talk to me again?

"Okay, I'm sorry," I say, giving in to the idea that I might never know exactly why I should be sorry.

I see tears come to her eyes, and she falters, nearly drops the cat. I want to go to her. I want to comfort her, but it will be some time before we're both on a break at the same time, and I see suddenly that it will be too late by then. It simply won't matter anymore.

My replacement comes in and sweeps up. Then the buzzer sounds. I step aside.

Lucy isn't crying anymore.

I reach for the door.

Steven Spruill

Steven Spruill was born in 1946 in Battle Creek, Michigan. He began writing in 1976, producing four science fiction novels and a novella. Since 1990 he has written the medical thrillers *Painkiller, Before I Wake,* and *My Soul to Take. Rulers of Darkness,* a modern vampire novel/ medical thriller, was published in 1995. He has also written about half a dozen short stories. He and his wife have had cats all twenty-five years of their marriage.

Spruill's métier is the slick, fast-paced thriller. "Humane Society" transfers that talent to the short form just dandily.

Humane Society

STEVEN SPRUILL

IT AGGRAVATED DR. Paula Parks that she could never face them without fear. She could feel it now, swelling against the walls of her stomach as she walked through the short, narrow hall to the holding cell. The guard peered at her through the diamond of tempered glass. The clack of the key twisting over in the lock sent an icy shock along her spine. Absurd. No matter what Louis Wingo had done, he could not get at her in here. And soon he would be where he could never hurt anyone again.

Paula thought of Susan. Thirteen years old, walking out the front door to buy cake mix at Ginger's Market. The plan was to surprise Mom when she got home from work. Susan telling her "No, Paula, you stay home and get the pans out," and her minding, not because she was only nine, but because she'd have done anything Susan said. Susan's red hair bouncing in the sun as she hurried down the front sidewalk. Only four blocks to Ginger's but it was the last time anyone saw her. Except whoever killed her.

Okay, Paula thought. Squaring her shoulders, she strode into the holding cell, conscious of the staccato tap of her heels on the concrete. Wingo, dressed in the Day-Glo orange jumpsuit worn by all inmates, sat on the other side of the wire-mesh barrier. As always, he was turned away from her. In profile, his rangy, muscular body clung rigidly to the straight angles of the chair. This was the way he sat each time, refusing to look at her, gazing instead at the high, barred window on his side of the barrier, as if by a concentrated act of will he might be able to float up and out of that window to freedom. Relief that he seemed unable

to look at her again today opened a momentary hole in her
fear and she saw him with a strange, cool detachment.
Anyone who did not know what Louis Wingo was would
think him good looking. Thick black hair, a golden tan
that had survived even the dark caverns of prison. He had
the smooth, angelic handsomeness of a Lucifer newly
fallen from heaven. What had made him so sure that any
living women would reject him?

She only had seven more days to find out.

Paula set the pet carrier on the desk on her side of the
screen. The guard opened it, took Rip out, and handed him
through the small open square in the mesh. Rip let out a
loud meow of greeting and Louis Wingo turned to take him.
His mouth remained expressionless, but he looked at the cat
with intense concentration. He pulled Rip against his chest
and buried his nose in the cat's black and orange fur. Rip endured this for a moment, then began to squirm. Wingo put
him down at once. The tomcat stalked around the concrete
enclosure, sniffing at the corners, trying to stick his paw into
the crack beneath the door behind Wingo. Wingo watched
every move and Paula watched, too. She was getting more
and more fond of the cat and hated bringing him here, but it
was the only way Wingo would talk to her.

And, after all, Rip belonged to Wingo.

Odd that Wingo seemed so attached to the cat. Abuse
of animals was a common feature of the serial-killer profile. On the other hand, Wingo could hardly have been attached to the mice and gerbils whose bones had been
found in his apartment. Apparently he'd bought them and
set them loose so he could watch Rip stalk and kill them.

The cat walked back to his owner and rubbed against
Wingo's leg. Drawing back a little, Rip sniffed at the orange pantleg. The tomcat's eyes narrowed and his jaws
opened slightly so he could taste the odor. His rapt look
reminded Paula of his master. She wondered what he was
sniffing so ardently. All she could smell was the pervasive
piney odor of disinfectant that rose from the pores of the
concrete floor like perfume on a corpse.

"He looks heavier," Wingo said. His voice was soft,

slack with depression. It sent a chill through her. She knew
why he was depressed, and it wasn't just being on death
row. It was going without the thing he most loved to do.

"The pound feeds him well," she said.

"I wish you'd take him yourself, Doctor."

"I told you, I can't do that."

"Can't, or won't?"

"I travel a lot. It wouldn't be fair to the pet."

"Rip is not a pet. If you worked hard on it, he would
consent to be your friend. He's very independent. Just
leave some food down for him. Or, better yet, put one of
those cat portals in your back door and he'll go out and
find his own food."

Alarms went off in her mind. What made Wingo
think she lived in the country? Had he, somehow, been researching her while she was researching him?

She said, "I told you, I live in an apartment on the
twentieth floor."

"Yes, you told me."

For a second, it seemed he had glanced at her, but no,
his attention had merely grazed the side of her face on its
way to the ceiling. Sometimes she almost wished he would
look at her. If he was truly ignoring her, it would be one
thing, but he was obviously acutely aware of her. He never
missed a thing she said. She'd had to stop putting on perfume until evening because four weeks ago she'd seen him
inhaling it, his nostrils dilating, eyes half closing with a
look between pain and rapture.

Paula put her Sony on the table and pushed RECORD.
"Last time, we were talking about how you selected your
victims."

"Were we?"

"Don't be difficult, Louis. I'm keeping to my end of
the bargain."

"What will happen to Rip?"

Paula suppressed a sigh. She did not want to talk about
the cat. If Wingo guessed what she'd already done about
Rip, she'd have nothing further to bargain with in case he
clammed up again. Next week, after all the sessions were

done and she'd learned all she could, she'd tell him. Until then, best keep to her script. She said, "The pound has agreed to keep Rip until thirty days after your . . . sentence is carried out. He's a beautiful cat. I'm sure someone will adopt him."

"And if no one wants him?"

"They would put him to sleep."

"Like me," Wingo said in his empty voice. "The humane society."

"It will be very humane, yes." Who was she talking about, Rip or Wingo? In Wingo's case, the first claim to society's humaneness belonged to the women he would kill if he ever got out. Even with no parole, there would always be the possibility of escape. Louis Wingo had already broken out of Attica once. Four more women had died because of it.

Wingo said, "If the pound finds a home for Rip, will they castrate him first?"

Paula felt a stab of distaste, then reminded herself that Louis had no reason to cushion his words. "They'll neuter him, yes."

"Don't let them." The dead voice was suddenly sharp. "He's done nothing. He's only following his nature."

"Is that what you were doing?"

"Yes. But I'm not small and cute. I don't have nice soft fur."

Paula checked the recorder, making sure the spool was still crawling around. "Do you think a human life is the same as a mouse's?"

"Of course not. A mouse is more innocent. And mice aren't overrunning the earth."

"So you're just a predator, a sort of big furless tomcat, helping keep the population in check."

Wingo's shoulders lifted and dropped in a long sigh. "Are you making fun of me, Doctor?"

Paula swallowed. For a moment, her throat was too dry to speak. She could feel her heart pounding in her chest. With the fear, she felt a strange exhilaration. By God, yes. She *had* just made fun of him. And it had felt good. "Why did you kill those people, Louis?"

"Doctor, are you really that ignorant? Because if you are, there's no point in us talking."

"If I'm ignorant, why not enlighten me?"

"I think you already know why I killed them."

"Because you wanted to."

For a second, he looked at her mouth. His eyes were black, dead as buttons. Paula felt cold monkey claws of fear digging into her shoulders. She realized she wasn't breathing very well. She took a long, slow breath, keeping it quiet so he wouldn't know.

"You say 'want' as if it were a whim," Wingo murmured. "Tell me, Doctor, what is the thing *you* want most in all the world? The thing for which you'd give up everything else?"

"We're not here to talk about me."

"Even if that is how you'll find your answers?"

Paula tried to control her repugnance. Did this murderer, this beast in human form, really think he had anything in common with her? She did not want to give him anything of herself, no trophies like the lingerie and the photos the police had found under a board in his closet.

"You doctors are all the same," Wingo said softly. "You probe and grope us and all the while your eyes are pinched shut. High incidence of brain injury, you say. Brutal fathers, mothers who did not protect. You do not see the nonkillers all around you who had brutal fathers and unprotective mothers—the priests, the teachers, dare I say, the psychiatrists. You write that we're below average in intelligence. You forget that the group you are studying is made up only of the ones you can *catch*."

We caught you, didn't we? Paula wanted to say, but the words stuck in her throat. She'd already taunted him once. Even in here, with seven days to live, Wingo was not a creature to antagonize. And he was right. Whether from cleverness or luck, some of his kind were never caught. Like the one who took Susan so many years ago. Paula looked at Wingo. I wish it was you, she thought. I'd come watch you die.

"What do you want, Doctor, more than anything? It

takes courage to come sit in here with me. You despise me. I terrify you. And yet here you are."

Paula felt a boiling pressure in her chest. "If I could discover why you are the way you are," she said, "if I could stop it from happening to even one man, I'd save a lot of women."

Wingo nodded sagely. "You want to be the one who cracks the code on serial killers. Sounds good. But I find it somehow too ... abstract. Who are you really trying to save? Yourself? Are you trying to escape your fear?"

Paula stared at him. He was staring at the window again, in another world, and yet inside her head, too.

"You're so beautiful," Louis Wingo said. "I would like to play with you after I've cured your fear. We could be good friends. Until you began to smell."

Paula nodded at the guard. He pushed a button and the door behind Wingo opened. Another guard came in, scooped Rip up, and handed him through the wire. Paula put the cat in its carrier and walked out. She did not throw up until she was safely out in the hall.

That evening, in the warm, bright safety of her kitchen, Paula was surprised to find herself hungry. She washed some romaine lettuce in the sink, enjoying the silky flow of water across her hands. Outside the window, the corn shocks in the north field glowed like molten gold in the setting sun. A crimson maple leaf batted the screen on its way down. Sniffing, she caught a cidery hint of overripe apples. Every year, she promised herself she'd pick them, but when the right moment came she was always busy with work and they plopped down to molder in the tall grass. Ah, well, she rather liked the smell.

Paula made a salad of scallions, romaine, and the big beefeater tomatoes she'd found on the way home at the roadside stand at Hickory Corners. As darkness fell, she felt the need for a human voice and turned on the TV on the counter. She took out the chicken from yesterday and put it in the microwave. Great devices, microwaves. No farm kitchen should be without one ...

And what had made Louis Wingo think she lived where she could let his cat out to hunt?

Relax, Paula told herself. In seven days it will be a moot point.

She took a chilled bottle of Bordeaux blanc from the fridge and settled at the table. The salad was delicious, the chicken less so, reminding her of Wingo's conceit that he was just another of nature's predators, like his cat. He was wrong, of course. Cats did not hunt and kill their own kind. Cats were capable of love—both giving and receiving. And Louis Wingo might not have fur, but his outsides were not the ugly part of him—

". . . escaped from Attica a few hours ago," the TV said, and she knew at once it was Wingo. Her fork clattered to the floor. She stared down at the piece of chicken impaled on the tines. Steel bands closed around her chest.

". . . not Wingo's first escape," the announcer said. "Two years ago he took a guard hostage and . . ."

All at once, Paula's paralysis broke. She ran to the phone and dialed. Busy. Frantically, she punched redial, again, again—

"Warden's office."

She recognized the voice of Edwina Reese from public relations. "Edwina, this is Paula Parks. He'll come here."

"Dr. Parks?"

"Yes. I'm at home. Louis Wingo will come here."

"Just a moment, Doctor."

Paula stared frantically around the kitchen. Get a knife, she thought. The big Sabatier in the third drawer. Her gaze slid across the window over the sink. *God, open!* Dropping the phone, she ran to the window and pulled at the sash. Humidity had swelled the boards; the window refused to budge. She pushed at it, grunting, and it slammed down. The front door—had she locked it?

". . . Dr. Parks? Dr. Parks?" A tinny voice from the dangling phone receiver.

She snatched it up. "Yes."

"This is Warden Pelosi. I've already called the state police. They're on the way to your house. Lock your doors and windows. Do you have a room with a phone where you can lock the door?"

The question required thought, she had to think, she could not think—the bedroom. "Yes."

"Good. Don't hang up the phone. Just put it down and go to the room you can lock. Pick up that phone. Stay on the line—"

The phone went dead in her hand. One second the line was open, sound and warmth and life flowing through it, and then it closed up, like a tunnel sealed by a cave-in. "Warden? Warden?"

Swallowing a sob, Paula dropped the phone and ran to the drawer. She yanked it so hard it pulled free of its tracks. Knives and spatulas and rolling pins clattered across the tile. On her hands and knees she sorted frantically through the mess, trying to spot the black handle of the Sabatier.

"Looking for this?"

She screamed and scurried back until the kitchen cabinet rammed her heels. He stood under the big arched doorway to the dining room. He held the big knife up to the light, but the black button eyes that had always avoided her in prison now looked only at her. They were hungry. She gasped at the air. Her lungs seemed filled with sand. He stepped toward her. "You're afraid now but soon you won't be. Don't worry, I won't cut you unless you make me. It's not my way."

No, she thought. Strangling is your way. "The p-p-police are coming."

He smiled. "Nice try, Doctor. But they won't think of you. Last time I hitched rides and got a hundred miles in the first two hours. That's what they'll expect again."

She could make no sense of what he was saying. His eyes made words unnecessary, those terrible unblinking eyes, staring his fill now that he knew he could have her. She tried to get her legs under her. She felt his hand twining into her hair, pulling her up. She struck out with her fists, pounding his chest. He laughed. She kicked at him, connecting with his shin. He spun her around and clamped his arm across her throat. His sweat filled her nostrils, a horrible, goatlike smell. She felt him muscling her across the floor, and then she was staring at their reflections in the black kitchen window. His gaze locked on her face and she felt his forearm tighten across her throat. *Going to die, please help me, Susan, SUSAN—*

"Neeoweep."

The arm slackened on her throat. Wingo spun her around, so that their backs were to the window. Through a red haze, she saw Rip picking his way through the spilled cutlery to where her fork lay under the table. Daintily he picked the piece of chicken free and chewed it, eyes narrowing to pleasured slits.

"Rip!" Wingo said. "You did take Rip."

Paula felt a desperate surge of hope. "Yes. I took him. I'll keep him. But if you kill me, he *will* go to the pound. He'll die. Or they'll castrate him."

She felt Wingo's body tense against her, but the pressure on her neck eased some more. "You know, Doctor, this is the longest I've held a woman without killing her."

Rip finished the chicken and walked over to rub against Wingo's ankle. Then he rubbed against Paula's ankle. She could hear him purring. Rip, as in Jack the Ripper.

Rip as in Rip Van Winkle.

"He likes to sleep all afternoon," she said. Her voice was very high. She forced it lower, controlling the quaver. "Then, around sundown, he likes to go out."

"And hunt," Wingo said. "Does he bring you back mice?"

"Sometimes."

"What do you do?"

"I pet him and give him a treat. The cat books say you should do that. He's trying to give you something of value and you shouldn't punish him. I put the mice in the garbage, but I don't let him see me do it."

"I could take Rip with me," Wingo mused.

"On the run? He'll slow you down. When they don't find him here, they'll know you took him with you. The police can have people watch for a man traveling with a cat. And what will happen to him when they catch you? They did last time and they will again. . . ." Paula's teeth chattered. She clamped her jaw. "Two female cats live in the barn," she said. "I think Rip does more than hunt at night."

Wingo sighed. She felt his body sag against her back. "I want you so bad. But there are other women in the world. I'm free again. I can have anyone I want." His breath in her ear made her shudder. No, she thought savagely. Not me, and not other women.

"Promise you will never put a bell on him."

"Yes."

"Never let him be castrated?"

"I promise."

"That you will keep him until he dies of old age?"

"I would have done it anyway. He's a good cat."

Wingo laughed, a short barking sound, harsh in her ear. "He's a killer, just like me."

And then he was gone, running out the door. Paula sank to her knees, sobbing in fright and relief. A megaphone blared, *"State Police. Stop or we'll shoot,"* and then she heard a loud bang, followed by a horrendous clamor of gunshots. Rip scrambled in panic, his claws spinning and slipping on the slick tiles. He got his feet under him at last and bolted upstairs, kicking the rag throw rugs on each landing out of alignment in his frantic need to get under her bed.

Later, after the body had been removed and the police were gone, Paula picked up the clutter on the kitchen floor and put it in the dishwasher. She still felt afraid, but not quite so much. He came for me, she thought, and he's dead. I'm still here. So are some other women. She wished she knew whom he would have killed. Just their names so she could watch from a distance as they picked up their kids, or got groceries or drove to work full of plans they'd get to finish.

Rip rubbed against her leg, then went to the door and meowed at her and she let him out.

Joel Lane

Joel Lane was born in 1963 and brought up in Birmingham, England, where he now works as a freelance editor and writer. His stories have appeared in *Ambit, Panurge, Critical Quarterly*, the award-winning anthologies *Darklands* and *Darklands 2, Sugar Sleep, Little Deaths*, and elsewhere. A selection of his poems appeared in *Private Cities*, a three-poet anthology from Stride Publications. A short-story collection, *The Earth Wire*, was published by Egerton Press and won the British Fantasy Award. He is working on a novel titled *Neighborhood Watch*.

"Scratch" takes place in the richly imagined parts of England that Margaret Thatcher helped create—pockets of poverty, grayness, violence, and depression. Lane has written several futuristic stories in this milieu.

Here a young man tries to survive with the help of a few friends. His strongest and perhaps most important relationship is with his cat, an animal many see as the ultimate loner.

Scratch

JOEL LANE

DO YOU KNOW, I can't remember the name my mum gave her? All I can remember is my secret name for her, Sara. Without an "h." It was my sister's name. Don't get me wrong, I wasn't trying to pretend she *was* my sister. Unless what you call things changes them. But I don't even believe that. I just think there are patterns. Like music or revenge or love.

I never knew my father. Or if I did, I didn't know it was him. My mum only knew him for a few hours. He never left his phone number, and she couldn't contact him when she found out she was pregnant. The only thing she ever said to me about him was that men who didn't have the sense to use condoms weren't fit to be parents. Which made me laugh. Sara's dad hung around a bit longer, a few months I think. So she was my half sister really. But she always called me her brother. She was about eighteen months older than me.

We lived on a council estate in Oldbury. Oldbury's a nice town but the estates aren't part of it: They're stuck out among the factories and power generators, where there's nonstop traffic but no shops or houses. There were two main housing estates. One was a street lined with three or four layers of identical cubes, like something in a nursery school. Now they're all smashed up or burned out, and hardly anyone lives there. The other one was a group of tower blocks clustered together on some sloping wasteground. That was where we were. On the ninth floor. All the windows had wire grids to protect the glass. Any time of year, the building was cold.

After I was born, my mum got depressed and had to be treated. The neighbors helped look after us for a while. After that, she had an operation to stop her conceiving again. One of the ways people are different from cats is they go on fucking whether they can make babies or not. Lots of different men stayed in the flat when me and Sara were little. Sometimes just for the night, sometimes for weeks. There was one who came on and off for about a year. I know he was married, because he and my mum used to row about what he was going to do: leave his wife or not. He didn't.

Some of the men brought things for my mum. But she was never on the game. Some of them took things, I mean apart from what they all took. All I can say for our many daddies is they didn't usually outstay their welcome. But one did. It happened when Sara was eight. She was off school with flu. I was just starting at the local primary, the same one she went to. When I came home, there were police in the flat. Mum was very pale. She was trying to drink a cup of tea, but her hands were shaking too much. When she spoke her voice sounded torn, as if she'd been screaming for hours. I don't remember what she said. When I tried to go through into the next room, where Sara and I had our beds, a policeman stopped me.

They never caught him. Mum never forgave herself for trusting him to look after Sara when she was at work. I'd liked him: He'd been nice to me and Sara. I suppose he would be. When I went back to school after the funeral, they all seemed to know more about it than I did. I learned two new words: *raped* and *strangled*. But nobody talked to me much. Kids who'd picked on me were afraid of looking bad, and kids who'd been friendly were afraid of saying the wrong thing. Or they thought I was bad luck. Mum didn't say much to me either. All she talked about was the chance of finding him, and what she'd do. She started to collect things like knives, razor blades, and pieces of broken glass. Sometimes she'd spread them out on the table and look at them, test how sharp they were by scratching her arm. All I could think of was Sara. Every day, wherever

I was, I could see her smiling, hear her voice when she told a joke, feel her hands when she shook me awake in the morning. It was all too bright, like the things you see when you've got a temperature.

There were no more men for a long time. A social worker came round every Tuesday and talked to my mum. A few times, she talked to me on my own. Asked me if I'd be happier somewhere else. I didn't know. Mum had told me if I was taken into care I'd probably get beaten and used. I went on a fostering list for a while, but no one wanted me. Later I realized if you've been through shit, people don't like you because you're not innocent. Most people want innocence because they like ignorance. Some people want innocence so they can abuse it. I wasn't either ignorant or innocent. I was just kind of shut off. Looking back on it, I realize I hardly spoke to anyone for three years.

Except Sara. The cat, that is. My mum bought her for company in the flat. The council were going to rehouse us, but there was nowhere to go that wasn't worse. If we'd moved outside the area, it would've been harder for my mum to keep her job and look after me. It was only packaging on an assembly line, but unemployment was getting really bad in the Black Country.

The cat was a smallish female. She was mostly black, with a few patches of white: upper face, front paws, and tail. And these narrow gray-green eyes that never stopped watching you. My mum put a gravel tray out for her on the landing. A tower block's a fuck-awful place to keep pets, but she managed to find her way around. In spite of the security system that kept strangers out of the building. She wandered round the estate a lot, sometimes bringing back dead sparrows or mice until my mum discouraged her. In the flat, she just sat a few feet away from the electric fire and did nothing at all. Neutered cats are generally like that. I don't think she ever forgave the human race for taking her identity away.

People say there's no such thing as a domestic cat, and it's true. Females in particular. Whatever you feed them, they still hunt. When they bring you something they've killed, it's not a gift. It's a lesson. They're trying to train you, like you're a kitten. And when they rub against you, it's not love: They're leaving their scent to mark you as part of their territory. A cat's world is full of territories, friends and enemies, safe roads and dangerous roads. Patterns.

I don't know why I started calling her Sara. Or why she took to me so well. Sometimes she'd follow me round the flat and come with me if I went out for a walk or to buy something. At night, she'd often curl up at the end of my bed. I got used to her almost silence, and the careful way she moved. Without her I felt—not alone, because I always felt alone, but like I wasn't all there. My mum was quite happy to let me feed Sara. She had other problems to worry about. Boyfriends came and went like before, but now there were often screaming matches in the middle of the night and the sound of things being thrown or smashed. Sometimes there was blood in the hallway, where a man had left injured. Some of them hit back—she was hospitalized twice. I used to cover my head with the pillow and lie there, with Sara curled up on the other side of the duvet like a kind of guardian angel. My mum must have got a reputation for being crazy, because the men became less and less frequent.

Years went by and nothing much changed. Just being able to carry on seemed enough, to both of us. But it wasn't. Sometimes it's easier to be a victim than a witness.

After I started at the secondary school in Warley, I was out of the flat a lot more. I used to go into Birmingham and just wander around, window-shopping or drifting through music and video shops with enough money to buy a can of Coke. Evenings were better, I could take Sara with me— except on the bus—and visit friends or hang around the town center, watching people. It was a bit like cable TV: as many different faces and voices as you wanted. Making friends outside school was hard. My age scared some people off and attracted some others I didn't like. But I was quick on my feet, and good at hiding. I didn't know what I was looking for. There was some image in my head of an extended family, people who belonged with each other but nowhere else.

My mum got used to me staying out at weekends. Sometimes I'd sleep on friends' floors or in spare beds. Girls my own age liked me because I was quiet and seemed grown up. I didn't have sex much. A bit. At thirteen it seems strange, like a dance to music you've never heard before. I liked being in groups, where you all sat together and went to sleep in one room, and I could feel myself slipping from one mind to the next. School was a waste of time. My teacher called me the Invisible Man because he never saw me. I wasn't being a rebel, I just didn't care. But after they sent the truant officer round a couple of times and my mum hit the roof, I had to try and keep them happy. Not that they ever expected anything of me. It was a circus: sawdust on the classroom floor.

What I really liked was walking in the town at night. Or between towns—industrial estates and bypass roads and canal routes. With Sara. She made me see things I couldn't see on my own. Telegraph wires like webs stretched out between buildings. Splinters of glass across empty windows. Pieces of electricity generators left out to blacken. Things moving on the ground until the rain nailed them. The silver. The red. I used to stop in doorways, fall asleep, wake up with an erection and a mouth full of dust. Crying. I found a pack of cigarettes and smoked them all for warmth. Those nights seemed to go on forever, and I hated them but didn't want them to end.

One night on Snow Hill, I was standing outside Hamleys, the big children's toy store that closed down a few years ago. The building's gone now. But then there was still a big window display of toys and posters and things. The street was quiet, only a few dazed-looking kids waiting for the night bus and a vagrant hunting through the litter bins. Then I saw the mice inside the window, walking in a line. A mother and about six children. There was a strange high-pitched sound, like someone screaming a long way off. The mice disappeared into the wall. A few moments later, the mother crawled out through a ventilator near street level. Her children followed her.

The crying sound was coming from behind me. It was Sara. She was perched on a low wall, beyond the grass verge at the opening to the subway. Her mouth was wide open, and her shoulders were quivering with tension. Her eyes followed the mice as they came toward her slowly, one after another. As if they were walking into a blizzard. Sara jumped down onto the grass, where a drainage ditch ran close to the wall. The mother stepped awkwardly past the edge of the ditch and fell. Sara struck once. One by one, the others followed. It occurred to me that I'd never seen her kill before. It was only when a whole dead family of mice lay there that she started to eat. And the high thin voice became silent.

She kept one baby for me. No, I didn't eat it. When I told Mikki about this, she said Sara was the Pied Piper of Hamleys. But that was much later. When I was trying to go back to the things I'd escaped from.

A few days after the Hamleys incident, I spent a night with a stranger in Birmingham. My mum and me were getting on really badly, and I didn't want to go home. But I had no money and hadn't eaten since the night before. It was getting late in the evening. I was sitting on the wall of a car park, watching Sara try to catch a starling. As the bird finally took off for the roof of a Chinese restaurant, I noticed this guy looking at me. He was about to get into his car—a white Metro. Feeling really embarrassed, I asked him if he could spare a quid. He came closer, looking nervous. In fact scared, but not of me. He was about forty, cropped dark hair, glasses.

"Are you hungry?" he said. Pause. "Would you like to go for a pizza, maybe?" I left Sara to fend for herself. He didn't ask my age, and I didn't want to scare him off by telling him. At that time I was fourteen, but looked older because I spent so much time on the streets. I murdered the pizza (ham, pepperoni, and black olives) and he asked me if I wanted to come back for a drink. In the car, I told him I needed somewhere to stay the night. His face lit up with relief.

It was different from when I'd gone to bed with girls. Not really because he was a man, more because this wasn't about what we could share—it was about his power over me and my power over him. In that way, I had an instinct for it. In the final moments I seemed to be watching myself through a mirror: crouched over him, my fingernails dug into his sides, my head down like a cat lapping up milk. When I woke up, he was fast asleep in the bed beside me. It wasn't yet dawn, but I could see okay. My clothes were wrapped up in a bundle on the floor. Next to them, his jeans were lying half under the bed. I checked the pockets: twenty-five quid plus some change. I took a tenner, thinking he might not realize he'd been robbed. And if he did he'd see it was need, not greed. When I looked up I could see him watching me. I pocketed the money and left the flat. Somehow I already knew the way back into town. Sara found me within an hour. All that day, no matter what I ate or drank, I couldn't get rid of the taste. After that I always asked for money.

It was me that found her. One cold still day in March. I'd come home just before dawn and gone straight to bed. When I got up around three, the flat was silent. I sat watching TV with the fire on, wondering where my mum had got to. It was Sunday, so she'd normally be there. Lately she'd been threatening to get rid of me, have me classified as *estranged*. The flat was a mess. I thought if I went round with the vacuum cleaner, it might put her in a better mood. The last room I did was my mum's bedroom. She was lying there on the bed, unconscious. No breath. No heartbeat. I gave up trying to revive her when I realized how cold she was.

They told me she'd died of a morphine overdose. Asked me if she was an addict. I said no, but I didn't really know. The police contacted her sister in Bromsgrove, who I'd never seen before. She was like an older, heavier version of my mum. Lived with her husband in a little terraced house, no kids. They looked after me and Sara for a while. I didn't cry at the funeral, not until a few days afterward when I went back to the graveyard on my own. Suddenly I began to remember what it had been like at first, before my sister was killed. Her grave was there, too. When I found it I started crying, then screaming. A kind of white numbness grew in my head, like scars. I fell onto my hands and knees. Then I punched myself in the face until the gravestone blurred. I begged my mum to forgive me for not helping her. The only answer was the scream in my head. It was a quiet morning, bright, really cold.

A week later, I got moved to a private hostel in north Birmingham. It was like a place for teenagers with "problems." All the rooms were painted a kind of frog green, with spots of damp like warts. The windows were tiny. There was always rubbish on the stairs that nobody bothered to shift. The kitchens and bathrooms were all smashed up, nothing worked properly. It was run by three fat men who sat around all day in an office behind a heavily barred glass screen, talking about their legendary fighting and fucking exploits.

At least I kept my room clean. Had some old photographs and some pictures I'd done in school. I used to light cheap candles and imagine I was in a cellar under a bombed city. Because I was still fifteen, a social worker came round to see me every week and check I was going to school. She hated the building, too. Most of the other kids were older than me and like complete deadheads. Slow, I mean. Or they'd got that way from boredom or solvents. Or they were too scared to face the world. A few were dangerous. One threatened me with a knife to get a blowjob. Whenever I went with anyone in that place I seemed to end up with crabs or scabies or some not quite accidental injury. I collected apologies the way some people collect empty bottles. Going out onto the canal towpath at night was better. There was a huge stone bridge with alcoves half full of rubble. The police never went down there. Some of the men were drunk and clumsy, others were almost romantic. I used to stare at the black water and imagine swimming out through the tunnel into the glowing red and silver of dawn.

What I hated most about the hostel was they wouldn't let me keep Sara. I had to leave her with Mikki, a friend from school. Mikki was the only person I trusted enough to talk to about Sara. They got on really well. Usually Sara was very cautious with anyone except me, but she settled down at Mikki's house without any problem. Everyone needs a home, I suppose. Me and Mikki had always been close, but the kinds of shit we were going through stopped us getting together. She liked going out with older boys who had jobs and motorcycles and things. They kept dumping her or getting her pregnant. She was a year older than me, dark haired, with strong cheekbones and a spider-web tattoo on one side of her neck. I knew she got on really badly with her mum and dad. When she was fourteen, she'd gone round the house and broken all the windows. To let the truth in, she said. Her mum had told her "You'll end up in a mental home." She'd answered "You'll have to get me out of this one first." Then her dad had beaten her. She never broke anything in the house again.

When I turned sixteen, I started making plans to find a job and move out. As soon as my school year ended. Then Mikki turned up on my doorstep with Sara and a big suitcase. Told me she'd been thrown out. I blagged some cans of lager off a neighbor who owed me a few favors, and we had a long talk. We also slept together, for the first time. When we woke up in the morning, Sara was lying curled up between us on the blanket. It was like a sign. The family.

But neither of us had jobs. We stayed with some friends of Mikki's on the top floor of a house in Balsall Heath for a few weeks. I managed to get some casual work in the Bull Ring Market, cleaning up the stalls at the end of the day. We were caught in the usual trap—no job without a home, no home without a job. At least the school weren't after me anymore. Once you're sixteen, they don't give a fuck. You don't even qualify for benefits. It's like you're not the innocent anymore, you're the problem. By now it was late spring, so we weren't that worried about keeping warm. Sara was used to fending for herself by now.

There was only one way we were going to find a home of our own. In the backstreets on the town side of Balsall Heath, the red-light district, there were some old terraced houses that had been boarded up for ages. Probably whoever owned them couldn't sell them and hadn't bothered to get them done up for renting. So we broke into one of them at the back, where a concrete yard was half full of loose bricks. Inside the floorboards were rotten, and the paint was flaking away from some wallpaper that was streaked with damp. We moved in candles, a mattress, some bedding, our suitcases and boxes. The water supply was still connected. There was no electric, but Mikki got some batteries for her radio. From the front, you'd have thought the house was still empty.

That was the best and worst time. The best because it was so different. We were finally in what I'd always dreamed of as the cat world. No need for talk or money or daylight. We used the showers at the local swimming baths. A lot of homeless went there. Mikki got some cheap paints and covered the walls of our room with trees. Big, muscular trees with tangled branches. And in between them, some thin buildings that looked shattered and empty. Heaps of dead leaves on the ground. The nights were best. We'd huddle under the blankets and make love in the dark, staring with our mouths. Or go for long walks in the city, holding hands, with Sara stalking along behind us. There was a built-up housing estate on the edge of the city center, a ring of tower blocks around an empty carpark and a children's playground. Just beyond that was a massive construction site where they'd almost finished pulling down a line of houses and were starting to plan out some new buildings. First there was just a lot of wooden posts and trenches in the mud, then they brought in metal troughs full of new bricks and sand. The tower blocks were half occupied, half empty. Lots of smashed and boarded windows. We got to know a few squatters from there who were around at night. In the middle of the night, me and Mikki used to go down there and play about in the small concrete playground. It was like a black-and-white film. We'd ride on the swings and the seesaw, hang upside-down on the climbing frame. That was best of all.

The worst thing was the mornings. What had seemed so mysterious at night became dirty and worthless. Dust glittered in the air and made a skin over everything. Sara was asleep or off somewhere, and I didn't have her eyes anymore. On my own I could have coped, but me and Mikki just snapped at each other and forgot how to talk. That was the only time we needed to drink, the early mornings. Daylight was a threat. But not just daylight. Every contact we had with the outside world, we came off worse. The DSS told us our families were the only people responsible for our welfare. And that was the office in Moseley, where you didn't need a fixed address to sign on. By this time, we were both having sex for money. I coped with it better than Mikki did, but she got more work. Balsall Heath was full of teenage prostitutes, hundreds of them. They stood around in little groups, wearing T-shirts and tight jeans or miniskirts. Like me, Mikki learned to avoid the drunken punters. But she still got raped a few times, once by a policeman. And one guy beat her up and didn't even pay extra for it. I tried to comfort her when she was upset, but it wasn't in me to say *let me take you away from this*. It was like violence was a part of life, you couldn't rise above it. I've felt that way since I was a child. Kind of numb. If you learn early enough, you don't need morphine.

One morning, Mikki told me she'd met a guy who wanted her to move in with him. "So I'm going to," she said. I laughed, but she just looked at me and I realized she meant it. We sat down together on the mattress and she put her arms round me. "I can't stay here," she said. "It's nothing, it's like dying. We'd freeze to death in winter. You'll do better on your own, Sean. You'll get a room in a hostel, no problem. This guy—he's okay, he's got money, he wants me. There's no choice, Sean. No choice at all." She tried to kiss me, but I pulled away. She started packing her suitcase while I thought about the "on your own." Mikki knew what I was thinking, she always did. "I'm taking Sara," she said. "I can look after—"

"Are you, fuck. Sara belongs with me. She's not property." At that moment, I felt so weak and lonely that I started to cry. Sara was curled up in a corner of the room, asleep. Like a child. But also like a wise woman who was older than either of us and had seen every kind of betrayal. I put my coat on. "See you." Outside, I couldn't believe the sun was shining. The city felt so dark, full of empty spaces where nothing could live. I walked for hours and fell asleep on a park bench in Yardley Wood. When I got back to the house, Mikki and Sara were gone. I had some money from a trick the night before, so I bought four cans of Special Brew and drank them. In the dark it felt like the room was empty. Like I wasn't there.

A day later, Sara came back. She was waiting for me in the yard at the back of the house, and she had that strange obsessed look in her eyes that I'd seen outside the toy shop. When I picked her up, she was purring. Sara never used to purr. I brushed some bits of dead leaf and twigs out of her dark fur. And a few days after that, I saw Mikki waiting on the street in Balsall Heath. She was on her own. It was nearly midnight. As I got closer, I could see a freshly healed scratch down her left cheek. She hugged me. "It's good to see you," she said. "Won't be here much longer. He's sending me to London."

"Sending you?" I looked at her face. New makeup. A new perfume. The scratch.

"Yeah. I work for him. There's two kinds of men, Sean. Bastards and more bastards."

I squeezed her hand. We kissed good-bye—gently, the way you kiss someone you care about. I touched her cheek. "Did Sara do that?"

"What?" Mikki laughed. "God, no. That was him. James." She tensed up suddenly. "Here he comes now. Checking up on me."

He was a chubby middle-aged man with short hair,

like Friar Tuck in the *Robin of Sherwood* TV series. I walked up to him and said, "See you've got a new pair of legs opening this week." He didn't get it. That was the last time I saw Mikki. A couple of days after that, the owner of the house I was living in got someone to throw out my stuff and brick up the windows and the back doorway.

I was on the streets a few nights. Even in summer, it's cold. All that concrete stores up cold like a massive fridge. Made me think of my mother and finding her dead. I really wanted a safe place to stay. Not another squat. So I went to the Salvation Army hostel in town and they gave me a room. Simple rules: no drink, no drugs, no pets. Everyone broke the first two rules and got away with it.

I thought Sara could manage for a couple of days while I found someone to look after her. But I was getting drunk all the time. The past was blowing into me like dead leaves. My sister. My mum. All those men. Mikki. I was getting Valium off one of the guys in the hostel, in return for the usual things. It was all blurred. Then I went back to the flat where me and Mikki had stayed when we were together at first. Two new people had moved in, but one of Mikki's friends was still there, Janice. I talked her into looking after Sara for a bit. Gave her some money to buy cat food. It was all okay. But Sara was gone and I couldn't find her.

I searched all that day and all that night. And just after dawn, when the traffic noise was starting up again, I found her. She wanted me to. It was in Nechells, that housing estate with the children's playground. As soon as I got there and saw the cold sunlight flashing from the top windows of a tower block like a distress signal, I knew. Sara was on the low wooden fence at one side of the carpark. She'd been fixed to it with nails through her neck and paws. There was a shadow of dried blood on the fence, almost black. Flies were crawling over the stiff matted fur. Her eyes were gone. But I could see them inside my head. Close up, the smell was unbearable. I started retching and had to walk away before I could stop. The carpark was empty. No one with any sense would park there.

It was a while before I could make myself go back to the fence and pull out the nails. Her legs stayed in place, stretched out like she was flying. She was cold. A stuffed toy left at the back of the cupboard. Flies crawled over my hands, and I wanted to scream but couldn't open my mouth. I took Sara to the building site just beyond the flats, dropped her in one of the trenches, and pushed some earth down over her. Then I went back to the playground, sat on a bench, and waited. It was cloudy that morning. Every now and then the sun came out and lit everything up, so bright it made the streets unreal.

Sometime in the evening, a group of kids came out of the nearest tower block and started playing football in the carpark. I counted eight of them. The youngest would have been about five, the oldest about nine or ten. As it started to get dark, one of them went indoors. Then two more turned up and joined in the game. The bigger kids were getting most of the action. They were a scruffy bunch. All white. Several of them with plasters or bruised faces. I wondered how many of them had been beaten or fucked by the adults they lived with. How many useless tears had crossed those pale empty faces. Then I stood up, walked over to the wall between the playground and the carpark, and climbed onto it. The kids stopped playing and turned to look at me. I stared back at them. Then I sang, in a high thin voice I'd heard only once before. Like a scream from a long way off. A place where the crying never stops.

They came toward me. Slowly, like they were moving underwater. I walked along the edge of the wall, jumped down, and started to back away, still singing. They followed me between the tower blocks. Their faces were blank. Their eyes were dull, like they were watching TV. I walked up ahead of them onto the building site and jumped the nearest trench. There were mounds of sand and earth on the far side, and a stack of loose bricks. I stood there and kept my mouth open for the sound to come out. The children looked right into my eyes. The youngest came on first. I'd already removed the wooden barrier. They were silent. Nine children. Nine lives.

When they were all in the trench, I started chucking bricks down onto them. They didn't struggle, most of them didn't move at all after they were hit. I felt like crying but I didn't, any more than they did. I just sang. Then I pushed earth and sand over them until they were all covered. It felt like part of me was being buried with them. I went on throwing in dirt until it was more or less level. Then I walked back to the hostel and slept all through the next day.

There are patterns. You have to finish what you start. Make it level. Even. Scratch.

I left the Midlands after that. Hitched a ride to London. There's a whole town of homeless kids down there, but I'll get by. You know how the Red Indians would each have a special animal as a totem, a spirit being? Sometimes a family would be under the same totem, sometimes a whole tribe. How many lives are part of me? Will I end up splayed out on a bed or the roof of a car, with a knife in the back of my neck? I can seek out food and keep myself clean. I like people, but I don't need them. And I'll never trust anyone. My claws are sheathed. They're deep inside me.

Joyce Carol Oates

Joyce Carol Oates is the author of over twenty-three novels, numerous short stories, poetry, and plays. Her most recent collections are *Haunted: Tales of the Grotesque* and *Will You Always Love Me?*, and her novel *What I Lived For* was nominated for the Pen/Faulkner Award. She is the 1994 recipient of the Bram Stoker Lifetime Achievement Award in horror fiction. Her work has appeared in *Omni, Playboy, The New Yorker, Harper's Magazine, The Atlantic*, as well as literary magazines and anthologies such as *Architecture of Fear; Dark Forces; Metahorror; Little Deaths; Ruby Slippers, Golden Tears;* and *The Year's Best Fantasy and Horror* series. She asserts that she has long been owned by a succession of cats.

This is another story from a child's point of view. In it, her family has recently been "blessed" with a new arrival. Oates uses one of the many superstitions surrounding cats to illuminate the pain and jealousy suffered by parental neglect of the firstborn.

Nobody Knows
My Name

JOYCE CAROL OATES

SHE WAS A precocious child, aged nine. She understood that there was danger even before she saw the cat with thistledown gray fur like breath, staring at her, eyes tawny golden and unperturbed, out of the bed of crimson peonies.

It was summer. Baby's first summer they called it. At Lake St. Cloud in the Adirondack Mountains in the summerhouse with the dark shingles and fieldstone fireplaces and the wide second-floor veranda that, when you stepped out on it, seemed to float in the air, unattached to anything. At Lake St. Cloud neighbors' houses were hardly visible through the trees, and she liked that. Ghost houses they were, and their inhabitants. Only voices carried sometimes, or radio music, from somewhere along the lakeshore a dog's barking in the early morning, but cats make no sound—that was one of the special things about them. The first time she'd seen the thistledown gray cat she'd been too surprised to call to it, the cat had stared at her and she had stared at the cat, and it seemed to her that the cat had recognized her, or in any case it had moved its mouth in a silent miming of speech—not a "meow" as in a silly cartoon but a human word. But in the next instant the cat had disappeared so she'd stood alone on the terrace feeling the sudden loss like breath sucked out of her and when Mommy came outside carrying the baby, the pretty candy-cane towel flung over her shoulder to keep the baby's drool from her shoulder, she hadn't heard Mommy speaking to her at first because she was listening so hard to something else. Mommy repeated what she'd said, "Jessica . . . ? Look who's here."

Jessica. That was the word, the name, the thistledown gray cat had mimed.

Back home, in the city, all the houses on Prospect Street, which was their street, were exposed, like in glossy advertisements. The houses were large and made of brick or stone and their lawns were large and carefully tended and never hidden from one another, never secret as at Lake St. Cloud. Their neighbors knew their names and were always calling out hello to Jessica even when they could tell she was looking away from them, thinking *I don't see anybody, they can't see me,* but always there was the intrusion and backyards too ran together separated only by flower beds or hedges you could look over. Jessica loved the summerhouse that used to be Grandma's before she died and went away and left it to them though she was never certain it was *real* or only something she'd dreamt. She had trouble sometimes remembering what *real* was and what *dream* was and whether they could ever be the same or were always different. It was important to know because if she confused the two Mommy might notice, and question her, and once Daddy couldn't help laughing at her in front of company, she'd been chattering excitedly in that way of a shy child suddenly feverish to talk telling of how the roof of the house could be lifted and you could climb out using the clouds as stairs. Daddy interrupted to tell her no, no, Jessie sweetheart, that's just a dream, laughing at the stricken look in her eyes so she went mute as if he'd slapped her and backed away and ran out of the room to hide. And tore at her thumbnail with her teeth to punish herself.

Afterward Daddy came to her and squatted in front of her to look level in her eyes saying he was sorry he'd laughed at her and he hoped she wasn't mad at Daddy, it's just she's so *cute,* her eyes so *blue,* did she forgive Daddy? and she nodded yes her eyes filling with tears of hurt and rage and in her heart *No! no! no!* but Daddy didn't hear, and kissed her like always.

That was a long time ago. She'd only been in pre-school then. A baby herself, so silly. No wonder they laughed at her.

The terrible worry was, for a while, they might not be driving up to Lake St. Cloud this summer.

It was like floating—just the name. Lake St. Cloud. And clouds reflected in the lake, moving across the ripply surface of the water. It was *up* to Lake St. Cloud in the Adirondacks when you looked at the map of New York State and it was *up* when Daddy drove, into the foothills and into the mountains on curving, sometimes twisting roads. She could feel the journey *up* and there was no sensation so strange and so wonderful.

Will we be going to the lake? Jessica did not dare ask Mommy or Daddy because to ask such a question was to articulate the very fear the question was meant to deny. And there was the terror, too, that the summerhouse was after all not *real* but only Jessica's *dream* because she wanted it so badly.

Back before Baby was born, in spring. Weighing only five pounds eleven ounces. Back before the "C-section" she heard them speak of so many times over the telephone, reporting to friends and relatives. "C-section"—she saw floating in geometrical figures, octagons, hexagons, as in one of Daddy's architectural magazines, and Baby was in one of these, and had to be sawed out. The saw was a special one, Jessica knew, a surgeon's instrument. Mommy had wanted "natural labor" but it was to be "C-section" and Baby was to blame, but nobody spoke of it. There should have been resentment of Baby, and anger and disgust, for all these months Jessica was *good* and Baby-to-be *bad*. And nobody seemed to know, or to care. *Will we be going to the lake this year? Do you still love me?*—Jessica did not dare ask for fear of being told.

This was the year, the year of Mommy's swelling belly, when Jessica came to know many things without knowing how she knew. The more she was not told, the

more she understood. She was a grave, small-boned child
with pearly-blue eyes and a delicate oval of a face like a ce-
ramic doll's face and she had a habit of which all adults
disapproved of biting her thumbnail until it bled or even
sucking at her thumb if she believed she was unobserved
but most of all she had the power to make herself invisible
sometimes watching and listening and hearing more than
was said. The times that Mommy was unwell that winter,
and the dark circles beneath her eyes, and her beautiful
chestnut hair brushed limp behind her ears, and her breath
panting from the stairs, or just walking across a room.
From the waist up Mommy was still Mommy but from the
waist down, where Jessica did not like to look, the thing
that was Baby-to-be, Baby-Sister-to-be, had swollen up
grotesquely inside her so her belly was in danger of burst-
ing. And Mommy might be reading to Jessica or helping
with her bath when suddenly the pain would hit, Baby
kicked hard, so hard Jessica could feel it, too, and the
warm color draining from Mommy's face, and the hot
tears flooding her eyes. And Mommy would kiss Jessica
hurriedly and go away. And if Daddy was home she would
call for him in that special voice meaning she was trying to
keep calm. Daddy would say *Darling, you're all right, it's
fine, I'm sure it's fine*, helping Mommy to sit somewhere
comfortable, or lie down with her legs raised; or to make
her way slow as an elderly woman down the hall to the
bathroom. That was why Mommy laughed so much, and
was so breathless, or began to cry suddenly. *These hor-
mones!* she'd laugh. *Or I'm too old! We waited too long!
I'm almost forty! God help me, I want this baby so badly!*
and Daddy would be comforting, mildly chiding, he was
accustomed to handling Mommy in her moods. *Shhh!
What kind of silly talk is that? Do you want to scare
Jessie, do you want to scare* me? And though Jessica might
be asleep in her room in her bed she would hear, and she
would know, and in the morning she would remember as
if what was *real* was also *dream*, with the secret power of
dream to give you knowledge others did not know you
possessed.

* * *

But Baby was born, and given a name: _____. Which Jessica whispered but, in her heart, did not *say*.

Baby was born in the hospital, sawed out of the C-section as planned. Jessica was brought to see Mommy and Baby _____ and the surprise of seeing them *the two of them so together* Mommy so tired-looking and so happy, and Baby that had been an *it*, that ugly swelling in Mommy's belly, was painful as an electric shock—swift-shooting through Jessica, even, as Daddy held her perched on his knee beside Mommy's bed, it left no trace. *Jessie, darling—see who's here? Your baby sister _____, isn't she beautiful? Look at her tiny toes, her eyes, look at her hair that's the color of yours, isn't she beautiful?* and Jessica's eyes blinked only once or twice and with her parched lips she was able to speak, to respond as they wanted her to respond, like being called upon in school when her thoughts were in pieces like a shattered mirror but she gave no sign, she had the power, you must tell adults only what they want you to tell them so they will love you.

So Baby was born, and all the fears were groundless. And Baby was brought back in triumph to the house on Prospect Street flooded with flowers where there was a nursery repainted and decorated specially for her. And eight weeks later Baby was taken in the car up to Lake St. Cloud, for Mommy was strong enough now, and Baby was gaining weight so even the pediatrician was impressed, already able to focus her eyes, and smile, or seem to smile, and gape her toothless little mouth in wonderment hearing her name _____! _____! _____! so tirelessly uttered by adults. For everybody adored Baby, whose very poop was delightful to them. For everybody was astonished at Baby, who had only to blink and drool and gurgle and squawk red-faced moving her bowels inside her diaper or, in her battery-operated baby swing, fall abruptly asleep as if hypnotized—*isn't she beautiful! isn't she a love!* And to Jessica was put the question again, again, again *Aren't you lucky to have a baby sister?* and Jessica knew the answer that must be given, and given with a smile, a quick shy smile and a nod. For everybody brought presents for Baby, where once they had brought presents for another baby. (Except, as Jessica learned, overhearing Mommy talking with a woman friend, there were many more presents for Baby than there had been for Jessica. Mommy admitted to her friend there were really *too* many, she felt guilty, now they were well-to-do and not scrimping and saving as when Jessica was born, *now* they were deluged with baby things, almost three hundred presents!—she'd be writing thank-you notes for a solid year.)

At Lake St. Cloud, Jessica thought, it will be different.

At Lake St. Cloud, Baby won't matter so much.

But she was wrong: Immediately she knew she was wrong, and wanting to come here was maybe a mistake. For never before had the big old summerhouse been so *busy*. And so *noisy*. Baby was colicky sometimes, and cried and cried and cried through the night, and certain special rooms like the first-floor sunroom that was so beautiful, all latticed windows overlooking the lake, were given over to Baby and soon took on Baby's smell. And sometimes the upstairs veranda where pine siskins, tame little birds, fluttered about the trees, making their sweet questioning cries—given over to Baby. The white wicker bassinet that was a family heirloom, pink and white satin ribbons threaded through the wicker, the gauzy lace veil drawn across sometimes to shield Baby's delicate face from the sun; the changing table heaped with disposable diapers; the baby blankets, baby booties, baby panties, baby pajamas, baby bibs, baby sweaters, baby rattles, mobiles, stuffed toys—everywhere. Because of Baby, more visitors, including distant aunts and uncles and cousins Jessica did not know, came to Lake St. Cloud than ever before; and always the question put to Jessica was *Aren't you lucky to have a baby sister? a beautiful baby sister?* These visitors Jessica dreaded more than she'd dreaded visitors in the city for they were intruding now in this special house, this house Jessica had thought would be as it had always been, before Baby, or any thought of Baby. Yet even here Baby was the center of all happiness and the center of all attention. As if a radiant light shone out of Baby's round blue eyes that everybody *except Jessica* could see.

(Or were they just pretending?—with adults, so much was phony and outright lying, but you dared not ask. For then they would *know* that you *know*. And they would cease to love you.)

This secret, Jessica meant to tell the thistledown gray cat with the fur like breath but she saw in the cat's calm measuring unperturbed gaze that the cat already knew. He knew more than Jessica for he was older than Jessica, and had been here, at Lake St. Cloud, long before she was born. She'd thought him a neighbor's cat but really he was a wild cat belonging to nobody—*I am who I am, nobody knows my name.* Yet he was well fed, for he was a hunter. His eyes tawny-gold capable of seeing in the dark as no human being's eyes could. Beautiful with his filmy gray fur threaded just perceptibly with white, and his clean white bib, white paws and tail tip. He was a longhair, part Persian, fur thicker and fuller than the fur of any cat Jessica had ever seen before. You could see he was strong-muscled in his shoulders and thighs, and of course he was unpredictable in his movements—one moment it seemed he was about to trot to Jessica's outstretched hand to take a piece of breakfast bacon from her and allow her to pet him, as she pleaded, "Kitty-kitty-kitty! Oh, kitty—" and the next moment he'd vanished into the shrubbery behind the peony bushes, as if he'd never been there at all. A faint thrashing in his wake, and then nothing.

Tearing at her thumbnail with her teeth to draw blood, to punish herself. For she was such a silly child, such an ugly stupid left-behind child, even the thistledown gray cat despised her.

Daddy was in the city one week from Monday till Thursday and when he telephoned to speak to Mommy and to speak babytalk to Baby, Jessica ran away to hide. Later Mommy scolded her, "Where were you? Daddy wanted to say hello," and Jessica said, eyes widened in disappointment, "Mommy, I was here all along." And burst into tears.

The thistledown gray cat, leaping to catch a dragonfly and swallowing it in midair.

The thistledown gray cat, leaping to catch a pine siskin, tearing at its feathers with his teeth, devouring it at the edge of the clearing.

The thistledown gray cat, leaping from a pine bough to the railing of the veranda, walking tail erect along the railing in the direction of Baby sleeping in her bassinet. And where is Mommy?

I am who I am, nobody knows my name.

Jessica was wakened from sleep in the cool pine-smelling dark in this room she didn't recognize at first by something brushing against her face, a ticklish sensation in her lips and nostrils, and her heart pounding in fear—but fear for what, for what had it been threatening to suck her breath away and smother her, what was it, who was it, she did not know.

It had crouched on her chest, too. Heavy, furry-warm. Its calm gold-glowing eyes. Kiss? Kiss-kiss? Kissy-kiss, Baby?—except *she was not Baby*. Never Baby!

It was July, and the crimson peonies were gone, and there were fewer visitors now. Baby had had a fever for a day and a night, and Baby had somehow (how? during the night?) scratched herself beneath the left eye with her own tiny fingernail, and Mommy was terribly upset and had to be restrained from driving Baby ninety miles to a special baby doctor in Lake Placid. Daddy kissed Mommy and Baby both and chided Mommy for being too excitable, for God's sake honey get hold of yourself, this is nothing, you know this is nothing, we've been through this once already, haven't we?—and Mommy tried to keep her voice calm, saying Yes but every baby is different, and I'm

different now, I'm more in love with _____ than ever
with Jessie, God help me I think that's so. And Daddy
sighed and said, Well, I guess I am, too, it's maybe that
we're more mature now and we know how precarious life
is and we know we're not going to live forever the way it
used to seem, only ten years ago we *were* young, and
through several thicknesses of walls—at night, in the summerhouse above the lake, voices carried as they did not in
the city—Jessica sucked on her thumb, and listened; and
what she did not hear, she dreamed.

    For that was the power of the night, where the thistle-
down gray cat stalked his prey, that you could dream what
was real—and it *was* real, because you dreamt it.

Always, since Mommy was first unwell last winter, and
Baby-to-be was making her belly swell, Jessica had understood that there was danger. That was why Mommy walked
so carefully, and that was why Mommy stopped drinking
even white wine, which she loved, with dinner, and that was
why no visitors to the house, not even Uncle Albie who
was everybody's favorite, and a chain smoker, were allowed
to smoke on the premises. Never again! And there was a
danger of cold drafts even in the summer—Baby was sus-
ceptible to respiratory infections, even now she'd more
than doubled her wight. And there was a danger of somebody, a friend or relative, eager to hold Baby, but not
knowing to steady Baby's head and neck, which were
weak. (After twelve weeks, Jessica had yet to hold her
baby sister in her arms. She was shy, she was fearful. *No
thank you, Mommy*, she'd said quietly. Not even seated
close beside Mommy so the three of them could cuddle
on a cozy, rainy day, in front of the fireplace, not even
with Mommy guiding Jessica's hands—*No thank you,
Mommy*.) And if Mommy ate even a little of a food wrong
for Baby, for instance lettuce, Baby became querulous and
twitchy after nursing from gas sucked with Mommy's
milk and cried through the night. *Yet nobody was angry
with Baby.*

* * *

And everybody was angry with Jessica when, one night at dinner, Baby in her bassinet beside Mommy, gasping and kicking and crying, Jessica suddenly spat out her food on her plate and clamped her hands over her ears and ran out of the dining room as Mommy and Daddy and the weekend houseguests stared after her.

And there came Daddy's voice. "Jessie?—come back here—"

And there came Mommy's voice, choked with hurt. "Jessica!—that's *rude*—"

That night the thistledown gray cat climbed onto her windowsill, eyes gleaming out of the shadows. She lay very still in bed frightened *Don't suck my breath away! don't!* and after a long pause she heard a low hoarse-vibrating sound, a comforting sound like sleep, and it was the thistledown gray cat purring. So she knew she was safe, and she knew she would sleep. And she did.

Waking in the morning to Mommy's screams. Screaming and screaming her voice rising like something scrambling up the side of a wall. Screaming except now awake Jessica was hearing jays' cries close outside her window in the pines where there was a colony of jays and where if something disturbed them they shrieked and flew in quick darting swoops flapping their wings to protect themselves and their young.

The thistledown gray cat trotting behind the house, tail stiffly erect, head high, a struggling blue-feathered bird gripped between his strong jaws.

All this time there was one thing Jessica did not think about, ever. It made her stomach tilt and lurch and brought a taste of bright hot bile into her mouth so *she did not think about it ever.*

Nor did she look at Mommy's breasts inside her loose-fitting shirts and tunics. Breasts filled with warm milk bulging like balloons. *Nursing* it was called, but Jessica did not think of it. It was the reason Mommy could never be away from Baby for more than an hour—in fact, Mommy loved Baby so, she could never be away from Baby for more than a few minutes. When it was time, when Baby began to fret and cry, Mommy excused herself, a pride and elation showing in her face, and tenderly she carried Baby away, to Baby's room where she shut the door behind them. Jessica ran out of the house, grinding her fists into her tight-closed eyes even as she ran stumbling, sick with shame. *I did not do that, ever. I was not a baby, ever.*

And there was another thing Jessica learned. She believed it was a trick of the thistledown gray cat, a secret wisdom imparted to her. Suddenly one day she realized that, in the midst of witnesses, even Mommy who was so sharp-eyed, she could "look at" Baby with wide-open eyes yet not "see" Baby—where Baby was, in her bassinet, or in her perambulator or swing, or cradled in Mommy's or Daddy's arms, *there was an emptiness.*

Just as she was able calmly to hear Baby's name _____ and even speak that name _____ if required yet not acknowledge it in her innermost heart.

She understood then that Baby would be going away soon. For, when Grandma took sick and was hospitalized, Grandma who was Daddy's mother and who had once owned the summer place at Lake St. Cloud, though Jessica had loved the old woman she'd been nervous and shy around her once she'd begun to smell that orangish-sweet smell lifting from Grandma's shrunken body. And sometimes looking at Grandma she would narrow her eyes so where Grandma was there was a figure blurred as in a dream and after a while an emptiness. She'd been a little girl then, four years old. She'd whispered in Mommy's ear, "Where is Grandma going?" and Mommy told her to hush, just hush. Mommy had seemed upset at the question so Jessica knew not to ask it again, nor to ask it of Daddy. She hadn't known if she was scared of the emptiness where Grandma was or whether she was restless having to

pretend there was anything there in the hospital bed, anything that had to do with *her*.

Now the thistledown gray cat leapt nightly to her windowsill where the window was open. With a swipe of his
white paw he'd knocked the screen inward so now he
pushed his way inside, his tawny eyes glowing like coins
and his guttural mew like a human query, teasing—*Who?
You?* And the deep vibrating purr out of his throat that
sounded like laughter as he leapt silently to the foot of Jessica's bed and trotted forward as she stared in astonishment to press his muzzle—his muzzle that was warm and
sticky with the blood of prey only just killed and devoured
in the woods—against her face! *I am who I am, nobody
knows my name.* The thistledown gray cat held her down,
heavy on her chest. She tried to throw him off, but could
not. She was trying to scream, no she was laughing helplessly—the stiff whiskers tickled so. "Mommy! Daddy—"
She tried to draw breath to scream but could not for the
giant cat, his muzzle pressed against her mouth, sucked
her breath from her.

    *I am who I am, nobody knows my name, nobody can
stop me.*

It was a cool sky-blue morning in the mountains. At this
hour, seven-twenty, Lake St. Cloud was clear and empty,
no sailboats and no swimmers and the child was barefoot
in shorts and T-shirt at the edge of the dock when they
called to her from the kitchen door and at first she didn't
seem to hear then turned slowly and came back to the
house and seeing the queer, pinched look in her face they
asked her was she feeling unwell?—was something wrong?
Her eyes were a translucent pearly-blue that did not seem
like the eyes of a child. There were faint, bruised indentations in the skin beneath the eyes. Mommy who was holding Baby in the crook of an arm stopped awkwardly to
brush Jessica's uncombed hair from her forehead, which
felt cool, waxy. Daddy who was brewing coffee asked her
with a smiling frown if she'd been having bad dreams

again?—she'd had upsetting dreams as a small child and she'd been brought in to sleep with Mommy and Daddy then, between them in the big bed where she'd been safe. But carefully she told them no, no she wasn't sick, she was fine. She just woke up early, that was all. Daddy asked her if Baby's crying in the middle of the night had disturbed her and she said no she didn't hear any crying and again Daddy said if she had bad dreams she should tell them and she said, in her grave, careful voice, "If I had some dreams, I don't remember them." She smiled then, not at Daddy, or at Mommy, a look of quick contempt. "I'm too old for *that*."

Mommy said, "No one's too old for nightmares, honey." Mommy laughed sadly and leaned to kiss Jessica's cheek but already Baby was stirring and fretting and Jessica drew away. She wasn't going to be trapped by Mommy's tricks, or Daddy's. Ever again.

This is how it happened, when it happened.

On the upstairs veranda in gusts of sunshine amid the smell of pine needles and the quick sweet cries of pine siskins Mommy was talking with a woman friend on the portable phone, and Baby who had just nursed was asleep in her heirloom bassinet with the fluttering satin ribbons, and Jessica who was restless this afternoon leaned over the railing with Daddy's binoculars staring at the glassy lake— the farther shore, where what appeared to the naked eye as mere dots of light were transformed into tiny human figures—a flock of mallards in an inlet at the edge of their property—the tangled grasses and underbrush beyond the peony bed where she'd seen something move. Mommy murmured, "Oh, damn!—this connection!" and told Jessica she was going to continue her conversation downstairs, on another phone, she'd be gone only a few minutes, would Jessica look after Baby? And Jessica shrugged and said yes of course. Mommy who was barefoot in a loose summer shift with a dipping neckline that made Jessica's eyes pinch peered into Baby's bassinet checking to see Baby *was* deeply asleep, and Mommy hurried downstairs, and Jessica turned back to the binoculars, which were heavy in her hands, and made her wrists ache unless she rested them on the railing. She was dreamy counting the sailboats on the lake, there were five of them within her range of vision, it made her feel bad because it was after Fourth of July now and Daddy kept promising he'd get the sailboat fixed up and take her out, always in previous summers Daddy had sailed by now though as he said he wasn't much of a sailor, he required perfect weather and today had been perfect all day—balmy, fragrant, gusts of wind but not too much wind—but Daddy was in the city at his office today, wouldn't be back till tomorrow evening—and Jessica was brooding, gnawing at her lower lip recalling now there was Baby, Mommy probably wouldn't go with them in the boat anyway, all that was changed. And would never be the same again. And Jessica saw the movements of quick-flitting birds in the pine boughs and a blurred shape gray like vapor leaping past her field of vision, was it a bird? an owl? she was trying to locate it in the pine boughs, which were so eerily magnified, every twig, every needle, every insect enlarged and seemingly only an inch from her eyes, when she realized she'd been hearing a strange, unnerving noise, a gurgling, gasping noise, and a rhythmic creaking of wood, and in astonishment she turned to see, less than three yards behind her, the thistledown gray cat hunched inside the bassinet, on Baby's tiny chest, pressing its muzzle against Baby's mouth. . . .

The bassinet rocked with the cat's weight and the rough kneading motions of his paws. Jessica whispered, "No!—oh, no—" and the binoculars slipped from her fingers. As if this were a dream, her legs and arms were paralyzed. The giant cat, fierce-eyed, its filmy gray fur lifting light as milkweed silk, its white-tipped plume of a tail erect, paid her not the slightest heed as he sucked vigorously at the baby's mouth, kneading and clawing at his small prey who was thrashing for life, you would not think an infant of only three months could so struggle, tiny arms and legs flailing, face mottled red, but the thistledown cat was stronger, much stronger, and could not be deflected from his purpose—*to suck away Baby's breath, to suffocate, to smother with his muzzle.*

For the longest time Jessica could not move—this is what she would say, confess, afterward. And by the time she ran to the bassinet, clapping her hands to scare the cat away, Baby had ceased struggling, her face still flushed but rapidly draining of color, like a wax doll's face, and her round blue eyes were livid with tears, unfocused, staring sightless past Jessica's head.

Jessica screamed, "Mommy!"

Taking hold of her baby sister's small shoulders to shake her back into life, the first time Jessica had ever really touched her baby sister she loved so, but there was no life in the baby—it was too late. Crying, screaming "Mommy! Mommy! Mommy!"

And that was how Mommy found Jessica—leaning over the bassinet, shaking the dead infant like a rag doll. Her father's binoculars, both lenses shattered, lay on the veranda floor at her feet.

Harvey Jacobs

Harvey Jacobs is the author of the short story collection *The Egg of the Glak* and three novels, *Summer on a Mountain of Spices, The Juror,* and the satire *Beautiful Soup, a Novel for the 21st Century*. His stories have appeared in many major magazines, including *Omni, Esquire,* and *Playboy,* and in some forty anthologies, including *Blood Is Not Enough* and *Snow White, Blood Red*. He contributed several scripts for the TV series *Tales of the Darkside* and *Monsters*. Two film scripts, *The Juror* and *A Race for the Cup,* are in development. He is currently at work on another film script, *Toonerville,* and a new short story collection. He lives in New York.

In this story a cat does what cats do—and her mistress learns to cope. . . .

Thank You for That

HARVEY JACOBS

> *Thank you for that, thank you for that*
> *You are a gentle and generous cat.*

DARLEEN KRANTZ WAS no poet. The song just popped into her mind and stayed. She was no singer either, her one attempt at choir was a fiasco, but she sang her cat song whenever Jubal brought her a gift. Nobody but Jubal ever heard so what did it matter in the infinite scheme of things?

Darleen spent most of her time involved with small things around her house. A lifestyle of solitude was her choice in a world of trauma and turbulence. Her own quiet city had become a battleground. When the sun set and the moon rose its peculiar gravity seemed to reach down and pull slime from the sewers. It simply wasn't safe to go out after dusk. That was one reason she got herself a cat. She wanted a companion in her self-contained universe.

Jubal's gifting began when she was a kitten, hardly the size of a saucer. She would tumble through the grass and come home with a leaf or a twig and sometimes a fat worm or slug that she laid at Darleen's feet. Darleen understood the gesture. She always made a fuss over Jubal's prize, pretending to treasure it, whatever it was, and wait to throw it into the disposable until after Jubal was out of sight and the present forgotten. That's when the song came to her, soon after Darleen chose Jubal from the City Pound, almost before the cat had a name.

> *Thank you for that, thank you for that*
> *You are a gentle and generous cat.*

* * *

After singing, pretending delight, Darleen feted Jubal, offering a gift for a gift, usually a bit of food, sometimes a new toy from Kmart. Then Jubal would roll onto her back and ask for her belly to be scratched. Darleen knew that some people thought cats cold and indifferent, proud and aloof, incapable of any real feeling. She wished those silly critics could see Jubal's eyes while their little ritual played out.

Jubal grew quickly. She became a rather large cat, well formed, black as night with a touch of white that sat like a cap on her head. Jubal was a basic cat, a no-nonsense descendant of alley cats, not a contender for a blue ribbon but with her own special beauty. And she *was* a gentle and generous cat, an ideal pet for Darleen who lived on a small inheritance, who helped make ends meet by clipping coupons for supermarket advertisements and resisting temptations like cable TV.

Darleen would watch Jubal's antics while pretending to busy herself, waiting for her cat to stretch and arch its body. She thought Jubal looked like a living cathedral in those moments, one of those splendid tributes to a moody, loving God. Even Jubal's exercises were a kind of offering.

> *Thank you for that, thank you for that*
> *You are a gentle and generous cat.*

As Jubal matured, her gifts changed. More innocent presents were replaced by mice and even small birds. It was, of course, the nature of the beast and no sign of special malevolence. Darleen would accept the gifts with a mild censure, trying to communicate to Jubal that dead rodents and sparrows were not the most cherished trophies. But Darleen was always careful to acknowledge the gesture and reward the intent. She wiped blood and feathers from her cat's puzzled face and sang her song.

Jubal's new surprises were not always easy to dispose of since the clever cat began to watch Darleen for what seemed like hours after bringing home a treasure. She would lie down and stare while Darleen carried on her charade of satisfaction even after the rolling over and the scratching were done with. When Jubal finally wandered into another room or left the house through her pet door to browse the yard, Darleen would drop a rigid corpse into a Hefty bag and tie it securely. At least time did not seem to expand Jubal's memory. The cat never sulked over those mysterious disappearances.

The Hefty bags went into a metal can that was emptied twice a week by the town collector who came at dawn to harvest Darleen's degradable garbage and the recyclable paper, plastic, bottles, and cans. If the sanitation man had any complaint about the bags filled with tiny tails, wings, legs, and beaks it was never voiced. Darleen left him a tip and a fruitcake for Christmas.

> *Thank you for that, thank you for that*
> *You are a gentle and generous cat.*

After Jubal was spayed, on the advice of the veterinarian, Darleen watched Jubal mope around the house. For a time her spirit sagged. Darleen felt her own share of guilt but realized it was for the best. The vet said it was a miracle that Darleen hadn't become a grandmother what with Jubal's wanderings. Kittens were a drug on the market. It would have been impossible to place Jubal's litter and insufferable to stand by while they were destroyed. Darleen did not have the temperament to become one of those cat ladies the neighbors joke about. One cat was quite enough for her.

But Jubal's recovery was quick and complete. In a matter of weeks she was her old self, though a bit less frivolous. Her frame thickened, her fur became stiffer, darker, her golden eyes peered out of deep caves. She became a more serious cat, even more of a companion to Darleen.

Jubal spent more time in the house. But when she ventured out, her former borders—the fence, the gate, the road—dissolved to wider horizons. She began to roam through the town. Darleen, who liked nothing better than being inside her own tight perimeters of house and garden, was anxious about Jubal's new geography.

In the market, a church, people would mention that they'd seen her cat running along distant streets, through strange neighborhoods, crossing dangerous highways. Darleen thought about sealing the pet door but she rejected the idea of keeping Jubal prisoner. As much as the cat's migrations worried her, there was also a positive feeling of pride in Jubal's curiosity and courage. Danger, Darleen knew, was the price of freedom.

There were no gifts for months, no bugs, mice, or birds, not even the dry leaves Jubal once loved to crunch in her mouth. Darleen realized she hadn't sung her song through a whole fall season. But then, in winter, Jubal's thoughtful affection returned. Darleen was in her kitchen when she felt a chill at her ankles. She knew it was a sudden wind from the pet door. Sure enough, there was Jubal, after a night on the town. She crouched near Darleen's shoe and shook something from between her teeth. Darleen sighed. She thought it was a small animal but quickly realized that it was a human finger. For the first time, Darleen struck out at her cat. Then she gathered Jubal up and offered an apology. How the ghastly thing came to be wherever Jubal scooped it up was no fault of the cat.

> *Thank you for that, thank you for that*
> *You are a gentle and generous cat.*

Darleen grabbed up the severed finger in a paper towel and put it in her sink. While Jubal watched, she went to call the police. When a voice answered she hung up. She was putting herself and her cat in jeopardy. Who could say what the police might do or say? At best the story would be in the newspaper and probably with a picture. And what would be the purpose? The finger was already lost. It seemed too shriveled to be reattached, even with modern medical miracles.

When she was released by Jubal's eyes, Darleen found a fresh Hefty bag. But that made no sense. Wind could tip the garbage can. Raccoons were foraging everywhere. If the garbageman found a finger sticking out of a ripped plastic bag, there would be no way to explain it. Even she laughed at the ludicrous confrontation such a discovery would demand.

Darleen put the finger in aluminum foil, then into the freezer. She needed time to think things through. She found Jubal stretched on a rug in the bathroom and lectured to the cat in a loud voice, more firm than harsh. Naturally, the cat had no idea of the reason for Darleen's long speech and rolled over to get its belly scratched.

Three nights later Jubal brought home another token. It was hidden inside her jaws. She rubbed against Darleen's leg, then coughed out somebody's eye. The eye was intact, a brown jelly eye, lying on the rug. It seemed to gaze at the wall where Darleen had grouped family photographs. The eye was not easy to handle. It was holding together but when she poked at it with a napkin it began to ooze. She had to devise a scoop made from aluminum foil, slide the eye into an empty horseradish jar, and lay it sideways in the freezer.

Darleen was so disturbed by the eye she forgot to sing to Jubal. The cat carried on, yowling and jumping from the table to the floor. It was rather sweet knowing that Jubal was really aware of the jingle and felt so deprived.

> *Thank you for that, thank you for that*
> *You are a gentle and generous cat.*

Darleen looked out of her window at the misty moon, the magnet that drew so much evil from its hiding place. She scratched Jubal's gut and explained to the cat that this was a difficult time, that it was especially important in difficult times to set a standard if only for oneself. Bits and pieces of some horror were certainly tempting but must be resisted, left where they lay. The dander of random violence should not be mistaken for trinkets or flowers. Jubal yawned.

Darleen decided not to watch the TV news anymore.

Though she didn't quite believe that news influenced Jubal, it just might. Every story was of urban rot, of clash, of awful accident, atrocity, or deceit. On the advice of friends, she installed a security system designed to set off alarms if any intruder broke its invisible seal. She also bought a larger freezer since Jubal continued to harvest the alien streets.

In jars, wrappers, bottles, cans, paper bags, Saran Wrap, and wax paper, Darleen had the makings of a felon or victim, or both, frozen inside her own fridge. She had bits of a face, a chunk of scalp, ears, toes, a leg tattooed with constellations, an elbow, hands, organs she didn't recognize, a full set of male genitals, and a liverish-looking heart. No matter how often she reasoned with Jubal, her message was lost in the flood of the cat's urge to please, to give something back in exchange for the love and warmth Darleen radiated. And to earn a just reward.

> *Thank you for that, thank you for that*
> *You are a gentle and generous cat.*

From time to time, Darleen would examine her cache of gifts, rigid, silent, purified by cold and time, made peaceful, healed, forgiven, made magic, redeemed, turned to icy crystal. She gave a name to her collection, Errol, endowed Errol with a history, a past, a present, most important, a future. She blushed to admit she felt less lonely.

Jubal was growing old and lazy but Darleen urged her to hunt, gave goodies and praise and, of course, the song.

Martha Soukup

Martha Soukup is one of the dwindling number of writers who only write short fiction. Her stories have been published in many science fiction magazines and anthologies, and she recently won the Nebula Award in the short story category. Her fiction has also been nominated for the Hugo and World Fantasy awards. Her story "Over the Long Haul" was adapted for Showtime. She waits for more Hollywood money to fall into her lap at her home in San Francisco. She has had the same cat, Scaramouche, since 1980, without ever doing anything terrible to her (the cat).

Here, like "White Rook, Black Pawn," is another, but very different, story of obsession—this one concerning the cat's nemesis: the rat.

To Destroy Rats

MARTHA SOUKUP

THIS IS THE only way to destroy rats.

I have lived with mice, in a sort of tolerant hatred, or hateful tolerance. I have laid traps for them, and they have laughed at the traps. In the night I could hear them whisper to each other, almost catch the mousely details of their plans for snatching bits of cheese, or even smears of peanut butter, from the fateful lever, the one meant to trip death down onto their necks. I could hear them giggle as it fed them instead.

Hateful, fateful: Mice love rhymes, love all manner of trivial foolish games; mice put these idiot rhymes into my head. That is another reason I do not like mice. But I can live with this inanity. Mice are fools with their foolish games, and the best they can hope for is stalemate, petty irritation, which I, man to their rodent, am evolved past regarding.

Rats make war. It is rats or you, you or rats. Rats will win by any means necessary. You must fight by any means necessary.

I must win by any means.

First I tried the things they suggest, those hardware-store men who do not know war except as a field for commerce. I tried the bigger, crueler, rat-size cousin of the spring tapes the mice had giggled at. The rats relieved them of their treats and temptations, quietly, guerrillas stealing in and out of battle before their enemy—I—could see them, not a blur of visible movement, not a whisper of noise.

I poisoned the bait, and with hideous rattish intelligence they let the poison be. I bought catch-ems promised by the hardware men to stick and pull their cunning, ugly hands and feet, and in the morning I would look for the baleful stare of an immobilized rodent that never was there. A rat knows the difference between the careless bounties of man and his lies. Rats do not joke and do not giggle, but somewhere hidden in my walls they mocked me.

Before I had attained the will necessary to ignore the mice, I once purchased a cat, for five dollars, from a banal little housewife down the street, reasoning that suffering the intrusion of one alien creature in my house would be more tolerable than the presence of dozens of chattering, asinine little rodents. The cat was plump and white, with blank blue eyes, bearing some grotesque name—Fluffy or Muffins—that I dismissed as soon as the silly woman pronounced it to me, along with her protestations that she would have pampered the creature until its eventual death of obese old age had her snot-nosed daughter not developed an allergy.

After I had brought it in its carry case to my home and told it to earn its keep with slaughter, I had soon learned it was no more than vermin itself. The creature would sit at the foot of my chair or my bed, staring as though it expected something of me. Feed yourself, I told it.

But it had refused. Though fat mice scampered through the walls, the hapless brute expected to feed off me just as they did: yet with the gall to demand I cater to it willingly. Its presence became more insistent, as though this were its house, not mine. It stared at me hour after hour. Intolerable. Finally I had been compelled to shove the scrawny thing back into its carry case, using a broom I later discarded, and take it out to a scrubby little wood miles from my house.

There is no good in this mendacity, I told it, when it refused to come out of the case and find its way in the woods. You are a man, beholden to no one, or you are vermin. And I walked away, knowing I might have to live with mice, but at least I would never again share my home with anything that selfishly presumptuous. Mice, at least, behind their bravado, are cowards.

But I had not then calculated on rats.

The mice had taken little notice of this feline incursion. Only the arrival of the rats drove them off. After the rats came, I never heard another giggle. The mice knew which was the real threat.

To destroy rats, it would take much sterner measures than those that had already failed against mice.

I purchased guns. I sat in the kitchen late one night, the next night, the next night, the next. I slept days, calling in sick, because rats are patient and can wait one night, two, or three. On the fifth night one walked calmly in front of the stove. I could hear its claws click on the linoleum. Slowly I raised the barrel of my nine-millimeter pistol. The creature stopped in its path and looked at me. It was nearly the size of my two fists, its eye calmly baleful. I centered my aim on its dark and scruffy body and squeezed the trigger. The noise deafened me and it was some moments before I looked for the fragments of its corpse. What I saw was a sharp black hole in the broiler door of the oven. The rat was gone.

Over the next three nights they came and went as they pleased through the kitchen. Foam plugs in my ears, I fired at every shadow of their movement. My hand is steady and my eye good, but I killed not one of them. The third night the officers came to my door, and after I finally managed to send them away, the smaller of the two darting a suspicious look back at me, I unloaded the clips from the guns. Defending one's home against intruders should not fairly attract the attention of the law, but there it was.

The rats would accept a victory won that way, though it was not of their own merit, the dishonorable cheaters, but I would not give it to them. This war is man against creature: They take me down or I take them. I would not let them make allies of my fellow man. I shut the guns away in the closet.

I put the brightest lights in every socket, floodlights in

the single-outlet ceiling fixtures and 150-watt incandescent bulbs in the multiple-socket chandeliers, and left them on all night and all day. I bought lamps, and armed them, likewise, with 150-watt bulbs. I wore sunglasses; I slept, by day, with a black cloth tied around my eyes. Even with dark glasses the light was staggering. I found myself stumbling on a simple walk to the bathroom. This torture would surely drive them, screaming, to thrash helplessly on my floors. Behind the wallboards was the dark they craved, but if they stayed there they would starve. And they could not leave.

And yet, I would grope my way through the overheated, overbright air of my house to a cupboard to take down a box of cereal and find new holes gnawed through the cardboard box and plastic interior bag. Deposited beside spilled crumbs of flaked wheat were several hard dark turds, the carelessly confident signature of an insolent parasite.

What were they doing? Squeezing their beady eyes tight against radiation and navigating my home by cunning memory? I tried to find out but could not see their passage in the blinding electrical glare. They had turned my offensive to their own advantage, again.

If I could not starve them out indirectly I must do so directly. I removed every bit of food from the kitchen. I ate pizza and Chinese food that I had delivered to my door, wrapped the remains in plastic, and drove them by night to deposit in back-alley Dumpsters half a mile from my house.

The rats did not leave. I could hear them. Turds began to appear in the middle of the floor, where, horribly, before I learned to look, I stepped, slipped, on them. By my bed, in the hallway, in the center of the bathtub. Insolence.

I scrubbed the kitchen down. Not a dried spill of orange juice down a cupboard, not a crumb of toast remained. I ran the vacuum cleaner for hours. There was no place in my house that could not be used to perform surgery.

Except that there was still the spoor of the rats, trailing across my path.

There was no mirth in their joke: There was dead serious purpose. They announced themselves masters of my human domain; they would settle for nothing now but my total defeat, my total acquiescence. It was written in the toothmarks they left nibbled on the legs of my furniture. In rattish code these marks demanded surrender. Though I had not fully seen one since the rat who evaded my first bullet, their takeover of my house was thorough and unmerciful. I had failed to destroy them.

How could I destroy them? Rats are not prey for humans, but their unwelcome beneficiaries. Before there were humans, rats scraped a miserable existence, forced to compete among a hundred honest beasts. When man appeared, the rats rejoiced. Human civilization was the making of them. It would be justice to tear civilization down, if only to spite their lazy, criminal triumph.

Thinking that, I sat in my kitchen, a room cold and bright and sterile, but still the playground of vermin. There was no visible hint they were there, or that the mice they had driven away with their bullying muscle had been there before. But I could feel their presence. I knew they were now so bold as to walk through every room of my house, just outside the edges of my vision; but the kitchen, empty as it was of food, remained their stronghold. I sat in my kitchen with a lighter and a candle and the last two weeks of morning newspaper, bundled neatly in a paper shopping bag. That neatness was marred. They had shredded and stolen paper from one corner. Somewhere it was made into a nest, for hideous pink naked rat infants to squall in.

I flicked the lighter on and off. I lit the candle and held it to the bag. An inch away; closer. I turned off the light switch and moved the candle again, watched the torn newspaper glow by orange flame. If I burned down the house they would die, roasted between the wallboards, shrunken charcoal corpses. Firemen's hoses would wash them, crumbling, into the gutters.

I touched the flame to the bag. I could feel tiny eyes staring at me. Then I knew that they were in no danger from the fire, that they were already deserting, as rats always desert. The flames would not outrun them. They would watch the fire from the bushes in the back of the yard, and when the ashes cooled, they would return to steal final spoils from the ruins.

Yellow flame licked from the shredded newspaper. I stamped it out. Even man's first and deadliest tool means nothing to rats. Blackened ripples in beige linoleum remained as witness to a last rodent victory.

As long as man walks the earth, the parasite rat will prey on the fruits of his labor. To destroy rats I would have to destroy every human artifact. That is out of my power.

Yet this is war. To quit is to surrender, to surrender is to be enslaved.

The chemical stench from the bubbled linoleum wafts around me. I can feel them peering around cabinets and appliances, looking to see what has become of my fire. Disappointed, no doubt, that I have not finished the job, failed to burn myself homeless or burn myself up, while they simply moved to the next house down the block. One less man, two dozen more rats.

I can hear them scuttling restlessly. I think I see a whisker twitch. They are all around me, wondering what I will do next, what pathetic failed attempt it will be. Their stubborn insistence on life at any price now teaches me that animals indeed have more vital force than we do. I thought I had invested everything in this war, but they had more to give than I did. In this moment I nearly gave in to despair. I did everything the human mind can devise, and their sheer animal persistence defeated me.

I nearly give it up, but instead I give it over.

No human effort can touch them. Their animal world is too small, pervasive, vital. I cannot reach down from my lofty world and point destruction at them.

Only in their animal world can they be caught and rent and killed, yet in that world there is not the matching hatred of my human soul. Only a human's soul can match a rat's for hatred. Only human hatred and animal hunger together could match their hatred and hunger. To kill any one of them would be worth any price. The hunger to kill rats grows. It consumes me. I follow the hunger where it leads.

I must be smaller to follow them when they run from me. I must be agile to turn their corners. I must smell them. I must hear them. I push my broad face into a hunter's point, a carnivorous spearhead. I pull my ears high, high to hear their rancid breathing. I open the pupils of my eyes high until no darkness could hide a rat from my sight. I bend my legs to springs. I curl my hands to claws. I am tooth and nail. I hear them running in all directions. They are too late.

I am destruction.

The cat tears at the confining cloth, tangling sleeves, and fur-catching zippers, until it is free, leaping with one fluid motion behind the refrigerator.

For hours there are strange sounds, hisses, growls, and high, tiny screams, from basement to attic.

Eventually the authorities declare the house abandoned.

When it is put up for sale and the buyers' contractor inspects it, he says that, except for the bullet hole in the kitchen, it is the cleanest property he has examined in years.

Sarah Clemens

Sarah Clemens, like many writers, has had a checkered career, working as a medical illustrator, writer of bogus horoscopes, portrait artist, and film critic. She lives in Florida, which she finds very inspirational for writing horror. Her first story was published in 1988 in *Ripper!* and her second in 1994 in *Little Deaths,* UK edition. This is her third.

This story is inspired by a trip to Rome during which Clemens says, "The cats were everywhere, as were the Gypsies. The Romans love their cats and feed them daily. They are very independent felines that may or may not deign to come to your outstretched hands. It is quite obvious that the ruins of ancient Rome belong to the cats."

I Gatti di Roma

SARAH CLEMENS

"SO THIS IS hell," said Melina as she turned and saw Renata glaring at her. Wearily she took her leave of Constantine's Arch, making her way through the afternoon crowds to the older woman, who stood with her puffy feet spread apart and her lips pursed. As usual, Mario stood behind Renata, smoking and staring straight ahead. He might as well have been in Tupelo. It was summer and the tourists were like overweight gnats swarming around the arch and the Colosseum. Melina had finished a shoot here a few weeks earlier, but even so, she couldn't just ignore the splendid and imposing structure with its original carvings and its sculptures taken from earlier monuments. Romans filched shamelessly from earlier works to build whatever they fancied, but seldom did this work out as beautifully as Constantine's Arch. In the blinding sunlight Melina approached Renata, who was clutching a frayed shoebox under her arm.

"What were you looking at?"

"You mean which particular scene?"

"Don't start," Mario said. "Let's just get this done."

"Take the ashes."

"Okay, Mama."

She handed him the shoebox and reached out for Melina's arm, clutching it as they crossed the street. Renata's hand was soft and clammy, her nails like bright red talons. What Melina hated most was the way Renata's fingers twitched constantly, as if they had a life of their own.

They crossed over into the shadow of the Colosseum

and stood in line with a group of dowdily dressed Hungarians.

"Your father loved Rome," said Renata, releasing Melina's arm and patting at her stiff hairdo. "He would be happy to know his ashes are goin' here." They were moving out from under the ground-level arcade and into the Colosseum itself. They climbed stone steps to a landing—and there they were, looking out over the awesome decay. You had but to be still and shadows of the past would take on color and noise. You could see the arena floor, weapons plunged into jerking bodies; feel the heat and copper smell of the blood. The Colosseum echoed with violence. On a more practical side, the pictures Melina had taken here launched her career in photography. She shot them as part of her thesis on Roman architecture and her professor had suggested she show them at a gallery.

"How about here?" asked Renata.

Melina turned to see her looking down over the railing. The arena floor was long gone and broken rows of underground walls filled the vast space like jagged teeth. "This is okay," she said softly.

"I want to be alone for a few minutes," said Renata, crossing herself.

Melina and Mario wandered away, following the railing.

"You think it's as big as the Astrodome?"

Melina took a deep breath. "It could hold seventy thousand people. Which is more than I know about the Astrodome."

"Mm. Pretty big." Mario finished his cigarette and flicked the butt over the railing. "Did your mother tell you about the letter Dimi left?"

"No." Her mother had called her a little over a week ago, telling her that Papa had killed himself by cutting his wrists and that she had inherited all his money. As Melina listened in shock her mother added, "Sweetheart, you should come home now. Your cousin Nick works for a big studio, he makes good money taking pictures of high school kids for yearbooks. He could get you a job there, you could be with your family. . . ." By habit, Melina declined and said good-bye. Then she had broken down. But after the first wave of grief she wanted to know more. The *why* of it.

"He knew Mama was superstitious," Mario continued, lighting another cigarette, "so he left a letter saying there would be a curse on her if she didn't dump his ashes on the Acropolis. But being as pissed off as she was about the money . . ."

"She didn't go to Athens. She came here." To Renata, there was no difference between one old place and another, so she came to Rome, where she could understand what people said. Melina smiled faintly. "If only Renata knew. In the 1500s Benvenuto Cellini was supposed to have held a séance here. He and a priest drew a magic circle and did all the incantations, then demons were supposed to have appeared—"

"I'm ready," Renata announced.

"Okay, Mama." Mario set the shoebox on the railing and lit another cigarette.

Melina peered over the edge and saw a cat stretched out on the dusty flagstones, a regal yellow tiger with a white chest. He basked oblivious to the throngs above. He stretched out like a small version of the lions that had fought here, then looked straight up at Melina, holding her glance for a moment. Then he turned and began grooming.

Renata picked at the tape holding the shoebox, muttering under her breath. *"Come sei stato crudele a trattarmi in questo modo? Come potresti fare una cosa del genere?"*

. . . how cruel of you to treat me in such a way . . . how could you be so cruel? Melina fought back tears. How *dare* Renata say that of her father. After spending over twenty years with Renata, Melina would have slashed her wrists, too.

The box fell from the balustrade as Renata gripped the plastic bag of ashes it contained. The tomcat was on his feet in a blur of motion as the cardboard hit the ground, but recovered just as quickly and raised his tail in inquiry as he strode over to sniff.

"Good-bye, Dimi," Renata said with an unconvincing quaver in her voice. She turned the bag over and the ashes cascaded down. Melina watched, appalled, as the grit and powder hit the cat full force.

"What's that cat doing there?" shrilled Renata.

"Jesus, Renata!" Melina yelled back. "Didn't you see him?"

The cat had yowled and bolted, shaking off clouds of white powder. He stopped to lick a paw, then dart off again. Suddenly he turned and glared balefully up at them.

Mario was laughing silently, cigarette smoke snorting out his nose.

Melina looked away, fighting to control her rage.

"That damn cat!" cried Renata. "What if he stole Dimi's soul?"

"Don't start, Mama."

"Jesus, Mary, and Joseph, what am I going to do?"

"Cats don't steal souls, Mama."

"Maybe a priest will know."

"Stop it, Mama."

"Melina, we have to find a priest."

She turned abruptly to face them. "He killed himself, Renata! A priest won't help."

"Oh, Jesus help me," moaned Renata. "Lord Jesus help me."

They got Renata back to the hotel, where she could be fussed over by Mario and given a couple of highballs. Melina stalked off to catch a bus back to her apartment. She had almost forgotten how draining it was to be around Renata, an effect compounded by bad memories. Dimitri Pappas had left his wife and eight-year-old daughter for Renata Testa and her ten-year-old son. Husband number one had died several years before, keeling over from a stroke as he was preparing Renata's breakfast. Maybe Melina's mother was a nag, but whatever had Papa seen in Renata? Granted, she had once been attractive, in a heavy-lidded Italian sort of way, but Melina had always seen through her. The way she pinched Melina's cheek when she came to visit and said, "Such a fat little girl!"

Renata took delight in Melina's childhood obesity and her blunt, ugly looks. Her son Mario was so handsome.

Every possible surface in the house was covered with plastic, except for an expensive couch in the living room that no one was allowed to sit on. Even worse was her obsession to control everyone around her. She had no concept of privacy. Every time Melina had visited she remembered Renata jerking the bedroom door open several times a night, staring at her in bed before slamming the door shut. She wasn't allowed to lock the bathroom door, and Renata often came in there, too. And Mario went through this all the time. He never had toys; Renata wouldn't waste money on them. The one puppy he was allowed was taken to the pound when he got too large, and she told Mario it had been hit by a car. He couldn't go on the class field trip to Washington, D.C., because five days was too long to be away and it was a waste of money. Though Melina suffered the many exquisite forms of torture children inflict on their ugly peers, she particularly dreaded being around Mario. Having no control over his own life, he made her his special project. When they were sent out to play, he would pin her down, spit on her, kick her, and grope clumsily at her crotch and breasts. Melina finally worked up the courage to tell her father when she was twelve and he went to Renata, who screamed at him without stopping for two hours.

"The only way I can protect you," he told her afterward, looking down at his hands, "is to send you home to your mother." The shame she felt was terrible, and she didn't see her father for several years because she couldn't deal with his weakness. Of all the emotions she felt upon hearing that he was dead, the anger had taken her most by surprise. She wanted to go back in time, shake his shoulders, tell him to slap Renata, walk out on her—something. She found herself clenching her fists when she thought about it.

At seventeen the fat vanished and a beautiful face emerged, one of lean Greek lines and expressive dark eyes. Just like that she became another person, one treated more like a human. At first, she went to college to escape her family, who had her whole life planned out because she was overweight and would never find a husband. Now the future seemed some marvelous adventure, and school just the first step. Renata had been stunned when Melina visited before leaving for college. Mario was getting homely and putting on weight; and he had the same conquered look about him that Melina saw in her father. But where Papa looked sad and distant, Mario was taciturn and tense. The first time they were alone together he had backed her into a wall, pinning her as he had years before.

"Remember how I used to do this?" He grinned, groping for her breasts.

She twisted away and by sheer luck rammed her elbow into his solar plexus. As he crumpled to his knees she felt a joyous surge and said, "Don't ever touch me again. Not ever. God, you make me sick."

Papa had walked in at that moment, taken it all in, and his face creased with pain. Melina read the look and felt pain, too, remembering that day when she was twelve and he had been so impotent, realizing that he still was.

Melina boarded the bus for her apartment and sat next to an old Roman woman in black, her silvery hair pulled back into a bun just like Melina's. As the streets went past, unbidden tears fell silently as Melina stared ahead, overwhelmed by a wave of memory and emotion. The old woman tapped her knee and Melina slid sideways to let her leave. She grasped Melina's shoulder for support as the bus stopped and said kindly, *"Sei troppo belle e giovane per avere lacrime negli occhi."*

You're too young and beautiful to have tears in your eyes.

Melina watched her climb off the bus, and the knot inside loosened a little. What if a cat *had* stolen her father's soul, his *animus*, as the Romans would say? Dimitri Pappas would like nothing better than to roam the Colosseum as a tomcat, taking naps in the sun, dreaming about fights in the arena ... Beautiful Rome, with its narrow streets and its terra-cotta colors, the Baroque grandeur and ancient ruins. With its warm people. *Good-bye, Papa*.

She ate supper that night alone with Mario. Renata was resting in her room, probably moaning in Italian.

"So how long are you staying here?" he asked her.

"Until late summer. I have an exhibit in New York this fall of the pictures I've been shooting."

"Pictures of all those cats?"

"Yes. There will be a book coming out."

"Why?"

"Lots of people like cats, Mario."

"So how much money will you make?"

"I don't talk about money."

They ate for a while before he spoke up again. "She's resting all day tomorrow, so I can go sight-seeing with you after all."

In a moment of weakness she had promised to show him the sights. He had looked pretty harmless at the airport. "Just remember I'm having lunch with my girlfriend at the American Embassy. You'll have to fend for yourself for an hour or so."

"No problem."

No problem, hell. He'd probably stand at the gates of the embassy and wait for her. He was used to having women take care of things for him. Mario smiled a lot around his mother, an indulgent "Oh, now, Mama" sort of smile. But away from her, his eyes glazed over and his mouth never so much as twitched. He was in his thirties and completely lost around people his own age, especially since Kelly, his wife of short duration, had left him. Pretty, straightforward Kelly who had seen good in Mario and brought it out. It must have driven Renata crazy not only to lose control of her boy, but to a woman who saw through her and ignored her completely. Melina had always wondered why Mario and Kelly broke up. Whatever the reason, he had gone downhill badly. The patchy way his hair was cut, the cheapness of his clothes; everything about Mario was a little . . . wrong.

Her mother had recently described Mario to her in a

letter as "doing just fine. He has turned out to be such a nice boy, living with his mother after his divorce." Keeping her distance from family definitely sharpened Melina's perspective and firmed her resolve to ignore her mother's pleading to come live in the old neighborhood. Recognition as a photographer had given her a new world to live in. She had friends who never covered their furniture or had plastic holy shrines in their halls. People who treasured books and conversed intelligently.

The next morning they started near the embassy on the Via del Quirinale with the church of Sant'Andrea, a small gem of Baroque architecture designed by Bernini. The oval church told the story of St. Andrew's martyrdom and ascension into heaven, and all the lines of the architecture carried the eye up to the sculpture of the saint surrounded by putti and garlands and symbols of the fisherman—nets, oars, shells, reeds . . .

"You learn all that in college?" Mario wanted to know when they were outside. On the steps of Sant'Andrea a cat brushed against her legs and she bent to stroke it.

"Most of it. Ah, just a few blocks more and we reach the corner of the Quattro Fontane. There's a fountain on each corner, and each intersection gives you a different view." Papa had lavished money on her education in ancient history, including several years of graduate study in Rome. She was the only one on either side of the family with a college degree, and she felt like an alien when she visited them in their cheaply furnished houses and watched them watch game shows. Melina had tried very hard to get her mother to visit Rome so she could understand her new life. But Mama refused, afraid of anyplace away from home.

Mario followed her, craning his neck to look where Melina would point, looking straight through every stone and statue. She had never known anyone as incurious. Only during his brief marriage had he shown any signs of coming alive.

"We're coming up on the Fontana del Tritone, also by Bernini," she said. "It's in a big piazza, the Piazza Barberini, and you might think about eating lunch here while I go see Heather."

Two cats floated past them with that lean and confident look of Roman strays. Melina made a mental note to bring back scraps from lunch.

"There's enough cats in this city," said Mario.

Melina swung once more into lecture mode. "*I Gatti di Roma*. They're as famous as anything else here. The Romans brought them from Egypt and took them on to Britain. They mostly live around ruins protected by the government, like the Forum and the Colosseum, and Romans feed them." There was a black-and-white one perched on the upwind edge of the fountain, where the spray from Triton's conch wouldn't get her.

"So where's the embassy?"

Melina looked past the cat and pointed. "Just up that street, Via Veneto. That's where they filmed parts of *La Dolce Vita*."

Mario looked at her blankly.

"Never mind." She couldn't help looking at her watch. "Anything else to see before you go to lunch?"

"Well, there's the Fontana delle Api, fountain of the bees—" She broke off.

"Yeah?"

"I almost forgot. Santa Maria della Concezione."

Mario looked tired. "Another church?"

"Not like any other."

He shrugged and followed her across the piazza, and out of the crowd came a plump girl of about thirteen, a pitiful look on her round face. She was holding out a magazine. She came straight up to Mario, jabbering at high speed. Everything about her was unusually washed out, from her skin to her brown, greasy hair. Her clothes were a strange mélange of outdated styles crudely patched together.

"She's a Gypsy," said Melina. "Ignore her and she'll quit bothering you."

The girl gripped Mario's pants and tugged.

"Her parents taught her to beg. Usually they work in

teams, so one can distract while the other one picks your pocket. She's just trying to sell you a week-old magazine."

Melina walked ahead and Mario pushed the girl away, his face contorting with revulsion. She backed away and the pitiful look vanished as she searched for another mark.

He caught up with Melina on the shaded sidewalk of Via Veneto and she pointed up the hill to the imposing Palazzo Margherita, which housed the American Embassy. "I'll meet you by that gate there, where the guards are. Okay?"

"Yeah. That kid was one of the most disgusting things I've ever seen."

"Everyone here hates them. They pick pockets, beg; but they don't get much into serious crime. My European friends think I'm crazy, but I just feel sorry for them."

"She makes me wanna puke."

Melina resisted a response. They were mounting the steps of a gray, ordinary church. Inside, in a small vestibule, a monk stood pointing to the donations box and a sign that read NO PHOTOGRAPHS ALLOWED.

"What's the deal?" asked Mario.

"You'll see."

She stuffed some notes into the box and led him downstairs into the Capuchin crypts. "There are over four thousand monks resting here."

The monks had arranged the bones of their brothers to decorate four cramped chapels. Stacks of age-darkened skulls climbed the walls and formed arches. White plaster ceilings were covered with rust-brown ribs and vertebrae in macabre arabesque tracery. Femurs and scapulae made up a chandelier, a clock, and an altar where a skeleton in monk's garb slouched, hemmed in by walls of bones.

"Holy shit," said Mario after several minutes.

The first time Melina had come here she was convinced there would be a smell, perhaps a rotting odor. There was none, of course, just a mustiness from the earthen floors. The bones were far too old to smell.

"This is great!" he said. "What did they do, boil down anyone who croaked?"

Melina shrugged. She'd never dwelt on that, as if it were too private. "I have to go, Mario. If you want post-cards, they have all kinds out there where the monk is."

"And let Mama find them?"

He had a point. Renata went through everything Mario owned.

"Enjoy," she said, and left.

He watched her go, slim and polished where she had been so fat and ugly as the child he terrorized. Mama hated Melina because of her education and contempt for them, and she had nearly gone insane when she found out Dimi had left Melina all his money. The old man could never stand up to Mama when he was alive, but, oh, what he had done to her dead! Mario didn't care. What he thought about was pulling down Melina's tight bun of long, black hair and holding her so she couldn't get away as she had the last time. He'd thought a lot about it since then, and coming to Rome was a momentous occasion that made him feel . . . strong, ready. For a long time he looked at the multitude of stacked bones. Thought about all the deaths they represented. Then he left and went down Via Veneto to the fountain that looked like all the others. The plump Gypsy girl was still there, annoying people with her shrill voice and her magazine. He could imagine what Mama would say about her, how she would yammer on and on and probably compare her to his ex-wife, Kelly, and inside he felt a shell cracking open, its thick acid trickling down his spine, into his lungs, making each breath heated, la-bored. The Gypsy girl was fat, like Melina used to be, be-fore she spurned him. Fat, like Mama.

"What you got there?" he asked her. She rushed up, speaking Italian. He jingled the change in his pocket and smiled at her. She returned the same empty smile.

Breathing a little more quickly, he turned his back on her, rattling his change again. Without looking, he knew she was following. Up a side street and into someone's doorway. Into a shadow.

She held back now, no doubt aware of the dangers.

On a sudden inspiration, he pulled out a 50,000-lire note pantomiming that she should lift up her dress to let him see underneath. She pulled the dirty skirt up and down her fat little tongue sliding out of her mouth. Then she reached for the money. Grabbing her by the nape of the neck, he jerked her small, smelly body against his and squeezed her throat with both hands while she writhed and twisted. The life pulsed away so easily. But he held on a little while longer, just to be sure. Her tongue bulged from her mouth and a thin line of drool touched his fingers. Jerking his hand back, he shoved her to the floor of the alcove, wiped the wetness on her blouse, and scanned the shadows for the 50,000-lire note. There was a cat sitting on it, glaring up at him with brilliant yellow eyes, pupils like black pits. He kicked out and the cat merely moved away with its ears laid back, leaving dusty white footprints. Snatching his money, Mario looked back at the doorway before he left, and there were three cats sitting there, whiskers thrust forward, tails lashing.

He was waiting at the gate.

"Did you get something for lunch?" she asked. There was a funny, slack look on Mario's face, but his eyes were strangely alive, and he looked straight at her. "Nah. just—looked around some."

She shrugged off the vagueness of his answer and brought him a sandwich.

"I'm going to the Vatican tomorrow. All those shops along there, I can get me a new crucifix at a good price." Renata dabbed with a napkin, which smeared spaghetti sauce on her lips. She was wearing her good dress, a blue and-white polyester affair that stretched tautly over her belly and breasts. Her plastic beads and clip-on earrings almost matched the blue of the dress. With a knobby blue-veined hand she pushed her glasses up her nose and peered toward the bathroom, where Mario had gone. They were eating at a *tavola calda,* where the buffet food was cheap and there were no waiters to tip.

"You two going somewhere tomorrow?" Renata asked.

"In the morning."

She smiled ingratiatingly, which made Melina a little queasy. "He wants to be with you more, honey. He never loved that Kelly, you know."

"Oh, I think they were a nice couple. Mario seemed very happy."

"Nice girls aren't in the army and they don't go to Arabia to be in some war when their place is at their husband's side." Renata paused to suck at her wine. "She sent him letters, you know, but I was home when the mail came and I hid them all." She winked heavily. "He thought she didn't write."

Melina felt sick to her stomach. "Oh, my God."

"He yelled at her when she got back, and she told him she did write and that I probably hid the letters. And Mario stood up for me, so she left."

"Does Mario know what you did?"

"He found out. But by then I had shown him what she was really like. You can't understand because you've never had a baby, dear. He was inside of me, a part of my flesh, and no one could love him like I do."

In stunned silence, Melina watched Mario heading for their table. He seemed oddly animated this evening.

"No desserts? Well, I want one, so let me get out some money . . ." He was digging through his pockets, and brought out a crumpled 50,000-lire note with a lot of white grit on it. "Picked up a lot of dust today," he mused. "Funny how Rome dust looks like ashes, doesn't it, Mama?"

Melina took him to Ostia Antica the next morning. She had the feeling that if she asked Mario, he'd just go back to the Capuchin crypts. They took the subway, then the train, and Mario gaped out the window as shoddy apartment buildings whipped past.

"Whoa! What's that?"

She looked out in time to see a highway overpass sheltering rows of derelict campers, most without wheels. It was a squalid encampment, littered with trash. "Gypsies," she told him.

He craned his neck until the trees obscured it from view. "They live like animals."

Shrugging, she said, "They live anywhere they can because people shun them."

The train drew up to a station and she noticed Mario looking at the name of the stop. After that it wasn't a long ride to Ostia Antica, the port city excavated out of the silt and mud of the Tiber. They explored the ancient avenues, peered into crumbled buildings, and admired the mosaics and worn sculptures. Ostia slumbered beneath the quiet tread of the curious, and Melina began to relax for the first time in days. With Mario in tow, she pointed out the firemen's barracks and the temples. They rested at the theater Septimius Severus had rebuilt, sitting halfway up the stone steps to watch gray clouds drift over the sun. A cool breeze hushed past and she looked down a few steps to see a regal tomcat, very much like the one at the Colosseum. No, *exactly* like the one at the Colosseum. He looked at her with melting warm eyes before jumping up the steps to rub against her. She extended her hand politely, and he brushed his face against her fingers, his deep purr booming.

"How did you get here from the middle of the city?" she wondered aloud.

He blinked blissfully, guarding his secrets. Then he looked at her again, and Melina felt something stirring from deep inside, a recognition—

"Cats," said Mario, lounging on the steps above her. "I'm getting sick of them."

The tomcat stiffened when he saw Mario, his eyes dilating so they were almost completely black. His ears flattened and his purr seemed to shift to a deep rattling growl, as if from the throat of a lion. Then he darted past Mario and vanished behind the stonework.

They left soon after and it seemed that everywhere Melina looked, there were cats, more than she'd ever seen, even here. And they all watched Mario. From under stone benches they stared at him with huge eyes, their lean bodies tensed and their tails twitching low to the ground. From crumbling windows and doorways they glared at him, their ears flattened. They eyed him from holes and crevices until he hunkered his shoulders and quickened his pace, hastening their departure from Ostia Antica.

Mario came out of the hotel bedroom drenched in sweat. "Mama, why did you turn off the air conditioner? I woke up because I was so hot."

She heaved herself up from her chair and turned the dial. "It's on now." She sat back, her hands folded in her plump lap, staring at an Italian soap opera on the television. She could sit like that for hours, never stirring.

"If you knew Italian, you could watch with me," she said, taking her eyes from the screen for a minute.

"You know I don't understand a word, Mama." When he was a child, she had boasted he only spoke American.

"Melina speaks Italian and Greek."

"Good for Melina. I'm going out."

"But it's almost dark! Where could you go?"

"I'm a big boy, Mama. And Rome's a lot safer than Miami. Melina says so."

"That Melina doesn't know anything. You're not going out."

"I'll see you when I get back."

"Don't leave me alone! You don't know what could happen to a woman if a man found her alone."

He smiled a private smile.

"Mario! I want you *here*. What if I have one of my spells? Lord Jesus help me if my son goes away and anything happens."

"Shut up, Mama."

"Are you sick, that you talk to me like that? You've been strange all night. Like you're happy."

"I am happy, Mama. I can do things here I never did at home." And with that, he left. She was crying after him, calling on Mary, Mother of God, then cursing him when he closed the door and headed for the elevator. Her recriminations were as unimportant as the rain that fell on his shoulders outside. Once on the subway, he sat in the starkly lit subway car, looking around at the tired blank faces of commuters and trying to stay calm, look like one of them. He got off at the stop by the Gypsy camp. There was no real pain, but taking care of the little Gypsy girl made him feel so good, as if he had attained a magic power. Power enough to talk back to Mama. It was completely dark now, and he wandered away from the station to find himself on a road dotted with dilapidated fences, tiny houses, and cats flitting through the shadows. Soft rain kept falling. There was lightning on the mountains around the city and he could hear thunder cracking across great distances.

A girl stood under a streetlight, the rain illuminated like silver needles. She was a Gypsy, wearing that odd mix of clothes the first girl had worn—out-of-date styles patched and decorated with bright bits of ribbon and fabric. Like any teenager, though, she defied even Gypsy convention by sporting punked hair and lots of piercings in her ears. She also wore too much makeup. He offered her cigarettes and lit it for her when she snatched one from the pack.

"Speak English?" he asked, not expecting her to.

"A little," she said. "You American, eh?"

"Yeah," he answered flatly.

She dragged hungrily on the cigarette and looked up at him. "Not many American cigarettes. Much money."

He pulled out the pack and gave it to her, amazed at how calm he could be.

"How much for you?" he asked.

"Oh, well," she said, smiling, running her hands through her necklaces. "Not much."

He reached into his pocket and pulled out a large note. Cocking an eyebrow, she took it and pointed into the bushes. She pulled him along through the dripping leaves to a crude lean-to. There was an old sleeping bag on the ground and they lay down together, her body pressed against him, her hands squeezing his growing hardness. He looked up and saw two iridescent yellow eyes, staring at him from the ebony shadows beneath the dripping shrubs. There was a hiss and the eyes winked away. He breathed the wet, earthy smell of the ground, heard the rain fall harder. And then his hands were on her warm throat, pushing the absurd necklaces out of the way, caressing her skin. He rolled on top of her and tightened his grip. She flailed out, but he was much heavier and his hands were strong. It was a simple matter of holding on, digging deeper, until she finally quit shuddering. Letting go, he gazed at her thoughtfully, then reached into her pocket to retrieve his cigarettes and money. It was wonderful, how helpless she was, and he pushed her skirt up as he decided what he wanted to do next.

"Come sei stato crudele a trattarini in questo modo!"

Renata's words kept coming back to Melina. *How cruel of you to treat me like this!*

It was a bright morning of clear air and cool dripping shadows. Last night's rain and thunder had played themselves out before dawn, and Rome seemed serenely quiet. In her darkroom Melina flicked through several photos without seeing them. Angrily she pulled her attention to the pile of proof sheets and prints. The wonderful shots she had taken of cats resting on fallen columns in the Forum, lounging about the baths of Caracalla.

"Come sei stato crudele . . ."

Something about the way Renata had said those words, the way they resonated with an anger beyond her usual pettiness.

With a sigh, Melina put down her pictures and her grease pencil. What had set Papa off, made him want to slash his wrists? Something must have pushed him over the edge. She couldn't ask Renata, but Mario might know. Reluctantly she picked up the phone and dialed.

"Oh, hi, Melina. Mama's gone to the Vatican for mass."

"Well . . . I just wanted to know if you still want to do some more sight-seeing. You're leaving tomorrow."

"Ah . . ." He made some rustling sounds and Melina knew she had woken him up. "Sure. If you want to."

"You said you wanted to see the Forum."

"All that stuff near the Colosseum?"

"Uh . . . yes. But, Mario, is it possible to do it without your mother? I need to ask you about a few things." She winced at the very idea that he might think her interested in him.

"No problem. She's going to visit friends after mass. They'll probably bullshit all day in Italian."

"Okay, then, see you in an hour?"

"Sounds good." He hung up without saying good-bye.

They made it to the Forum by early afternoon.

"Not much left, is there?" was all he said as they descended the steps to the Forum and wandered from one fragment to the next.

She pointed out the Arch of Septimius Severus and where some of the temples had stood and the massive remains of the Basilica of Maxentius, surrendering herself to the futility of getting Mario interested in anything. Sitting on stones near the Temple of Vesta, she looked out across the weeds while Mario lit a cigarette from a crushed pack.

"So what's up?" he asked her.

"I know Papa—cut his wrists, I know I got the money, but I seem to be missing some pieces."

He snorted with amusement. "He . . . did it messy, you know? He bled all over the bathroom, all over the carpets, all over that fucking couch she likes so much. The one she won't let you sit on. Christ, he bled so much in the bathroom, she's going to have to get it regrouted."

Melina fought back tears, and her hand fell slowly to rest on something soft, the back of a cat. Numbed with sadness, she simply stroked it and it looked up at her with familiar eyes. *Eyes like Papa's.* The tiger with the white chest. "So that's it?" she said finally.

"Almost." Mario stood up and moved away from the cat, who watched him. "Dimi took out a huge insurance policy, made a big deal out of it, made Mama the whaddayacallit—"

"Beneficiary."

"So Mama goes to cash it in the day after he dies, along with all the others she keeps in that safety deposit box, and guess what? All the older policies, they're not made out to Mama anymore, you get it all. And the new one? Since he committed suicide, it's no good."

A small black cat brushed Melina's legs as she absorbed this.

"I have to tell you, I'm getting sick of cats," said Mario. "Is there anyplace where there aren't cats?"

"Pompeii is full of dogs," she said distantly, unaware that a third cat had joined the other two.

"I thought Mama was going to have a heart attack right there on the spot. Old man Kallikrates, the insurance man, he looks at me like 'Get her outta here before she dies on me!' She was moaning in Italian all the way home."

Melina became aware that Mario was relishing all this, grinning as he talked. "Dimi, he was okay. But Mama had him under her thumb, just like me. He sure as shit got the last laugh, though."

"Why . . . did he do it?"

"I dunno," he said vaguely.

She really looked into his eyes for the first time since he had come to Rome. He returned her gaze with eyes empty of emotion, like those of a statue. What did she expect? To share feelings with him? They had never shared anything, probably never would. One of the cats, a calico, hissed at him—one of the seven or eight that now lay at her feet, and she was struck by their plaintive faces and wide eyes. They looked at her as if they understood her sorrow. Yet the same soft faces and gossamer whiskers were flat and hard when they turned to Mario. Their lithe bodies were eloquent in their hostility.

"I'll take you back to the bus," she said. "I just want to be alone for a while."

He shrugged and followed her.

Melina sat for several hours at an outside café, far enough away from the Forum and the Colosseum to avoid the tourists. She sipped absently at her mineral water as it lost its sparkle and watched the waiter light the table candles as another famous Roman sunset fell into darkness. From the still isolation of her grief she finally woke to the

bustle and night sounds of the city. To the honking cars
and motor scooters and overlapping voices speaking Italian in fluid cadenzas. The waiter approached her, but not
to hasten her departure.

"*La signorina desidera un giornale? C'e un signore
che ha laschiato il suo . . .*"

It was a kind gesture, to offer her a departed customer's paper. She smiled her thanks as she took it and
opened it.

"*Scoperta Seconda Vittima Zingara.*"

"Second Gypsy Girl Found Murdered." She read
about the first strangulation near the Piazza Barberini and
the second one by the encampment. No suspects so far, the
police were following several leads, would probably have
someone in custody soon. . . .

She tossed a wad of money on the table and found
herself walking along the street, the din of traffic and conversation remote once more. Modern Rome was tame
compared to the city of the ancient world, in which two
such murders would scarcely cause ripples. Still, it seemed
a shame to see this sort of crime here. She almost expected
the soft brush of fur against her leg, and leaned down automatically to stroke her tiger cat with the white chest. He
reared into her hand and arched his body with pleasure.

"It would be nice to think you were my papa." She
sighed. "You certainly have his eyes." He trailed ahead of
her, then turned and meowed for the first time. Melina
quickened her pace to keep up with him as he trotted
along the street. After a few turns, she realized they were
heading for the Colosseum. When its dark form loomed
into view, she scooped up the cat, crossing the busy street
with him in her arms, purring blissfully.

The Colosseum wasn't brightly lit at night, but it didn't
stop people from wandering up to the iron bars and peering in. She put the cat down, watching him flow through
the bars and look back at her, as if she were to duplicate
the feat.

"Humans can't just walk through bars," she whispered, and his eyes glowed soft yellow from the shadows.

A hand touched her neck and she jumped.

"Mario! You scared me!"

His eyes were shadowed, and sallow light from above cut his face into angular patterns. "I got off the bus and watched you at the café. There was something I wanted to tell you."

"What?" she asked, drifting away from the arch.

"Dimi found Kelly's letters. Mama stuck them under the carpet in the bedroom, and just after Kelly got back from the Gulf, Dimi was cleaning, and there they were. He brought them to me, but Kelly had already said those things about Mama—" He turned away. "Kelly was gone, because I took Mama's side."

"It was a terrible thing for Renata to do."

He turned back around. "Well, Dimi thought so, too. I said I didn't know, when you asked me why he offed himself. Well, I think finding those letters was the last straw. He couldn't take the kind of shit Mama pulled anymore."

"I didn't know." She couldn't stop the tears.

He edged closer and she could only step back, almost to the bars. "My mind seems so sharp tonight, Melina, like I could see right into the darkness. Like I could see all those ghosts, or whatever they were."

"What!"

"You know, what you told me about that guy who had a séance here." He moved closer, out of the light, his face a black silhouette.

"Benvenuto Cellini. He brought a priest—" She backed up, touching stone with one hand, wiping her tears with the other as her throat tightened. "He brought a priest and a boy and they drew a circle and said some incantations."

They were far back under the arch now and she wondered where the cat had gone. If only she could follow him and become invisible in some crevice.

"So what happened?"

"Uh, well, the priest said he saw demons and the boy said he saw a million warriors." She felt around frantically, unable to come in contact with the bars she should have backed into by now. The night was silent, as if there were no one else alive.

"What did Cellini see?" His words echoed and hissed in the stone hall.

"Smoke and shadows." Completely disoriented, when she saw a light, she ran for it. She should have run into a wall, an upcropping of stone, but there was nothing but empty space and a sandy floor. . . .

She could hear Mario behind her and they fell together as he tackled her. She went berserk, kicking out and spitting coarse sand. His hands were climbing toward her throat and she lashed out with her nails, scoring his face and screaming between gasps.

Light and space. She could sense it as she gripped his wrists and twisted under his heavy body. There was a booming sound, purring that couldn't possibly come from a little cat—a deep cacophony of rumblings that wove in and out of snarls of large animals. Mario let go of her and tried to crawl away from the sound. The oval arena of the Colosseum stretched out ahead in gray light, coursing with the restless shadows of a million feline warriors.

The lions. Multitudes fought here every day, along with panthers and even tigers, a warm-up show for the gladiatorial games. For almost five centuries they faced the *bestiari* and devoured the hapless, the criminals, then defiantly faced their own deaths.

The echoes of their roars surrounded Melina as she crouched in the sand and felt the warm body of a cat rise up under her arm, a noble beast with yellow eyes and a tangled mane and white chest. Her cat, enormous and leonine, looked at her, blinked and then padded away to join the others as they stood staring at Mario. Overwhelmed, she felt her vision cloud. The oath of the gladiator rolled through her head like thunder: *"Uri, vinciri, verberari, ferroque mecari patior."* He willingly swore to be burned, bound, beaten, and slain by the sword, a sacred vow to go to a violent death. Melina saw a *bestiarius* emerge from the smoke, a lowly gladiator whose specialty was fighting animals. He carried short sword, shield, and arm guard, and the lions stalked him hungrily as he turned uncertainly, holding his sword as if it were an alien thing. A cat sprang so fast Melina could only gasp as it knocked the man to the ground and ripped off his helmet. It was Mario. She could see the abject terror on his face, the blood on his cheek where she had scratched him. Struggling to his feet, he held the sword and shield out awkwardly. A panther moved closer, ears back, eyes glittering. It raked the shield from Mario's grasp, lithely twisting away from the sword. Mario's lips formed words as several lions attacked, slamming him down. They surrounded him, and the faint sound of his screams bled from the din as pale shapes assaulted him, snarling as claws caught on flesh, ripped through bone and muscle. With frightening grace and speed her lion leapt, snapping his jaws shut on the exposed throat. He tore upward, his muzzle dripping blood like dark jewels.

Melina watched paralyzed, sickened, aware of the occasional lion drifting through her to circle their prey. They tore Mario apart as if he were made of paper and the sand soaked up the blood as they finished off what was left, crunching bone and gulping sinew.

Then they relaxed, lying down, washing. Their low purrs made the ground vibrate. Her cat drifted toward her, his head swinging as he walked, licking the blood from his muzzle. Sniffing her hair, he put a colossal paw on her shoulder, then drew away. He let out a soft crying sound and sank to the ground next to Melina as she drew shuddering breaths and put a hand on his mane. He turned and held her gaze with those great yellow eyes.

"Melina . . ."

"Baba." She called him by the old Greek endearment she had used when she was little and he was a strong, wonderful father who carried her in his arms and protected her from the world. She gripped his mane and wept, shuddering as he purred softly and supported her. Finally she let him go, and like so many vanishing whispers, the lions faded, their golden coats metamorphosing to many colors—black, orange, calico, striped . . .

When she looked back at the arena Mario's torn carcass had faded, too, the roiled, wet sand clinging to the
arms and face of a prone figure that moved, just barely.

Melina rose and went with *I Gatti di Roma* out
through the dark arcade and onto the sidewalk. Leaning
against the ancient stones, she closed her eyes for a moment, then opened them to see cars whizzing past, people
walking by. The bars were where they would be, closing
her off from the Colosseum. Inside, one small pair of eyes
looked at her and blinked. The heavy musk of lions hung
in the air.

"Melina!"

She had hoped never to hear that voice again, grating
in the morning air like claws on slate. Melina went to the
window and looked out. Renata stood below, hands on
hips. A taxi idled at the curb.

"You gotta come down and say good-bye!"

"I don't gotta do nothing," she muttered, pulling
away from the window. The overriding urge was to stay in
her apartment, but there was something about going
down, a sense of completion. After all, she would never
see them again. "I'll be right down!" she yelled out at Renata, and moved as slowly as she could to rack up their
taxi fare.

Somehow she made it home the night before. As she
walked on uncertain legs across the sidewalk she saw her
cat, hanging back by the Colosseum. Back at her apartment, while numbly pulling off her clothes, sand from the
arena spilled from her pockets. On impulse she emptied it
into a bowl and stirred it with her fingers. It was so dry, so
coarse. Like ashes. In the next few days Melina would buy
a ticket to Athens.

"Mario won't get out of the car," shrilled Renata. "I
don't know what's wrong with him. He doesn't want to
say good-bye to you."

"No problem." Melina smiled, looking toward the
shadowy shape in the back of the cab.

"Did you have an argument or something?"

"No."

Renata pursed her lips, ready with questions, yet when she spoke, she was strangely quiet. "He came back last night with scratches on his cheek. Never said a word." Behind her glasses, her eyes looked huge and unnaturally wet. "He's *changed*."

The taxi driver revved his engine.

"He told me he was never going anywhere again."

"Rome has that effect on some people," Melina said.

She waited silently while Renata twitched and simpered. "Well, dear, a girl with money should travel, so come and visit. Miami is such a nice city."

Melina smiled faintly and looked one last time toward the back of the taxi. Renata went around and clambered in and the taxi lurched.

Mario flicked a cigarette out onto the sidewalk and leaned out the window. His cheek was greasy with ointment and the scratches seemed to glow red underneath. He looked at her, his eyes vague and tunneled in his head, lost to the relentless memory of the night before. She too remembered, and at last the two of them shared something. Then he looked down, and she saw real emotion, the fear that would shackle him, hold him in its smoke and shadows forever. The feel of soft fur against her legs told her why.

Nina Kiriki Hoffman

Nina Kiriki Hoffman lives in Eugene, Oregon. Her first novel, *The Thread That Binds the Bones,* won the Bram Stoker Award for First Novel. Her second novel, *The Silent Strength of Stones,* came out in September 1995. She also wrote and published a collaborative young adult novel with Tad Williams, *Child of an Ancient City.*

Her short stories have appeared in many magazines in the science fiction, fantasy, and horror fields and in the anthologies *The Ultimate Witch, The Ultimate Zombie, Bruce Covillle's Book of Aliens, Weird Tales from Shakespeare, 100 Vicious Vampires, Sisters of the Night, Heaven Sent, The Year's Best Horror* series, *Best New Horror* series, and *The Year's Best Fantasy and Horror* series.

While at a convention a few years ago, Nina and I had a drink and I told her about the various anthologies I was working on. In mentioning the cat horror anthology, I said that the cats didn't have to be central figures in all the stories and I wouldn't be averse to an "incidental" cat or two. This is what I received from her.

Incidental Cats

NINA KIRIKI HOFFMAN

IT WAS NO great trick for the first and most important cat to read the history of the comes-from-mouth stuff. The cat spent all day reading the histories of things through their scents, learning each being it encountered anew; nothing was allowed to get close to the cat without being smelled. Even if the cat already knew the person, the person needed to be smelled, because each new experience the person had added to the person's collection of scents.

The person the cat smelled the most often was the one it lived with, its tree-legs. The cat needed to know if the tree-legs had encountered any other cats besides the second and somewhat important cat who lived with the first cat and its tree-legs.

Of the other things the cat smelled, comes-from-mouth stuff particularly demanded action. When the cat smelled it the cat had to bury it even if the cat didn't have any dirt; if the cat didn't bury it someone else might get a whiff and find out everything the cat knew. And it was important to be the one with the most information.

Most comes-from-mouth stuff the cat encountered was either the eat-too-fast kind or the kind that licking the cat's own hair produced. Sometimes the eat-too-fast kind was so close to the eating that the cat could eat it again.

But this comes-from-mouth stuff was different.

The cat found it on the floor in the front room after returning from a forage and pushing through the pet door. A chair had fallen over, and a lamp had broken, and there was the cat's tree-legs lying there with this wrong comes-from-mouth stuff. This comes-from-mouth stuff had no food smells in it, just dark nose-burning scents, dead blood, and something else.

This comes-from-mouth stuff came from the cat's tree-legs, and the tree-legs ate all kinds of things the cat would never touch, such as oranges, and other things the cat would eat only if it wanted to make its own comes-from-mouth stuff—grass things—and yet the tree-legs didn't usually make stuff come from its mouth afterward.

This comes-from-mouth stuff had death smells in it.

The cat circled around the fallen tree-legs, sniffing it. The tree-legs' face lay in its comes-from-mouth stuff, which was wrong. After scratching at the carpet for a while and trying to bury the comes-from-mouth stuff, digging up only carpet threads and small curls of its own shed hair, the cat crept close to the curved-to-fit side part of the tree-legs and curled up against it. Usually when the cat did this, the stroke-scratch parts of tree-legs would perform their cat worship, but this time they didn't. The cat knew by the smells on the tree-legs and on the floor that everything had changed. Since the cat hated change, it pretended for as long as it could that change hadn't happened.

Even with the cat leaning against it, though, the tree-legs was losing heat. When the key rasped in the door the cat ran to hide under the couch with its bell-balls and bite-toy. The cat peeked out through the fringe.

Even before the door opened, the cat knew who it was. Tree-legs-who-stole-the-cat's-place-on-the-bed always had the scent of animal sex parts and dead flowers so strong that the cat didn't like being in the same room with her. The cat watched.

The door nudged the cat's tree-legs and stopped moving. It closed, then opened with more force, pushing the cat's tree-legs across the rug a little. Stole-cat's-place came in, closing the door and stepping over the body's legs. She stood and stared down at the cat's tree-legs. After her smell had filled the front room, she headed toward the room with the bed. Keeping low, the cat crept after her. It watched from the doorway as Stole-cat's-place opened and shut the drawers of the dresser, feeling through the things in each drawer that the cat loved to sleep on or pull out and play with when it had the chance, silky things that snagged on claws, stiff cloth the cat could dig into, other things the cat desired merely because its tree-legs tried to keep them hidden from the cat.

Something struck the cat from behind. The cat turned, hissing, to find that the other cat had snuck up on it. It boxed the other cat. They moaned and growled at each other. The first cat jumped on the second cat and bit the back of its neck, holding it down for a long moment as it growled, until both of them knew who was boss.

The dead flowers and animal sex parts of Stole-cat's-place was very near now. The first cat jumped off the second cat and whirled to find Stole standing over them.

She said something in a growl and kicked at the cats. The first cat jumped; the second cat flew from Stole's boot to hit the wall. The first cat yowled and leapt at Stole's legs, digging in with all claws, climbing Stole in a way the cat usually reserved for trees. Stole swung her purse, which smelled of the things she had taken from the cat's tree-legs' dresser. She hit the cat with it, over and over. Things came from the purse, falling to the hall carpet. Stole was screaming and strong. Despite the cat's grip on her she managed to beat it off.

She ran from the house before the first cat could decide whether to attack her again or run and hide. The first cat's ribs hurt; it tasted its own blood from something Stole had done to its face.

The first cat crept to the second cat and smelled it. The second cat lay quiet, its eyes shut, but its sides still moved and air went in and out of its nose. The first cat licked the second cat's face, then ventured back to the front room. Stole had left the door open.

The cat waited under the couch for a time, watching through the fringe. No one else came into the house. The cat went into the kitchen and smelled the food dishes. They were empty. The cat clawed at the cupboard where the tree-legs kept the food, but it wouldn't open. The tree-legs had put a lock on it after the cat had opened it and bitten through the food bag a couple of times. The cat kept wishing the door would act the way it used to, but it continued to resist.

All the cat's scratching didn't make the cat's tree-legs come in and open the cupboard. The cat went to the front room and smelled its tree-legs and the comes-from-mouth stuff again. Change, horrible change.

The cat went back to the hall and smelled the things that had fallen out of Stole's purse. One was a thick wad of soft paper that carried the smells of many different places and tree-legs. The cat sank its claws deep, ripping through the resisting but helpless paper in an orgy of delight, tossing it in the air and capturing it before it landed. The cat batted the paper wad up and down the hall.

When it had shredded the toy it went to sniff the second cat again. It licked the second cat's face until the second cat woke up and licked back.

They both went to the kitchen. The second cat tried a different cupboard and managed to claw it open. Behind the door was the trash can. The second cat tipped it and both of them fought to creep inside the bag. The first cat could smell fish bones and chicken things. And then, suddenly, mixed with the tempting chicken smells, the edge-of-death smells like the one in the tree-legs' comes-from-mouth stuff. Faintly, the dead flowers and animal sex smell of Stole-cat's-place, too.

The first cat yowled and ducked out of the bag. It ran from the kitchen into the front room. It smelled the tree-legs and the comes-from-mouth stuff again.

No change.

The second cat came and smelled the tree-legs and the comes-from-mouth stuff. It sneezed and shook its head. After a moment it jumped up onto the couch, where the cats were not supposed to go when the tree-legs was home. The first cat waited for the yell, the clapping noise, the swat with a rolled newspaper to drive the second cat from the couch, but none of them came. The first cat glanced at the tree-legs, then jumped up on the couch with the second cat.

They waited.

Who would feed them?

The first cat fell asleep.

Tanith Lee

Tanith Lee was born in London, started writing at the age of nine, was first published in her early twenties, and has been prolific in fantasy, science fiction, and horror ever since. Her most recent novels are *Elephantasm; Darkness; I, Vivia,* a vampire novel; *Eva Fairdeath,* a futuristic novel; *Reigning Cats and Dogs,* a parallel Victorian gothic; *Gold Unicorn,* a novel for young adults; and "Louisa the Poisoner," a novella chapbook from Wildside Press. She has twice won the World Fantasy Award for her short stories, most of which are collected in *Tales from the Flat Earth: Night's Daughter; Red as Blood, or Tales from the Sisters Grimmer; Tamastara, or the Indian Nights; The Gorgon and Other Beastly Tales; Nightshades;* a novella and stories, and others.

Lee's ability to create a strong sense of place helps make those of her stories set in the past especially effective. "Flowers for Faces, Thorns for Feet" occurs during a particularly inhospitable period for cats—and certain women. Lee weaves an intricate tale of horror, cruelty, kindness, and forgiveness in her stories within stories—all of which illuminate the varied relationships between felines and humans.

Flowers for Faces, Thorns for Feet

TANITH LEE

IN A VILLAGE near the roof of the world, held fast by mountains whose tops were swords of snow, lived two young women. One morning the younger woman came to the elder.

"Annasin," said the younger woman, "I'm here to warn you."

"Warn me of what?"

"They say the snow has gone from the pass, and a man is coming."

"What man? What should I care? Do you think I want a husband?"

"No, he's a finder of witches."

Then the elder woman, who was all of three and twenty, sat down on her stool. She said, "I am not a witch."

"Are you not? Others say differently. And besides, I have been everywhere in the village, telling this thing, and many women I told have gone white and said, '*I'm not a witch.*'"

Annasin said, "Mariset, go away. This is all nonsense."

Mariset nodded, and she left the house.

Annasin sat on her stool, and she thought. She thought of the winter when she had made the fire burn by snapping her fingers. She thought of the summer nights when she had danced on the high meadows, and later how she had floated, as it seemed, up to the moon. And she had cured some of toothache and coughing. And one man, who had put his hands on her in the wood, she had made double over with a pain in his belly.

Annasin put biscuits to bake in the oven, but her heart was heavy and beat like lead. An hour later into her house through the open door walked a slim gray cat pale as first morning.

"Come with me, Annasin," said the cat. "Come with me you must." It spoke in the human tongue, and as she heard it, Annasin felt herself shrink down, and then she was on four feet on the floor, with her pointed ears up on her head, her tail in the flour, and the smell of burning biscuits in her dark gray nose.

"A pail of water on you, Mariset," said Annasin.

"Come away," said Mariset.

And together they trotted out of the house door and along the street.

None paid them any heed, two cats. They ran behind the wood stores and under the shadows of goat pens, and even the goats, with their yellow eyes no yellower now than the eyes of Annasin and Mariset, did not try to stop them.

Annasin and Mariset reached the hill above the village. They ran up the hill, and up another hill, through the wood of pines, until they were in the high pastures, where, in summer, the goats were brought to feed. Little grass was there as yet, and all about the sworded mountains rose, and then the sky.

"Let us go to the waterfall," said Mariset.

So they ran on up the wet turf sides of the hills, to the feet of the mountains, where a white gush of water sprang. And behind the waterfall, in a cave of blue flowers, they sat on the mossy stone, the two gray cats.

"Now we're lost," said Annasin.

Mariset answered, "Now we are safe."

But Annasin remembered very well how she had left her own young body sitting in her house before the oven, and she knew Mariset had left her own younger body in her own house near the church.

"What will they think of us?" said Annasin.

"They will say our souls have gone out of us," said Mariset, "and they will leave us alone."

"I don't believe so."

Mariset washed her paws. Then she rolled on her back in the flowers. "There are worse fates than being a cat."

Annasin agreed. "To be dead, for one."

"Who knows," said a voice, "if to be dead is worse than to be living."

And there before the cave stood a third cat. He was a male, and they were well able to see this, his balls in a sheath of smooth black fur, firm as walnuts, for he showed them, courteously, first. Then, letting down his black silk tail, he turned about and coming up, touched both their noses with his own, politely. He was black all over, even his tongue, all black but for one spot of bright yellow, like a primrose, between his jet black eyes.

"Now," said the male cat, "we will speak in the cats' speech."

"I regret, sir, we don't know it," said Mariset. "We are not true cats."

"Oh, then it is time you learned," said the male cat, "for you seem true enough to me. First," he added, "I will tell you my name. I am called Arrow."

Annasin and Mariset glanced at each other from their primrose eyes. It was a fact, the cat had spoken in another language, but both women understood it perfectly and at once. And trying this language out, both found they could speak it pretty well.

"Arrow is a fine name," said Mariset. "But who called you that?"

"I myself, for I had another name, once. I named myself for the straightness of my fall."

"Your fall," said Annasin. "Did you fall from somewhere?"

The black cat looked at her quizzically. "Indeed I did. And need I tell you where?"

Mariset gave a nervous chirrup and Annasin searched for a nonexistent flea. Both grasped they were in conversation with a fallen angel.

Arrow, though, was all at ease, and lay down among the flowers. He said mildly, "It was a great argument over one small thing. Can you guess?"

"You would be king," said Mariset riskily.

The black cat laughed, as a cat does. He said, "Why should I, or any of us, want that? The king must do all. We were happy enough. No, it was this way. You see, we had beheld them in the garden, the woman and the man. And we said amongst ourselves, 'Look, *he* has created them unequal. The man is almost but not quite as wise as the woman. That is surely unfair.' So then we spoke to *him*, for in those days *he* was very approachable. *He* seemed surprised and told us we were wrong, for it had been *his* plan to have them, the woman and the man, the other way about—she less than he. And our prince—you will know his name—he laughed, he laughed until he fainted. How handsome he looked, lying at the feet of—*him*, his golden hair and wings spread out. Then I fear *he* became angry. *He* cast us out. We fell. But then, we had jumped first from those crystal casements."

Annasin washed behind her ear. She did not venture a comment. But Mariset, the younger, ran out and began to play with Arrow, who was a fallen angel. They rolled and kicked, biting and cuffing and laughing in shrill meows.

Annasin said eventually, "We're true witches, then."

"And almost true cats," said Arrow, leaping on a stone before Mariset could nip his tail. "But cats too are not always well thought of. They have pretty faces like the flowers, but sharp teeth in their mouths, and sharp claws in their feet, quicker than, but extremely like, thorns."

"Our two bodies," said Annasin, "are sitting in our houses."

"Perhaps no one will find them," said Mariset.

Then they ran to the stream that broke below from the waterfall, and here they fished and caught their supper. They ate it raw, of course, and never had fish tasted so delicious, cold and sweet from the mountain stream.

When they were done, they walked back down the hills, and in the dusk below they saw the village, its flat red lights burning and smoke on most of its chimneys. A pair of horses were by the hospitable house, where travelers stayed, and in that window stood a bright lamp.

"He has come, that witch-finder," said Annasin.

"It's good we are cats," said Mariset.

"I will tell you one story," said Arrow. And he did.

The First Story—The Hearth Cat

There was a woman who had never seen a beautiful thing in her life, except perhaps the sky, and she had little time to look at that. Since her birth she had lived in a bleak barren land, and at thirteen she was wed to a cruel oaf, who treated her like his slave and often beat her. She went in terror of him. He for his part hated her and everything but to eat and sleep and drink. It is a fact, he did not even lie with his wife after the first few times he had her in his bed, he was too lazy. But she was glad enough to be left alone that way, and slept on the floor, on the bare boards beside his couch, with her head on a bundle of straw and an old blanket to pull over her.

There came a winter then that was terrible, like a long breath from the hells of ice. In that region the snow fell thick and froze like glass. Upon the ugly house of the man it fell, too, and covered it up so it was like a lump of dirty sugar. Each morning the woman would make her difficult way to the well and break the ice with a stick. All day she would tend the fire on the hearth. In summer she had gone often to the market and brought back, on her shoulders, a sack of logs, for there were no trees nearby. And now she fed the logs to the winter fire so that the man could sit in his chair in comfort. And on the fire she cooked his food, and mulled, with a hot iron, the ale for him to drink. But she drank the cold water from the icy well and ate the scraps he left. Through the rest of the day the woman went about her tasks, cleaning the house and scouring the pots and washing out the clothes, but these two last things she did in the outhouse, in the bitter cold, for he did not like her to disturb him.

In the evening, which came quickly from the low gray sky, she lit the lamp for him and prepared his supper. Then he would climb the stair to his bed, and if she had not angered him at all that day he would not strike her. But often he did strike her, and sometimes her red blood fell on the floor of the house.

Once he had gone to bed, the woman would sit alone by the dying fire, for she was not allowed to keep it alight after the man had retired. Nevertheless, she would look into the golden embers, and sometimes she would dream a little, but not really of any proper thing, for she had never been told of, or seen, anything worthy of a dream. And though the embers themselves were in their way beautiful, they meant to her the coming of the cold night, and her hard sleep on the bare boards above, and the thankless tomorrow.

One morning in that winter, the woman woke as she always did at the first chill light of dawn. She got up stiff and sore from her wretched nest, and the man stirred in his furs and sheets and said, "Not so much noise, you cursed cow."

Then she crept down and, going to the hearth, she laid the logs and lit them from the tinderbox, and when she had done that she warmed herself for a few hasty minutes. When she opened the house door, there the winter lay before her as always, as if now the summer had died and would never return. Blank as death that white plate of the land stretched away to meet at last with the low white sky. The woman took her pail and stepped out, and the cold struck her as the man did, sudden and vicious, and she stood alone with her misery in the middle of that wilderness, and in that moment a finger of cold sun pierced from the cloud. The woman saw that something moved on the face of the dead world besides herself.

Amazed, she stared, and presently she saw it was a cat. Now, she had never seen one, she had only heard of them, but not, she thought, of one like this. For it was a cat the color of an orange, sleek as silk, and in its head it had two amber jewels for eyes. And seeing her, standing in her rags at the door, the orange cat ran to her, and as it came it made a sweet and musical noise.

The woman's empty heart filled at once. She bent and touched the cat. It felt better than silk, and it was warm as a pie.

"Oh my beauty," said the woman.

But just then she heard the loud steps of the man coming down through the house, and in a moment more he was in the house door behind her.

"What are you idling at, you pig?" he said, and clapped her about the head. "Go fetch the water. Where is my brew? What do I keep you for, you bitch?"

At which he saw the cat that burned so brightly in the white snow, like a piece of the summer sun.

"And what filthy thing is that? Eh, you mare, have you been keeping a darling cat all this while? Giving it too my food?" And he awarded the woman a push that knocked her down, and at the cat he aimed a great kick, but the cat was off like a flame over the snow. Then the man picked up a stone by the house door and flung it, but it missed the cat, who was gone around the outhouse, from sight. "Learn this," said the man. "I'll catch that thing and skin it. It shall make me a collar." And so saying he went back into the house, for it was cold work, raining blows in the doorway.

The woman had never thought to weep, but now, as she stumbled to the well, she did, and the tears froze on her face. She thought, What would the cat do, out in the bitter cold? But then she reached the well and broke the ice and hurried back to make food for the man.

All day, the woman thought of the cat. She thought of it in astonishment, and in fear, for how could it survive in the markerless snow? And when she went to scour the pots, she left open the door of the outhouse, in case the cat might come and shelter there, but she did not see it.

As for the man, he said no more about the cat, but he had taken down his slingshot, and his knife, and he sharpened the blade till the blue sparks flew. As the day slackened from its gray to its dark, he got up even and went to the door, but he did not venture out. The snow was so hard, there were no footsteps in it, not even the woman's from her trudges to and fro, let alone the cat's light paws.

The woman mulled the ale and brought it to the man, who drank and drank again, and then he went to his chair, and she thought, Perhaps he will forget.

But she did not forget. She wondered how the cat would be faring.

When he had eaten his evening meal, the man took himself up to bed. As he passed the woman, he smote her, so a ribbon of blood came from her lip. He said, "That's for your bloody worthlessness."

She listened to his steps ascend, and huddling by the perishing of the fire, she gnawed some crusts and rinds. But near his chair he had left the slingshot and the knife.

Presently the fire sank and there was only a smudge of red upon the hearth. The woman rose and went to the house door, and quiet as a whisper, she opened it. She had no lamp, for she was not allowed one, but there was a glimpse of watery moonlight over the land. Above, she heard the man snoring.

She looked at the waste, and there, like a wish, by the outhouse wall, she saw a color shining in the snow like a golden coin.

She thought this: I will bring the cat into the house and warm it for one night. Then, before he wakes, I will take the cat away. I will take it to the place where the road starts to the market, and perhaps someone will chance on it and give it a home. But at least he will never go so far to catch it.

Then the woman went out into the snow and she walked to where the cat lay curled up by the wall. When she bent and touched it, it felt cold now, and so she raised it in her arms. The cat opened its amber eyes and looked at her. "How beautiful you are," she said. "I have never seen one like you." And she carried the orange cat back to the house, and took it inside.

Upstairs the man still snored, and grunted in his

turgid sleep, and the woman noiselessly took a little broth
from the cauldron over the cooling fire, and this she gave
the cat, though it was the man's food. The cat watched
her. And then it licked up the broth. At last it made a wonderful low noise, but the woman put her finger to her lips,
and the cat fell silent.

"You are so cold," she murmured. "Look there, the
fire is all out, but the cinders are warm. I will put you there
in the hearth till morning."

And she put the cat into the warm dust of the fire. It did
not struggle, and feeling the heat it snuggled itself in and
curled itself round, and closing the suns of its eyes, it slept.

Then the woman crept upstairs, and she lay on her
straw pillow, wide awake, for the first hint of dawn, so she
could hasten the cat away before the man should think to
get up. Wide awake she lay, tense as a stick, and then she
heard a loud creaking. A wind had sprung up like a ghost
over the snow, and it was blowing the outhouse door,
which she had forgotten to shut. Over and over the door
complained. Until at last the man shifted in his bed.

"There is the door outside," he said. "Go and close
it, you damnable bitch. In the morning you shall have a
beating."

So the woman got up again and went down. In the
room below all light had failed, and on the hearth was
nothing but a shadow. She hurried to the house door and
slipped out, for she must stop that other door from making its noise, before he in his turn descended.

Over the hard white earth she ran. And coming to the
outhouse, she secured it. And then from the veil on the
moon she heard a voice call to her, from out of the night
itself, from over the hills, from out of the ground.

> Stand in the snow like a stone
> Until your trouble is gone.

The woman was afraid, and she tried at once to fly.
But it was as if iron hands held her feet rooted to the spot
and there she must stand, her teeth chattering from the

frigid night, and in the house she saw a light spring up, and she cried aloud in terror, for she thought he had come down and lit the lamp and he would find the cat upon the hearth.

But it was not the man. Oh no.

On the house hearth, the fire had burned up again. The old cold cinders had come alight. Or so it seemed. For on the hearth a bright fire was sparkling, yellow-red, like a hectic sunrise. But the shape of the fire was this way, it had a sleek body and four legs, and a face like a heart with two pointed ears, and a tail like a blazing stem.

And off from the hearth the fire stepped, dainty as a maiden in a golden dress. But it was a cat, a cat made all of fire.

Into the lower room of the house it moved, and there, at the touch of it, the floor burst into flame. And reaching with one paw, it rapped the man's chair, and the chair became a burning bush.

Then lightly up the stair darted the cat of fire, and the stair lit bright behind it. While above the man coughed on the smolder, and roused himself, and called out, "What are you doing, you cow? Haven't I said you are never to light the fire save for me?"

And the fire cat answered, "Oh, but it is for you," yet it spoke in the cat tongue, and the man did not understand.

Even so, how light his house had grown, the bitch must have kindled all the three lamps, and so he sat up in bed and he readied his fist, and just then, in through the door danced the cat of fire, and all the room went up like a flowering tree of gold.

"God—God save me!" cried the man. But God is sometimes off on business, as so many know to their sorrow.

The fire ate through the bed and through the flesh of the man. First his feet burnt, and then his legs. Then his body was a bonfire, and black smoke came from his nostrils, and from his eyes tears of flame. He burst like a bad fruit, and the house fell down, and the white snow dropped sizzling into the core of it, so a cloud went into the sky and put out the moon.

All this the woman had watched and she sobbed and screamed, thinking only of the poor cat she had left in the cinders to be warm and that she had killed the only thing she loved.

However, when the last timber of the house had settled, out through a hole in the ruin walked a golden fire, and it had the shape of a cat. At this the woman's feet were free, and she ran to meet the cat, and, leaning down, she held its fiery fur to her heart until she was warm all over.

Then this pair, the woman and the orange cat, walked away across the plain of snow, and the footsteps of each were deep and black, one by one for the woman, and two by two for the cat, and smoke rose from the footsteps and rose from them, up and up, long after the cat and the woman were gone.

The night had come, and the three cats on the hill had settled on the bare earth. Above, the stars were like the eyes of black mother cats, who watched over them.

"Why did you tell us this story?" asked Annasin.

"To show that cats are not always what they seem," said Arrow.

Mariset said, "But this we know. We of *all* cats."

"Then," said Arrow, "to show that one does not always know the heart's desire."

They slept awhile, but the moon came up. The night was now all lit like a ballroom, but in the village the lamps were out and every head on its pillow. Just so had Annasin and Mariset slept, some nights of the year.

"No others have joined us here," said Mariset. "I would have said that in our village, there were at least three others who were witches."

"Or they told that they were," said Annasin. And she thought of the crone Margotta, who put spells on the goats and sent the milk sour, or so she said. And of the girls Vebya and Chekta, who claimed that they could fly. But Annasin, as she drifted past the moon on summer nights, had sometimes glimpsed Mariset, but never Vebya or Chekta. Though the sour milk she had tasted, and she thought Margotta had thrown something in it.

Arrow got up, and so did Annasin and Mariset, the gray cats. They played together under the moon, and ran to chase moths in the vast pine woods, which glittered with moonlight as if hung with silver and diamonds. All night they played and chased, and in the last patches of the white snow they left the prints of their flowery feet that had thorns in them.

When the pink dawn came, they watched it. Then they drank from a pool, all three, and how Arrow's black tongue lapped. They slept in an ancient burrow, breast to back. And Annasin lusted after Arrow and was ashamed, but somewhere in the drowse of day, he mounted her, she felt him, and her whole body seethed with joy. At length, and it seemed long enough to her, he left her, and then came a sear of pain. She turned and struck him in the face. He bowed and went to spray the ferns outside the burrow.

"Thorns," said Annasin. "Not only in the feet."

"*He* planned the world," said Arrow. "It's a wondrous deed, and we could never have done it. Alas, in the rush to get things done, *he* left certain acts untested and particular elements unkind. *He* did not mean to harm. *He* never does. You must not blame *him*."

In the afternoon, the wood was warm. They rose all three and groomed each other tail-tip to nose-end. Then they hunted mercilessly and did terrible things, which were not their fault, nor God's, simply a flaw in the too-hasty planning of a great genius. They ate well, and the sun descended like a flaming eye.

During the sunset, there was a commotion from the village. Then Annasin and Mariset ran to see, from the vantage of the nearer hill, and Arrow sat behind them.

A tall old man was in the street. He was swarthy and dark and clad in rusty black. In his hand was a cross that shone as the wood had done by night, so they knew that it was silver. From the houses strong men were roughly dragging out some women. Old Margotta came, cursing and spitting in her stenchful garments, and next white

Vebya, and brown Chekta, sobbing. Then there strode u
the woodcutter, from the house of Annasin, and over hi
shoulder he bore the limp form that Annasin recognized to
be her own human body, its long hair down his back.

"See, she's bewitched," said the woodcutter.

But the grim old man, the witch-finder, he said, "No
in the witch-trance. Her soul is off at some mischief. Fly
ing over the chimneys on a stick, or sucking the bloo
from lambs and children."

"Old fool," said Mariset. But she had eaten a whol
mouse, she could hardly pass judgment.

Annasin said, "I am in jeopardy. I'd best go back."

Just then there were fresh cries, and the door o
Mariset's house by the church was beaten in. Out they
dragged her charming body, by its very hair, and Marise
wailed.

"What shall I do?"

Into the hospitable house, which already blazed with
lamps, as if the coming night were dark, the five witches
real and false, waking or unconscious, were hauled, and
the door slammed.

Silence came to the hill, until an owl with a cat's eye
went sailing overhead.

They looked up at the owl, Arrow and his ladies
Then Arrow said, "I will tell you a second story."

"There's no time for tales," declared Mariset in a piti
ful mew.

"There is always time," said Arrow, "for time only
exists by the grace of *him*."

The Second Story—The Sea Cat

The ship of the thieves was painted black, and it had for
figurehead a wooden man with upraised sword and, in hi
other grasp, a severed hand. They sailed about, the com
pany, and reckoned they were fair enough. For when they
came on another ship they robbed it, but only killed those
who resisted them or tried to hide away their goods.

They had besides, these thieves, a sort of lucky thing, or scapegoat. The mate, who liked to carve, had made it from a piece of driftwood, and it was a very rough and graceless wooden cat, with one eye big and round and the other long and narrow. When they had had fortune, the thieves would spill drink on this lucky cat, and when matters had not gone well, they would stick nails in it, kick it, and spit in its face. They called it a name that meant Ratter.

It happened that they had extreme luck for a whole month, and robbed four ships and got away with many excellent prizes, bolts of velvet and necklaces of pearls, and some casks of wine, which they liked a great deal. And one evening, when the sun had just gone down, they saw a storm go by them on the horizon like a moving cliff of wind.

So then they anointed Ratter and sat down to eat. As they were doing this there came a great shouting from the watch above.

The captain of the thieves ran to discover what went on, and most of his men with him, and looking out from the rail, they beheld something floating on the cradle of the black night sea.

"It's a barrel of rum," cried one.

But another said, "No, for it cries. It's a baby."

Over the sea it came, the floating, crying thing. And the moon began to rise in the east.

Now, they were miles from land, and nothing anywhere in sight. Not an island, not a sail, or anything that they knew of. But there on the water drifted, never going down, a shape like a bluish flower. And raising its head it meowed to them. It was a cat.

"How does it stay up there?" said one of the thieves.

And another said, "It must swim."

The captain said, "Make haste and draw it up. It's lucky, and bad luck to leave it there. But don't say its name."

So they cast a net and caught the blue cat, and brought it up into the ship. There on the deck it shook itself, and was quite dry. A pretty cat, and small, with a pointed face and wide eyes.

"Call it Rum," said the captain, "for that was what we thought it to be at first."

Then they gave Rum a dish of fish, and Rum sat purring under the masts, and looked at them gently, and washed behind her ears.

"See, she's calling a soft wind," said one of the thieves, and sure enough this benign wind came, and blew them on where they wished to go.

When they had dined, the thieves sought their bunks, and only the captain and the mate stayed in the cabin, where Ratter stood in the corner. Soon enough Rum came in, and purred, then curled to sleep on the captain's bunk.

"Look," said the mate, "how the lamp seems to make Ratter's eyes move about. He's jealous of Rum."

The captain laughed, and just then there began to be shouting again, up on the deck. The captain and the mate went to see, and so they found the thief, who had relieved the watch, standing bellowing, and the thief who had kept the watch lay dead beside the wheel, not a breath in him, not a mark upon him.

"Men die," said the captain. "One less is one less to share with. Throw him over the side."

So they did, and leaving the new watch at his post, rolling his eyes, the captain and the mate went to their rest. Rum was gone, like a virtuous cat, to patrol the deck, and over the ship the cool moon stared. Like a lullaby, slowly rocked the vessel.

At sunrise, there came another loud shouting. Now several turned out. And going up to the wheel, they saw the third new watch had found the second dead, as the second had found the first. And he too lay there, like a log, and not a mark on him.

"Now something goes on here," said the captain. And he set three men to watch and keep the wheel, and had the other one, the second corpse, thrown over the side. Then he went to breakfast, and he and the mate kicked Ratter and slung some dregs of wine into his face. But they ate well, and sat long, counting the money from the last of the robberies, and seeing how it would go further now.

And once or twice there was shouting up on deck, but often the thieves shouted at each other, for they drank by night and were quarrelsome all day until they drank again.

At noon, a man came to the captain, and he was very pale. "Curses on Ratter," said the pale thief, "I have gone the length of the ship, and every man on her, but I and you two, is lying dead, and no mark on him at all."

Just then, through the door walked Rum, and sat to wash herself at the paws of Ratter. The captain looked at this, and he said, "Rum has not been good luck to us, after all."

And the mate said, "She must go over." At this Rum gazed at him with her pretty round eyes, and the mate said, "But I have no heart to do it." Though he had sliced the throats of fifty men.

"Besides," the captain said, "What can Rum do? No more than Ratter can, who's a block of wood. This is some pestilence. Let's drink wine, for that is a fine medicine."

So the three of them, the captain, the mate, and the last sailor-thief, drank cups of wine, and then they went up and looked at all the dead men on the ship.

Some lay at their work, where they had been scrubbing or mending sail. One lay up in the lookout even, head tilted back as if at his ease. The wheel had moved a little from the course, but this they tended to. The captain said, "They must all go in the sea or they will stink." Accordingly they took each of the men and cast him from the side and the water received him kindly in her long blue arms. "Now," said the captain, "we'll make course for the nearest port. Think how rich we will be, the three of us." And he sent the last sailor to trim the sails and himself took hold of the wheel.

The captain stood then at the wheel of his ship through the heart of the afternoon, and now and then he quenched his thirst by means of the cask of wine at his side. Once or twice he saw the bluish shape of pretty Rum go up and down, though he paid not much heed. But then in the end, he heard no sounds from the ship but for the voice of her timbers and the murmur of the sails above. So he shouted for the mate and next for the other thief, the last sailor left. None answered.

As the sun went over, and the sky deepened, and the calm smooth wind blew on, taking them to port, the captain tied the wheel where he would have it, and drew his knife, and went to see.

He found the last sailor lying amidships, dead as a nail, and a smile on his face and no mark. And the mate the captain found lying against the money chest, with some coins in his hands, and smiling, and unmarked.

Then the captain went to Ratter, and he spat on Ratter and then he gave Ratter some wine. "I shall be," said the captain, "the richest man since the old days. If I live."

But the captain did not live, for as the sun went down, pretty Rum came softly to the cabin and looked at the captain. And the captain gazed into her shining eyes, and never, it seemed to him, had he beheld so deep and sweet a sea. And on the sea he sailed, lost in the calm air, and Rum purred, and it was a song better than sirens make, or the mermaids who lure men to their deaths. So the captain lay back on his bunk, in a dream, and Rum came gently up his body, and lay on the captain's face. So as he dreamed, he was suffocated, and died in the same way as all the others.

When the captain was quite dead, not a mark on him, Rum jumped down and washed herself, and the wind dropped and the ship stood becalmed on the ocean.

Rum gazed about with her bright eyes and saw wooden Ratter looking at her.

Ratter said, in the tongue of cats, "Now you will go back into the sea and wait for the next one."

"Just so," said Rum politely.

"Take me with you," said Ratter.

"Alas," said Rum, "regretfully, you can be of no use to me. I am very sorry."

"There you are wrong," said Ratter. "Only grant me the power to move, and I'll show you what I can do."

Then Rum flicked Ratter with her silken tail, and Ratter came alive, all wooden, and rough with splinters, with, sticking out of him, all the nails that the thieves had stuck in him, and stained on him the marks of their kicks and cups.

But Ratter stalked, like an old worn chair, down the length of the ship. And reaching the bow, he slipped over. Rum sat by the rail and watched.

To the wooden figurehead, with the sword and severed hand, Ratter went, and climbed upon its face. And there Ratter curled up, as Rum had done upon the faces of the thieves. And presently the sword dropped from the wooden grip of the figurehead, and next the severed hand dropped. And then the figurehead began to buckle and to bend. As Ratter sprang away, the figurehead fell over into the sea, and after this, the ship groaned, and she broke apart as if on a rock, and soon she went down.

Ratter said to Rum as they floated in the sea, "You can kill men. I can kill ships."

Rum said, "Then come with me, brother."

Mariset sighed and said, "Why tell us this story?"

"So you may notice," said Arrow, "that men fear cats."

"If it was true, your tale," said Annasin, "they have some cause."

"Perhaps they do."

In the village below the lights still burned, though it was late. Noises came dim and fearful from the house of hospitality, and once or twice, even over Arrow's melodious meowing, they had heard the ranting of the witch-finder, though not his words. And later, screams.

"How sweet it is," said Mariset, "here in the hills."

"How safe it is," said Annasin. "But I keep thinking, what have they done to me, down there."

Mariset said quietly, "I have never had a lover."

Annasin said, "You don't want one, they are clods." But then she remembered Arrow and his velvet, and the thorn of pain after the tumult of desire.

And Mariset had stood up, and she rubbed her face against Arrow's face.

Annasin curled herself into a ball of fur and closed her eyes and slept calmly, until she heard Mariset screech and the sound of Arrow jumping backward through a briar thicket in order to escape her claws. Then Annasin got up and went to Mariset and washed her, and they laughed, and Arrow pranced about, spraying the bushes, the moon in his eyes.

"Is it a fact now we have slept with the Devil?"

"Who knows?" said Annasin. "Who cares?"

Then all three played again on the hill, but at last the moon set, and then the night was darker. They drank at the pool, and Annasin said, "I don't mean to be abrupt, but I must go back to the village. I must go back into my shape of a woman. Perhaps I'm a fool to do it."

Mariset said, "I was fair of face, I had shining hair. But I haven't the courage to go back at all. I'd rather stay here on the hills. How cold the mountains look against the stars! I release you from my spell, Annasin, so you can go back into yourself. You yourself know well enough how to get out again."

Annasin picked down the hill like a sleek gray shadow. She stole in among the byres and huts, and never a dog barked. She came into the village street, and there her house was, black as a hole, and all the other houses lit with their lamps.

She ran four-foot to the hospitality house, and outside the horses standing tethered whinnied and widened their eyes. So Annasin loosed herself, and her cat form melted away. One moment she was in the air, and then inside her skin, and inside the house.

The light was dull and low, a sort of brown, and she lay among a heap of groaning, whimpering women, and she hurt.

She realized they had been sticking pins in her and touching her with hot irons, to try to rouse her. Her body was scraped over, in and out of her clothes. Besides she had been tied, by a strong rope and too tight, to a hook in the wall that was meant for meat. And all those other women had been done up similarly.

"Look," whispered a voice. It was Vebya, who bled from her temple and her wrists and feet. "Annasin is awake. Oh, Annasin—save us. Call a demon to set us free."

"That I can't," said Annasin. "I'm no witch."

"Yes you are," cried Vebya. "For I saw you float over the meadow."

"Yes you are," said Chekta, who had been whipped, her dress and her back all ribbons, "you light fires by a word. I spied on you."

"There is a limit to what I can do," said Annasin.

And nearby, filthy Margotta hawked and spat. Her fingers were broken on her right hand. She said, "I've called the lords of Hell, but they won't come, the traitors. Forty years I've served them all. And the Devil has had me in my own kitchen. I told it all, to stop the hammer. And I have been loyal, but where is he now, the demon who filled me?"

Then there was a rush of movement, a chair thrust back, and out from the brown light stormed the shadow of the witch-finder. His evil tortured face loomed over Annasin, yellow from the candle that he held. He lifted high the silver cross, and Annasin bowed to it, at which he snatched it back.

"Do you mock God, you bitch?" he yelled.

Annasin said nothing.

The witch-finder spat as old Margotta had, but into the sinking fire. He said, "Speak up now, witch, since you have woken. Where have you been on your broomstick or your nightmare horse? Who have you poisoned? Has the Devil had you?"

Annasin compressed her lips. She said, "You would do better in the church, Father, praying for nicer health."

"Rein yourself in, woman. Don't try to put your curse on me. I am safe in the arm of God."

"You will die in seven months," said Annasin. And she could have bitten out her tongue. What had possessed her? But it was true, for she saw his skull through his head like a stone in the soup.

The witch-finder struck her hard in the belly, and Annasin fell back. She fell against Mariset's vacant body, and Vebya shrilled, "Make her tell where the other witch is. Make her tell of Mariset."

But Annasin could not speak, and the witch-finder now was not concerned anymore with confession.

"Tomorrow you will burn, all five of you. Burn and go down to Hell where you belong, and the Devil awaits you with his forks and knives."

Then the old man went back to his chair and poured more spirits into his mug.

The injured women moaned and muttered and grew still.

Annasin thought of how they would burn her as a witch. Her heart broke. There was nothing she could do, nor anything for the others, nor anything for Mariset. Each must save herself as she could, if she could.

And through the cracks in the door and window came the scent of night, over the stink of blood and useless pain and fear and human flesh.

When she had got up the hill again in her slim gray fur, Annasin found Mariset and Arrow at the stream, splashing starlit ripples with their paws.

Mariset ran to her, and Mariset asked, and Annasin told her, bit by bit, unwilling, but holding nothing back. Cats cry. Of course not with tears. Mariset and Annasin wept by the stream and then they went to Arrow and he curled against them, and they laid their heads on his taut male belly as if for the milk of their mothers.

"I will tell you now a third story," said Arrow, as the stars wheeled slowly overhead.

The Third Story—The Tower Cat

When people heard the sound, echoing over the long fringed grain fields and up to the bony hills beyond, they would say, "The ravens are noisy today," or they would say, "Listen, it's thunder." Or they would say nothing. But in secret they had a name for it, that sound: the *grinding*, they called it.

What was ground? It was like bricks, like stones, mashed over and over. Like little stuff worked down to littler stuff. Yet it was never done.

What then did they suppose made the *grinding*? A church lay on the plain, and in the church was a priest. He was a fat man, tall and black-maned, and he ruled the land about like a king. Every holy day his church was full; none dared stay away. And he preached harshly. There was no kindness in him. He told them of their vileness and how they would be made to pay for it by a God who, in his mouth, became like a ravening dragon. Then he would pass a silver bowl among them and they would each put in a gift, all they could afford and more. And at other times he would visit them, the priest, their huts and houses, their farms, the mills and the inns. And whatever he asked for he was given, food and drink, keepsakes, wine and cloth. Even gold rings he was given off their fingers if they had gold rings, and now and then he would take a fancy for a girl, and then she must go to him. They hid their sisters, wives, and daughters where they could, but it was not always possible. He was a hungry man, their priest.

He was more than that, for sure. How else did he so terrify them? He was a magician.

Some nights, from the top of the church tower, which was high and rimmed like a castle, cold lights reeled off into the sky. And those that had to pass that church by midnight did so by going off the road, walking away over the fields, so a new track was worn there.

From the tower, too, from its top, came that sound they called, in secret, the *grinding*. They did not know what it might be and did not care to know. "The owls," they said. "A storm," they said, and pulled the blankets over their heads. Some prayed he would die, but bad things happened to those that prayed in this way. One had an ax fall on his foot, and the blade severed it, and he was a cripple. One met something on the hill at dusk, and he went mad; they had to chain him. "God bless the good priest," they said.

There was a girl the priest had seen when she was only ten, but he waited, he did not like them so young as that. Her father and her mother hid her away, it was true, but then her hair shone like copper in the sun, and he remembered it, the priest, as he rode by the farm.

"What is that which glimmers?" said the priest.

"It's the old pan on the kitchen wall."

"No, never any pan. Answer me again."

"The sun catching on the window."

"Answer again."

"My daughter's hair."

"Send her," said the priest, "to me. Let her come just after sundown. She will be thirteen now."

The mother spat in the dust, but she said, "Excuse me, holy Father. I have a bad taste in my mouth from eating unripe fruit."

And the father said, "I will set her on the road to you."

And, what use to hesitate, on the road they set her, their copper-haired girl, when the sun was burning low as a candle and the shadows reaped the fields.

She walked all the way, although the tears dropped shining from her eyes. Like gold her tears were as the sun declined, but when it was down, like silver. And in the moonlight, glass.

Then she stood by the church door, and the priest called to her to come in.

He had his will of her under the altar, and she knew better than to complain. When he was done her tears were spent. She sat against the side of God's table, and she heard above her, softly, the *grinding*.

"Shall I tell you," he said, the priest, "what it is makes that noise?"

The girl said, "The old church stones rub together."

"No," said the priest. "Come up and see."

It was his whim, and she could not resist, so in great pain, for he had forced her, she climbed up the winding stair of the church tower and came at last out onto the roof.

Open it was, that roof, to the high sky, and the moon shone down on it. There was the strangest sight. At the center of the roof, all about which stood up huge gargoyles of gray granite, there was a pattern marked on the slates. And in the middle of this was a grindstone, a huge stone wheel. And tied to the wheel was a small creature, which walked round and round, and the wheel ground something small and smaller and smallest, but it was never done.

"It's a cat," said the priest. "Do you see?"

The girl said that she did. And it was. The creature tied to the wheel that went round and round and never stopped. It was a tabby cat, thin and silent, like some everyday mouser of the farms, and its eyes were cold as the stars.

"I will tell you the truth," said the priest, "for tonight I'm fearful, miss, you will die. Out on the bony hill. A shame."

The girl said, "I don't care."

"Perhaps you will," said the priest, "for I have given you to a demon. But, even so, you too shall have something. A little knowledge. Understand then that this ordinary cat, a common tom I found upon my travels years ago, has inside it the great magic all cats possess. And I can let such magic out. I secured tom to my magic grindstone. The wheel goes round and grinds away anything that is against me. No illness, no ill will, no mishap may come near. Old age is crunched, bad luck is squashed of juice. And all this my dear cat does for me."

"Can it never rest?" said the girl, for she had a sweet heart.

"No, it never rests. Never feeds. It has no life but as my thing. And now you may go and meet the demon. Greet him for me."

The copper-haired girl went down the stair and out through the church and away into the dark fields, which the moon had sliced with silver. She walked straight up to the bony hills. She did not hang back, not she.

But when she felt the rough grass under her feet, a sickly fire was there, in the distance, and she knew when she met with it, she would die. Then she paused. She turned and looked back at the church. And she said this:

> Pussycat, pussycat, turning his wheel,
> Either the world or the wheel must stand still.
> Pussycat, pussy, by power of my will,
> The world, or the wheel, for I die on the hill.

And then she laughed and ran toward the sickly flame, and nothing was seen of her again.

But the priest ate roast meat and grapes, and drank wine, and slept deep in his soft bed. And all the while the *grinding* went quietly on, on the tower above.

What of the cat, then? Well, he had, of course, bewitched it. He had brought out the magic of which it was made, which is old as the earth. And as it walked round and round, under the circling sun and the moon and the arrow-tips of the stars, it had nothing in its head, not a memory or a want. But then, that night, as the priest slept, a shooting star sped down the black sky, like a falling soul. And the cat looked up. In that moment it became a cat. It stood on its hind legs and it clawed at the air, at the curtains of the magical air that hung there about the wheel, it clawed and rent, and so it called, in the way of cats, a storm.

Dim were the first flashes of the tempest, smooth as blue blushes on the cheek of night. And faint the thunder. But then the storm rolled in.

Around the tower, the highest thing upon the plain, the storm glanced and battered, and the wind rocked. Rain sprang like swords. The priest turned, careless, in his sleep. But all about, in the houses and the huts, in the mills and inns, they were afraid.

For it was a storm like an animal that beat in the sky, maybe even something like the horrible God the priest ranted of, wicked and unreasonable and full of jealousy and wrath.

The cat walked on about its eternal stroll, pulling the grinding wheel, but its head was lifted into the rain it had raised, and its fur was soaked through, black now as soot. It was wet as an eel.

Then lightning hurled from the sky, and it struck the tower a crack like a whip. Stark blue, the fire, and it broke on the gargoyles, one by one. Now there burned up a thing like a bear with the tail of a snake, and now a thing like a man with the mask of a weasel. But then the lightning-strike burst full on an upright shape of stone, lean and winged, and it had the head of a cat.

The thunder bowled away down the sky like a great soft ball. The flickers of the lightning paled and stilled. The rain ebbed.

Smooth now, the night. But up there, on the church tower, the cat walked on and on, round and round, half drowned, with its eyes blue as sapphire.

It had ground a deal of badness that day, for the sound had grown low, the sound of the *grinding*.

Yet then there came another grinding sound. It was the note of a stone arm that ended in a granite paw, stretching out. And next, another. And then a patter like pebbles skimming down into a pool, that was the rain-wet wings of the cat-gargoyle, all the flinty feathers shaken out.

It stepped from its plinth, the gargoyle, and its cat face moved, and it spoke, while it looked down upon the priest's magical cat. "Will you be here?" it said. "Or will you come with me?"

"What are you?" said the cat, in the language of cats, which the gargoyle itself had impeccably spoken.

"I," said the gargoyle, "am an angel of your kind."

"How beautiful you are," said the tabby cat.

"I was about to say the same."

Then the angel bent and bit through the tether with strong stone teeth, and taking the cat in its arms, the angel rose into the sky, up, up, where the stars were, and beyond. Do not doubt there is a heaven for their kind. There is always a heaven.

Yet in his sleep, the priest did not even turn, he felt no trouble, had no warning. Nor had the world stopped spinning. It was only his wheel.

However. When he woke, it came to him at once that some awful thing had happened. He did not hear the *sound*, that sound familiar to him as his own breathing. The sound of the *grinding*.

It occurred to him that perhaps no bad thing was near and so the wheel had nothing to work on—but always the wheel worked. So he rose and dressed himself, and went up the stairs of his defiled church, and when he reached the roof, he saw.

The cat was gone, and the wheel was still. And a crowd stood waiting beyond.

Old age was there, with his broken teeth and hoary head, and smiling, and bad luck with his claws, and disease with his pitchers and needles, and at the back of them all, a shadowy thing that had no face.

The priest screamed. He ran down from his tower, and on the way he fell, and his leg was shattered. He lay then in the hollow of the church, howling.

As he did so, out on his body broke sores and pustules, he sweated and turned green with fevers, snot ran from his nose and blood from his lips. His black hair shriveled and dropped out. Lines were drawn in his face as if a plow had riven there. The seeds of death were planted, and presently death came down.

Death stood above the priest all morning, as he shrieked and spewed and tried to crawl and could not, and the sunlight dappled over the floor.

At last the sun stood high above the tower, and then death touched the priest. And the priest arched backward until his body was a bow, and he snapped in the middle. From his belly and his genitals ran serpents, and out of his eyes long worms that could not see. Then he melted and was a filth on the floor. But the sun dried it.

On holy days thereafter the church was unfilled. Rumor had gone around. Three seasons passed before any came to see, and by then there was no sign but for a dry black stain under the altar.

They shut the church and planted trees about it, to overwhelm it and pull down the stones, which in the end they did, but that was long after, when the priest had been forgotten, and the sound of the *grinding*, too.

It was the dawn in the sky, so soft and yellow, and Annasin and Mariset looked up into the face of Arrow, their lord.

"And why *this* story?" asked Annasin.

"To show," he said, "that vengeance is usually possible, as is escape."

The clouds were golden, and curly as fleece. How mild and ready for the spring that high land near the world's top. Even the mountains glowed, and the waterfall was like a jewel.

But they washed themselves, and then they went down, down to the place on the hill where the village was to be seen.

Already villagers were busy. They were building up, on the open space before the church, a huge pile of wood and sticks, old broken furniture, and posts torn from the walls of barns and pens. It was the pyre for the witches the witch-finder had found.

They worked with a will. The women, some of them were singing. Happy songs. And the children danced about squeaking, "Burn the witch! Burn her to a stitch!"

There was a man Annasin had cured of a chest-rot, heaving in long planks of dry wood. And there the woman whom Mariset had blessed with a baby. But there too were the women whose husbands Vebya and Chekta had lain with, and there the man whose goats had given sour milk, and there the one who said Margotta had made him cut off his big toe with the scythe.

Yes, they worked with a will, and before the sun was very high, all was prepared.

Then the witch-finder came from the hospitality house, and on the wind blew his smell of liquor. He held in one hand his silver cross and in the other a black book.

The witches were brought after.

Vebya and Chekta screamed and soiled themselves, Margotta cackled curses. Mariset and Annasin were like the dead already, their two young bodies limp as the rope that trailed from their ankles. All were tied among the posts of the pyre.

Only Vebya went on screaming for reprieve. Poor thing, she had never learned.

The witch-finder spoke some words, but the wind broke them and carried them about. A jumble came up the hill. *God,* said the witch-finder, over and over. As if God was a name that might be forgotten and must therefore be repeated frequently.

It was the witch-finder who lit the pyre. He did it with a torch one of the men had made. The witch-finder walked all about the heap of wood and women, and put the red flower in here, and here, and finally threw the flower down on the feet of Mariset, who lay on her shining hair.

Mariset could not bear it. She saw her flesh evaporate, and she ran away, away into the wood, screeching. But Annasin stayed and carefully beheld her human body consumed, its petals falling, its bones clothed only in smoke.

The cries and shrieks of the three waking women were terrible. Annasin prayed they would soon die and find peace. At last, bitterly, she said to Arrow, "Can you do nothing?"

The black cat answered: "Alas. We have some power over *him*, for *he* is reasonable. But none over men."

At last the noises were stopped. At last the pyre fell in.

Some of the villagers took bones from it for good luck. The witch-finder went back to the hospitality house. He seemed shrunken and very tired, as if he had lost hope.

Annasin and Arrow ran to find Mariset. They discovered her easily, wailing under a pine tree.

They licked her and kissed her until she lay down. They slept all three in a ray of sunlight, while the birds flew overhead.

In the late afternoon, Arrow went hunting alone, and brought back for them three of these birds. It was a wicked dance they had with them. But no one's fault, and in the end they fed. Poor world, it had never learned.

The sun sank in fire, but the fire did not crackle or shriek.

"We are cats now till the end of our days," said Annasin.

Mariset replied, "I have never been anything else. But am I still a witch?"

"We will have to see."

Arrow laughed.

"And if you are," he said, "what, with your witch power, will you do to the village that burned you?"

Annasin and Mariset gazed into each other's primrose eyes and then at the third primrose eye on Arrow's forehead, between the two black ones.

"I will tell you," said Arrow, "the fourth story, and the last."

"Why?" said Annasin and Mariset.

"To help you to decide your vengeance."

The Fourth Story—The Tomb Cat

In the midst of a desert, a green river ran, and on its banks cities and towns of marble had bloomed like lilies. But beyond the river, the desert stretched mysterious and ungenerous, and out of it came many tales. Statues rose there that touched the sky. Wells sank there into the underworld. Strange beasts existed, winged lions, and dragons, and curious magicians lived among the rocks. From the desert presently there traveled the story of a tomb. It lay at the base of a mountain whose shape was like that of a giant's head. And in the tomb were heaped incredible riches, room after room of them. But at the center of the tomb stood, in great magnificence, a vacant couch. Though readied as if for a king, none slept there. The tomb was empty.

Certain lords and nobles of the cities began to covet the tomb, its wealth and glory, which would go with them into history, and also into another life beyond death.

They sent, to find the place, their captains and warriors. But none returned.

There was a princess in a town of tall gates. She was old and wicked in her ways, but she, too, knowing that soon enough her time would come to die, wanted to secure for herself the mystic tomb in the desert, for her mages had assured her it existed. "But," they said, "there is some guardian who bars the way. For this reason no man returns from there."

"Men," said the princess, "are expendable." And she

summoned the first of her three most powerful and accomplished knights.

This first waited before her. He was young and strong; he bore the scars of many battles and the marks of much favor. She thought, since he was young and strong, it would serve him right if he perished. She commanded him to get for her the tomb, warning him only that there would be a guardian, and doubtless he would have to fight with it. At this the warrior grinned, showing his strong young teeth. The old woman laughed, showing her elderly and carious ones. Pitiless, she sent him out.

The first warrior rode from the town, where girls threw flowers to him, and came into the desert, where only the hot wind blew and whistled down the dunes of white sand.

He set his course, as the mages had prescribed, by the sun and by the moon, when it appeared. He did not listen to the voices that called in the wind, or to its songs, he drank sparingly from the water and the wine he had brought, and on the fifth day, as the light was going out, he reached the appointed spot.

Against a lavender sky, there bulked up the yellow mountain that was in the shape of a giant's head. And at the foot of it, a silver fountain broke from the rock and poured into a gleaming pool. But no trees, no plants of any sort grew by the pool, and behind it was a round dark opening in the rock. A pillar defined either side of this, each with a plume of stone for its top. But inside the darkness there was nothing to be seen.

The first warrior dismounted and led his horse to drink from the pool, but it would not. Looking down, the man saw his reflection in the water, but it was no longer himself, it was a skull.

"I have known magic," said the first warrior. "I'm not afraid of it. Nor of darkness."

Then he lit a torch and went straight forward into the cave between the pillars.

To begin with the way was narrow, though on either side the walls were carved, with flowers and stems, weapons of war and animals, and even the phases of the moon. At last the corridor widened out and the first warrior, holding high the torch, discerned he was in a chamber made all of pink marble, and in the walls now were set scrolls of gold, and emeralds and amethysts of vast size. In the middle of this chamber, which was otherwise empty, stood a marble trunk with a flat top, and on this rested a face made of gold.

"What is it," said this face, parting its golden lips with strange ease, "that you want?"

"To claim this tomb for the princess, my mistress."

"Go back to her and tell her," said the face, "the tomb is not made ready for *her*."

"She is a great lady," said the first warrior. "She is rich as three kings, knows sorcery, and will soon die."

"Yet the tomb is not for her. Go back."

"Never," said the first warrior.

The face said, "Ascend into the second room."

So the first warrior walked by, his sword drawn now, and the torch upheld, and crossed the threshold of the room of pink marble, and came into a room of black marble. Against the walls rose enormous boxes and urns of gold, and they were piled over with jewels that flashed rosy and blue and green and purple. On a trunk of silver sat only this: a pure white cat, which washed itself quietly.

But then the cat spoke to the first warrior, and not in the language of cats, but in the tongue of men.

"Go back," said the cat, "or you must fight with me."

The first warrior laughed. And then the cat laughed, too. It jumped down light as a feather, and when its four feet touched the ground, it swelled. It grew to the size of a dog, and then to the size of a lion. It glowed in the torch-fire, and its eyes were palest green.

"Still I will fight you," said the first warrior.

"Look about you. See those that have fought me."

The first warrior turned. He noticed that among the urns and boxes of gold were rolled ivory sticks and rounded pitted ivory balls, and these were the bones and skulls of men. But the first warrior knew that he was too young to die. He threw away the torch and raised the sword.

Then the white cat leapt straight at him, and it was not like muscle or skin or fur, but like the thunderbolt. The young man's spine broke, splintered at the impact, and as he fell the claws of steel put out his life.

When the first warrior did not return, the old princess had his family thrown into the streets without recompense. She was amused to think of his youth and valor lost, but angry, too. She had not got what she really wanted. So then she sent for the second warrior.

He, too, was strong, though not so young as the first. His scars were more various, and he wore jewels that he had won. She sent him out with only a wry brown grimace. And in the streets, children pointed and stared in awe, but in the desert only the wind blew and he took no notice of either.

Five days he journeyed. And on the fifth day, at sunset, when the sky was vermilion, he came upon the mountain like a giant's head.

At the pool, the horse would not drink, and glancing in, the second warrior saw reflected nothing at all, and took this for a trick of the light.

He entered the tomb fearlessly with his torch, passed through the corridor and into the pink marble chamber, and there spoke with the golden face, defied it, and went up the sloping floor into the second room of black marble, and there the urns and boxes and bones were, and he saw the bones at once, and then a white cat washing itself on a trunk of silver.

He ran to the cat and swung his sword to cut off its head. But the cat sprang down, and next it was as big as a dog, and then big as a lion, and it spat in his eyes and he was blinded, the second warrior. And as he fell, its paw, like an ax, crushed in his chest.

When the second warrior did not return, the old princess walled up his family to starve to death. Then she summoned her third warrior.

This man was no longer young; he was aging, yet not so old as herself. He had scars to be sure, but no jewels or honors. He had sold these to maintain himself, since for years the princess had given him no wages.

"What do you think?" she said to him.

"That, madam, you will not get this tomb," said the third warrior.

The princess's hard eyes flashed with venom. It had been said her bite could kill. "You are a coward and afraid to chance yourself for me."

"I will go," he said. "I have no family for you to murder or abuse. I have no special wish to die, but then no special wish to live. Why not?"

In the town of tall gates, no one noticed the old knight as he walked along, for his horse had long ago been sold. He left the streets, and in the desert, he heeded the voices of the wind. He heard women weeping for lost love and pitied them. He heard men shouting in anger and would have calmed them if he could. He walked for thirteen days among the sands, and all his meager food and water were gone.

In the dawn of the fourteenth day, he saw the mountain like a giant's head, but gazing at it, it seemed to him it was more like the head of an old woman with a wicked mouth.

Going to the fountain, he drank gratefully, and the water was sweet as wine.

Then the third warrior drew his sword. It was ancient and cut and battered, dull, but on the hilt was a figure in iron, an iron cat. And this he kissed for luck, then put the sword back into its sheath.

In darkness he walked into the tomb-cave, and darkness took him in, and after a while, he began to see in some uncanny way, as if it were allowed him. So he beheld the carved walls, and the walls of the pink chamber strewn with jewels, and then the face of gold, which said to him, "What is it that you want?"

"There is an old bitch," said the third warrior, "wants this tomb to lie in for her comfort in death. But for myself, I'm only curious."

"Ascend," said the golden face, "into the second room."

So the third warrior, the old knight, walked into the chamber of black marble. He glimpsed the jewels and gold and bones, but then he saw the white cat washing itself on the silver trunk.

"My respects to you, sweetheart," said the third warrior. "May I come close and stroke your fur? For I've heard of a thing called snow, but never till now have I seen it."

"Approach," said the cat, in the tongue of men.

The third warrior did so, and he stroked the cat over and over, head to tail, many times. And the cat looked at him with pale green eyes, and purred.

"Never in my life," said the third warrior, "did I meet one who made me so welcome."

"Never in my life, my life as here it is," said the cat, "did I meet one who was worth a welcome."

"That is a shame," said the third warrior. "May I serve you in any way?"

"No, for I have, like yourself, my task. I keep the tomb for one who will come. However, you may serve yourself. Take anything you wish from this place, any gem or trinket."

"Give me instead," said the third warrior, "one of those snow-white quills that sprout from your face."

Then the cat shook itself, and a long white whisker fell into the knight's hand. It grew then, and was the length of a palm branch, and from its end sprang buds and flowers of emerald and diamond.

The third warrior said, "God bless you, white cat."

The white cat bowed, and the third warrior left the tomb in the desert. For thirteen days he walked over the sands, and on the fourteenth, he walked into the town and went to the palace of the princess.

She shrieked when she heard the knight had returned. She ran to him without her wig, bald as an egg.

"Is it mine?"

"No, madam. It is not."

The princess's face shriveled horribly, as if she had aged yet another ten years. "What is there, then?" she screamed.

"A cat is there that purrs," said the knight.

Then the princess jumped up to kill him with her bare hands, and it was too much for her, for usually she allowed others to work her deeds of violence. She fell dead on the floor, and the third warrior left the palace and lived the rest of his life a wealthy man beside the river.

But one morning it chanced the knight saw a poor beggar, a leper boy, wandering in the street, and he went out to feed him. But the boy paid no heed, and strayed on. Then some of the townspeople came to stone the boy, because he was a leper, and a beggar, and innocent. The old knight drove them off. He walked behind the boy to the tall gates of the town and allowed no one to hurt him. But here the boy went out into the desert, and it seemed to the knight he must be let go, the desert now would care for him.

It did so. From the sky ravens flew and fed the boy small pieces of honey. And from the rocks small streams of milk ran.

The wind sang to the boy, and urged him gently on, and the moon and the sun guided him.

After fifteen days he reached the mountain that was shaped like a giant's head, and he paused only to look into the pool, but what he saw he did not understand. The sunlight led him forward into the shadow of the tomb.

In the carved corridor, the carvings touched the boy softly. They drew away his rags, laved him with water and ointments. In the chamber of pink marble the golden face smiled in silence and closed its eyes.

The boy paid no attention to the jewelry walls, and in the chamber of black marble, when he entered this in turn, no attention to anything at all, but for the white cat, which rubbed against him.

"Everything is prepared for you," said the cat, in a tongue that perhaps was the tongue of men. "Come with me now."

The cat led the beggar boy into a third inner room. It was of green jade, set with beryls and rubies, and in the middle of it stood a beautiful bed of ebony formed like a lion.

"Lie down, dear child, for soon you will sleep," said the cat. "Here you will be safe. And I shall guard you as I have guarded your bed all this while, against your arrival."

So the boy lay on the bed, which was the couch of the tomb, and the cat lay down at his side.

"Once," said the cat, "there was a young god, the son of God, and he was so perfect that many loved him, and many more feared him. And so in the end, because every word he said was too marvelous to be borne, they took him and scourged him and killed him, so that he expired in agony, mocked and reviled, on a far-off hill. Yet he died forgiving them. He had promised, this god, that after death he would return, return in the flesh, out of the tomb, to prove death had no power. So it was, he descended first into all the hells, and there the demons kneeled to him, for they loved him even better than his father. And then he rose again into the flesh, and he woke in his tomb, and the door of it had been opened ready for him to leave and go back into the world of men, and show himself whole. But he lay exhausted in the twilight of that place. He said, I asked before that I might not drain this wine of death, but I did drain it. Now spare me this last labor in the flesh. I am so tired. Surely I have done enough."

The boy smiled as he lay upon the lion, and the cat smiled, as they do. The white cat said, "As the young god thought this, it happened that a cat stole in at the open door of his tomb. It had no fear, for the cat is always curious, and seeing the radiance of the young god's soul through his flesh, the cat jumped lightly up on him and stood there, staring in his face. Then the god thought, seeing the cat's face like a flower, *There is still beauty in the world*. But the cat, curious, flicked her tail, and the tail brushed the young god on the lips. He thought, *There is still softness in the world*. And the cat, for cats will, went close and began to lick and groom the young god's hair, which had been torn and smudged by dust and blood. Feeling this motherly washing, the young god thought, *There is still tenderness in the world*. But then the cat, not considering, trod on his neck, with one of her claws that were like thorns. He knew too this touch. He said aloud, *And there is still pain in the world. I must return.* So he rose then and went out into the garden beyond the tomb."

The boy smiled, and as he smiled he died in fearless serenity, with the cat lying at his side.

A storm beat over the desert. The sky was black as night. Rocks fell and closed the mouth of the tomb in the mountain, and the shape of the mountain now, it was not like anything at all, formless, wild, and silent.

But in the pool before the tomb was the reflection left behind by the beggar boy, a face like gold and crowned with roses that had no thorns. Until the darkness passed, and the reflection faded, and only water was there, clear water.

The last story had taken a great while to be told. Days perhaps, and nights. Maybe half a year. But when it had ended, the night had come and gone, the stars were closing their eyes, the east was lined with crimson.

"Not fair," said Mariset. "You are not fair to us."

"It was after all a gentle story," said Annasin, "mostly."

"But have you decided on what shall be done to the village?" asked Arrow.

Mariset yawned. "Let the sky drop on them," she said.

And Annasin said, "Let them burn like us."

Then both laughed. Arrow said, "Perhaps it would be much funnier to have such power over them that you could make them glad."

"Do you hate God?" inquired Mariset boldly.

"I presume to love *him*," said Arrow, blushing cat-like even through his black fur. "It is, I agree, a great impertinence."

"Then the tales of your kind are not true."

"Few tales are entirely true."

"But you love another better," said Annasin slyly.

Arrow said, "Young people are always the same. They cleave together. Sons of fathers . . . Do you see?"

"But you said that *he*—"

"Perhaps I did not speak of *him* in the tomb," said Arrow, washing his tail. "Did I name him? No. Well, then."

They played with sunbeams in the wood. Then they magicked up some mice that were not real but that behaved as if real, and that, being greedily devoured, tasted real, and filled their bellies.

Then they magicked a stream from a rock, drank from it, and put it away again.

They went down, to look at the village.

It went on as it always had. Goats milked and children slapped. Women cooked and gossiped, and men gossiped and mended things. Even the houses of Mariset and Annasin had smoke coming from the chimneys.

"This is my vengeance," said Mariset. "Let blue flowers fall on them."

At once a rain of blue flowers, thick as snow, drifted down upon the village, covering the roofs, powdering the street, catching in the women's hair.

The villagers shouted and screamed. The words came up vaguely to the hill: "God save us, the sky is falling!"

And they were flinging themselves on their knees, crying and praying.

Annasin said, "Golden flowers, then. How can they mistake those?"

The golden flowers fell.

The villagers roared in panic, scrambled up, and fled into their houses. "The air is full of fire!"

Quietness arrived, and the rain of flowers had stopped. They lay lovely and scented on the street and roofs. None came to pick them up.

"It is often hard," said Arrow, "to do good to those that hate you."

And then they rose up in the air, the three cats, into the air where the flowers had been, they rose up and they flew away, and who knows where they went?